Oliver Harris was born in London but now lives in South Korea. He is the author of the Nick Belsey series of crime novels, plus two novels featuring MI6 officer Elliot Kane. He teaches creative writing at Manchester Metropolitan University.

Praise for *The Shame Archive*

'Oliver Harris is an outstanding writer'
The Times

'Harris writes with compassion or satirical glee, depending on which his characters deserve, and this third Kane novel puts him firmly in the Mick Herron class'
Telegraph, Best New Crime Thrillers to Read This Summer

'Harris has crafted an enthralling tale about a secret repository of bad – sometimes criminal – behaviour ... Harris steadily cranks up the tension, relating Sinclair's and Kane's stories with skill and verve until they meet in an explosive climax'
Financial Times

'Harris's deceptively understated style powers a relentless thriller that deep dives into the digital battlefields where future wars will be fought'
Irish Times

'*The Shame Archive* is a flawless political thriller: gripping, smart and hugely enjoyable'
Charlotte Philby

'Captivating and horrifying at once ... Oliver Harris is squarely in the territory of the greats: Greene and le Carré but also the modern masters, Mick Herron and Adam Brookes. There can be no higher accolade'
Manda Scott

'One of our finest thriller writers'
Evening Standard

Also by Oliver Harris

THE SHAME ARCHIVE

OLIVER HARRIS

abacus
books

ABACUS

First published in Great Britain in 2024 by Abacus
This paperback edition published in 2025

1 3 5 7 9 10 8 6 4 2

A CIP catalogue record for this book
is available from the British Library.

ISBN: 978-0-3491-4522-8

Typeset in Palatino by M Rules
Printed and bound in Great Britain by
Clays Ltd, Elcograf S.p.A

Papers used by Abacus are from well-managed forests
and other responsible sources.

Abacus
An imprint of
Little, Brown Book Group
Carmelite House
50 Victoria Embankment
London EC4Y 0DZ

The authorised representative
in the EEA is
Hachette Ireland
8 Castlecourt Centre
Dublin 15, D15 XTP3, Ireland
(email: info@hbgi.ie)

An Hachette UK Company
www.hachette.co.uk

www.littlebrown.co.uk

For my parents,
Elaine and Charles

ONE

The first message came in at 6 a.m. Rebecca Sinclair was already up, cradling a tea on the balcony, claiming her five minutes of peace before the week began. When, in the coming days, she thought back to this moment she was grateful that her phone had been on silent, that she didn't see the message immediately, and had enjoyed a last few breaths of summer before her life collapsed.

Robert was downstairs. She could hear him practising the speech he was due to deliver today in the House of Commons. No other sounds but the birds; her daughter remained asleep, her stepson and stepdaughter stayed with their mother in London during term times. Rebecca's companion was the quiet drama of the Chilterns: the sheer edge of Watlington Hill tumbling into the grass beneath it, the inviting darkness of the beech wood across its back like a pelt. Then, as the new sun tiptoed across Christmas Common, a revelation of wildflowers dusting the chalky soil. Mist lingered here. On quieter days she could go out and try to catch it in her hands, but not this morning.

She lifted her phone to check the time and saw a new WhatsApp message from an unknown number. No name, no picture, just one line: *I know who you really are.*

Rebecca stared at the words. She went to delete the message but placed the phone face down on the balcony's table and turned back to the view. Then she picked up the phone again. The brevity of the message gave her a chill. Some scam, she wanted to think, but that didn't feel right. Scams deceived. There was no deception here, just a forthright claim. Rebecca wondered if she should show it to her husband, but knew at once that she wouldn't, and felt sick.

When she came downstairs Robert was pacing the kitchen, in a crisp shirt and blue silk tie, arching carefully over his coffee with each sip. The day's newspapers were piled up on the table, unread. Rebecca scanned the front pages for anything worth alerting him to, knowing he had teams of people to do this now but wanting to preserve her role as filter and messenger. Being a member of the Cabinet didn't just bring official cars and red boxes and TV interviews but also a whole new level of scrutiny. She placed the *Guardian* down.

'Michael De Souza still gunning for you.'

Her husband drained his coffee cup and placed it squarely over the journalist's byline.

'I don't want to see his face at this time of day.' He grimaced, kissed her, glanced at the clock. 'Thanks for the warning.' The MP scanned his speech a final time as he dropped it into his briefcase, then straightened and addressed the kitchen. 'A family, at its best, teaches us our values, shapes our identity and nurtures our sense of responsibility,' he said.

'You used my line.'

'That's why today we will improve the Troubled Families programme, to provide vulnerable families with the intensive support they need—'

Their intercom chimed. Robert checked the security screen, saw his governmental ride and buzzed the gates open.

A Range Rover pulled up outside Howe Cottage, beside the five-hundred-year-old yew tree. Here when Chaucer was still a twinkle in his father's eye, as Robert liked to tell guests. Robert's driver emerged, gave Rebecca a friendly salute through the window.

'Don't forget the reception tonight,' she said, as her husband tied his shoes. 'Black tie. Have you got what you need for that?'

'At the office. I'll message you.'

Another kiss, then he was gone. Only when the front gate had whirred closed behind them, did she look at the message again. *I know who you really are.* This was what she was, she thought, glancing around the wooden beams and antique furniture of her home; the evidence surrounded her, exhaustingly so. Wife of a politician in a Grade II listed cottage, with an eight-year-old daughter she really needed to rouse and feed. But what a perfectly chosen message. She tried to smile. If you had to choose six words to strike fear into someone ... How many people could look at their life and think: this is everything; I have nothing to hide?

Rebecca wasn't sure, and continued to wonder as she packed her notes for the talk she was to give today for new beneficiaries of the charitable trust where she worked. She dressed, considered herself in the wardrobe mirror. Following her marriage she had decided to stop dyeing her hair blonde, in a spirit of perversity. She had resisted the MP's wife look, and similarly the Chilterns lady, the Barbour and gilets, and had started going to second-hand stores for surprising items, discreet expressions of independence. Her hair was dark, and today her eyes seemed particularly bright; fearfully bright.

Her daughter, Iona, woke protestingly, before being reminded that her class was going on a field trip to an Iron Age hill fort today, which stirred some enthusiasm. They breakfasted together – Rebecca forced herself to eat – then loaded themselves into the Tesla. The drive took them between wheat fields to Watlington. Laughing children in red sweaters stood out against the grey stones of the market town like little drops of blood. The primary school was the epicentre of their dawn chorus. It was a beautiful day, but the light and sound felt uncomfortable, and

Rebecca found herself staring longingly at the trees and fields beyond. The heart of their own beauty was an indifference that gently obliterated you. This she had recognised for several years.

When her daughter had disappeared into the school, Rebecca looked at her phone again. A second message had arrived.

I know what you did. I have pictures.

The message concluded with instructions: *Download the Whispr app. It makes all communication secure. You don't want your family to find out about this.*

Rebecca crossed the road, past the Chequers pub to the cricket club, where she sat on a bench outside the main gate. She checked that none of the other parents or school staff were nearby, then she folded over her lap and pressed the palms of her hands into her eyes. After a moment she straightened. Anyone could claim to have pictures. Why was she taking this nonsense seriously?

She googled the anonymous phone number. Nothing came up. Rebecca dialled the number and it rang but no one answered.

She had received some training on identifying what Robert's security advisers had named phishing attacks: people who persuaded you to click a link and suddenly your devices were riddled with malware. The possibility was comforting. She imagined some scrawny young man in Lagos or Mumbai or Beijing, reaching out to the Western world; or not even a person, but a bot, an algorithm, dragging a net through humanity's guilt.

Whispr appeared to be a legitimate, highly encrypted messaging app offering total anonymity. Fuck that.

She blocked the number and drove to work.

Three years ago, St Peter's Church discovered it had a sizeable trust set up by a Victorian businessman and staunch temperance campaigner intent on providing the men of Henley with alternatives to alcohol abuse. In the hands of its current chairman, Reverend Jeremy Palmer, the trust had become a charity and expanded to provide services to local youth and those in need generally: helping with CV writing, job applications, offering support for families battling mental illness, after-school activities for teenagers. Rebecca had joined shortly after Robert won his seat, one of only three paid employees. Robert had liked the look of it from a PR perspective, so long as she didn't get too involved with food banks, and beneath the raffle sales was a mission she believed in.

Today, they were welcoming a handful of selected mentees to a morning of interview training. Some were already waiting outside the church as Rebecca arrived. She managed a smile and headed for her office in what had once been the vicarage. She always loved this, entering her own office. The space was a trophy in itself, testament to years of nocturnal study and self-belief – to a struggle that no one would ever fully know, and no one needed to. It held her up and it held her apart from her husband's orbit.

Her phone was busy now: a Westminster spouses' group, the school Board of Governors, a local children's hospital that she was encouraging to apply for funds – the cloud of activity that usually arrived with a sense of the fullness of her life and now seemed so many points of vulnerability.

At 10 a.m. Rebecca gave an introductory talk to the mentees in the church, grin fixed, trying to savour the smell of old stone and wood and wax. She didn't believe in God but she believed in this smell, which had never failed to calm her until today. Her introduction was followed by an inspirational talk from one of their alumni, then it was back to her office for a video meeting with the children's hospital. She managed to forget about the messages for an hour or so. Then, at midday, the first pictures arrived. From a new number this time, still no name. The first showed her dancing in a G-string, her bra in her hand. The second showed her blindfolded, on all fours. In the third, there were drugs visible:

a mirror on the bed with lines of cocaine, alongside which she lay on her side, naked apart from a pair of heels.

I have hundreds, the accompanying message claimed.

Rebecca locked her office door. She sat down on the floor with her back against it, then crawled over to her wastepaper basket and vomited.

Her phone beeped a minute later. This message was a list of email addresses. It included her parents' Hotmail accounts, those of her closest friends and some co-workers at the Church trust, her husband's constituency account, then contact details for several of his friends and colleagues. Finally, there were names she recognised as members of the press. Whoever was behind this had collected all the pieces of her life.

Rebecca was so used to interpreting the world through the prism of Robert's career, her first thought was of the various enemies who might turn on her by association: enraged constituents, the Labour Party, half of Fleet Street. These were the sharks that circled her family. But this was not how they operated.

For the sake of doing something, Rebecca changed her passwords and privacy settings. Her hands were shaking. She checked the news. Robert's speech had been well received, loyal media suggesting he appeared increasingly prime ministerial. He looked good at the despatch box, notes rolled like a baton in his hand, pumped with outrage and vision. Messages from other MPs' wives sat on her phone, congratulating her, which meant they'd assessed the value of her stock. Most satisfyingly, perhaps, his attackers in the left-wing press were momentarily caught on the back foot, stories on various donations and lobbying rendered petty beside his competence and compassion. She found Whispr on the app store, downloaded it and signed up. Within seconds, her tormentor had found her on there and sent another message.

Transfer 10.15 BTC by midnight tonight, followed by a long string of random letters and numbers. She had never seen a Bitcoin address before but understood the basic concept: you could use it to send and receive money anonymously; no banks or apps involved, just this code. She found an online currency conversion calculator, typed in 10.15 BTC and it came to £250,000.

Rebecca sat back, winded. What kind of resources did they think she had? Did they imagine this kind of sum would be straightforward for her given her privileged existence? At least now she knew what they wanted. From a quick search it seemed easy enough to set up a Bitcoin wallet – you just installed some software. But obviously you'd have to buy the coin, exchange your brazen sterling for this shadow currency. And she wasn't going to do that.

If there was one thing she'd learned about the powerful it was that they fought back. They played dirty, and saw the world as adversarial, a zero-sum game in which you destroyed your opponents before they destroyed you. When Robert first became aware of Michael De Souza, the pitiless *Guardian* hack digging into his business affairs, he set about trying to ruin the journalist personally and professionally.

She needed to buy time.

Who are you? Rebecca wrote.

One word came back: *Eclipse*. It sat there on her screen, insolent, unwavering. Still, she had initiated some communication. That had to count for something.

I need a few days to raise that, she messaged. *I don't have it to hand.*

The longer you take, the more people get sent pictures of you.

Then I won't be in a position to pay. I need to be able to get the money discreetly.

24 hours.

Rebecca felt ludicrously grateful. She took a breath. What was she going to do? Out of instinct, she took a piece of paper and pen; brainstorm, she thought: options, strategy. After a moment, she smashed the pen into the paper, breaking the nib and denting the desk below.

No solutions occurred to her over the course of the afternoon. Rebecca collected her daughter from school, managed to chat to one of the other mums and arrange a sleepover, all while the pieces of her world were tumbling through the air around her. Their nanny was already at home – a muscular Australian woman in her forties – cooking Iona's supper. Rebecca dressed for the reception, did her make-up on autopilot. She looked unintentionally striking: pale, haunted. She chose more jewellery than usual, then a burgundy lipstick, then she went to the living room drinks cabinet, downed half a glass of vodka and called the taxi.

'No more than an hour's TV,' she said, kissing her daughter farewell.

As they approached the junction with the M25, she told the taxi driver to divert: she wasn't going straight to the Lord Mayor's reception. There was something she needed to collect from a house in Croydon first.

Once upon a time, she would have felt embarrassment as she directed him deeper into the humble streets of south London, to the family home that had always seemed to her such a worrying expression of life's scale. It had never been clear to her what inspired this anxiety; rich in a previous life, perhaps; in possession of a disproportionate soul.

Her father answered the door, startled. He retained his permanent flush of apparent anger, but beneath it there was a new frailty. Her mother was visible through the living room doorway, lying on the sofa; her default position. She propped herself up on an elbow. Both stared at Rebecca in her black satin off-the-shoulder dress.

'I was passing. Thought I'd say a quick hello.'

'Well, come in, Becky. Don't just stand there.'

'I needed to grab something, from my old stuff.'

'Of course.'

Entering their home always felt like an affront. There was an instinct to stoop, as if she might not fit through the doorway. The place was unchanged. Over the years, she had offered various forms of refurbishment and even, very gently, suggested that they might move to better premises entirely. But this was them. She had always marvelled that such a modest structure could house someone's existence. Yet it now contained her old life adequately enough. In fact, one suitcase held it.

It was in Rebecca's old bedroom. She brought it down from the broken wardrobe, caught a glimpse of herself in the mirror. She looked like some exotic bird that had got into the house, a fragment of wild night. A fairy tale curdling.

Rebecca unlocked the suitcase out of which she had conjured so many identities before burying one in it. Schoolwork, old photos, books; her first twenty-three years squashed together so that the later stages were barely separable from childhood, all entangled in one stale knot.

Her old life. Her real life.

Hidden inside an old make-up bag was a business card. Or, at least, it was the size of a business card but handwritten. She wasn't sure why she had kept it. Because of the man who gave it to her, perhaps. It was yellowed now, but the message, in flowing black ink, was perfectly legible: *If you ever need me*, followed by a number, then the name 'Elliot'.

She tried to call, standing there in her old room, staring down at the darkening street, but the line was dead. Of course it was. Why had she thought this might work? Every line should be dead, every door closed. Otherwise what did time mean?

Did Elliot even exist any more?

TWO

'White van,' the boy said. 'It's been behind us for five minutes.'

Elliot Kane glanced in the rear-view mirror then back to the Pentonville Road.

'Seen it before?'

The boy shook his head. 'It's a Ford, one man in it. Nothing written on the side.' He looked at Kane with a ten year old's desire to impress. Kane had noticed the vehicle a few minutes earlier, slipping through the Monday-morning traffic behind them, down towards Kings Cross.

'Get its registration?'

'I've memorised it.'

'Good work.'

The boy smiled. Kane squeezed the accelerator and watched for a reaction from the van. He was in a sleek black Audi, which he'd bought as part of the new role: private spy. It had been a year now, working for himself, and he'd learned that a private spy got a lot of attention, sometimes from the people you were targeting, equally often from your own clients whose trust declined in proportion to how much they were paying you. And both sides were inevitably loaded; everyone had the resources to fund a tail team, and plenty of former spooks lined up to provide the service.

'Going to lose him?' the kid said.

'Not sure that's wise. We don't want to draw too much attention, remember.'

'Yeah.'

And there was a risk assessment involved: Central London, with a child in the car, heavy traffic and a lot of police about – Kane wasn't going to initiate a chase. But at Great Portland Street he got lucky with the lights, cutting them fine and leaving the van stuck on red.

'I knew it,' the kid grinned.

He was Mason Bell, son of Kane's partner in the investigative firm. Partner in more than that, it was turning out, which was both convenient and complex. Kane turned off Piccadilly into a sleepy Mayfair: boutiques, hedge funds and private clubs nestling behind gold plaques and sharp railings. He felt good, lucky, with the dizzy brightness that comes at the end of luck. And this was his favourite part of London, he could admit that to himself now; the most beautiful and blood-soaked corner of the world. Kane parked alongside the sports cars outside the Westbury Hotel.

'We're going to be quick,' he said. 'Have a good swim. Don't cause any trouble. I'll pick you up when I'm done.'

The kid grabbed his towel and trunks, strode past the door person towards the spa area. Kane went to the Polo Bar at the back.

The bar was plush, bland and very Mayfair, with polo sticks on the wall and low chairs spaced out of eavesdropping distance. Waiting for Kane in the far corner was a shaven-headed man in a bright, short-sleeved floral shirt. It showed thick forearms but hid the old military tattoos that Kane had glimpsed once, if not for long enough to determine which country had enjoyed his service. Bob or Bobby Spears was the name the man used, which didn't sit entirely straight with his Eastern European accent and an investigations company registered in Montenegro. Kane took a seat opposite him, ordered black coffee from the hovering waiter.

'How's life, Elliot?'

'Good.'

'About to get better.'

Spears slid a flash drive across the table. His gold rings winked. Kane let the drive sit for a moment and looked around. A couple of suits by the windows talking French; three middle-aged women in jewellery close to the bar. Kane had been meeting in the Westbury for fifteen years. He remembered the early days, feeling like he was getting a glimpse into a dark and exclusive realm. After fifteen years haunting these places you have to accept you're the darkness. His coffee arrived and he took a sip, thinking, as ever, that you'd expect better coffee. He picked up the flash drive.

'It's a full criminal record,' Spears said. 'Plus tax investigations, files on his wife and children, private flights, even some videos with prostitutes. There's enough dirt there to put your man out of business.'

'You always impress me, Bobby. Thank you.'

For the last six weeks Kane had been on a job for a billionaire in a big legal fight with another billionaire. Caught in the middle was a bank that both men claimed to own. It must have meant a lot to them, because each side had put millions into the quest to block and criminalise the other. Kane was digging dirt for a fee of five grand a day. It was a stupid, morally blank life and he was richer than he'd ever been and planning his exit.

Spears poured tea into a china cup. Kane turned the drive in his hand, then pocketed it. Kompromat was more than he'd asked for, and a testament to Spears's enduring connections. Kane assumed most of the data had come from Moscow, a contact inside the FSB – maybe some official saving up to escape the current shitstorm. Kane handed Spears a padded envelope containing eighty grand in euros, and the investigator dropped it into the case beside him. A decent payday, minus whatever he passed on to his sources. But Kane knew what he really wanted was protection. Most people assumed Kane was still attached to MI6 in some capacity and therefore to the British government.

'You are keeping an ear out for me?' Spears said.

'Of course.'

'A lot of my friends are nervous. My Russian friends in particular. They are upset and confused.'

'If they're still here now, I reckon they're safe.'

'No one's safe. You know, the Alenichevs have left. The Mishinskys sold their mansion. You were happy enough to take their money when times were good, now they are scapegoats.'

'I haven't seen honest people getting nervous.'

Spears laughed, then wiped his mouth and dropped the linen napkin onto his plate. Kane imagined his web of acquaintances, powerful men and women waiting to find out if they were pariahs. Londongrad was over. Sanctions had sunk their teeth through the expensive skin of the capital's oligarchs. He'd last seen the Mishinskys' Notting Hill mansion on the news, occupied by squatters, a banner from its windows: BLOOD ON LONDON'S HANDS; OCCUPY UKRAINE AND WE OCCUPY YOU. A rock had been overturned, leaving a lot of reptilian creatures blinking in the light.

'You heard about the Bolshunovs,' Spears went on.

'About the horses.'

'Twenty of them. Shot. Couldn't bear to leave them behind.'

Kane had heard all the stories: closing up the big houses, shooting the racehorses, scuttling the yachts. He'd heard about the classrooms of elite schools languishing half empty, lawyers shutting up shop. Parasite London, starved of blood, was supposedly withering away. He hadn't noticed it yet.

'I'll tell you if I hear anything specific,' Kane said.

'I am still a helpful person to know. There's a lot of material

13

available at the moment, a lot of power to those who know where to look.'

'I value your acquaintance, Bobby. I'll keep an ear out for any trouble.'

This seemed to be enough.

'The videos are quite something,' Spears said as he got up to leave.

Kane picked up Mason from the pool and waited for him to change. They left the hotel together, squinting into the sunshine. The day crackled with the electricity of leaving a successful handover. No obvious watchers, but Kane performed some light counter-surveillance anyway, driving back a different route with a few wrong turns. Reluctantly, he acknowledged the buzz. He had always told himself that what he loved about espionage was hiding himself in other cities and identities, but integral to that kick was the possession of secrets. You weren't hiding unless people wanted to find you.

His personal phone rang as he was turning onto the Euston Road. A landline. He didn't know the number and was about to kill it when he saw it began with 721: Whitehall. Government.

Kane pulled over.

'Hello?'

'Elliot?'

'Speaking.'

'Do you have a moment?'

Kane recognised the voice of Alistair Godfrey, even though it had been several years. Head of P5, the Operations Section in MI6's Russia department. He was one of the few former colleagues Kane liked and trusted.

'What is it?'

'Are you in a position to speak?' Godfrey asked.

Kane glanced at Mason.

'Briefly.'

'Does the name Anthony Zachariah mean anything to you?'

It took Kane a few seconds to realise who he was referring to. Realisation came with a shot of unease.

'Yes.'

'He was killed last night at his home in Surrey. I'm at the scene, wondered if you could throw some light. It's a nasty one, Elliot. And the only information we've got about him came from you.'

Kane felt a darkness return. Godfrey gave him an address on a private estate entitled Magna Carta Park. Kane hung up, stared at the traffic, then swung the car around and began back west.

'Where are we going?' Mason asked.

'There's something I need to see.'

It took forty minutes to get to the crime scene. Kane left the M4, skirting Windsor on one side, Legoland on the other, to a different kind of make-believe. A sign for Magna Carta Park promised 'a private estate for the twenty-first century'. It led away from the main road to a grandiose set of gates and a security lodge beneath a flag with a coat of arms.

The first police cordon was here. Kane gave his name to the officer, who radioed through and then waved him on.

Half a kilometre further, a surreal assembly of homes appeared, imitations of Queen Anne and Regency style, only untouched by time, their bravado garish. Acres of parkland surrounded them, jewel-perfect cross-hatched lawns, a golf course, six tennis courts. Ten police cars.

Kane left his car alongside the police and told Mason to wait. An inner cordon had been placed around the home that contained the murder. Godfrey met Kane at the tape. He wore a white forensic suit, with the Borough Commander in full uniform beside him. Both glanced uncertainly at Mason in the passenger seat.

'You're in company,' Godfrey said.

'He'll be okay for a minute.'

'Is he yours, Elliot? I haven't kept up.'

'No.'

'Okay. Well, we won't have long anyway.' Godfrey was a large, gentle man who had survived both Eton and Oxford without losing an innate sense of tact, a good reader of people and situations, which was why, behind the soft façade, he occupied one of the most frontline roles at MI6 and was tipped for the top. The Police Commander stood beside him, alert and concerned.

'Bit of background is there?' he said to Kane, hopefully.

'I need to see what happened.'

Kane was given his own protective suit and shoe coverings. He told Mason not to leave the car. Godfrey led him to the home at the centre of the activity.

'Mercifully, their children are away with grandparents,' Godfrey said, 'Anthony Zachariah, as far as anyone here can tell, was a successful businessman who moved to the UK almost twenty years ago. His wife was a primary school teacher. So there's a lot of people wondering why they've been targeted for assassination.'

Kane passed beneath the lucky horseshoe over the entrance, into a corridor lined with family photos, through to a smart new kitchen with children's drawings on the fridge. Zachariah lay on his back on the slate tiles, eyes closed, in a bed of treacly blood. He wore jogging bottoms, white socks and a sky-blue polo shirt that had ridden up to expose the lower half of his stomach. His throat had been hacked at viciously, exposing a dark, wet mess of larynx and trachea.

Anthony Zachariah was what he'd become, but Kane knew him as Anton Semonovich Zakharyan. The best source he'd ever had.

No spray or splatter or smear that Kane could see, none of the traces in which you could begin to read a narrative. The butchery was narrowly contained.

A second body lay at the bottom of the stairs.

Police watched Kane as he approached it. Irina, Anton's wife. She lay awkwardly, her feet still on the stairs, a white nightie ridden up her thighs, hair in a blonde plait. Her mouth was open so that you could see what was obscured in her husband's corpse: their tongues had been removed.

Kane flinched, then forced himself to look closer to confirm he'd seen correctly. Corpse signalling. That was what they used to call it. Murders as messages. Now he saw the tongues themselves on the floor, a foot or so away from each body.

Colourful plastic building blocks spilled from a box in the living room. Drawers and cupboards stood open. So not just a hit; the attackers had been searching for something. Kane stared, puzzled, at a small doll on the living room floor, its head stained as if it had been dipped into the victims' wounds. Then he turned and saw the living room wall, across which a Russian word had been written in blood: *Podkulachnik*.

Kane was staring at it when Godfrey came over.

'I feel I should know what it means,' Godfrey said. Kane eyed the police who watched their every movement but remained respectfully out of earshot.

'It's an old Soviet term: *Podkulachnik*, sub-kulak. Means traitor to the government.'

'Of course. Was he?'

'Once upon a time. Any suspects?'

'None so far.'

'Any recent contact from him at our end?'

'Not as far as I'm aware. Not many traces at all. But we ran some checks and he's been receiving payments from us for the last sixteen years: two thousand a month to a Swiss account. Your name comes up as authorisation.'

17

'Who discovered the bodies?' Kane asked.

'One of the estate's security guards. They noticed the gate into the back garden had been left open, then looked in through the window.'

'And you haven't picked up any intelligence on this? Nothing from sources in Moscow?'

'Nothing yet. We're hunting fast, as you can imagine. What can you tell me?'

Kane walked over to the French windows. They were outward opening with mortice lock, double-cylinder deadbolts, security screen rolled up, vibration sensors on the panes. A large garden led to a high brick wall: roses, towering delphiniums, then the open gate. He counted three security cameras, all with red lights showing, suggesting a connection had failed. Kane stepped into the garden, careful to avoid the route any intruders might have used. Godfrey followed. They were briefly alone.

'His original name was Anton Zakharyan,' Kane said. 'I recruited him shortly after he came to London. He worked for a department of Russia's Main Intelligence Directorate called Unit 22195. It concentrated on overseas assassinations. But he was retired; this was a decade and a half ago.'

'Looks like the news might have finally reached Moscow, nonetheless,' Godfrey said.

Kane studied the open gate, then turned back to the house, flush with its dream of another age, another England. If it was a hit team, they'd be out of the country by now. No shortage of flights in the last five hours to Cyprus, Georgia, to Moscow itself via Istanbul or Baku. Zakharyan would have known as well as Kane, you don't retire from treachery. And not returning to the motherland, staying within the timid landscape of Surrey, would have raised red flags. But why now? With such open viciousness?

'I'm late for HQ,' Godfrey said. 'I need to speak to them, then

I'll be in touch for more background.' He hesitated, seeing Kane loiter. 'I'll tell the police to let you have another minute.'

'Thank you.'

When Godfrey had gone Kane turned back to the stairs. He asked the Crime Scene Manager if he could look at the first floor and they led him past Irina's corpse.

The children's bedrooms were themed: pirates and princesses. On the floor above was an adult bedroom and study. The bedroom contained a king size bed with oyster-coloured silk sheets, but only one side had been slept in, a few long blonde hairs on the pillow. Irina had been coming down in nightclothes. But what was Anton waiting up for?

The study was neat, modern and relatively bare: a PC, ledgers, a filing cabinet. On the desk beside the computer Kane saw a hardback book with a cream cover: *The Oxford Anthology of English Poetry*. Kane had given it to Zakharyan as a gift shortly after they had begun meeting regularly. Something had been wedged in halfway through, like a bookmark.

Kane picked up a pencil with his gloved hands and used this to lever the book open. It wasn't a bookmark but a sheet of notepaper containing the word *Eclipse* and a string of letters and numbers.

The alphanumerical chain looked like a cryptocurrency address. Kane took a photo on his phone, closed the book and looked around the study a final time before returning downstairs. The crime scene tecs and Murder Investigation Team were watching him more impatiently now. He'd been allowed a paying of respects. Kane was grateful for that. He left them to it, knowing they weren't ready for where the trail was going to lead them.

Eclipse.

The estate had become crowded by the time he left the house, its crime scene swelling, a collision of urgency and artifice that gave the impression of a film set. Reporters who had somehow breached the fortifications of Magna Carta Park were being steered back towards the tennis courts. Kane took off his overalls and handed them to a woman who marched over and introduced herself as the senior investigating officer. Kane apologised for not being able to help further at the moment, explained that he had a child waiting for him in the car, and continued towards the Audi.

'Can I get your name, at least?' the SIO called.

'I'm afraid not,' Kane said. He couldn't think of a single question about Anton Zakharyan that he'd be prepared to answer, not without speaking to C first. Mason stared at the officer as Kane gunned the engine and reversed away.

'Did someone die?' Mason said.

'Two people.'

'People you knew?'

'People I used to know.'

'What are you going to do?'

'Go home. There's not much else I can do now.'

THREE

The evening was a daze. Rebecca met her husband in front of Mansion House, the Lord Mayor's official residence in the City of London. She could see Robert was puffed up by the day's success but glad to see her, glad to see her dress. The City itself was more captivating than ever, its banks as elegant as its churches, all wrapped in the magic of enduring power.

Mansion House was the cathedral of pomp among all this, its grand entrance consuming an elite stream of guests, who trickled through, past deferential security, to the Egyptian Hall, where banquet-style tables had been set between white columns topped with gold. The Lord Mayor's Dinner for Bankers & Merchants of the City of London. Rebecca scanned for familiar faces, then for those she could endure conversation with. Everyone crowded around the Chancellor, trying to get his attention.

Robert introduced her to his new private secretary, a young woman with dazzling teeth who seemed almost too nice to realise that Robert would eventually try to fuck her. Rebecca's jaw was starting to ache from smiling when they were interrupted by the presence of Lord Lazenger. The boss, Robert had on occasion called him. The puppet master, he had been called in the press. It had taken several meetings for Rebecca to realise that Lazenger was not in fact short but, rather, hunched inwards as if sunk into an armchair out of which he wasn't going to rise to greet you. And why should he when he had given approximately half a million to Robert over the course of three general election campaigns. He kissed Rebecca on both cheeks with a hand on her waist. His New Britannia think tank had been on the email list of contacts Eclipse sent through, and the thought made her want to retch. She had long deduced what the twinkle in his eyes meant when he studied her: that he considered her beneath Robert, and that this degraded status was a source of arousal. She had encountered no shortage of Gerald Lazengers in her previous life.

Lazenger took Robert off to discuss their ongoing litigation against the *Guardian* and she was left making small talk with the private secretary, chatting about their upcoming holiday in Santorini and Robert's long hours and the awkwardness of having to diarise someone's marriage for them. Rebecca felt like she was watching her life from a distance, through the wrong end of a telescope. There was an odd sensation of lightness. She had had a cancer scare a couple of years ago and it felt similar: everything vivid and yet slippery beneath her gaze, as if the world's solidity depended on your own, and she was fading.

Dinner was served. Rebecca allowed herself to become background, ignored as people spoke to her husband. It allowed her to think and observe. No one could take that from you. Even when an object for others, back in the day, she was watching. Watching them more than they realised, the clues to the life they left outside the door.

When the main course of organic lamb was over, Rebecca sneaked off to the toilets, locked a cubicle and checked her phone. No more messages. She looked at the three images of herself sent by Eclipse. Why did these exist? That was the question that had emerged from her initial horror. She had not photographed herself. The men she slept with did not record her in any way. There were clients who had wanted to, for some kind of trophy or masturbatory souvenir. Rebecca always declined. The beauty of each job was that it ended, they parted ways and she could control whether that man had anything more to do with her life. She didn't leave traces, didn't give them more of herself than they paid for. Once, she had caught a client with his phone recording on the bedside table and made him delete the video.

But these camera angles were not from phones on bedside tables.

I know what you did.

She had done many things in many places, but these three images related to a specific building. The only one she had tried to forget.

The hall erupted in fulsome applause, like a shower of coins rattling down on the stone floor.

Robert drank heavily. When things were going well he drank; when under stress he drank. Rebecca monitored his inebriation, assessing how deeply he would sleep. In bed, she waited half an hour, eyes open, watching the crown of the yew tree visible between the bedroom curtains. Then she went down to the kitchen and sat in the dark.

Rebecca allowed the memories to return, and they seemed clearer for having been stored away so long; preserved far from the light, unhandled. A house near Victoria, Central London. She had been there eight or nine times, each time for 'parties', as people called them, or orgies, which is what they were.

She studied the pictures again on her phone: the men themselves, then the details around them – high ceilings, long drapes, picture rails. Three images, all from the same house, two from the same bedroom. She was sure. On the wall was a painting of a nymph. Or this was what she had always believed it to be, the ivory flesh of a young woman caught bathing up to her waist in a river, half-turning away towards the fecund darkness of a grotto, shielding herself as best she could. Rebecca had felt a certain affinity with her, posed awkwardly, enacting someone else's fantasy. What is your story, she had wondered. What got you into nymph work?

She had no idea whose home it was. The house had always seemed more like a stage set, or a gallery in which she was an exhibit; somewhere you visited rather than lived. The agency had given her the address; other girls had shown her the various bedrooms and told her which were en suite, which locked, which were soundproof, which had straps on the four-poster bed.

Now she retrieved her laptop from her bag and opened it. The glow of its screen bathed her in guilt. She couldn't remember the name of the road, but she remembered the area, of course: Belgravia. Rebecca brought up a map and travelled the streets, memory hand in hand with the digital map until they arrived at Eaton Square.

That was it. Rebecca clicked to Street View. All the houses looked identical. But their austere, ghostly elegance gave her a kick of obscure terror that told her she was on the right track.

Twenty-four hours, Eclipse had said. That was at 4.30 p.m. If he was serious, it meant she now had fifteen hours left. Until what? All night she had thought through the possibilities. The best-case scenarios seemed flimsy: this Eclipse character was joking; he gave up. The worst-case scenarios were vivid. Exposure. What would that mean? Being a prostitute was nothing to be ashamed of – she had seen the social media accounts and marches, the young sex workers, in an age where every identity was a flag to wave. And she had felt an odd sense of parental care, that mixture of envy, protectiveness and pride. But *having* been a prostitute brought back the implication of shame. You are allowed to be one thing, that was the lesson she had learned while trying to protect Robert from scandal. It doesn't matter if it is good or bad, the crime you must avoid is changing, which is never distinct enough from a lie.

Besides a general bonfire of her identity were more specific concerns. Was it a resigning matter, having unwittingly married a prostitute? Downing Street would be involved. She could imagine the calls from Kate and Marcus in the Press Office. Papers loved this kind of thing. They wouldn't hold back on the details: the number of partners, the drugs, the exact activities. Speculation would follow: had she been on the game when she met Robert? Let's say they rode it out. *I'm standing by my wife at this difficult time; we ask for privacy.* A seat with a 15,000 Conservative majority – it could hold. But no more promotions, their collective brand would be tarnished for ever. And Robert's own identity was his career. Resentment would eat their relationship from within.

Her job would have to go. Probably any other jobs for the foreseeable future. Every acquaintance would be cast into a form of pain, no one knowing where to look; the nanny, her teenage stepchildren, and her parents, so successfully preserved in ignorance all these years, with their weak hearts and small minds, neither of which would be able to withstand the flood.

But the reaction she feared most was her own daughter's. Rebecca could not begin to imagine how she might explain her past to the girl, explain to her why people were whispering, why a silence had gathered around them at the school gates, why she was no longer receiving invitations to friends' birthday parties. *What is a prostitute, Mummy?* A child was a conscience reborn. The defiance Rebecca had always counted on evaporated in the light of this puritanical innocence.

Yet some form of revelation had always been a possibility. Her knowledge of this had shadowed Robert's rise: the more successful he became, the more cash someone would get from a tabloid. Rebecca had changed her appearance as much as possible, kept a low profile. The longer she had gone without anything surfacing the safer she had felt. There had always been a chance that an old client recognised her, or one of the other girls, but in exposing her they would have had to expose themselves as well – that was the balance of power she had counted on. There was an immense amount of trust involved in the world of high-class prostitution, an unspoken pact that it occurred in a different world altogether, one where individuals could come and go freely, anonymously, and a shared understanding that a single crack could lead to the entire dam collapsing.

Rebecca googled 'I'm being blackmailed'. It turned out there was an industry devoted to this predicament: sponsored ads, 24-hour chatbots, advice sites. Confide in someone, they all said; tell police; go to police, no matter how embarrassing or explicit the material is. Businesses had been set up to get your money by other means, shrill private investigators: *Don't Let Sextortionists Destroy Your Family Life, possibly even leading to divorce or loss of parental rights. Your professional reputation could be destroyed. You could lose the trust of friends. They might never look you in the eye again.* Then they asked for your email, phone number and post-code for a free quote.

Don't pay your tormentor, everything said. Resist the temptation to pay. Keep evidence.

The last site she visited was a charity named after a sixteen year old who'd killed herself. *Our role is to raise awareness of image-based sexual abuse and support victims.* Rebecca left a message on their voicemail: 'I need to remain anonymous but could do with some advice.' She gave her number and hung up, then closed the windows on her laptop until there was just the map left. Eaton Square. After another moment spent staring at it, Rebecca emailed her colleagues at the charitable trust and cancelled tomorrow's mentoring session, citing possible food poisoning. A plan was forming, an appointment in London.

FOUR

Kane got home at midday, to the Islington townhouse he had shared with his partner, Juliet Bell, for the past five months. As he unlocked the front door, with Mason beside him, he realised his heart was beating fast. The Magna Carta crime scene had burned itself on his retina, and he instinctively looked for blood on the floor of his own home. When Bell appeared from the kitchen, smiling, Kane felt a disproportionate amount of relief.

'I was worried about you,' she said.

Bell had been in a meeting with a prospective client and still wore her suit, looking by far the smarter and more professional of their two-person team. She tried to hug Mason as he hurried past, then caught something in Kane's look.

'You okay?' she asked.

'Just about.'

'What happened?'

'We had to make a diversion. I'll tell you about it later.'

'Someone got killed,' the boy said, heading upstairs. Bell frowned.

'It's nothing for us to worry about,' Kane said.

'Really? Something to do with Bobby?'

'No, Bobby was fine. He says there are details of all sorts of contacts and payments here. Maybe some dirty videos.' Kane smiled as he gave Bell the flash drive, to show her everything was okay. Mason's bedroom door slammed closed.

'No computer games until after lunch,' Bell called up the stairs, then she turned back to Kane. 'What does he mean, someone got killed?'

'I got called to something connected to the old days. We were on the way back. Mason didn't see anything. I had to go visit a crime scene.'

'Oh, God. What happened?' Kane felt the intensity of Bell's stare. She was trying to balance her concern with their unspoken agreement on not probing pasts. 'Can you tell me who?'

'An old source. And their partner. It doesn't really matter who. It's a complicated one. Let's see where it goes,' Kane said. 'I'm not going to keep you in the dark, but I just don't know if it's anything we need to think about at all. I don't want to worry you unnecessarily.'

Kane went up to the box room at the top of the house he used as his personal study. It was their agreement that while he supplied contacts and advice, the bulk of the intelligence work and money went to Bell. His ad hoc study was crowded with literary magazines and the remnants of his PhD. He turned on his laptop and searched for news. On the BBC website, a female reporter stood by police tape. The chyron read:

POLICE SEEK LEADS IN 'HORRIFIC' DOUBLE MURDER.

The reporter spoke to camera. 'What appears to have been a targeted killing has shocked residents on this exclusive private estate in Surrey. Neighbours describe the couple as quiet and friendly. As of now, the Metropolitan police say no arrests have been made and they are urgently appealing for anyone who has information about this crime to come forward.'

The police had kept details of the victims' mutilations to themselves. No mention of the message in blood on the walls, either. The news cut to a helicopter shot, the white forensic tent sitting amid the manicured landscape like a wedding marquee.

Kane imagined the faces of those men, somewhere deep in Russian foreign intelligence, who had commissioned this – who had, somehow, discovered that Anton betrayed them fifteen years ago and decided time meant nothing. Cold, delayed revenge is best not just because you catch your target unawares but for what it says about your commitment. It is a devotion, and every intervening year an offering of patience. A revenge also upon time, and time's presumption that we will forget and so lose ourselves. No, revenge says, something in me is harder, will not be eroded. It endures more than grief itself.

Podkulachnik.

Kane emailed Godfrey, using the secure protocol he had sent through.

Anton Zakharyan, codenamed COURTESAN, was an agent in place at a senior level in Russian military intelligence, recruited in late 2007 after he came to London to coordinate the targeting of dissident Russians in the UK. He was a high-ranking non-declared officer, under cover as a businessman investor. His department, Unit 22195, is based at the headquarters of the 161st Special Purpose Specialist Training Centre in eastern Moscow. They are very well-trained special forces fighters, financed from a budget separate from the Ministry of Defence. It's possible someone's using the current political situation to settle scores.

At the time I left, he was no longer in regular contact with MI6, but I received no indication that his work for us had been discovered. From what I understood, he retired from the Unit in the following years but remained in the UK. Obviously, you'll know whether he was still in

any way active on behalf of British intelligence. I'd also
like to know if he was still involved in any Russian activity.
Check for traces of surveillance on the property and
his electronic communications. It is likely he was being
watched long before the attack.

Finally, he wrote:

I found the word 'Eclipse' on a piece of paper in Zakharyan's
study, along with what looked like a code, possibly for a
cryptocurrency account. Worth running a check.

And that was all he could do for now. Kane sat back and felt,
for the first time since leaving the Secret Intelligence Service, an
immense frustration at being locked out. He couldn't concentrate
on the reports of corporate espionage he was meant to write,
which seemed tawdry by comparison, so he went for a walk.

Outside, his mind was flooded with memories; as if he hadn't
just walked into the world but into the past. Lean, dark-eyed
Anton; the hollows of his stubbled cheeks and his elegant fingers. Details he had omitted from the report to Godfrey: in May
2008, Kane and his team at MI6 had identified Zakharyan as a
non-declared officer of the Russian Intelligence Directorate. But
he was clearly more than that, involved in something specialist.
So they began a dive. And it was a deep dive: electronic surveillance alongside 24-hour monitoring. And they found a life split
three ways between business, intelligence and sadomasochism.

Zakharyan's erotic obsessions revealed themselves in his
internet history, in participation in drug-fuelled group sex, and in
visits he made to both male and female prostitutes, using some of
the millions at his disposal to recreate elaborate fantasies involving being stripped and beaten, far removed from his everyday
persona as a conservative family man. Kane remembered being

shown the footage and knowing at once it would be enough to break him. His father was a former member of the Russian parliament, instrumental in creating an organisation called Russian Choice, which pushed to outlaw all portrayals of 'non-traditional sexual relations'. It promoted the idea that decadent European values contradicted traditional Russian morality.

Zakharyan, it seemed, had European values.

They staged a raid during one of his chemsex marathons, claiming to be police and that some of the men present were underage. Kane, from the start, presented himself as Zakharyan's saviour; this was crucial to their strategy. He turned up as Zakharyan waited outside West End Central police station, introduced himself as a representative of the British government and expressed his desire to prevent this becoming 'a diplomatic incident'. Kane said he understood Zakharyan was a person of significant value, and offered to arrange for the whole thing to be buried in return for the opportunity to talk.

The beauty of it was that, once a source starts talking, they can't go back. They are a traitor, they have broken the oath that bound them to their life. Three months and seven meetings later, Kane explained to Anton Zakharyan that he had become an asset of the UK's Secret Intelligence Service, MI6. If Anton wasn't genuinely compromised before, he was now. Talking to Kane had signed a suspended death warrant.

But, whatever manipulation had been involved, their bond was genuine. On long walks in the Lake District, Anton spoke about a childhood in Russia and his desire to return there one day, even expressing hope that it might reform, that he might be a part of that process. On darker days, he said: *You know they will kill me eventually.* He always said it calmly, as something necessarily accepted. *I think you are a good man. I trust you. But there is a limit to what you can do.*

Everything Kane had hoped to leave behind had returned. And

31

he was caught powerless. The sources forcibly retired, imprisoned or still hiding – Kane thought about them every day. It became a tinnitus of the soul. MI6's HQ, Vauxhall Cross, was a nightmare, a citadel of inaction, but at least it was the heart of things, and turning up there each day was a laying of flowers, a candle lit. If you could do nothing for your old sources, you could still maintain the cause for which they had risked their lives. It made the act of moving into private work feel like a relinquishing of responsibility. So many did it, Kane wondered if that was the point.

At 5 p.m. he was back staring at emails, no response from Godfrey, when Bell came in holding two glasses of white wine. She'd changed from the suit into a summer dress.

'Mason's dad's on his way. Still want to go out? We could relax at home.'

'Let's relax. I want to talk about where we go from here,' Kane said.

'Okay.' Bell smiled cautiously. 'That sounds interesting.'

'I was thinking about being less interesting. Next steps.'

'I'm intrigued. Not sure I can be less interesting, though.'

'That's what I'm worried about.'

She touched the back of her hand against his cheek. He kissed it and wanted to be far away from everything. Just the two of them. And he knew, part of this craving for purity – the fantasy of drifting away – was because he didn't want her ever finding out the truth about why he'd walked into her life.

Two years ago, Kane had been called in by his boss at MI6, John Broughton, and told there was a journalist getting dangerously close to some uncomfortable truths. She was fearless, well connected and out to expose the dark side of the British intelligence service. Her name was Juliet Bell.

'Make friends,' Broughton said. 'You're good at that, befriending women.'

Bell had just got a publishing deal for a book looking at illegal

MI6 activity. It was to be titled *Under the Cover of Darkness*. Kane read some of the material they'd liberated from her computer and it was good. He agreed to make enquiries into this ambitious reporter, and justified the operation to himself on the basis that he could make his own decision about the threat she posed and thereby control how MI6 responded.

MI6 found a mutual contact who arranged for him to be at a dinner party with her. She wasn't what he'd expected, which immediately made him feel naïve and made him realise why she was good – candid, flirtatious, with shoulder-length dark brown hair streaked with flashes of white. They didn't talk much then, but Kane ensured she learned enough about his background to invite him for coffee later that week.

'I'm writing a book,' Bell said. 'Talk to me. It will be fun, and I'll respect all due sensitivities.' There was a disarming twinkle in her eye. 'A chat off record. Background.'

'I shouldn't,' he said, 'but okay.'

She was right, it was fun. Coffee became dinner. Bell's intelligence was underpinned by moral cause, and it made her forceful, unapologetic, and she enjoyed trying to provoke him into revelations. They talked for over three hours. Kane kept the details of his governmental role vague, but she knew what that meant and read him as a disenchanted spook, which was easy enough to play. Kane gave her some tantalising crumbs from inside the intelligence world: MI6–Saudi collaborations, Yemeni connections, the training of spies in Egypt and Turkey, all of which she scribbled down in a black notebook she kept on her person, even when she went to the bathroom.

She was good company: wry, with a fizzing, aggressive energy. Kane enjoyed being the audience for her. At one point she took an incoming call and he saw her husband's name on the screen. When she came back, she downed her glass of wine then forced a smile.

'Where were we?'

A fun night with a steep bar bill. Kane had his theories about people who placed themselves in dangerous situations as a matter of professional routine: they inevitably had an element of danger within them. They were natural risk-takers and therefore vulnerable to risky propositions. Kane saw that lack of inhibition in Bell and liked it. As they went on to a basement bar for cocktails, he tried not to think of the report he was meant to write.

At the end of the night, she said, 'That was more pleasant and informative than I expected.' She shook his hand as her Uber arrived. The handshake lingered. Then she got into the vehicle and didn't turn as it pulled away.

He told MI6 to back off. He said there was no justification for maintaining surveillance on Juliet Bell, or accessing her communications, and that further actions posed a risk of reputational damage for the intelligence service. He had no idea if they listened to him. A year passed, and Kane thought of her often. Then their paths crossed again. Close to the end of his time in government service, he had attended a talk at an art gallery about facial recognition technology. Bell was there, giving a presentation. She saw him in the audience and her eyes widened.

'Concerned about government surveillance or doing it?' she joked, afterwards, when they approached one another.

'Concerned. Off duty.'

'Does anyone here know who you are?'

'No one knows who I am,' Kane smiled. Bell looked at him quizzically. 'Want to walk for a bit?' he asked.

They walked from Old Street through Angel. Neither of them talked shop. At one point they heard piano coming from a basement window and she slipped an arm into his as they listened for a while. Kane considered the various approaches open to him. He couldn't see how something would work between them. But then it had been a long time since his last relationship, and he couldn't see how anything would work with anyone. Enjoy the moment, he thought. Midlife had its own intensity. Eventually she said, 'My home's not far.'

They continued into the tree-lined streets behind Highbury Fields and arrived at a handsome townhouse. Bell invited him in and paid off a babysitter. No mention of the husband. There was an upright piano, a lot of books, her awards: Courage in Journalism, the Martha Gellhorn prize for investigative reporting, an inscribed plaque from Spotlight on Corruption. Bell poured vodka tonics then sat down at the piano and, after a hesitant start, played the piece they'd heard. When she'd finished Kane clapped and she came and sat beside him. Their knees touched. She set her drink down on the coffee table and looked him in the eye.

'We're being watched,' Kane said. A shape flickered in the piano's gloss.

'What?'

'Look over my shoulder.'

'Oh, for God's sake,' Bell said. 'Mason. How long have you been there?'

That was the first time Kane saw him, crouching halfway down the stairs. Eyes dark, sandy-haired. Something about his stare reminded Kane of street kids everywhere from Naples to Karachi: hungry, distrustful, poised to run. Kane winked, but he didn't respond and Bell got up, moving to him.

'How are you feeling, Mason?' she said.

No response.

'This is a friend of mine,' Bell said. 'He's called Elliot.' After another moment she muttered to Kane: 'You should go. He's not been well recently.'

And that was that. Kane messaged her the next day and didn't hear anything back. There were enough reasons for her to have second thoughts. It wasn't long before he walked out of MI6 altogether. He took his interest in Middle Eastern languages into academia and began a PhD.

Oxford proved just as cut-throat as Moscow or Kabul. Kane hadn't sought any status but, after he won a competitive grant, a jealous colleague started spreading rumours that Kane's seminars on literary transmission constituted some sort of radical cell, that Kane had a criminal past which he hadn't declared to the university and, more accurately, that in the midst of debates around the restitution of colonial antiquities held by the college museum, Kane had proposed that they steal them, even discussing the museum's poor security. Kane declined to counter the rumours. Indeed, he returned the grant and proposed they give it to his colleague instead, who was nothing if not eager. But the damage was done.

The university asked him to suspend teaching activities. He began spending less time on the PhD and more time taking long walks into Oxfordshire. Money ran low and he found it hard to care, sensing, at least, some financial urgency approaching that would give him a purpose.

Bell's name appeared on his phone while he was sitting in a damp public library, applying for work as a translator.

Looking for new ventures and wanted to pick your brain.

Kane smiled. They arranged to meet for dinner at a modestly priced Italian. Bell turned up late, breathless. She asked enthusiastically about Kane's life, very curious about its genteel collapse. Kane didn't push her about her own situation. His money was on a divorce, which turned out to be true but only part of the truth. Over dessert, she said, 'You once talked about a couple of reporters who'd moved into private intelligence. They were in the States, set up a company.'

Kane remembered the conversation. Bell had been talking about the decline of newspapers; he mentioned two journalists who'd quit and established a successful private intelligence outfit.

'No,' Kane said, when he saw where this was going. He ignored the bite of personal disappointment at why she'd contacted him.

'No what?'

'Don't do it.'

'I'm in real difficulty, Elliot.' She looked pained.

'I'm sorry to hear that. Why are you coming to me?'

'I have some irrational trust in you. Perhaps that makes me naïve. I could do with some advice.'

'That was my advice: it's not something to get involved with. The world needs your journalism.'

'Oh, please.'

'I mean it.'

'And if I don't have a choice?'

'Definitely don't do it.' He saw her body tense with anger. 'I can give you some names,' Kane said. 'You don't need me to introduce you.'

'They'd think I was investigating.'

'Maybe. Worth a try, though.'

'Okay.'

'You're too good for it, Juliet.'

'Great. I must have imagined the fact that I'm about to find myself fucking homeless – because I'm such a good journalist I must be rich. Right? Because I've fought such a noble battle. That's how it works. Sorry, it's just … I've hardly slept for five days. I'm in the midst of a custody battle from hell. Meanwhile, Mason's been diagnosed with non-epileptic seizures which, as far as I can tell, means no one has any idea what's going on. It's been really bad. But I didn't mean to take it out on you.'

When they went back to hers, the piano was taped with bubble wrap and protective cardboard. A lot of belongings sat in open cardboard boxes across the living room floor. Mason was with his father and not due to be dropped off for another hour. As

Bell improvised cocktails out of the remaining bottles, Kane sifted bank statements on the kitchen counter. They had been covered with calculations, scrawled to the point of annihilating them. Underneath were lawyer's invoices and, finally, NHS letters detailing Mason's appointments with paediatricians and neurologists and psychologists.

'It's a stress thing,' Bell said, glancing over. 'Apparently you get it when something big has disrupted your life. He blacks out. But there's no meds for it or anything like that. He has a stone he's meant to grip when he thinks he's about to have a fit.'

'Does it work?'

'Sometimes. Maybe.'

They took their drinks to the sofa.

'It gets worse each week,' Bell said. 'And his mood swings are becoming more extreme. Last week, he hit a boy in school. The school insists on therapy but there's a year's waiting list unless you're willing to spend a fortune. And it still feels ridiculous taking a ten year old to therapy. What's he got inside him to be unpacked? The childhood I failed. My fuck-ups. It's not him who should be sitting there. And there's this bloody court case. Patrick, my ex, says he wants Mason living with him, which is odd, as he's made it clear he dislikes the boy and sees him as a failure. But he wants to sort him out, and he has money. And maybe that's what Mason needs: a rich, arrogant father. Maybe it's what we all need. I don't have to talk about any of this if you don't want.'

Kane learned details of the ongoing custody battle. Her ex was a lawyer and doing everything he could to damage Bell in a personal way. She'd borrowed twenty grand from her mother, but there wasn't going to be any more. She was selling possessions and planning to move home, downsize.

'Hence the piano. I hardly play it. And someone's offered five grand. That's a bargain, right? One piano, ten hours of lawyer. What a world.'

Kane didn't hear the exchange when Mason was dropped off, but the boy went straight to bed with a slammed door. Bell came back down, slumped with defeat.

'It's almost funny, isn't it? I've reported on wedding parties that have been hit by stray missiles, but I still thought there'd be some kind of moral fairness in life. It's a stupid comparison. I'm sorry.'

'You need to expect some fairness to be good. I've met the people who believe that life's a battle without any right or wrong and you don't want to spend too much time in their company. It narrows you.'

'But they win.'

'That depends what you mean by winning.'

'I can't even remember what I mean by winning.'

They drank with commitment. At some point Kane turned around and Bell was asleep, tumbler cradled in her lap. He prised the drink from her hands and covered her with a blanket, then went to the kitchen and poured himself another measure of vodka. He took a final look at her prizes for journalism then dialled a man in Dubai.

'Elliot.'

'Sebastian, I hope I haven't woken you.'

'Not at all.'

'I wanted you to be the first to know, I'm going to be dipping a toe into private work. So if you're still looking for any help, I'm here.'

'Wonderful news. What changed your mind?'

'Just life.'

'Ah, life.' Kane wasn't sure what Sebastian Rosenquist, youngest and most freewheeling son of a minor banking dynasty, understood by the word. Did he have much concept of financial necessity? Sebastian was a playboy but he was also smart, well connected and obsessed with the acquisition of geopolitical knowledge. They'd become close when Rosenquist had been arrested on drugs charges in Turkey. Kane was seconded to MI6's corporate liaison team at the time and had a strong working relationship with the Turkish intelligence service, so it wasn't difficult negotiating the billionaire's freedom. Rosenquist invited him onto his yacht the following week. Like a lot of rich people, he was obsessed with a more elusive power and had a connoisseur's hunger for intelligence product. Kane had been a useful contact, and Rosenquist was genuinely disappointed when he left MI6.

'Drove me mad, thinking of you sitting in a library,' Rosenquist said. 'With everything you've got to offer.'

'It was quite pleasant for a while.'

'Well, you've seen the light at just the right time. I have some lawyers I'd love you to meet who could really do with the kind of insight you'd provide. Going to one of the big names?'

'Staying independent. Setting up my own.'

'Even better.' Kane knew what that meant: one to one, Kane serving his needs. 'Who are you getting on board?' Rosenquist asked.

'All sorts. There are several old MI6 hands who will be interested. But it's early days. And there's a former journalist involved.' Kane said it carefully – careful to place subtle emphasis on 'former' but feeling regretful about it, as if carving a headstone.

'Who's that?'

'Juliet Bell.'

Rosenquist laughed again. 'Are you sure she's not just going to write about us?'

'She's in a hard place. Trust me.'

'Life.'

'Exactly.'

'And she's willing to use her address book? Her sources in finance and the energy industry?'

'Of course. We could do with some cash flow fast, though. Lock her in before she changes her mind.'

'What are we talking?'

'A few hundred k to start. I'd be happy if you took a 40 per cent share. Something like that. I'll email you figures, but this is really embryonic. Right now we don't even have a name.'

'The best ones keep it that way. Just let me know what you need.'

Kane emailed a request for five hundred grand of seed money and an initial estimate of profits. He finished the vodka and slept in the armchair, woke at 6 a.m. to a message from one of Rosenquist's lawyers with contractual paperwork attached. It had been followed by an email from Rosenquist himself, outlining a situation with a competitor who was trying to sue him and against whom he was launching counter-legal actions.

There was a noise in the garden. Kane thought Bell was awake, looked up to see her son with a knife, prowling the bushes. A squirrel darted away. Kane stepped out. It was a crisp, blank dawn, the kind he liked. Mason pocketed the knife when he saw him.

'Hunting?' Kane asked. The boy shook his head. 'Can I see the knife?'

Mason handed it over. It was a fold-out pocket knife. Kane resisted the urge to ask how he'd acquired it. He tested the blade then gave it back, which surprised the boy.

'Ever caught anything?'

Silence.

'Brushed your teeth recently?'

'Why?'

'Animals have a powerful sense of smell. It can be one hundred times more powerful than ours. If you've washed with soap or brushed your teeth in the last twelve hours, there's a chance they can smell it from half a mile away. Their sight's a lot better too. Can I borrow the knife again?'

41

Kane took the knife to the end of the garden, where some long branches from a maple tree had been sawn off. He showed the boy how to strip the branches to Y shapes, sharpen the ends to a point and then stick them into the ground. Over the next twenty minutes they built a bivouac. When they had struts and a crossbeam, Kane told the boy to bring two old blankets out and they put one over the structure and the other inside and lay down.

'See the steam of your breath? Try to breathe so your breath is as invisible as possible,' Kane said. 'Try using your nose rather than your mouth, see if that makes any difference.'

It was cold and damp, but the boy didn't seem to mind. Out of the corner of his eye, Kane saw Bell at the back door, staring. When he went in she was making coffee.

'A morning of miracles,' she said.

'Is it?'

'Why is there a hundred grand in my bank account?'

'It was the maximum transfer allowed.' Kane found mugs and plunged the cafetière. 'I can do another hundred tomorrow.'

'What is this?'

'Investment in our private intelligence company. If you're not still interested, you can keep the money anyway. I'll figure something out.'

'Of course I'm interested. It was my idea. How did you know my bank details?'

'They're all over your kitchen.'

She nodded slowly, poured two coffees and handed one to Kane, appraising him with a new, inquisitive intensity. Then she looked at Mason, still lying belly-down in the bivouac, then the clock on the wall.

'Mason needs to get to school. I'm meant to be at my lawyers in half an hour.'

'I can take Mason. Then we can meet for lunch and discuss details.'

'Really? You can manage that?'

'Can I manage a school run? One day I'll tell you about the time I got ten men out of Afghanistan across the Hindu Kush.'

She smiled. He thought he knew how attractive she was, but that smile took him by surprise.

On the way to school, Kane asked Mason if he wanted to play a game.

'You walk this route each day,' Kane said. 'So you're in a good position to see how one day differs from another.' The boy stared at him. 'Trust me, it's an interesting question: what's always here and what's different; what's out of place?' The kid still acted sceptical, used to being the butt of jokes, but he soon joined in, noting cars, people, even flowers. He was sharp. Whatever lay beneath his silence it wasn't a lack of cognition. When they arrived at the school he asked if Kane would be collecting him and when Kane said it was unlikely, he turned away, embarrassed to have asked.

Bell arrived at their scheduled lunch looking keen. She'd applied make-up as if it was some kind of interview.

'How were the divorce lawyers?' Kane asked, once they'd ordered and their drinks had arrived.

'Delighted to be paid. What now?'

'You ask me whose money it is.'

'The question crossed my mind.'

Kane talked her through the details: their investor, his business empire, his expectations.

'This is Rosenquist money?' Bell said. 'Fuck me. I slipped out of the ethical pretty quickly.'

'That's how it happens. But Sebastian thinks we can be useful.'

'Sebastian.'

'We're acquainted.'

'And now I'm working for him?'

'We're working for ourselves, advising people where we

43

choose. At least you are. I'm backseat, doing a bit here and there informally.'

'And is your acquaintance, Sebastian Rosenquist, correct? Can we be useful?'

'Of course. Between us, we're about two connections from every major player out there. And if we're not, we can find someone who is and persuade them to talk. You're very good at that. You've got the ability to pick up the phone to pretty much anyone in business or government or law and have a convincing reason to speak to them. On my side, I can get us people to do surveillance, access emails, call data, all that kind of thing. We're not employed directly by Sebastian but by his lawyers.'

'What do they want us to do?'

'Find out about this rival of his and destroy them.'

Bell nodded thoughtfully, casting her eyes around the restaurant. He hadn't seen her this contemplative before. She looked like someone imagining themselves in a new role rather than someone weighing up ethical decisions. Their food arrived.

'My proposal is that I help you,' Kane said. 'I can use my contacts, act as a go-between, but this is on your request. You're right, it's good money and you'd do it well. I'm involved with a centre for victims of torture and would love to get them what they need to renovate their premises. But I don't need much money and I don't want much of my time spent spying.'

'I understand. I appreciate you doing this.'

'The rest wouldn't be too difficult to set up. You know the score: an intelligence company is a front. It connects the client to people who can do certain things they want done discreetly.'

'What else do I need to know?'

'In terms of craft? Nothing. I'm guessing half your address book is already encrypted. You're used to manipulating people. You protect sources. Most importantly, you know that someone is always going to try to stop you and you have to act accordingly.

We don't get hired for open goals. But that's not the biggest challenge you'll face,' Kane said.

'Go on.'

'A private spy sells themselves on their reputation. Clients will buy my association with the Secret Intelligence Service. They'll want to use your reputation for being good. You won't just be selling your investigative skills but your halo. And some people might pay you to close stories down. A lot of the big money is about concealing the truth. It's a different endgame. That might be especially tough because sources will talk to you on the basis of what you've achieved before; because they want a story out there.'

Bell nodded. 'I get it.'

'If you can really handle that, then let's make some money. Obviously, we'll select who we work for,' Kane continued. 'But there's not an infinite amount of people willing to pay money for private intelligence work, and they're rarely the nicest people in the world.'

'I know all this. I've been researching it for years.'

'I want us going in with our cynicism intact. It can be ugly work.'

'I understand.'

Bell's determination remained. She hadn't just been flirting with the idea. This would be an education, Kane reasoned. If she wanted a walk on the wild side, he could lead the way. Maybe, further down the line, solvent and disgusted with herself, she'd write an exposé and it could blow the whole industry up and he could get out of town with some cash and memories. Besides, this gave him reason to spend more time with her, and he wanted to see that smile again.

'All I care about is Mason,' she said.

'He's not all you care about, he's what you care about most. It's different.'

'Not right now, it isn't.'

KX Global Insight was born the following day, the name as meaningless as they could manage while being enough to head an invoice. That afternoon, they met Rosenquist's corporate lawyers at their thirtieth-floor offices on Threadneedle Street, windows staring insolently down at the stone scalp of the Bank of England. The meeting went well. The lawyers described how helpful it would be to achieve reputational annihilation of their competitor. Kane said he could get them full access to phone, bank and credit card details for all the major players by the end of the day, establish the nature of any rival private intelligence operations within a week. Bell laid out the placing of a piece about corruption in a national newspaper, which would get global syndication plus over a million hits guaranteed across social media platforms. The team were keen. When they asked rates, it caught Kane and Bell unprepared. Kane said an initial payment of a hundred thousand pounds plus a monthly retainer of ninety thousand plus expenses. Success clause of half a million if they provided evidence that materially contributed to a victory in court. The clients agreed on the spot.

Bell stared at the lift doors as they descended back to ground level.

'Ninety grand a month?'

'Should I have gone higher?' Kane said.

'Jesus Christ.'

'How do you feel?'

'Dirty. But I think I like it. What do we do first?'

'Unwrap the piano. That's my vote. You?'

'Do you mind if I complicate things?' she said, and she placed a hand either side of his face and kissed him.

That was six months ago. Sitting there now, on the dying grass of her lawn, he saw how idyllic it had all been. Monetising your past told you it had been worthwhile. Using that money to support a home and a family was like laundering it. He had relaxed about the idea of selling out and allowed himself to consider that it had been the right thing to do. Bell had transformed herself. She bought new clothes, the black reporter's notebook disappeared. She never tried to unpick the strange fate that meant their paths had crossed. Not to his knowledge, anyway. And in the rush of success Kane had shelved his plan to tell her everything. This was what normal people do, he realised: lose control of their lies. As a spy you had to own them, manage them, file them. He needed to reset their relationship on a basis of total honesty, now that it was real and he didn't want it to end.

'Bobby got us great stuff,' Bell said, lying down on the picnic blanket, head resting on Kane's stomach. 'Did you have a chance to see it?'

'Not yet.'

'It's dynamite. You can never start to imagine what other people are into. Until you spy on them, I guess. Did you find that?'

'I always had an inkling what people were into.' Kane stared at the sun. He imagined it rinsing his sight.

'Mason didn't get in the way this morning?'

'Not at all. You know, some of the most effective communist spies were women with children.'

'Never heard of that.'

'Exactly. It's not a problem. I like his company.'

'I think you're the first person to say that.'

They lay in silence for a long time. Kane was conscious of his breaths, her head rising and falling with each one. The sun tangled itself in the branches of the garden's apple tree and the light became softer, colder.

'Your old source,' Bell said. 'I saw the news. It looks awful. The wife as well.'

'It's certainly awful. But it's not my problem any more.'

'Are you sure?'

'I sincerely hope so.'

'He was an agent of yours?'

'Yes. I was called to the scene because they wanted some background. But that's all.'

'Okay. So what was it you wanted to talk about? Being less interesting, you said.'

'We always discussed getting out sooner rather than later. I'm going to propose we do it as soon as possible. Take a break, at least. I was saying to Mason I'd like to take him travelling.'

'He'd love that.'

'Let's go away. When we get the money from this job, let's get out of London.'

'You saved my life, Elliot. I'm happy to go on holiday with you.'

'I got you money. It's not quite the same.'

'You got me more than money.'

Bell lifted herself on an elbow and kissed him.

'Keep me warm,' Kane said, wrapping his arms around her body.

The evening chill woke them where they lay interwoven on the blanket. They went inside, upstairs to bed. Around 5 a.m. Kane's phone rang. It was Godfrey. Kane got up and saw Bell's eyes glinting in the darkness, watching him as he left the room to answer it.

'We need to meet,' Godfrey said.

London wasn't a city of panoramas but Alexandra Palace boasted one of the few. A Victorian pile on a three-hundred-foot ridge overlooking north London, roughly equidistant from their homes, it was deserted when Kane arrived but for the lights of the city stretching into an indifferent grey dawn.

Godfrey was already there in the parking lot, standing by his Mercedes. He looked drained, unshaven. No other cars around, the abandoned gravel scarred by handbrake turns. Seclusion made the place popular with lovers and joyriders, but it was theirs for now, the dark expanse of Alexandra Park beneath them, then the forms of the city beyond it, glass blocks against a bruised, uncertain sky. Street lights began blinking off.

'We fucked up,' Godfrey began. 'Zakharyan tried to contact us in the days before he was killed. Four days ago, then again on Sunday. He called various governmental numbers, couldn't get through to anyone who would take him seriously. Eventually, a junior officer spoke to him, and a meeting had been set up for today.'

Kane swore. Prevention missed. Nothing was more agonising. And his absence from HQ was to blame.

'Any idea why he wanted to speak to someone?'

'No. At the weekend, he called his brother in Moldova. We tracked the brother down and he said Zakharyan was very worried: something had got out and he was in a situation. Zakharyan said that others might be in danger too.'

Godfrey added the last detail carefully, watching Kane's face.

'Something had got out?'

'Yes. I don't have any clarity on what he meant by that. There had been a threat of some kind, or a suggestion that if he didn't do something then information about him would be released. That's all the brother knew. Zakharyan was searching for you as well, according to his internet records. He emailed your old university address.'

Kane's heart sank. He stared at the gravel. When he looked up again the city was still there, rising out of torpor; a city he had sought to defend in various ways for many years without expecting thanks, just the chance to stop eventually. Anton Zakharyan had been searching for him. In his terror, in his last days.

'Any leads on the killings?' Kane asked.

'Very little. There was a good security system installed, with cameras, but it was reliant on Wi-Fi and it appears the killers used some kind of jamming device. Nothing so far from

49

forensics,' Godfrey continued. 'No sign of the weapon used. The attackers were careful. We've pulled five hundred hours of CCTV and there's no trace of them. We're still trying. There are ninety officers knocking on doors and chasing dashcam footage. So far, it seems clear they approached from the back garden. The estate is well guarded, of course, but it's also huge, with a lot of perimeter, and a lot of parkland. Beyond it's countryside, more golf courses, A-roads. It would be possible to avoid cameras altogether if you put thought into your route.'

'What else have you got on Anton's life recently? Anything that stands out? Travel? Finances?'

'He hasn't left the UK in the last eight months. That was a family skiing holiday in France. His business dealings all seem healthy. In terms of his intelligence work for Russia, it looks like he genuinely retired. After you left MI6, he didn't do anything more for us in terms of briefings. I think he turned his back on that world altogether. How did you recruit him, if you don't mind me asking?'

'Why?'

'You know how rare it is. And you were one of the few who could do it.'

'I filmed him fucking other men, then threatened to show it to his family.'

'I see.' Godfrey gave the slightest grimace, rapidly replaced by professional equanimity. 'Needs must.'

'Anton had some pretty intense erotic obsessions. Did you come across those? Internet searches? Use of male prostitutes? Sadomasochistic stuff.'

'No. But there's one thing that's puzzled us. We found an encrypted messaging app on his phone: Whispr. Ever use it with him?'

'Not me. Whispr wasn't around when I was running him.'

'He downloaded it three days ago. Maybe he felt his regular

channels had been compromised. I don't know, we can't find any evidence that he was under surveillance. But it's not helpful from our point of view – the app doesn't retain any content or metadata. The company itself doesn't even have access, so the servers are a non-starter. Whatever he used it for is gone.'

'Might it connect to the Eclipse note I mentioned?'

'Anything's possible. The note matches his handwriting. The numbers are almost certainly a Bitcoin address, but that's all they tell us. The thing that concerns me is that we can't see any signs of the hit team themselves. We've looked at all entries and exits from the UK in the surrounding days. I'm starting to wonder if there's a possibility they're still in the country.'

'They wouldn't hang around unless they had more to do.'

'Exactly.'

Kane could tell there was something Godfrey was holding back. He thought it might be due to official secrecy.

'Tell me what else you've got,' he urged.

'Another name came up on Zakharyan's internet search: Christian Rivera. Know who he is?'

'He was my colleague, involved in Anton's recruitment.'

'He was the other person your man was trying to reach.'

Kane felt a new twinge of dread. A picture was coming into focus, the one picture Kane really didn't want to see: whatever got Anton Zakharyan and his wife killed, threatened all those who had worked with him.

'Anton was trying to find you and Christian,' Godfrey said.

'He was trying to warn us.'

'It seems so.'

Now Kane saw, with the precision of horror, the home he had just left: two unprotected souls asleep inside, two blameless people he had become close to and made very vulnerable.

'You say the men who killed Zakharyan and his wife might still be in the UK?' Kane said.

'That's right. And there's one further cause for concern, I'm afraid. After researching yourself and Christian Rivera, Anton printed out some of the material. It's in the printer memory, but we can't find the documents themselves, and we don't believe he gave them to anyone. We know the attackers searched the premises . . .'

'And took it.'

'That's what I'd assume.'

'What kind of information?'

'Everything he could find about you and Christian Rivera.'

'Home addresses?'

'I don't know. Not necessarily.'

They fell silent. The sun was almost up. Bell would be awake soon.

'Would you return to help?' Godfrey asked.

'To MI6?'

'Broughton's in Kyiv right now, but I know he'll want you involved. People say you were the only one who could do it last time: take on the Unit.'

And look where it got us, Kane thought. 'I'm not doing that any more,' he said.

'I'd like to tell the Russians that: to stay away, that you're out of the game. I'd really like to. But I'm not sure they'd listen.'

FIVE

By morning, Rebecca knew her next step. She woke early and tried to prepare herself, walked out, still in her nightclothes, towards the woods, into the night odours of soil and moss. She watched the day tearing itself from darkness with a silent scream, saw the red kites owning the skies and tried to draw inspiration from their gall. Then she returned indoors. Rebecca messaged work again: the sickness continued. A sickness called the past, she thought. She made breakfast, bid Robert goodbye, dropped Iona at school, then continued to the M40, into London.

That was when things became very strange.

She parked at Victoria Station, suddenly alone in the capital with the uneasy freedom of a truant. As she left the car, Rebecca felt herself stepping into an alternative life. She bought a pair of cheap sunglasses from Boots, a pack of protective face masks, tied her hair back and pulled a mask on.

The area around the station had taken itself apart and refashioned a new district entirely, blocks of glass and retail where she remembered there being streets. But just two minutes west was Belgravia, and Belgravia had no need to change. It had been born perfect, aloof from time and its insecurities, a Georgian vision of elegance that left the world around it looking crude. Eaton Square surrounded a long strip of private gardens, with creamy porticoed terraces on each side. Rebecca remembered being surprised on her first visit, finding this elegant paradise so close to the beggars of Victoria. But that was London – you slipped one block away from your usual route and fell into a different world. Only a prostitute could really know this city, she had thought.

The square, as ever, was unsettlingly quiet. No people visible through the tall windows, few lights on inside the houses. Wealth was a form of silence, she had come to understand, so deep here it made you conspicuous walking down the street. It demanded that you justify the unsavoury warmth of your body intruding on the neoclassical hush. These were ghost streets, owners evaporated, as if money had liberated them from the demands of physical existence. She saw now, as she had not done while fucking the inhabitants, that they weren't even homes but assets, they would continue to prosper while you were long gone, rotting inelegantly in the ground. That was why they looked down on you.

There was the church, at the northern end. So she was in the right place. It was a distinctive one, fronted by a row of six columns, with a clock tower on top. This gave Rebecca some orientation. She remembered being able to see its clock from one of the beds.

The houses were barely distinguishable from one another. Each looked opaque and mysterious. But the trees in the square were individual as fingerprints. Rebecca located the tennis courts, then the towering redwood tree beside them. And there was the window looking out onto it.

Number 62.

Yes, she thought. They had painted the door dove grey, where it had once been a lustrous black, but the single brass doorbell remained. No hint of the debauchery that had occurred behind it; the house looked as innocent as its neighbours. But she was sure. She remembered the undulation of the stone steps, with the comfort of history, all the feet that had passed this way before you, including other centuries' mistresses and courtesans no doubt. How many times had she come here? Eight or nine? Always admiring the effort put into these events, the girls doing their make-up in the rooms upstairs, the food and drinks lavishly laid out in the main reception room. Sex parties. The fantasy they were told to enact was that they weren't prostitutes but everyday women drawn to depravity. God knows, the organisers could have found some easily enough for free, but the idea wasn't simply that women might want to attend orgies, it was that all of them looked like models and signed NDAs.

Rebecca climbed the steps under the scrutiny of two cameras and pressed the bell. The door was answered a few seconds later by a man in his forties, clean-shaven, in an olive-coloured jacket and a tie just a shade darker. He looked bizarre, standing stiffly, a family home behind him with fresh flowers in vases and an airy daylight that did not chime with her memories. A child's Spider-Man rucksack lay on the floor beside a lacquered side table. It occurred to Rebecca that the man gazing impassively down at her may be some kind of staff.

What had she intended to say? Rebecca felt off balance, and decided to make an excuse and leave, then she smelled the place: that cocktail of floor polish, the velvet of the drapes, cold stone-work. It caught her like a hand around the throat.

'I realise this is a little odd,' she began, with an unthreatening and vaguely upper-class lilt to her voice. 'I used to visit this house some time ago and lost touch with the occupants. I wondered if they still lived here, if I could have a word.'

The man stared at her.

'And who might I say is enquiring?'

'An old acquaintance.'

Something about this resulted in his manner cooling.

'I'm afraid everyone's busy right now.'

Rebecca had a moment of self-doubt. Then her new self kicked in: educated, rich, an MP's wife.

'This is important,' she said. 'Could I speak to the owner? I've travelled a long way.'

Her tone gave the gatekeeper pause. He nodded once, closed the door. A few moments later it was opened again, this time by a man a decade or so older than his butler, with a white goatee and open-necked pink shirt. Sixty or so. Rebecca didn't recognise him. He didn't look like someone who had hosted orgies.

'How can I help?' he said, sounding distinctly unwilling to help.

'I'm interested in a group of people who used this house fifteen years ago. I wondered if you knew them. There were some parties and I wanted to obtain some more information about who exactly organised them.'

'Parties?'

'Yes. I attended some parties here. Was it your home fifteen years ago? Or could you point me in the direction of the previous owner?'

'I don't know anything about that. The building has been in the family for many decades.' He smiled tightly as he appraised her again. 'What exactly is all this about?'

Was she imagining it? No. The smell, the curl of stairs behind him, the floor tiles. Tiles which she had bled over. The image flashed and faded. Stairs down which she had run, trying to scream.

'A crime,' she found herself saying. Now he frowned, but it was the frown of someone with a madwoman on his doorstep.

'I'm so sorry not to be able to help,' he said, closing the door. Rebecca stepped back. She tried to say thank you in a measured way, to prove she was sane, but her voice was gone. She nodded to the door and turned.

Back on the pavement, Rebecca caught her breath. She moved away from the house, feeling she was still being watched. She intended to head back the way she had come, towards the station, but found her feet following a different route. Then she realised it was the one she had walked that last time, after staggering out of the house intending never to return, New Year's Eve 2009.

And, as if this unwilled change of direction was the turning of a key, her memory inched open. She remembered people staring at her as she passed; a group of young men, dark suits in disarray; a young couple arm in arm, the woman with red lipstick, laughing and then not laughing, peering into her face, asking if she was okay. And Rebecca realising she had no coat, the air biting her bare arms. Seeing blood on her arms.

Her adrenalin surged, a panic attack sweeping in, heart tripping over itself. Rebecca recalled the prescribed response: do not fight it. Stay where you are. Breathe deeply.

The gate into the square was locked. Rebecca made it to the church, which was open. It was surprisingly bright inside, empty, with lemon yellow walls and elegant white stone, as if offering a more upmarket God.

It helped. She sat down. *Remind yourself that the attack will pass. Focus on positive, peaceful and relaxing images.*

The images were currently battling in her mind: butterflies and beech woods assailed by darker fragments she had not realised she possessed. Or, at least, which she had packed away so efficiently she had forgotten they were there. The lipstick woman asking if she was okay, then recoiling. The lights of the main road glaring; thinking she should buy some water and not knowing where her purse was. And then a succession of rooms: one bright and white, like a clinic; one with the dusty yellow light of an uninhabited property, a basement flat with bars over the high windows, and a man in glasses with the turquoise sheen of an electric razor along his jawline telling her to forget everything.

There was a reason it was Eaton Square that had come back to haunt her. She just needed to understand what it was.

*

The grand Victorian public library on Elizabeth Street still looked as she remembered. She used to visit libraries on her way to and from jobs, and had popped in here on numerous occasions. The libraries were a form of armour and detoxification, a checking-in with the other part of herself. Little had changed in the library since 2009. Books and the destitute who sheltered among them were resilient to fashion.

Rebecca sat down, not minding the faintly urinary smell, borrowing its defensive cloak. She skimmed the day's newspapers, looking for any indication of her scandal. What was the joke Robert liked, about checking for your own obituary before bothering to get out of bed? That was how it felt. There was nothing about her, no allusions to an MP's wife's sordid past. Various wars continued. London was expected to hit thirty degrees over the next few days. Rebecca found her phone and got onto the library's Wi-Fi.

No more messages from Eclipse. Rebecca googled 62 Eaton Square. She got a postcode and a valuation on a property website: six and a half million, last sold 1980; freehold property. Same from a search of the Land Registry itself. Nothing more.

Her phone rang. Unknown number. Rebecca was about to reject it when she wondered if it might be Eclipse.

'Yes?' she answered.

'This is Helen Boyne from the Sarah Boyne Foundation,' the caller said. 'You left a message.'

'The what?' It took a second for Rebecca to recall what the name meant. She had forgotten last night's desperate enquiries. Helen Boyne, the Sarah Boyne Foundation. Was this the mother of a girl who'd taken her life after being blackmailed? Rebecca imagined grief hardened to a cause, to save others. Now she moved out of earshot of the other library users.

'That's right. I've been contacted by someone with pictures of me, threatening to share them if I don't pay. What are my options?'

'Well, first off, I'm very sorry to hear about your situation. It's vital you go to the police as soon as possible.'

'Can they do anything?'

'Possibly, possibly not. But you really do need to report it. Were you hacked?'

'Hacked? No, none of this had been on my phone or anything.'

'Do the images come from a partner?'

'From a hidden camera. I don't know who set it up.'

'You don't know?'

'I used to be a sex worker,' Rebecca said. It was the first time she had used the expression. In her day, they had preferred less industrious-sounding euphemisms: escort, call girl. Boyne, to her credit, reacted with no more than a hum of consideration.

'Well, I don't see that that should significantly change things. But I've not come across it before.' No, Rebecca thought, and probably not come across wives of Members of Parliament.

'Would I get anonymity?' she asked.

'Well, sextortion gets dealt with by Economic Crime. So-called revenge porn – men posting pictures of their former partners – is classified as a communications offence. That means victims don't get anonymity, unfortunately.'

'And what are the chances of catching him?'

'They struggle. To be honest, if it was easy for police to do anything then my charity wouldn't need to exist. But it's important you go to them. If the person targeting you is found guilty, they could face being locked up for up to two years.'

'Two years?'

'It's not much, I know. But, more importantly, by reporting it to the police, you might be able to stop them from doing the same thing to another victim.'

'Yes, I understand.'

'We have a support network. Perhaps I can send you the details. The most vital thing is that you don't confront this alone.'

'I understand. Thank you. I'll let you know if I need the support network.'

Rebecca hung up. *The same thing to another victim* ... The thought hadn't occurred to her. But there'd been plenty of girls in that house. Had anyone else been approached?

The girls. Sara, Lizzie, Precious, Vic, Dominique. The closest friendships she had experienced, and so suddenly and absolutely broken off. It had been the closeness of those clinging to a raft, she realised in retrospect, clutching one another, and eventually some made it to land and some fell in the sea, and none could afford to look back. But she had experienced nothing like that camaraderie before or since. Rebecca's faith in her own enduring humanity had depended on those friendships.

There was only one acquaintance from that life that she retained any kind of contact with, and it wasn't contact as such but a mild, mutual online stalking, enough for Rebecca to glimpse a life that had not been as fortunate as her own, though at least Michelle Weaver appeared to be clean now. And a lot more fortunate than when Rebecca had taken her to the A&E of St Thomas' during an overdose, registering her at the hospital, which was the only reason she knew enough of her real name to google her, which was the only reason she now knew Weaver ran a pet salon in Muswell Hill.

She should have kept in touch. This thought drummed in Rebecca's mind as she drove over. Part of Rebecca's monitoring of Michelle's social media was a scratching at her own guilt. She should have, at least, said goodbye, told her she was leaving. Disappearing left an open wound. Sometimes it felt like the transgression that haunted her was not the prostitution itself but walking out of that world without saying goodbye. This was a guilt shadowed by the distinctive, unnerving knowledge of being a semi-public figure: while her former companions had the luxury of disappearing, Rebecca had not entirely left their lives. Googling her revealed a very different story. It was possible that they might open a newspaper and see her face.

As well as occasionally checking Michelle's social media, she had almost bumped into her once. A couple of years after leaving that world, Rebecca had passed her former colleague in the street, near Oxford Circus. Rebecca hadn't believed it at first – she regularly thought she saw someone from her previous life, punter or prostitute, falling through the networks of London, adrift on their secrecy; more often than was rational. But this was Michelle. Their eyes met, Rebecca got a glimpse of the crucifix glinting in her cleavage, an unlikely looking partner beside her, then they were gone. Michelle had messaged a couple of years later about meeting up and Rebecca, to her shame, hadn't replied. She had suspected her friend was back on drugs. Why had she ignored her? Michelle, who had taught Rebecca how to put a condom on with her mouth, who had talked her through the choreography of threesomes, who had a child of her own and a history of abuse and shouldn't have been on the game.

Bow Wow Pet Salon and Spa was hard to miss, its neon pink signage enlivening an otherwise genteel high street, tucked away from London's extremes. A suburban village, generously supplied with pet owners. Through the salon's window, Rebecca could see a reception area with silhouettes of various breeds of dog around the walls. The actual business of grooming must have occurred behind the next door. As Rebecca was staring, wondering, this far door opened and a customer appeared, cradling a Yorkshire terrier, followed by Michelle herself, laughing. Michelle saw Rebecca at once through the window and her laughter stopped. Rebecca, caught in this bizarre act of intrusion, tried an awkward smile and a nod of greeting. Michelle just stared. After another second, feeling like she must look crazed,

Rebecca turned and walked away, back towards her car, cheeks burning. Then she heard Michelle's voice.

'Becky.'

Rebecca turned.

'Michelle.'

Michelle stood on the pavement in a clear vinyl smock, holding a dog brush, with the look of someone in perpetual fear, a child about to cry. That was why she had been popular with the punters.

'Long time,' Michelle said.

'Yes, I'm sorry.'

'You don't have to say you're sorry.'

'No, I suppose not.'

'Did you want something?'

Rebecca stepped closer. 'I've got a situation, Michelle. Someone's harassing me – about the past, those days. Has anyone approached you about any of that?'

'Like what?'

'Threats about leaking pictures. I wondered if you'd heard anything along those lines.'

'No. What's going on?'

'I don't know. Were you ever aware of being filmed at those parties – Eaton Square, near Victoria?'

Michelle shook her head.

'Any idea who ran them?'

'No. I remember there were a few men who could have been host – on different nights. I was never introduced to them.'

'Me neither.'

'Gloria would know,' Michelle said, quietly.

'I was hoping not to go there.'

'She's still running it. Platinum.'

'I'm sure. Where else would she be? Well, good to see you.'

Michelle pulled a face.

'Nice to see the salon thriving,' Rebecca said, in an attempt to rescue a human encounter from one that was otherwise just another exploitation. For a long time, Michelle appeared to be trying to think what to say, then she just turned and walked back to her business.

'I miss you,' Rebecca said, quietly.

The website was still online – London Platinum Escorts – offering elite companionship for elite gentlemen. In the first few years after leaving, Rebecca would occasionally check it, see who was still up, check she wasn't. She still looked at the website every couple of years and experienced the odd comfort that must compel criminals back to the scene of a crime: to reassure yourself that you are not still there, that you can watch from afar, like a god, or someone who has got away with it, which is much the same thing.

She called the number listed, got a receptionist whose voice she didn't recognise.

'I need to speak to Gloria.'

'Who is this?'

'Rebecca. I used to work for her. Something serious has happened.'

The woman took a number. A few minutes later Rebecca's phone rang.

'Rebecca, sweetheart.' The voice sent a shiver up her spine.

'Can we meet?' Rebecca said. 'I'm in a situation and I need to ask you about something.'

They met in Claridge's Foyer & Reading Room, home of the afternoon tea. It was where Gloria always met her employees, where Rebecca had gone for her initial job interview with the agency. Rebecca wondered what the place meant to her old boss, or if Gloria had some understanding with the staff that ensured extra discretion. Maybe it was a test of one's ability to look inconspicuous.

Gloria had already arrived when Rebecca got there, in her usual corner seat, typing on an iPhone, hair fashionably short, cream blazer over something blue and silk. She looked, as ever, a product of two opposing forces: smoking and surgery. A flawless forehead was betrayed by the lines around her mouth. And the thinness that constituted so much of her identity now seemed merely a product of ageing, a retreating of herself ever further beneath the glossy façade.

'So nice to see you, Rebecca,' she said, air-kissing, and Rebecca could see she was anxious. People didn't get in touch with their old pimps without reason. Gloria subjected her to the head-to-toe appraisal that always made Rebecca feel like cattle. Her dressed-down disguise was evidently a source of perturbation. 'Doing so well for yourself,' she said, uncertainly, as she sat back down.

They ordered black coffees and some pastries, which Rebecca knew neither of them would touch. She remembered the first time she came here, after answering an advert, nervous yet knowing there was one thing intruding between her and her own future: a lack of money. The older man with whom she had been living from the age of eighteen had departed her life when she turned twenty. He had taken her away from Croydon and left her nowhere. That was the last time she thought someone else could provide her future. She remembered sitting here, the idea of being cast back to her parents so horrific that she would have said yes to anything.

'How is business?' Rebecca asked.

'I am lucky, I have chosen a business that will not go out of style.' Gloria gave a wan smile. 'Business is good. But that is not why you asked to meet.'

'No,' Rebecca conceded. She wondered how to approach this. She wondered, as ever, at Gloria's life, looking at the woman's expensive face. What a career, sending women to fuck strange men. Rebecca had initially suspected there was a network of seedy men behind the cool, feminine front that Gloria lent the agency. Now she wasn't so sure. Was it no more than just a clever business idea? An obscure pleasure for the virginally neurotic Madam. God knew there was a story to Gloria. Her accent had the clipped, cut-glass clarity of a fake – Rebecca sometimes heard it in her own accent now. Gloria had a grown-up daughter, who sometimes helped run the agency, so she must have shared a bed with a man at some point. There was no wedding ring. Rebecca sensed sexual repression beneath Gloria's intrusive fastidiousness: advising girls on weight loss, good timekeeping, fashion. Making sure you looked very proper before hooking you up with a businessman who wanted to urinate in your face.

But they had made a lot of money together. Rebecca had always felt pride in being a good whore; lucrative, professional, willing to engage in a wide range of activity. When Gloria first sent her to those parties she hadn't needed to be very persuasive. *Something a bit different, Becky. You flirt, you dine, they dim the lights. Suddenly, voila, the ladies are all in lingerie. It is theatre. And these men are exceptional customers. There will be ten of you – only my finest – and you will be paid a flat fee for the night.* This last detail had made Rebecca hesitate until she was told how much.

One of the attractions of the agency was its vetting procedure. This was a combination of practical measures and instinct – the practical side involving credit card numbers, ID checks; instinct involving Gloria's analysis of men's phone voices, screening their requests, adjusting the price according to demands; she knew which hotels she would send girls to, and, of course, she blocked any punters that got bad report cards, no matter who they were.

Over time, Rebecca came to realise that the parties were not vetted. Men there were curt, presumptuous, usually drunk. They had a sense of entitlement even beyond what she was used to. On that first visit to the house, she was asked to sign a non-disclosure agreement. She recalled a young, attentive man in a dark suit, who handed her an expensive pen. Whose idea had that been?

'Someone has photos of me doing jobs,' Rebecca said.

'Photos?'

'From those parties, the ones on Eaton Square. Possibly stills from videos. I need to know why they were filmed, who did it.'

Gloria looked appalled.

'I've never heard of anything like this.'

'You never gave permission for that kind of thing?'

'Of course not.'

'Who put those parties on? Whoever made the recordings, it has to be someone with access to the place, someone who could hide cameras.'

'You think? I have no idea.'

'You do though, Gloria. You know who was paying. That's what I need.'

'Rich people. That's all I know. Rich, important people.'

'That's not all you know. I signed an NDA. Why was that?'

'For obvious reasons.'

'It never happened before.'

'This is so long ago, Rebecca.'

'But it's come back. Whose house was it?'

'I've told you, I don't know.'

'Okay. Who initially contacted you about setting those nights up?'

Gloria's phone rang. She checked the screen, then silenced it. Rebecca imagined the business of prostitution going on out there, timeless and relentless. She pressed further . . .

'Gloria, if something about me gets out it will be all over the papers. And if the papers start looking into those parties they will eventually get to you and Platinum, and they will find drugs and they will find some very young girls.'

'Rebecca—' Gloria began, sternly.

'And the thing is, by that stage I will have nothing to lose, no reason to protect you, to protect clients, anyone.'

'Are you threatening me?'

'I could, Gloria, couldn't I? You know Isabella was seventeen when she joined the agency.' Isabella was a high-spirited Costa Rican girl. Rebecca had no idea of her age, but she enjoyed the intensity of Gloria's stare as she processed this accusation. 'And the Vietnamese sisters didn't have visas, did they? What does that mean? I don't want to get anyone in trouble, but I'm saying we need to manage this, which means figuring out what's going on. What were those parties about, Gloria? They must have cost someone a fortune.'

'I can't remember.'

'Could you find out, please?'

Gloria sighed. She cast her eyes around the room, drummed her nails on the screen of her phone then glanced at it as if the answer was there, before placing it face down, hard.

'Opula,' she said, quietly.

'Opula?'

'That was the name of the company. That's all I know. Really.'

'Who are they?'

'I've no idea. Something to do with international business. Something with a lot of money to burn.' Now she fixed Rebecca with a stare of renewed vigour. 'Isabella was nineteen.'

'Sure.'

'Money's made you ungrateful.'

'I'm sure it's made me a lot of things.' Rebecca got up and prepared to leave, then she sat down again, lowered her voice, though to protect who from what, she wasn't sure.

'Did you know something happened to me that night? New Year's Eve.'

'No.' Gloria frowned. 'How would I? What happened?'

'I don't know.'

'All I know is you never answered my calls again.'

Opula. It rang a bell. Rebecca carried the name across to Grosvenor Square, repeating it, sometimes out loud, as if the very intonation might summon forth knowledge. She sat down in the square and ran a search for 'Opula' on her phone. Top result was Opula Lifestyle Services, *a one-stop concierge facility for London's High Net Worth Individuals.* That sounded right. But the company's website was down.

Concierge facility. Such oblique neutrality, she could well believe it included the staging of orgies. Did she have a lead? A dead end? Getting from this error message to the identity of her blackmailer felt like a long and implausible journey. She was running late. Iona would be getting out of school soon. Halfway back to her car, her phone vibrated. The Whispr icon had returned.

24 hours. Where's my money?

Eclipse followed this with three links, each to a different web page. The first was an Only Fans account in Rebecca's name. *Get to know me. Inside out.* It described what lucky subscribers would receive, how much Rebecca was going to charge. One was a Pornhub page entitled 'Westminster Wife', promising amateur videos. The third was a stand-alone website: BeckyX. co.uk. Each bore a holding message: *Coming soon.* Nothing had been uploaded yet.

Rebecca logged out of Whispr, tried googling them. They came up on searches, there for anyone to see.

Sites are ready for tomorrow. Eclipse messaged. *What do you think?*

Alongside despair, Rebecca felt an overwhelming fury at the one-sided nature of it all – that he could see everything and she had no idea about him whatsoever. The image that came to mind was the old Soho peepshows, men staring through a slot at a stripper. More than anything, she wanted to know who this was, to bring him out of the shadows.

I can get money to you, she wrote. *But it will need to be cash. I can't risk having a Bitcoin purchase show up on my bank statement.*

It felt good to at least try to set the agenda, to put him on the back foot. His response might tell her something, tell her if he was in the country, at least. When a few minutes passed without response, she elaborated:

I have managed to withdraw 50k in cash. A first instalment. It's just as anonymous as Bitcoin. I can leave it somewhere for you.

She sent the message, then walked down Tottenham Court Road to Mountain Warehouse camping store, to the glass case containing knives.

Among the cheerful Swiss Army contraptions was one with an altogether more sinister profile: Wolfcraft Leisure Knife. It was black all the way up the blade, folding, with a serrated edge and gleaming point. A knife for stripping the skin from an animal. For survival.

Eclipse messaged as she was staring at it.

Okay, but if you fuck me about I will destroy you. Go to the south side of Blackfriars Railway Bridge. There are steps down to the shore. Leave the money in a carrier bag on the stone steps beneath the bridge. This has to be done in the next hour.

Her stomach lurched. She hadn't expected her plan to come to fruition so quickly, and it made her sceptical. So was he a Londoner? Someone in the city with her now? It was too fast, too suspicious. But there was no going back. Rebecca went to the counter, where she requested the knife and a carrier bag. Once outside, she messaged the nanny, asking her to collect Iona from school, then she unpackaged the knife and checked it fitted in her back pocket.

Fifty minutes.

She got to the bridge early. The area was busy with tourists and city workers, cafés closing, pubs filling up. Across the water, EC1 looked peaceful, the dome of St Paul's offering its benediction to finance. Families passed her on the riverside, moving happily towards Shakespeare's Globe and Tate Modern.

Narrow stone steps coiled down to the silt.

Again, Rebecca thought: surely he wouldn't risk this. The tide was out, exposing stones, rubble, some crumbling structure of older stairs lapped by the brown water. She stepped down carefully, made her way under the bridge. It was deserted down here, cold in the bridge's shadow. It was a good choice of place.

Rebecca filled her carrier bag with pebbles and sand, placed the bag on the stone steps, then retreated. She didn't want to be down on the shore with him. She climbed back to the walkway and found a position far enough away to be barely visible in her mask, but close enough that her phone might zoom in on someone searching for the cash. The knife stayed folded in her other hand.

Five p.m. came and went. The streets thickened with commuters. No one went down to the river. Rebecca waited. After another half an hour, she checked her phone, unnerved by the absence of communication. At 6.15 p.m. she went home.

It was as she was walking through her door that the messages started coming in: one from a distant cousin, one from her boss at the trust, Reverend Palmer. *Call me*, the cousin said. *Have you been hacked?* asked the Reverend.

Rebecca relieved the nanny of her duties, kissed Iona and left her in front of the TV. Then she called her cousin.

'Is something going on with your email?' he asked.

'Why?' Rebecca asked, trying to keep her voice steady.

'I got an email from you asking if I wanted to see something interesting.'

'From what email address?'

'Your Gmail account.'

'I don't have a Gmail account.'

'Oh, is it some kind of spam? What should I do?'

'Block it. If you receive anything else, don't open it. Tell me. We've got a bit of a situation here. Some harassment. But I don't want to risk your computer getting infected if you open any attachments.'

'I'm sorry to hear that.'

The head teacher at Iona's school had left a voicemail. *Didn't want to alarm you, but we received an odd-looking email in your name, suggesting there was material you wanted to share with us. I wasn't sure if this was something you were aware of.*

Palmer WhatsApp'd again: 'Rebecca, just seen your email. What are these pictures you're sending tomorrow? Have I forgotten something?'

She was wondering how to reply when Whispr's icon appeared.

That was fun. Dumb bitch. You've got until midnight to transfer the whole amount. And now I know where you live.

SIX

It was a nervous 6 a.m. drive home from Alexandra Palace. Kane imagined the Unit team still in London, a cheap hotel somewhere, waiting, studying maps. Then, in his imagination, they'd escape the hotel and begin moving through the city towards his front door.

He walked the length of their street when he got back, looking for any signs of surveillance, but nothing stood out. Bell was still alive, asleep in bed. The previous night, Kane had made sure to lock the doors and windows; he'd placed a hammer and a kitchen knife in his bedside table drawer. He felt profoundly ill prepared for the arrival of a Russian hit squad.

Godfrey messaged from the office: Sir John Broughton, the Chief, was still out of the country. Meanwhile, it had been confirmed: Anton had printed detailed information on Kane and his former colleague, Christian Rivera, the day before he was killed. Someone had removed it from the property.

Kane hadn't spoken to Christian Rivera for ten years. He tried calling the last-known place Christian had been working, a brokerage on Moorgate, got through to a switchboard and asked for him by name. He was told Mr Rivera no longer worked there, and eventually elicited the information that he had moved to a company called Vaultec several years ago.

Vaultec's website promised world-beating system security solutions, and flaunted the fact that its staff had backgrounds in military and intelligence. It looked like a typically comfortable post-MI6 position. They refused to give out employee details when he called, so Kane tried a mutual friend who said they hadn't heard from Christian in years but had got the impression he'd settled down. When pushed, they suggested he was somewhere in Barnes, west London.

That was a start. Barnes made sense, as Vaultec's HQ address was in Kingston, a few miles south-west. Christian wasn't on social media but his wife was, which gave Kane the names and ages of his kids as well, along with dismay at the thought of them exposed to harm. With access to the electoral roll, he could locate their house: a detached structure at the end of a long street beside a wetland reserve.

By 11 a.m. Kane was parking beside it. Christian Rivera's was the last house on a broad, expensive road that fell peacefully away from the city, a new construction, with bold combinations of timber and brick, and conspicuous amounts of glass. Kane felt himself encroaching on this idyll like a disease.

Only a standard security system. Less state-of-the-art than Zakharyan's, not that that had helped. Kane stood on the gravel drive and thought of the last time he'd seen Christian, walking away down a Russian street. Three a.m. The aftermath of an argument. Bitter end of a mission and an era. Kane realised he was being watched. A woman stared at him through the front window of Rivera's house – Christian's wife, Amelia. A few seconds later the door opened.

'Elliot?' Amelia's expression was one of mixed wonder and caution. She looked well, in an expensive, well-preserved way: tanned and exercised.

'Amelia, so nice to see you. I realise this is out of the blue. I was in the area,' Kane said. 'Seemed opportune.'

'How nice. I didn't even realise you knew where we were.' Kane merely smiled at this. 'Chris is just on his way back.' She checked a thin watch. 'Shouldn't be more than a few minutes.

He was just picking the kids up from tennis. Do you want to come in?'

'Sure.'

But something made her stop before they got to the front door. She turned and studied his face again. 'It must be ten years,' she said.

'Surely not,' Kane said.

A car turned in to the driveway. Christian sat at the wheel of a metallic-grey Porsche Cayenne. He saw Kane and his eyes flashed with concern.

The children climbed out, all of them tanned and lithe in tennis whites and carrying racquets, followed by a German shepherd, then Christian, in a pink shirt, pale chinos and deck shoes. As ever, his towering presence was magnified by the square jawline, the sweep of tousled hair and broad grin.

'Well, I bloody never.'

He pulled Kane into a hug. Then they held each other at arm's length for inspection. Christian's hair had turned from blond to tarnished silver. His blue eyes had also paled. But the hale, hearty bearing hadn't changed, upon which Kane had once strived to model his own persona. Unchanged since Kane first saw him across the courtyard of Magdalene College, centre of a throng, magnetic.

'Not as haggard as I'd have expected,' Christian said. 'Lucky bastard. Kids, they're meant to keep you young – that's the lie.'

'Good to see you, Chris.'

The children studied Kane with something of their mother's circumspection, then ran into the house. Amelia grabbed the dog by its collar.

'You really are all looking well,' Kane said.

'Just got back from Saint Lucia. You caught us at the right time. Another few days and we'd be pasty-faced again.'

'Do come in,' Amelia said. 'When you're ready. There are

beers in the fridge.' She smiled and disappeared, ever the MI6 spouse, knowing when to vanish. Now the concern returned to Christian's eyes.

'What are you doing here?' he said.

Kane had imagined this reunion many times over the years. It was always a chance encounter, with an awkward laugh of recognition. They'd leave unspoken the victories they'd achieved, talk about the present only. In none of the versions did he turn up uninvited with bad news.

'Anton Zakharyan was killed. Have you seen?'

'I saw the news.'

'It looks like he was blown – but it's possible there's interest in us as well.'

Christian winced. 'Let's go to the garden,' he said.

They walked down a side path to a back garden. As they passed the kitchen windows, Christian's bonhomie flickered back into life.

'The plan at the moment is to extend the decking in an L-shape – around where the pool will be. The bottom will be space for outdoor Pilates, apparently ... ' Kane felt a familiar pleasure in his friend's ability to shapeshift. The lawn was the size of a football pitch, strewn with bikes, trampolines, a paddling pool. Settled, Kane thought: *Now my charms are all o'erthrown, And what strength I have's mine own.* The grass curved away from the patio to a secluded corner with a shed, swings and a wooden bench. They took a seat.

'What happened?' Christian asked.

'He'd been trying to contact us in the week before he was killed. Contact Six generally. He couldn't get hold of anyone.'

'Fuck's sake,' Christian muttered.

'I'm in touch with Alistair Godfrey. He's concerned that Anton might have been trying to track us down – that he knew something was coming. And if he had our details, then it's possible the killers took them.'

Christian briefly closed his eyes. Then he gazed at the back of his house. It looked like a monumental and ill-advised gamble. The back wall was entirely glass, so you could see right through: stone spiral stairs, a marble kitchen, the children moving about like toys in a doll's house.

'Does the Service know anything else?'

'Not that they've shared with me. Putin gave a speech last week, implying the UK would soon learn the mistake it had made. He talked about bringing the war to a new domain. That may have been literal. The Unit's back in the UK.'

'So what are we meant to do?'

'At the moment, that's up to us. Broughton's been away; he's on his way back. Run and fight, I guess. They were asking me if I'd get involved. I don't know.'

Christian laughed. He stared at the grass.

'Get the band back together? They want us to go hunting?'

'I don't know what they want.'

'Would Six give us protection?'

'We can ask. I wanted to tell you what was going on as soon as possible. Do you think you could get the family out of town?'

Christian gave an exasperated sigh.

'Just like that? Charlotte's got exams. I'm in the middle of a work project. Amelia's parents are frail. How the fuck did Anton get blown?'

'No idea.'

'I built this life because I thought it was all over.'

'I know.'

'Are you still with them?'

'Six? No. I left a few years ago.'

'Where are you now?'

'Working private.'

He laughed. 'You? What firm?'

'Independent. Just consulting.'

Christian shook his head with weary amusement. Then the amusement went. He picked up a toy car from the grass and spent a moment trying to fix a loose wheel. Kane had a flashback to Christian reassembling his Makarov pistol on the floor of a hotel room overlooking the Neva River, that last job together, stepping onto a balcony to see the dusky rose of the midnight sky, the mad, hallucinatory light of high latitudes before the summer solstice, with an insomniac sun unable to set. And Kane, briefly, feeling like he was in the centre of his own life, knowing what he was for as he had not known before or since.

'We need to speak to Broughton,' Christian said.

'I'm trying to get hold of him. Obviously, he's deep in Ukrainian business. Not easy to pin down.'

'If this is something to do with Operation Halcyon . . . '

Christian's eldest daughter came to the back of the house and slid the glass aside. Inside, food had been served. Kane wasn't going to stick around for it, even if invited. The girl saw them and waved. Christian waved back. The girl looked like she was considering running to them, but something stopped her, and the expanse of lawn seemed suddenly impassable as deep water.

'I should go,' Kane said. 'That's all I've got for now.'

'Do you have kids?' Christian asked.

'No,' Kane said. He didn't want to enter into the complexities of his personal life. Christian nodded, as if adulthood was one more act he had perfected, where Kane had been left flat-footed.

'If you hear anything concrete that suggests my family is in danger, please let me know immediately,' Christian said.

'I promise.'

'You got me into this, after all.'

Kane sat in his car but didn't drive at first. He thought about Christian's words, and the way people get us into things, and then we blame them for motivations that lie within ourselves.

Beginnings were as wishful as endings. But there was a moment that always came to mind when he thought about the start of all this, of Operation Halcyon and its frenzied uncoiling. He stared at Christian's model home, but what he saw was a newspaper headline: RADIATION POISONING KILLS EX-RUSSIAN SPY.

November 23rd 2006. Kane had never forgotten the date, or the cold, inadequate news accounts.

Alexander Litvinenko, the former KGB agent living in exile in London, died in hospital last night, three weeks after apparently ingesting a mysterious poison which has baffled doctors.

He remembered walking into Vauxhall Cross that fateful morning, sensing everything had changed. What the newspapers didn't know: Litvinenko had been a valuable MI6 asset for several years, supplying intelligence on Putin's connections with organised crime. The kind of detail that took them close to the heart of the Kremlin. The fact that he had been killed right under their noses, poisoned by polonium-210, was a source of shame and horror. An assassination on UK soil. A nuclear attack on UK soil. Kane felt the atmosphere of mortification in Head Office as soon as he walked in. The legitimacy of MI6 hung on its ability to protect sources. Russia had laughed in their faces.

Broughton was made head of Psychological Operations that very morning, in spite of numerous objections to his philosophies and working methods. It was the start of his rise to the top. The Service called for darkness. Broughton called for Kane.

When Kane arrived at his office that afternoon, it was the first time they'd met face to face. The new PsyOps chief had a file open in front of him. It was Kane's own report into the torture and execution of one of his sources, a Russian journalist working in London. Kane had established that a small team of designated

Russian hitmen were responsible. They had travelled into the UK assisted by Russian intelligence officers embedded in London's Russian émigré community, kidnapped the journalist, broken his legs with a sledgehammer, then disposed of his remains in Brent Reservoir before vanishing again.

Kane had put his own time into establishing who was responsible, calling in favours from the Service's top analysts and Kremlin experts. He had gone some way towards identifying the group. There was clear airport footage of the four men laughing as they waited to board a flight back to Moscow a few hours after the murder.

He had written this up a year ago, concluding his report with a warning: in response to the steady stream of dissident arrivals in London, Putin had loaded the British capital with spies. This had occurred in a period when the attention of MI6 was almost entirely consumed by Islamist terrorism. It had allowed London to become a crucible of Russian secret service activity, and therefore of easy, unaccountable killings.

Kane insisted his report go to the top. Which was a mistake, because the top served government, who served money, and a lot of the money coming in was Russian: twenty-seven billion pounds had been invested by Russian citizens in the UK in the past five years. Kane heard nothing for weeks. Eventually his line manager handed the report back with a shake of the head and one word: 'Politics'. But politics was a storm that changed direction.

Broughton closed Kane's file and nodded at the young officer.

'I'm told you're a languages man,' he said. 'Know the German word, *Zersetzung*?'

'Corrosion. Decay.'

'Yes. Used by the Stasi to mean a kind of water torture – incremental actions on a target over time, ongoing low-level harassment that drives you mad, makes you question your sanity. This is what they are doing. Drip, drip.' He pressed a finger to Kane's report. 'This isn't bad. But you underestimated the scale of the problem.'

He slid a sheet of paper across: nineteen names, with dates and locations. All were assassinations on UK soil. The majority of killings had been disguised as suicides, muggings and accidents. New autopsies had been carried out, on Broughton's instructions. Traces of poisons and evidence of torture were discovered in almost all cases. It was the first time Kane heard the name: Unit 22195.

'Unit 22195 is Putin's personal assassination squad. That's who you've stumbled upon. We think it's operated in secret since at least 2005. We don't have any doubt that it's controlled directly by the Kremlin. Last month, Russia's parliament passed a law allowing for the elimination of terrorists outside Russia's borders. Supposedly to provide legal cover for operations against Chechen militants, but it's London they've got their eye on. They think they're untouchable. I'd like them to think otherwise.'

Broughton spoke softly. He had a classless, nasal accent that Kane associated with non-commissioned officers and former grammar school boys. Physically, he was slight, with an energy that stiffened his body and brightened his eyes.

'What do you need from me?' Kane said.

'We're going to send a message back. I need to know if you're willing to help.'

It was another two weeks before the guiding principles of Halcyon were established. This time Kane wasn't the only one summoned to Broughton – not to his office this time but Fort Monckton, the grey-stoned stronghold on the Gosport peninsula that housed MI6's field operations training centre. Along with Kane, Broughton had gathered six operations specialists, two analysts, a surveillance officer and a representative of MI6's military intelligence department.

'Halcyon will have no formal structure and hence no

post-holder titles,' Broughton explained. 'It will be conducted on the same broad principles and methods as any covert operation. Orders will not be assigned to paper.'

To the outside world, Broughton maintained a façade of impotence and bureaucratic frustration. Behind the scenes, they got to work. First off, they needed someone to penetrate London's oligarch community. There were three hundred thousand Russians in the UK, most in London, and they included more Russian intelligence officers than at the height of the Cold War. Their tentacles stretched right through British politics. To get at the killers they had to start unpicking the infrastructure. So they needed someone comfortable with sleaze and wealth, who could seduce new arrivals to the capital, get on the inside of that world. A corrupt and well-connected Englishman.

'I know just the man,' Kane said.

Christian had charted a meandering course since university. But he was perfect. And Kane even had the sense that this was what their relationship had been waiting for – that, for the first time, Kane could grant someone their own fate. Christian was one of those people you encountered first in rumours. At Cambridge, these had included intellectual brilliance, a descent from fugitive Nazis in Argentina, and significant wealth from professional poker playing. He may have spent his gap year in a Moroccan prison. He had slept with the wife of a teacher at his public school, and most probably the teacher himself. And alongside the hint of sexual fluidity was his perfect rendition of the alpha male: rower, rugby blue, Officers' Training Corps. It was another year before, lying on his bed in halls, Kane asked him the truth about his past, and Christian confessed that his mother was an air hostess from Luton, his father a Chilean businessman who disposed of her soon after Christian was born. The financial pay-off got Christian through school but wasn't going to get him much further on its own. He had smiled regretfully at this – like a man forced to contemplate uneasy decisions – and Kane thought he saw his real face for the first time.

They'd been out of Cambridge for three years when Kane approached him to join Halcyon. By then, Christian had received the inevitable call to the City, EC1, kingdom of bluff. On the few occasions they'd met for drinks since leaving university, Christian had questioned Kane about his own career in 'government', sniffing for opportunity.

Kane put Christian's name forward as a potential front for Halcyon. MI6 initiated the vetting process. Whatever Christian was up to in the Square Mile it looked shady, involving a lot of elaborate offshore arrangements for wealthy clients. Broughton was pleased. It proved Christian was willing to stretch the rules, and there was a potential legal threat with which to confront him if he stepped out of line. The fact that he broke the law while chasing some kind of celebrity was even better in Broughton's book.

With Broughton's encouragement, Kane met Christian for drinks at the Travellers, a private members' club on Pall Mall. Originally a gathering place for the Empire's more footloose explorers, it was now established as the gentlemen's club of choice for Foreign Office and intelligence service heads. The interior was exquisite, and Kane sometimes visited just to look at the artwork. Christian paid little attention to the details of the place but lapped up the snobbery. He looked more dazzling than ever.

'Finally, government wants me,' he beamed.

'If you're up for this,' Kane smiled back, 'the government will never admit having heard your name.' He saw the intrigue on Christian's face. There was a distinct kick in being the one making the offer, and Kane realised how long he'd been waiting for this. At Cambridge, it was always Christian inviting him into exclusive circles, including a secret society which he had endeavoured to set up: the New Apostles. Kane laughed at the invitation – the whole university was a secret society as far as he was concerned, with its gongs and gowns and Latin – but Christian was unde-terred, and Kane secretly flattered by the invitation. He made a mental note of that, the simple power of an invitation. The New Apostles, it turned out, was more a cocaine-fuelled book club, although nights grew increasingly promiscuous, and the books leaned towards the erotic and esoteric. Christian, as host, hardly spoke a word, but proved good at the theatre of it. It was always interesting to see who he'd collected.

Now it was Kane inviting him into secrecy.

'You'll enjoy it. There's no feeling like breaking the law on behalf of the government.'

'What exactly would I be doing?'

'It wouldn't be too different to what you're doing now, only we'd set you up with your own company.'

Kane's memories were interrupted as Christian's front door opened. The man himself appeared, taking the rubbish out. He saw Kane and winced, caught in this act of humble domesticity, unhappy to find Kane still there. *You got me into it.* Kane started the car and began to drive.

When he got home, Kane ran a full series of security checks again. There was a plumber's van on the street, one he hadn't seen before, but he called the number on the side and got confir-mation of which address they were visiting.

Bell had left a note on the kitchen table: *Clients asking for update. Can you send?* She was meeting a source in a charity focused on corporate tax avoidance. Mason was at an activity centre. Kane checked this was all correct, everyone was where they should be, then he did the work. This mostly involved processing the data they'd collected: visitors to their target's various homes, caught on hidden cameras, generating a list of number plates, which Kane dutifully passed on to his police contact to run against the

DVLA. It was all searching for legal angles, for hostages in the ongoing negotiations, which resembled two states at war more than individuals. That was how the afternoon passed. But all the time his thoughts were on that febrile time in MI6, Halcyon days, beside which the private work was flat. Even in the worst of what they did within the Secret Intelligence Service there was a point of light in the distance to which they were moving, which resembled something like justice. Or, if not justice, then a larger goal at least. Speaking to an old colleague who had gone private they said you were only heading towards money, there was no North Star from which to take your bearings, and it was easy to get lost. *Not even lost, because you're not going anywhere in the first place. Disorientated.* Now Kane understood what they'd meant.

He'd been staring blindly at emails for several minutes when something caught his eye. The top partner at Rosenquist's law firm had sent through personal thanks for what they described as 'valuable audiovisuals', which, presumably, related to the kompromat Bobby Spears had acquired. This had proved a valuable asset in ongoing negotiations with the other team's lawyers. 'The Dorchester material has worked its magic,' they wrote. It took Kane a moment to realise that this referred to the videos. He had assumed the footage came from overseas. There weren't many people who got good kompromat from Central London. In fact it was a suite at the Dorchester in which they'd first entrapped Anton Zakharyan.

Kane took Spears's flash drive from the safe and plugged it in.

All you saw at first was an empty, upscale hotel room, then a man in a bathrobe walked in. It was the billionaire Kane was targeting, only several years younger. He answered the door and a woman entered the room. Kane recognised her from their research as their target's stepsister. She slapped him and he knelt down, removed her shoes and began kissing her stockinged feet.

Kane paused the video.

The furnishings certainly looked like the Dorchester. It felt like MI6 footage. It may well have been filmed by a colleague of his.

What had Spears said? *There's a lot of material available at the moment.*

The fixer answered somewhere loud, with music and laughter. 'Elliot.'

'The sex tape – I need to know where you got it,' Kane said.

'I can't speak now. I'm with a client.'

'Give me one moment.'

'Elliot . . .'

'It's important.'

Kane heard Spears make his excuses. The music became quieter.

'What's the problem?'

'I need to know where it came from. It's not footage that should be in circulation.'

'Obviously. But now it is.'

'You said there's a lot of good material out there at the moment. More than usual. You mean dirt? Videos?

'That's right.'

'Where from?'

'From places. This is just what my contact said.'

'Who is this contact?'

'I can't talk about it on the phone.'

'I need to know where it's coming from.'

'Why?'

'I think it's MI6 footage.'

Spears contemplated this suggestion.

'I'd have to make some enquiries,' he said, eventually.

'Do that. Bobby, this material is potentially dangerous.'

Another pause. In the murky world in which they operated, trust was everything, and they trusted each other. A warning like that wasn't given lightly.

'Give me an hour,' Spears said. 'Come to the Park Lane Nobu.'

SEVEN

Rebecca drew the curtains, locked the doors. Was Eclipse out there now? Outside her house?

Now I know where you live.

Every entry point was closed, but he was inside, on her phone, her laptop, in her mind, her clothing. Westminster Wife. BeckyX. The sites were up. Contact with her acquaintances had begun.

Rebecca moved the curtains and peered into the darkness. Nothing. Trees. A blanket of stars. If he was out there, he would be laughing.

She opened Whispr, typed, *You win.* She thought he'd like that. *I'll get you something to show goodwill.*

The money she had in her personal account was far too little: just under thirty grand. She was going to have to get her hands on more. Robert messaged as she was contemplating how. When she saw his name, Rebecca feared the worst – videos, weblinks – but he was just saying he was going to have stay in Westminster for a late vote. He would sleep in the MPs' digs at Portcullis House.

So she and Iona were alone tonight.

Rebecca let Iona eat her dinner in front of the TV. The girl was delighted at this luxury. There was the option of sending her to her grandparents. But then what if her tormentor followed her there? What if he found out where her parents lived, and knew Iona was there without her? In a flash of inspiration, Rebecca called the emergency number for Robert's security team. She said she thought she'd seen someone loitering outside their house and they sent a couple of men over immediately. They arrived twenty minutes later, asked her what she'd seen and she spoke vaguely about someone in the garden, possibly looking through the windows. They searched the surrounding area, rummaged around the appropriate bushes, reassured her that there was no one currently present but that they'd remain parked at the front just in case.

Robert messaged about the security: *Everything okay? I was told you had concerns.*

I was being paranoid, Rebecca messaged back. *Sorry.*

Okay darling, he replied, *love you*, with a picture of himself in the House of Commons lobby. He was trying to reassure her, which was sweet. He knew she needed something.

Rebecca checked the doors again, checked the security team in their car at the front. She put Iona to bed and lay beside her while she fell asleep, nose to the girl's shoulder, wanting some contact with her newness and the simplicity of her life. Feeling what she felt every time she lay here, only more so tonight: a desire to wrap her in privilege like an opioid cocoon.

When her daughter's breathing grew slow and steady, Rebecca left the room and set up a Bitcoin wallet. Then she went to Robert's study.

Walking into Robert's study always felt transgressive and vaguely erotic, the masculine smells of leather and wood and tobacco; ornaments from what she always felt was some other man's life: ships in bottles, cigar boxes. Blessed are those at ease in a stereotype, she thought. That was part of the security he had offered her; even his betrayals were predictable. The only personal touch was a framed photograph of the two of them on the desk, from the night they met, at a Christmas party in Chelsea. Her smile in the photograph looked anxious. She placed it face down, turned to the safe.

The safe was a Victorian antique, decorated with gilt tendrils. The combination for the lock was Rebecca's birthday, which should have touched her but instead made her feel abstract and functional. She opened it.

The rich, she had learned, don't just have more money but a whole infrastructure of wealth. Money became something you struggled to deal with, and which required pipelines, bridges, underground reservoirs. There was his personal account, their account for school fees, nannies; then the shares and ISAs. Then there were the more opaque entities, connected to private consultancy work: holding companies, limited companies. Rebecca suspected Robert didn't know where all his money was. On a couple of occasions, when her husband was away and she had realised that a bill was outstanding without sufficient funds in the joint account, he had instructed her how to retrieve funds from a Bank of Gibraltar deposit account in the name of a company, Watlington Hill Consultants. She didn't ask questions. Was it an option now, moving money out of this account? That was all she wanted to know. And besides, she reasoned, wasn't that what the money was for, ultimately: to maintain a façade? To bury your secrets?

She fired up his computer, went into a file he used to store passwords, then found the Bank of Gibraltar website and sat looking at the home page, a silhouette of the Rock. She could transfer to her own account – or would it be better to buy Bitcoin straight away? It would look glaring, but maybe that could work in her favour. It might seem lost in a scam. Which was sort of true. And, anyway, people believed what they needed to believe.

Rebecca typed in the account number and password. There it was: £1.5 million. It had gone up. She was already in the saved list of payees. She tried to transfer fifty thousand to her own account and a box appeared on the screen: *We have sent a security code to your phone.*

Shit. She felt a stupid instinct to check her phone. But whatever phone it went to wasn't hers. Rebecca looked for some kind of undo button. Of course, no such thing existed. She was still sitting there when her phone rang. Robert again. He must have seen the message. This time she ignored it, then threw the phone across the room and muffled a shriek by biting her arm. Tears were coming. She swept her arm across the desk and knocked the laptop to the floor. She punched the desk. The doorbell rang.

It was the security officers. She answered on the latch, conscious of her reddened eyes.

'Are you okay?' they asked. 'We thought we heard something.'

'I'm fine, thank you.'

Rebecca smiled apologetically, walked back to the study. The mess of the office felt like someone else's crime scene.

She picked up the photo of the two of them, the night they met. The Chelsea Christmas party. She had been sent there by the agency. The company throwing the party wanted attractive women around. Rebecca always liked these jobs: decorative background at events, a splash of glamour. You could keep your clothes on. Which meant she hadn't met Robert through sex work, exactly. That had always been important to her. She had noticed him watching her, though, and had been unsurprised when he approached holding a bottle.

'It's a tough life.' That was his opening line, said with a wry grin, refilling her glass.

He had seemed not too obnoxious. Charming enough to make her break a cardinal rule – she let him have her personal number. In the context of prostitution this was strictly forbidden, and implied you were taking customers away from the agency. But this felt different. And, in truth, she was already committed to departure from that life altogether. And the handsome, wealthy man only a decade or so older than herself had represented a clear getaway.

She had introduced herself as a model and a writer and a friend of the event organiser. This had been enough to sate any biographical curiosity, it seemed. Robert offered to show her around the House of Commons. He left early for another event. It was another fortnight before he called her – he had warned her he was away over New Year's. He was also involved in a complicated divorce. By the time he messaged her, New Year had happened – the undefined horror of it. After all that, it had been strangely comforting, miraculous even, to see his message – a message from a more innocent time – and she replied with tears in her eyes, feeling a numb disbelief shaded with irrational gratitude. Yes, dinner would be wonderful. I'm free most nights.

It offered her a fairy tale when that was what she wanted – a return of simplicity. Rebecca wondered if she would be able to bring herself to put on clothes and make-up. But at the same time she recognised another escape on the horizon, resigned now to her modus operandi. And almost being destroyed made you appreciate things. It gave you the strength to endure them. How useful it was to become grateful for the smallest kindness, which meant some setting aside of judgement.

In the photo, black and white helium balloons crowded the ceiling; a white Christmas tree with silver decorations rose monstrously behind Rebecca and Robert, her arm in his. She knew she had simply been doing her job at this point, but it looked like she was already gripping him to stay afloat. Wasn't love always survival? Didn't biologists say something like that? Deep within the ecstasy is an equation, and there was no shame in growing a love out of an escape attempt. That was what she had always told herself. Into what else would its roots sink? It had seemed fate that they were photographed together, and they did look a fine couple, even if they'd exchanged less than a few minutes' conversation at that point. Later, Robert sought out the photograph, had it printed and framed. Apparently, he had already told his friends: that is the woman I'm going to marry. Adding, perhaps: as soon as I've got rid of the first wife. The question of whose party it was barely seemed relevant. But now she saw, projected across the wall, five letters in a gold font: *Opula*.

Rebecca stared at the photograph, digesting what this meant. So that Christmas party had been Opula too – its more presentable face. It had seemed a world away from the sex parties.

Rebecca googled 'Opula' again, this time adding her husband's name into the search bar. She got a cryptic result: a political blog called *The Strangers' Bar*, 'tittle tattle from the darker corners of WC1'. They had written about Robert and Opula on 10 November 2017, or, at least, had found a way to conspicuously not write about them:

> 'A serving MP may have taken out a super-injunction preventing details of their activities being exposed,' rattles the Press Association this afternoon. The revelation came in the Commons as MPs debated creeping judge-made privacy laws and the spiralling use of gagging orders.
>
> We at the Strangers' wouldn't want to speculate which MP could have used the law to silence critics, let alone allude to the activities that needed to be silenced – after all, a super-injunction not only prevents publication of information but also the reporting of the fact that the injunction exists at all!
>
> So shh.
>
> And we're sure it couldn't be anything to do with Robert Sinclair, seen exiting the Commons at speed today. If he is overloaded with duties, could we recommend Opula Lifestyle Services, who seem to do whatever their clients wish. This gilded company might make his life much easier. Or possibly not.

Rebecca read the piece several times, unpicking its innuendo. She knew how super-injunctions worked. She also knew there was only one journalist with whom Robert was in legal battles – and those battles had kicked off around this time.

Rebecca went back to the safe and found the file labelled *Legal*. This, too, seemed to have grown – it was now, in fact, four cardboard files bound together with rubber bands. But it was organised, arranged in date order. She searched through for details of the injunction until she had it.

From William Temple Solicitors to the journalist Michael De Souza and the *Guardian*:

IF YOU THE RECIPIENT OF THIS ORDER AND ANY OTHER PERSON WITH NOTICE OF THIS ORDER DISOBEY THIS ORDER YOU MAY BE HELD TO BE IN CONTEMPT OF COURT AND LIABLE TO IMPRISONMENT OR TO BE FINED OR TO HAVE YOUR ASSETS SEIZED

UPON hearing Counsel for the Applicant without notice to the Respondents

AND UPON the Applicant by his Counsel giving the undertakings set out in Schedule 1 at the end of this Order

IT IS ORDERED that:

An injunction is hereby granted restraining the Respondents and any person with notice of this order from publishing or disclosing to any other person or allowing or causing to be published in any newspaper or to be broadcast in any sound or television broadcast

or by means of any cable or satellite programme service
or public computer network any association between
the Applicant, Robert Sinclair, and Opula Lifestyle
Services Ltd.

It went on for several paragraphs, without disclosing the
reason for their paranoia. Attached to this was a report made for
the lawyers into De Souza himself, a profile running to twenty
pages, exploring the journalist's lifestyle, financial connections
and potential legal vulnerabilities. It included De Souza's personal information and contact details. Rebecca put his number
into her phone.

EIGHT

Kane knew little of Spears's life outside of their meetings. Nobu was a surprise, though perhaps it shouldn't have been. Michelin-starred Japanese–Peruvian fusion, with all the sleek, low-lit, minimalist decor and politely defensive maître d' you'd expect. Popular with celebrities, wealthy tourists, anyone with a desire to spend half a grand on sushi. The place was crowded, but Kane saw Spears at a large table at the back, with twelve men and women, all looking international rich. Spears wore a blue blazer and was saying something that made everyone laugh. But evidently he was more alert than he seemed, because he noticed Kane at once, raised a hand.

'I'll wait for my friend outside,' Kane said to the maître d'.

He sat on a bench by Park Lane. The more he thought about the videos that Spears had supplied – 'the Dorchester material' – the more certain he was that it originated with the Secret Intelligence Service. They'd bugged the hotel enough times. What wasn't possible was for it to be floating around, for sale. Was someone in the intelligence service making cash on the side? If this was leaking, anything could, including details of Anton Zakharyan's treachery. But you didn't just leak MI6 material without a very good reason.

Spears emerged from the restaurant, a member of staff holding the door for him. Kane usually met the man in civilised hours. The night-time Bobby Spears was more wild-eyed, fleshy, with a sheen of perspiration. He clapped Kane's shoulder, and they crossed the road towards the park, out of sight of the restaurant windows.

'I'm not sure how much I'm going to be able to help you, Elliot.'

'I need to know how it's come into my possession.'

'I put a request out. My contact, one of my researchers, they felt around for me. Someone could help, and so we got the video. Standard.'

'I need a bit more, Bobby. Was this feeling around online or a human contact?'

'Online, I believe. Dark Web.'

The scenario came into more focus. Kane had some familiarity with the hidden corners of the internet where information changed hands for a price. They were valuable, if you could find them. Things were possible there that weren't elsewhere.

'How much did you pay?' Kane asked.

'Around twenty thousand euros in crypto.'

'So you know the supplier.'

'Not personally.'

'Any idea of nationality?'

'Not sure. Russian maybe.'

'I need you to find out and tell me.' Spears winced. This would be disclosing a lot. 'The British government would be grateful. And I'd make sure you're reimbursed for the trouble.'

'Why? What is this?'

'I'm trying to find out.'

'Give me a second,' Spears said. He returned to the restaurant, taking his phone from his jacket, came back a few minutes later with a message scrawled on a paper coaster.

'The site's called Night Market,' Spears said. 'This is the address.' The address was a jumble of letters and numbers, ending .onion, which told you it was a hidden service only accessible via encryption software.

'Do you know *who* on Night Market sold this?'

'A guy calling himself Eclipse,' Spears said. He caught something in Kane's expression. 'What is it?' he said.

'Come across Eclipse before?'

'No. It's just a handle. A vendor. Why? Do you know the guy?'

Kane locked the study door when he got home, even though Bell and Mason were still out. He downloaded Tor onto his personal laptop. This was the cloak that afforded entrance to the secret world. Devised by the US military in the '90s to protect defence communications, Tor bounced internet activity through endless layers of connections, each time encrypting it further. By the time a message reached its destination it was untraceable. Layers of obscurity, like the skin of an onion, hence its name, The Onion Router: TOR. The shift from military to criminal usage was as swift as ever. It became the gateway into the Dark Web.

Kane checked Spears's coaster, typed in the .onion address and arrived at Night Market. What appeared on screen looked like a '90s-style internet message board. The site was organised according to categories. 'Narcotics' had 273 vendors offering everything from mushrooms to medical-grade cocaine; 'weapons' hosted a more exclusive 89 sellers. There were just nineteen in the even more recherché market of 'data'.

Main offer under 'data' was stolen credit card numbers. Another vendor, targeting private investigators, claimed they could supply bank statements for customers at a range of high-street banks in Western Europe. Someone else could get mobile phone records. Prices ranged from fifty dollars for a check to five grand for someone's full call records over five years. There were clearly a variety of people making these offers – corrupt insiders, mercenary hackers, organised criminal networks – along with a lot of junk.

On the third page of entries Kane found Eclipse. They offered 'government files' from the UK: *classified docs, surveillance footage, intelligence reports. Contact for details and prices.* They listed these details in English, Russian, Arabic and Chinese.

Eclipse had been trading on Night Market for six months, attracting twelve reviews with a solid five stars each. Not many transactions, but they weren't selling a product quite as mainstream as guns or heroin.

Kane set up his own buyer's account, username 'Moskva'. Then he messaged Eclipse: *Hey. Want to run a check on someone – maybe UK govt employee. U help?*

A message came back in two minutes.

Got$?

Yes. How do we do this?

If you are any form of law enforcement you are wasting your time.

Kane typed: *Lol. Ok.*

Eclipse replied: *Give me names and I'll let you know what I can do.*

Kane looked out to the darkening sky then back into the abyss behind his screen. He typed: *Elliot Kane. UK civil service, poss MI6. Any info?*

The next message took twenty minutes to arrive.

I have extensive file. 0.67 BTC.

The promise alone gave Kane a jolt of uneasiness. He had to coax his scepticism back. Sure you do, he thought. Eclipse included a Bitcoin address. At current exchange rates, 0.67 Bitcoin worked out at just under fifteen grand.

Kane typed: *Steep.*

That's the price.

I need proof this isn't a scam.

Set up a Whispr account. Let me know number.

This was his man, Kane thought. Someone implicated in the death of Anton and Irina Zakharyan.

Kane put the Whispr app on his phone, then changed the user ID so it didn't show a functional phone number. He sent the ID to Eclipse. The sampler came through a few minutes later in the form of a compressed zip file. Kane opened it and stared at the contents. In his career he had received plenty of shocks but none quite as chilling as this.

The file contained a cover sheet with his name and date of birth. It was the opening page of Kane's enhanced security check for MI6, from the time of his recruitment in 2002. The document looked authentic, stamped by the security department: D6. Its date was accurate.

Offered openly for sale on the internet.

It was only twenty minutes or so since Kane had made his request. That was quick retrieval. Was Eclipse currently inside the MI6 system? Or sitting on a huge, searchable cache of data? Kane's file could have been pulled from the system anytime in the last twenty years. Only, it couldn't because it was one of the most secure systems in the world.

Getting the rest would cost fifteen grand. To test whether he really had the whole thing. Who did they think would pay fifteen grand for government files? Other governments, Kane assumed. Private intelligence companies. Maybe some press, if there was a story attached, or well-funded lobbyists if it gave them leverage.

Kane checked his finances. When Kane and Bell started the private intelligence company they set up an offshore account with the Atlantic Bank in Belize for the sake of discreet payments to contractors. It currently contained three hundred grand. He used fifteen thousand pounds from their account to buy the cryptocurrency and then transferred it to Eclipse. For ten minutes, nothing happened. He thought he'd been scammed after all, and part of him hoped that was the case. Then it arrived.

The vetting file began with a letter to the intelligence service from Kane's tutor at Cambridge, who had put him forward as a 'promising potential candidate for MI6; a linguist with the temperament for intelligence work'. This was followed by his

CV, which MI6 had somehow acquired – fairly threadbare at the age of twenty-two – plus those of close family members and the results of his initial two rounds of interviews, including the 'confessional', as he had heard it called, in which you sat in a room with a friendly and non-judgemental man and told them every secret you possessed. A confession without penitence. Kane had prepared himself for questions about sexual preferences, but not to hand over the names of all those he had slept with in the last three years. A lock of his hair was cut off to test it for drugs, in what felt like an oddly intimate violation.

Next in the file: interviews with eight people he'd volunteered as character references, and five close companions he hadn't. Then came the security department's independent investigations of Kane covering political beliefs, lifestyle, friendships, travel and religion. Kane had never seen any of this before. He scrolled through, strangely unwilling to peer too closely. Something about it seemed more intrusive than a contemporary investigation into him. The Elliot Kane of 2002 was no longer around to defend himself. Was that it? Or was it that this autopsy took place on the border of his childhood.

Whatever they'd discovered, MI6 had offered him a home, and after the vetting process there was the implication that no one would know him better. Kane would come to use the same psychology when recruiting agents: the sense of creating a sanctuary beyond the lies. At the end of the file there were photographs of his mother, a year or so before her death, some details of her alcoholism. Kane studied the photographs, which he had never seen before, then he messaged back: *How much of this kind of thing have you got?* Eclipse replied with a menu that ran to three hundred pages.

Kane scrolled down the list: intelligence officers, politicians, foreign dignitaries, royal family members, journalists, academics and business executives. Kompromat on most of the UK establishment. On an impulse, Kane typed: *Who are you?* The reply was immediate: *Who are you?*

Kane closed the laptop and went downstairs, where he poured himself a large scotch. Had there been a hack on MI6? He called a couple of officers in the UK's Cyber Security Centre, former hackers still plugged in to the digital underground. No one was boasting of a hack on any UK government systems, they said. But cyberspace was chaos right now, with feverish work from Russia and Ukraine in particular. The two countries had always boasted more than their fair share of elite hackers. The war had splintered that scene into warring factions. Kane's cybersecurity contact reeled off a list of gangs with varying connections to the Kremlin: Sandworm, who targeted banks and energy infrastructure in Ukraine; Ghostwriter, who operated out of Belarus and liked to take over official accounts in Europe to pump out pro-Kremlin propaganda. There was NoName57, who had turned their digital guns not only on organisations in Kyiv but those directly supplying military assistance to Ukraine as well.

'If a crew like NoName57 got into Ukrainian military intelligence, could they bridge to MI6 systems?' Kane asked.

'We can't see that capability. I doubt it.'

When Kane finally got through to Alistair Godfrey, the MI6 officer said there'd been no word of any kind of hack in Vauxhall Cross. Godfrey sounded concerned.

'Broughton's back, though. Is this something he should know about?'

'I believe so. I'd like to speak to him in person. ASAP.'

Bell had collected Mason from a friend's house on the way back from a celebratory meeting with their client. They'd caught a cab. She was tipsy when she got in, smiled when she saw Kane, and he desperately wanted to keep all his fears to himself, all the knowledge he'd acquired since leaving her bed that morning: the kill team with his contact information; Eclipse on Night Market with his past.

'Elliot, the clients are head over heels in love with us. The filthy videos had an immediate effect, and everyone's suddenly agreed to re-enter negotiations. It's in business news. You'll laugh. *Speculation regarding what lies behind change of heart.* Not sure many people will guess. A fetish for the feet of his nearest and dearest.' She took an open bottle of white wine from the fridge and poured them glasses, then regarded him with heavy-lidded eyes. 'I've got nice toes. You ever thought that?' She prodded him. He kissed her. 'Bonus day for us. As you never buy anything for yourself, I got you a present.' She reached for her handbag and brought out a wrapped parcel. 'A Rolex.'

'A Rolex?'

'I'm joking.'

Kane took the paper wrapping off. Inside was an anthology of contemporary Arabic poetry in translation.

'How did you find this?'

'I have my ways. It's good. I had a flick through. Maybe I'm starting to get poetry.'

Literature was an ongoing source of disagreement between them. She was a journalist, trained towards clarity. She said poetry was encrypted writing, and that was why he liked it. Kane said it was the clearest way of expressing complicated things.

'I think the book's got some of your PhD people in.'

Kane checked the contents. She was right. His PhD involved a study of poetry under the Ba'ath regime. The idea had been to compare and contrast different groups: the Arabic poets of Baghdad, Christians writing in Aramaic, a Kurdish woman who had worked with Kane as a fixer when he was in Kurdistan and whose long autobiographical poem Kane was now translating. He hadn't even been sure how much of this Bell was aware of, and the present was touching.

Kane thanked her again. Then, reluctantly, he said: 'You haven't noticed anyone around? Anything suspicious?'

'No. It's this thing, isn't it? It's not going away.'

'There's a possibility I'm of interest to them.'

'To the people who killed that couple in Barnet?

'Yes.'

Bell looked uncharacteristically distressed.

'What do we do?'

What Kane did was place his gift upstairs, then picked up the phone and dialled the most violent men he knew. Tactical Services called itself a security company, although that barely did them justice. Set up by a former Flying Squad police officer and a former SAS captain, with a lot of former everything else on their books. Not prestigious or slick, but they were the people the slick spies went to when they needed muscle – especially in a grey legal area.

'There's a possibility a job's turned nasty,' Kane said. 'I need you to run some security checks. Be prepared to step it up at short notice if a direct threat is made, or if I'm able to identify or locate the individual concerned.'

'You've got no ID for this guy?'

'No.'

'We'll come over, have a look.'

Dave Tarrant – former Squadron Sergeant Major Dave Tarrant – came within the hour. He checked the house security, installed some new cameras, looked for any signs of existing surveillance. Nothing. A 24/7 security posting would cost £300 an hour per person, he explained. Kane knew that most of their clients were visiting Saudis. Kane wasn't in that spending league. As a compromise, Tarrant offered to have a man drive by and run checks twice a day. The new security system would alert him remotely if anything suspicious showed up.

'And then?'

'We contact you, send someone over pronto.'

'Estimated response time?'

'Can't guarantee less than half an hour. Not crossing London.'

Kane agreed to this, knowing it was too little. When Tarrant had gone, he went to put Mason to bed. The boy didn't let his mother touch him, as if her presence had become a source of deep shame. Kane had tried to talk to him about it, to no avail. He wanted to say, there may be enough of life where no one will touch you. Don't rush it. In the end, it was easier if the bedtime routine was handled by Kane himself – not a duty he'd ever anticipated, but it worked.

Kane knocked on the bedroom door and entered. The boy was on his computer, playing a first-person shooter game, already in pyjamas. Kane watched him for a moment, wondering how different it would feel if he were his own child. Maybe not that different. Imagined watching him grow up.

'You're good,' Kane said, when the next level was cleared. Action took place in a simulated Iraq, remarkably realistic, down to the trees on the banks of the Euphrates, the bazaar, individual shops Kane remembered near the old cemetery. When he saw the sunset behind the domes of Haydar-Khana Mosque he couldn't stop himself muttering 'wow'.

'Good, isn't it?' the boy said.

'It's something. What's the idea? Kill as many people as possible?'

'Not exactly.'

'Where's the game where you talk to them?' Kane said.

'You can play an Iraqi family trying to escape, if you want.'

'Have you tried that?'

'Yeah. It's like a different game.'

'I bet.'

Mason turned the computer off.

'Listen, Mason, over the next few days, keep an extra eye out, okay? Let me know if you see or hear anything unusual – people, cars, you know the drill.'

'Sure.'

'Good man.'

Kane waited, always alert to the boy's changing moods. But it was Mason who said: 'Are you okay?'

'Me? I'm good. Don't I seem okay?'

The boy grinned. He got into bed. The routine was that Kane sat by the PC for a while. Mason was scared of the dark, although he wouldn't admit it, and liked having someone there, the glow of the PC screen, so Kane read the news or did emails until Mason fell asleep.

Tonight he watched the news. Ukraine. A Russian aircraft shot down, armoured vehicles destroyed. Liberated villages by the Dnipro River; an arms depot on fire deep inside Russian-held territories. Had something of this sea of troubles lapped at his life? Kane knew that a lot never made the news – aspects of war that were harder to film. The NATO Cyber Defence Centre in Tallinn and its Strategic Communications in Riga had both been busy since the invasion of Ukraine. They were targeting Russian social media around the clock, along with direct messages to members of the Kremlin elite, stirring fear and paranoia about defection. War happened in all sorts of ways, spilled out in all sorts of ways.

Kane waited until the boy was asleep then went to the top-floor study. No reply from C yet. He glanced through his own vetting file again. Strange to have all that honesty at the start of something, as if they were giving you the last chance to be open before a lifetime of deceit. He locked it away in his desk.

When he finally got to bed, Bell was still awake. He anticipated fear, but she slipped a hand over him, down his stomach, kneaded his thigh, then brushed her hand back to his chest. He found her mouth with his mouth, wove his fingers into her hair and let his other hand trail down her body.

Their bedroom was directly beneath Mason's. Bell tried to keep quiet as they made love, eventually smothering her face with a pillow. Afterwards, lying together, she said:

'Well?'

'Well what?'

'Now are you going to tell me what's going on? What you're doing upstairs?'

'Was that your interrogation technique?'

'I've got worse tricks. Talk to me.'

'I was just thinking about that plan to escape. Now is definitely the time.'

'Yeah?'

'Maybe immediately.'

And he saw that she understood this wasn't about a holiday. Bell propped herself up on an elbow and watched him. 'I'd like you and Mason to get well away from here, preferably tomorrow.'

'Just like that? Indefinitely? Until you decide it's safe for us to resume our lives? I mean, that wouldn't be easy, Elliot.'

'I'd come with.'

'And what do we tell the clients? We're not in a position to write off contracts. I still owe the lawyers, and there's a lot more legal stuff on the horizon. And the whole point of this work is to afford specialists for Mason. We've got appointments lined up.'

Kane understood; he thought of all those he'd known who had refused to flee, who had remained rooted in a war zone, paralysed. A paralysis called having a life, and knowing that leaving it behind for ever was an anaemic form of death in itself.

'I'm sorry, Elliot. I just ... I don't know what to think. This is very new to me.' Bell lay against him. For a moment he thought she'd fallen asleep.

'Where would we go?' she said.

'Anywhere. Where's the best place you've been?'

'A lot of the best places I've been are still at war.'

'Mine too.'

'Tuscany then.'

'Fuck Tuscany. Are there even schools in Tuscany?'

'Of course. Full of little Tuscan children.'

'Okay. Maybe.'

'And let's say we do go away, do you think we'll feel able to be open with one another? You're someone who I feel understands me. We understand each other. But, for obvious reasons, there's still a caution and I hate that. It's like we're on a leash.'

'Let's slip the leash, Juliet. I want it as much as you do. But I want us to be safe.'

Kane couldn't sleep. He kept thinking about Night Market, his vetting file. It felt odd in a way he wouldn't have been able to describe, knowing a part of him was out there for sale to anyone. Eventually it began getting light. The day looked unprepared. Something fundamental had malfunctioned, the mechanism of privacy that kept our souls within our skin, and the world hadn't realised yet.

NINE

Morning arrived and she'd hardly slept. Rebecca checked the guards outside, their car pimpled with beads of dew. Then she checked online. The adult websites in her name remained poised. The message on her phone from Robert, asking about a Bank of Gibraltar login attempt, remained unanswered.

Iona was still blissfully asleep. Rebecca knelt and touched her forehead to the girl's cheek in a position of prayer, then went downstairs and dismissed the security guards. They dutifully made final checks before leaving. She returned to Robert's study and tidied up all traces of last night's criminality. Then she called Michael De Souza. No answer on the phone number listed by Robert's investigators. De Souza's social media accounts were easy to find. Indeed, she'd been avidly consuming their attacks on her husband for the last two years. His DMs were open so she tried that approach.

This is Rebecca Sinclair. I want to speak to you. Then, in an enlightened moment, she sent a picture of herself.

Still no reply.

Rebecca woke Iona, did the school run. De Souza got back to her as she was driving away from the village. She pulled over.

'Hello,' De Souza said. 'Who is this?'

'Is that Michael?' she said.

'Yes. May I ask who I'm speaking to?' It was his voice – she knew it from radio and TV – a deep, confident drawl. She felt a frisson of excitement, as if speaking to a celebrity.

'Rebecca Sinclair,' she said. Then she added: 'I realise that may be hard to believe.'

De Souza went silent for a moment. 'What can I do for you, Rebecca?' he asked, when he spoke again.

'Thank you for getting in touch. You can appreciate this isn't a straightforward thing for me.'

'I'm sure.' He waited. She tried to imagine his thought process: was this some convoluted prank? An odd kind of revenge?

'I wanted to ask you some questions,' she said.

De Souza gave a quiet laugh. 'I see.'

'I mean, there's something I need to know about, something quite personal, and I think you can help. I recognise that in talking to you there may be material you find useful. To be honest, I'm not in a position to care too much about that. I think you'd find this conversation interesting.' She was gabbling, Rebecca realised. But perhaps this had its own authenticity.

'This all sounds slightly odd,' De Souza said, carefully, and she could sense his defensive radar turning.

'I want to find out about Opula,' Rebecca said.

'Opula.'

'Yes.'

'Right.' An intake of breath. 'What in particular do you want to find out about Opula?'

'Who they are, what they do, why you're not allowed to write about them.'

'So you are aware of the legal complexity here.'

'Yes. But I think I have a personal angle on Opula. I know something quite dark. I don't know the exact law on talking to you about it, or whether you can investigate ... '

'I'm not sure you should say anything more on the phone,' De Souza said.

'No.'

'Are you around this morning, in London?'

'I can be.'

'I'll message you,' he said, and abruptly rung off. The message came from another number: *This is Michael. Can you make 124 Kentish Town Road at 10?*

Yes, she messaged back.

124 Kentish Town Road, it turned out, was an independent art gallery. Rebecca walked straight past it, then had to double back and check the address he'd sent. Large windows at the front showed an unlit exhibition space with lurid oil paintings and vaguely sexual ceramics. A bike had been propped against the central pillar. The front door was locked.

Here, she messaged, and a moment later a figure appeared inside, crossing the bare room to unlock the door. It was De Souza. He was taller than she'd expected, in a fawn corduroy jacket and jeans. De Souza stared at her, glanced at the street behind, nodded.

'Rebecca, thanks for indulging the subterfuge. This place belongs to a friend of mine, it's as discreet as we'll get. Come in.'

She could tell he was excited, that he hadn't fully believed she was for real. De Souza locked the door behind her and led her down to a windowless basement office, with frames and canvases propped against the wall. There was a swivel chair at a desk and an armchair in the corner. He cleared a leather satchel from the armchair and gestured towards it.

'Please.' When Rebecca had sat down he pulled the swivel chair over and sat a few inches away from her. De Souza eyed Rebecca with a slight squint, uncertain whether he was looking at a hunting trophy or a hand grenade.

'So,' he said. 'Opula.'

She tried to compose herself. Here was their nemesis, a little dishevelled, handsome in a driven way, with a familiar Oxbridge languor, jet-black hair with the first touches of grey. A lot posher than she was, if not as posh as Robert. He cleaned his glasses on his shirt all the better to peer at her. Arrogant as any of them. Probably as lascivious. The journalist appeared to be revelling in the situation even as it puzzled him. He could smell her helplessness.

But that didn't mean he trusted her. She imagined what was going through his mind: luck didn't walk straight in. Perhaps he suspected some unspent fury at her husband's infidelities, one that might provide a rationale for this bizarre and dangerous scenario. The beauty of a rocky marriage was that anything could be possible. And, in truth, she had long considered various revenges, an affair of her own being the obvious option. This wasn't unlike how she had imagined it feeling.

'If I requested our conversation to be off the record, would that count for anything?' Rebecca asked.

'If there's something you want to share I can try to ensure it happens in a way that works for both of us,' the journalist said. 'If we're embarking in a spirit of openness, then I should be clear I have a duty to the public as well.'

'Yes.'

'Opula.'

'You've written about them. A lifestyle company.'

'Tried to write, yes.'

'Who are they? What do they do?'

De Souza watched Rebecca carefully.

'Why?'

'I have something to share about them, but I want to know some background first.'

The journalist took a breath, folded his glasses in his hand.

'Opula did whatever you wanted them to do. They closed down a couple of months ago. They were a place very rich people went to make their lives easier. Especially Russians. What exactly is it you want to know?'

'Why I met my husband.'

The faintest of smiles played at his lips.

'And you think Opula connects?'

'Yes.'

De Souza considered this.

'They were set up in 2008. There were a lot of oligarchs arriving in London, millionaires, billionaires, who needed to build a new life, to be shown the ropes. Opula styled themselves a concierge company, a one-stop shop for all potential needs. For a sign-up fee of around five grand, and another grand's subscription per month, Opula could find you places at top London schools, professional nannies, artwork to decorate mansions. Of course, they could also find sharp lawyers and tax advisers. A lot of their clients were on the run, to some extent. They were here to use our courts, to protect themselves, secure their illicit earnings.'

'Did you know that Opula threw parties?'

'Parties?'

'Sex parties.'

The journalist's absence of response suggested he had some awareness. No flinch, no startle. He stayed very still, eyes on her.

'Tell me about these parties.'

'62 Eaton Square,' she said. 'Have you come across the address?' De Souza frowned as he tried to recall.

'I know Eaton Square, of course. Who is at 62?'

'I'm not sure. But Opula threw parties there. And they were pretty wild.'

'Can I ask how you know about this?'

'I was one of their whores.'

She saw him speechless for the first time. In a curious way, the power had switched.

'I see. And did Robert attend these parties?' he asked after a moment.

'Quite possibly. We didn't meet at a sex party, though, but at

111

Opula's Christmas do. What exactly was his connection to this lifestyle company?'

De Souza nodded again, staring at the opposite wall. He bit the arm of his glasses. Things were coming together.

'One of the services Opula offered was to connect their clients with British politicians and other members of the establishment. A lot of these oligarchs wanted more than a home in the UK, they wanted to bury themselves in the ruling class. They had more money than some nation states, but it was dangerous money, stolen. Opula introduced them to powerful people who could protect them, and helped smooth ongoing relationships of various sorts, usually involving the distribution of some of this cash; political donations, carefully disguised in some cases, a few million to a university or a museum – these might be interests close to the politician's heart. Or directly to an institute or foundation with a more explicit political focus. Obviously, Robert's very involved with the New Britannia Institute. Several Russians gave to that, and to the Conservative Friends of Russia. I know Robert once helped Opula hire the Churchill Room in the House of Commons for the launch of a gold-tier membership scheme, or something like that. But he's far from the only politician who benefited. I think I'd heard that many of these people came together at a Christmas Party in 2008. I didn't realise it was organised by Opula. In answer to your question, that may partly explain how you met your husband. You were ... there professionally?'

'Yes.'

'And what do *you* know about Robert's relationship with Opula?'

'Nothing. Just that he had been there at the party. Robert's not an evil person.'

'The concept of evil is not of particular interest me.'

'Naïve, perhaps. A people-pleaser. He tries to be a good MP, and believes he needs backing.'

'Well, he's certainly got backing.' De Souza shifted impatiently in his seat. 'So what made you suddenly interested in it? You're risking your life here, to a certain extent. Why?'

'Someone's trying to blackmail me about those parties. I need to find out who they are, how they connect. How they have pictures of me. That means knowing more about the parties themselves.'

'I see.'

'Who ran Opula?'

'I don't know.'

'What happens when you try to write about them?'

'Legal pressure, and more.'

'From who?'

'Obviously, those implicated. But in my experience, once money has gone to politicians, things become extra complicated. You have a situation in which it's in no one's interests for it to get out. You don't have anyone on your side. To be honest, I hadn't originally been aware quite how well connected Opula were. That became clear once I'd started investigating. And in particular when I started looking into these parties.'

'So you knew about them.'

'Rumours. No details. But I was given a tip-off that Opula offered a top tier of membership, semi-secret; the gentlemen's club, they called it. And it involved some very important people, British politicians rubbing shoulders with shady characters from all around the world, Russia in particular. I made some calls, submitted some official Freedom of Information requests to the House of Commons. Within a matter of hours we were contacted by lawyers on behalf of Opula as well as several politicians. Robert filed a defamation lawsuit, preceded by two cease-and-desist letters demanding that we suspend all reporting while court proceedings took place. It was calculated harassment, of course. They poured tens of thousands of pounds into blocking us. They knew we couldn't afford to fight. My editor knew we couldn't fight. We had no choice but to back down.'

'Was there something in particular they wanted to hide?'

'I don't know. But, like you, I was curious. The interim injunction they'd been granted restrained anyone from publishing information about Opula whatsoever. Something had persuaded a judge at the High Court that this company deserved utmost privacy. The judgement itself was sealed. I sensed someone very powerful at play.'

'And did you have any idea what?'

The journalist shook his head. 'But I'd clearly touched on something very sensitive, something that made them think that even the slightest scrutiny was too much. It's such a blanket suppression. I'd stumbled upon a story that simply couldn't come out at any cost – that much was clear – but I've no idea what.'

'The sex?'

'Maybe. Sex itself is basic, though. There must have been something more to justify the injunction. That's what I always thought. But I was at a dead end. Until you called.'

Now it was over to her. But this didn't seem like a dead end that she could overcome. Judges, court orders – again, the sense of forces drawing a curtain over those scenes; curtains in her mind, those rooms: the bright one like a hospital, the one with the portable electric heater and a man saying *you realise the trouble you would be in*. Somewhere in all this, a police car. She remembered the plastic screen behind the front seats and the crackle of the radio. She could see the combination of beige and blue-grey paint at the police station, the peeling posters: *Know your rights* . . .

'Why did Opula close down?' she asked.

'Sanctions against Russia had really begun to kick in and the whole situation with oligarchs in London started to come under intense scrutiny. But I think it had been under new management for years. You mentioned something quite dark that you knew about Opula, when we spoke on the phone.'

'New Year's Eve 2008, there was a very big Opula party at 62 Eaton Square. A woman was raped.'

De Souza stared at her. Then he clicked his ballpoint. The gravity and sincerity of his gaze was a relief, a hint of vindication.

'At an Opula party.'

'Yes. I believe it was reported to police.'

His eyes lit up further.

'Okay. And what happened?'

'Nothing.'

'Do you mind if I write this down?'

'No.'

He slid a notebook from his jacket.

'A party at 62 Eaton Square,' he said.

'Yes.'

'Do you have details of the victim?'

'It was me.'

De Souza looked at her, then laid down his pen.

'I'm sorry to hear that, Rebecca,' he said. He watched her face very carefully now. 'Is this a story you'd like me to investigate?'

'Yes. I'd like to know who was there, what happened to me. You're the only person I could think of who's in a position to look into that.'

'That's flattering, and a responsibility I'd take seriously. But I can't make promises. You may be overestimating my powers. There's also the issue of your husband's ongoing legal action against me, and how that impacts all this.'

'You deal with that. Do what you need to, or not. Like I say, I don't have many choices.'

'If, let's say, this was to have an adverse impact on his career, if I was sued and people began asking who I'd been speaking to ... Obviously I have a responsibility to protect my sources, but I'm not sure, in this instance, how that would pan out.'

'I understand that.'

'What I'm asking is: are you willing to risk your marriage and your husband's career?'

'Yes.'

'Let's keep going, then. Do you know the identity of the man who raped you?'

'No. I've got nowhere to start. My memory's a total blank.'

'I see. Tell me about these parties, then.'

'Just ... parties. Orgies. What do you want to know?'

'Any suggestion whose property it was?'

'I got the feeling no one lived there. I never saw any personal stuff.'

'What was it like?'

'Very grand. At least seven bedrooms. There was an internal lift. That impressed me. The basement had a room like a club.'

'What were you expected to do?'

'Mingle, chat. Early evening, it was fairly convivial. There would be a meal, top-class chefs. We'd flirt and then, at midnight, the women undressed. Someone would turn down the lights and put on some music. People would go to a living room with a stage and we'd perform. Sometimes there would be games, or just a show. We'd mingle some more. Then, obviously, there were the bedrooms. There were at least seven in the property, plus a sauna, pool and a room set up for bondage, S&M.'

'And you're sure of the address?

'Yes. But I visited yesterday, and the man there now – I don't think I've seen him before.'

'Who was at these parties? Do you know any names?'

'No.'

'Any idea who attended on the night you were attacked?'

'Just a lot of wealthy people.'

'No one you recognised? Politicians? People like that?'

'I wasn't trying to recognise anyone. No.'

116

'Tell me about that night.'

'I don't remember. That's the problem. It's possible I'd been spiked. But then ... I was using drugs. And drinking.'

'And you remember having contact with the police?'

'I think I had some contact with the police later that night. I remember being in a police station at some point. That's all. I don't remember which one, or anything else.'

De Souza looked puzzled.

'You never had a reference number or anything?'

'No.'

'And they didn't follow it up?'

'Not that I'm aware of.'

He opened the notebook again, drew a small dot, thinking. 'That seems significant.'

'Maybe.'

'And you decided against taking it further.'

Rebecca thought of the prim, bespectacled man in the undecorated flat. A fragment that she could well believe had emerged from nightmare rather than experience. *Forget everything. It will be in your own interest.* And out of the fog that followed, Robert inviting her to dinner, a chance to close the door entirely on a night she didn't understand. Even now she wondered if, in pursuing the truth of it, she was breaking some seal that would unleash monsters.

'The only thing I had was that I could leave it behind, become a different person. I was very afraid, for a long time. I'm not now. I'm not that person.

'It sounds like there is an important story here. Just to be clear, I can't offer you much in the way of money.'

'I'm not after money. As I've said, my concern is to identify who may be blackmailing me.'

'You think they connect to those parties.'

'Yes.'

'I can ask around. We can take it from there.'

'I signed an NDA. Would that affect me?'

'Who asked you to sign an NDA?'

'I don't know.'

'No, I don't think that would affect you. But it does make me wonder what exactly was going on there. What I'll probably do first, if you want me to take this further, is to see if there's anything on the police system. I have contacts who can do that discreetly. We can retrieve information if necessary.'

'You can see the records?'

'Perhaps. We can try. I take it you don't have details of who you spoke to in the police?'

'No,' Rebecca said. Her phone vibrated with a message. Unknown number. The message said: *Rebecca, I'd like to see you. This morning? Can you call?* It was signed *Gerald*.

Gerald Lazenger? *Lord* Lazenger, Robert's think-tank connection? This added considerably to her fear and confusion. Did he know she was here? How did he have her number? Why was he messaging her directly? De Souza saw her concern.

'Who is it?' he asked. She showed him the message.

'Robert's puppet master,' she said. 'I think it was you who called him that.'

'What does Gerald Lazenger want?'

'I don't know.' Then it occurred to her: Robert will have told him about the security alert on the Gibraltar bank. Maybe he could see it directly.

'Is it possible he knows we're meeting?' De Souza asked.

'I don't think so,' she said.

'Be careful, Rebecca. You know more than me, but I don't think you know very much. Neither of us does right now.'

'No,' she said. 'Hardly anything at all.'

TEN

Kane's phone rang at 6 a.m.

'You've been trying to get hold of me,' the Chief of MI6 said.

Broughton, Kane thought. Finally. 'Yes. Has there been any kind of security breach recently? A data leak or hack?'

'No.'

'There's some material in public circulation that shouldn't be. I think it connects to the hit on Anton Zakharyan.'

'What kind of material?'

'I can show you. You really need to see this.'

'Come to VX now.'

Kane switched his phone off on Millbank, before he was within five hundred metres of HQ, as he'd been trained to do. Then he crossed the river. It was strange to be back. The guard at the staff entrance was uncertain. He recognised Kane but also recognised that Kane was now an outsider. He checked Kane's name off a visitor's list and directed him to inner security where Kane emptied his pockets, deposited his phone in a locker and submitted himself to the scanner. Kane said he needed to keep the laptop, that there was something on it he had to show John Broughton, and after several calls and a scan of the device this was permitted.

If Kane was hoping for some impromptu reunions in the corridors it wasn't going to happen. Once the security officers realised he was bound for the Chief, Kane got ushered along the VIP route to a dedicated lift with only one stop: Broughton's suite.

The guards that had accompanied him descended back down. Kane stepped into Broughton's wood-panelled, book-lined office, with its panoramic views of the Thames and Parliament. Broughton sat in front of the window, a slight man with a prominent Adam's apple and thick-lensed glasses that made his stare at once intense and cloudy.

'Sir,' Kane said.

'Elliot, come in. Shut the door.' He rose, shook Kane's hand, studied Kane's eyes. 'I was sorry to hear about Anton Zakharyan.'

'Me too. And his wife.'

'And his wife. We're looking into it.'

'Any developments?'

'Nothing yet. I'm being briefed by the police twice a day. The Russia desk's at a loss. So what's all this about? You said you had a lead.'

Kane opened his laptop.

'There's a site on the Dark Web offering files from our system. They look legitimate. I managed to buy my own service vetting file.' Kane brought up a screenshot of Eclipse's directory and pushed his laptop across the desk. 'You can also see the list of other individuals on offer. It's extensive.'

Broughton studied the laptop, expressionless. He clicked between the vetting file and the menu.

'And what are you suggesting the connection is?'

'Someone calling themselves Eclipse. There was a handwritten note in Anton's home naming Eclipse with a Bitcoin address. He knew of Eclipse. He might have known of the danger posed – to himself, to others. To us.'

Broughton moved the laptop closer to study the list again. Still inscrutable. Had Chiefdom changed him? No, he had always considered himself Chief. It was his genius to mask this ambition behind an utterly unprepossessing façade. Kane had seen him mistaken for staff in one of the grander clubs, and noted that Broughton had not been offended by this. The consummate grey man, he had the forgettable anonymity that could save your life when operating behind enemy lines. In a service filled with over-promoted public schoolboys, Kane had always admired him.

Still no signs of a family life visible. His bachelorhood had always had something monastic about it, devout in unspecified ways. The eunuch, Christian called him. It made the few clues to his personality all the more interesting. In their first meeting, Kane had scanned the spines of books in Broughton's office: works on asymmetric warfare, the Mau Mau uprising, ISIS, Chechnya, Mossad, two histories of Northern Ireland, one anthropological study of the Troubles. Rumours were that Broughton had been a student of Soviet techniques of psychological disruption, and had brought this fascination with KGB methods to the streets of Belfast with devastating effect. Broughton set up a massage parlour in the heart of Catholic Belfast for the purposes of getting compromising material, which he had used to set IRA factions against one another. He spread gossip about the behaviour of Republican wives while their men were interned. He took information gained from phone taps and claimed it came from moles within the organisation, watching as they tore themselves apart.

When Broughton became Head of PsyOps in 2007 he revived MI6's blackmail and propaganda department, under the title Psychological Operations Research Group One. Broadly speaking, PsyOps Research had two goals: controlling potential enemies and keeping vigilance over the British establishment. You had to know who was a security risk, which meant peering into the lifestyles of the powerful. The material contained in their archive stretched back to the dawn of the intelligence service, but under Broughton it grew from several hundred files to tens of thousands: photographs and video recordings, intercepted text communications, internet activity. Very few knew enough about Broughton's empire of voyeurism to object. Previously, it had been made clear that blackmail was beneath British sensibilities: messy, ugly, amateur. Broughton's conflict-hardened skills had seemed too wild in Vauxhall. In the wake of Litvinenko, the times began changing. But he divided people, with many who would be happy to see him fall, and Kane knew this lay at the heart of whatever happened now.

Broughton assessed Kane's material again, then he excused himself and went to the secure communications room at the side. Kane let his eyes rest on the view and imagined, wishfully, his own panic percolating down the building. The potential consequences were almost infinite. First and foremost, with any breach, there was the immediate threat to sources, sometimes deep inside enemy organisations, those who'd been turned, who were still operating as moles, and who would be tortured and executed if discovered. Second, there was the long-term damage to the service itself, reputationally and logistically. A compromise of this scale spelled meltdown, end of the MI6 brand for ever in terms of trust. Biggest fuck-up since the Cambridge Five.

Kane took a piece of paper and pen from his jacket and began writing up a list of agents, past and present, who might be threatened by Eclipse's cache – his own people, those he'd promised to protect, and who needed to be watched and potentially moved. Broughton returned while he was still writing.

'I'm getting no indication of a security failure,' the Chief said. 'No suggestion that there's other material out there. Nothing from the Russia desk; no suggestion from China, Iran, North Korea. The Americans appear oblivious too, and I'm keen to keep it that way. Who have you told?'

'Just Christian. He also came up in Anton's searches. Police believe information about him might have been taken by the hit team.'

'Christian Rivera?'

'Yes.'

Broughton's eyes flicked to Kane's list of names, then the sea of polished wood around them, finally back to Kane's own stare.

'I'm going to have Night Market taken offline,' Broughton said. 'But I don't believe someone could have removed these files from our system.'

'Nothing's secure indefinitely, and we've never been as strong as we could have been on that front. Taking Night Market down won't stop them. They'll just set up shop elsewhere.'

'The digital security's been tightened. We spent millions updating the system a couple of years ago. Do you know anything else about this Eclipse character?'

'They sound like a native English speaker. In terms of time zones, it's hard to tell. They communicate around the clock. They appear to be motivated by money – not just selling online, but it's possible they'd attempted to get money out of Anton Zakharyan. That doesn't rule out a state connection – someone who had been working for Russia, maybe. Obviously, elements of this are classic Russia: a hack-and-leak op, unattributable grey-zone mischief.'

Broughton turned back to Kane's vetting notes as if they could hardly equate to state-level aggression. But he was clearly unnerved.

'I need you to wait here again,' he said.

This time it was a long wait – over half an hour. Kane was on the point of trying to leave – wondering how far he'd get – when the door opened and Broughton returned with Gillian Rossi, Head of Technology at MI6, one of the three Deputy Generals who reported directly to Broughton.

Kane knew Rossi from back in the day, one of Broughton's

protégés – though she wasn't always so sharply dressed. A highly skilled operative, she had embraced the cutting edge of surveillance technology, and had overseen the collection of a hell of a lot of dirt. She carried a laptop, which she laid down carefully on the table and which remained closed for the duration of their talk.

'Elliot, good to see you.'

'So to speak.'

'So to speak, yes. I appreciate you bringing this to our attention. We've got forensic analysis of all internal networks under way. As John's mentioned, so far we haven't seen any evidence of a breach. No one's in our system now: there've been no alterations, no settings changed. We've received no ransomware demands. I've set up a honeypot in place, just in case.'

A honeypot was a replica system acting as decoy. From the outside, a hacker would think they'd penetrated MI6 but they'd be caught in a web. Then MI6's own hackers could pick them apart. But until then it did nothing.

'What about an insider? Someone in the building now?'

'We're going to be interviewing everyone. But the question remains how it would be possible to remove data even if someone wanted to. Obviously, the network's air-gapped. There's no means of plugging anything in. There's no connectivity to allow for downloading.'

'There have been cases of hacking air-gapped,' Kane said, although even Rossi – who had done her own experiments – looked doubtful. Getting data off an entirely off-grid computer was the Everest of hacking. Technically, you could leak it to a nearby device via the noise of an internal fan, or by changing air temperatures in a way that could be detected with thermal sensors. You could blink out a stream of information from a hard drive LED to a camera on a drone hovering outside a nearby window. But that was lab fantasy stuff. And none of it could deliver anything like the quantity of material apparently in Eclipse's possession. Rossi merely said: 'We're looking at all possibilities.'

'If someone's managed to penetrate our systems that deeply,' Kane said, 'they could have gone for military intelligence, nuclear security, anything. But they go for kompromat. That surely tells us something.'

'*If*,' Broughton stressed. 'First thing is to assess authenticity. We'll take it from there.'

'You need to go to GCHQ,' Kane said. 'They've got the skills. We need to move fast.'

'Of course we're going to move fast. But if this is Russia, some kind of inter-agency panic is precisely what they'd want. Going to GCHQ at this stage would mean involving the Joint Intelligence Committee, which means informing government. You understand the implications.'

Reputational embarrassment. Kane had forgotten what a force it was. Those who made it to the top never forgot. Broughton wasn't a coward, but he had a lot to hide.

'You can't close this down on your own,' Kane said.

'Let's see,' Broughton said. 'There's no guarantee they have everything they claim to have.'

'They had my vetting file,' Kane said. 'It's likely they blew Anton Zakharyan. We need preparation for a worst-case scenario.'

'That's under way. And I'm not convinced it's as straightforward as you think.'

'In what way?'

'Why did Anton have Whispr installed? Why did he have the Bitcoin address? There's more to this. We analysed thirty-seven murders by Russian teams together. Remember? None involved stabbing. None involved painting words in blood.'

He was right, of course. Broughton usually was. Defensive, but also clinical. Trust nothing, believe nothing: old mantras. Still, Kane felt maddened.

'The hits we analysed were fifteen years ago,' he replied.

'The priority is containing this.'

'The priority is protecting people.' Kane pushed his list across the desk. 'These are names of people out there who could be in danger.'

Broughton took it. He nodded to Rossi. Rossi got to her feet. 'I'm sure you'll be updated,' she said to Kane as she left.

When they were alone again, Broughton said: 'Does Juliet Bell know about any of this?'

The question caught Kane off guard. He chided himself for his surprise.

'Juliet Bell's not the issue here,' Kane said. He saw the first flicker of emotion on Broughton's face: a twitch on the right side.

'Wake up, Elliot. You're in a relationship with a journalist who's tried more than anyone to expose what she sees as the illegitimate side of MI6. What do you think she'd make of this kind of supposed leak?'

Kane found himself momentarily speechless. Eventually, he said: 'I'm sure she'd be very interested. Right now, she doesn't know anything.'

'Please remember, our work in Psychological Research was precisely the kind of thing she wanted to reveal when I assigned you to investigate her. Before you let her turn you.'

'Turn me.' Kane felt himself smiling in disbelief. A man is the sum of his vocabulary.

'Juliet Bell isn't the problem here,' Kane said, getting to his feet.

'We need to handle this very carefully.'

'I realise that.'

'I need to trust you to manage this situation.'

'Give it a go.'

Out of the building. Always a relief, as if humanity touched him along with the sunlight. As ever, the instinct was to march along the riverside, work HQ out of his muscles, so that was what he did. Wishing, not for the first time, a plague upon all houses, and sensing that he was going to have to find a way forward without institutional backing. Kane passed Parliament and felt the dynamite of its own corrupt desires smouldering beneath the chambers. How many MPs had been collected into the Research Group archive? Pinned and mounted in Broughton's collection?

He called Christian.

'There's been a huge leak, a lot of the Research Group files. Maybe all of them. I think photos we took of Anton might have blown his cover. I just met with John Broughton. He's saying there's no sign of a hack, so I don't know what happened. As you can imagine, they're terrified of this getting out. I don't think they're going to pull adequate resources for fear of making noise.'

'If this really is something to do with Halcyon,' Christian said. 'You and me are going to be a lot more sought after as targets – a lot more attractive to them than Anton. It's a matter of time. Someone's putting work into this. It suggests people in Moscow with long memories.'

'That's what I'm thinking.'

'There are men over there who will have been waiting for their chance. You know what I'm saying: men high up. They've got nothing to lose now. They'll have a green light, gloves are off. And we're not government any more. We don't have that protection.'

This had occurred to Kane. Diplomatic convention said that you handled one another's intelligence officers carefully. There were no conventions for former spooks cashing in on their glory days.

'We need to proceed on the assumption that we're next. I'm

going to keep applying pressure to Head Office, but also looking into alternative arrangements. Most of all, we need to be alert, and stay in touch.'

'Yes.'

'I'll keep you updated.'

'Likewise.'

As soon as he was home, Kane took his laptop and tried to log into Night Market. It was down. MI6's technical department had worked its magic. But it was weak magic. Kane tried a few rival sellers' sites, and sure enough Eclipse had popped up on one called Nemesis. Same offer of classified documents and footage: *Message with enquiries*. Migration from one shady message board to another was part of the scene. Sites got shut down, hacked, ransomed. You moved on under cover of darkness. It was how the community survived.

Kane set up a Nemesis account and gave it the username 'Admin'. He messaged Eclipse.

This is Nemesis admin. It's believed one of your buyers has broken site regulations. Please provide information on all transactions in last 48 hours, otherwise we will be forced to suspend your account and withhold any outstanding payments.

The reply was prompt: *Is that the best you can do?*

Kane realised he was operating without self-control. He had allowed Eclipse to rile him, and that meant carelessness.

You are getting people killed, Kane typed. *The material you are selling endangers lives.*

I think I know who you are, Eclipse replied.

Kane sat back, concerned. Eclipse sent a link a moment later. It was to a web page with the URL KaneXposed.com. No content yet.

Kane covered his face with his hands. He'd been too obvious, of course. Complacent because he wasn't on an official mission.

And he was out of practice. That could mean serious consequences now.

I don't know what you're talking about, he typed.

Do you want to play?

Play what?

Send fifty thousand dollars in BTC or I start to fill it.

Kane typed, *What is it you think you can expose?* then deleted
it. He was about to close the laptop when he saw the message blink in:

I know more about your life than you know yourself, Mr Kane.

ELEVEN

Lazenger had proposed coming to his office at the New Britannia Institute on Greycoat Row. Rebecca made her way from the meeting with De Souza, terrified, obedient. Her immediate suspicion remained that this summons connected to last night's failed attempt at transferring money. She was sure the Bank of Gibraltar account was connected to Lazenger's foundation.

Greycoat Row. The very name had acquired a sacredness, though the road looked superficially docile: narrow, cobblestoned, with neat townhouses either side. On the fringe of Westminster, just outside Westminster Abbey precinct, in a network of streets infested with think tanks and consultancies and institutes you wouldn't notice unless you peered very closely at the small plaques beside the glossy doors. They had various names for what they did: analysts, lobbyists, strategic advisers. All added up to being a front for real power – those with millions to spend – for which politicians like her husband were merely levers to pull. It was a shadow zone that existed to do the things that would have looked bad two hundred metres to the north in Parliament, in the same way that the city's brothels used to be situated just beyond its walls and therefore its laws.

What had become startlingly clear in her twelve years as wife of an MP was that the elite was a brothel of its own, split between those with money and those whose grip on power depended on seducing them. Robert would drop anything when summoned to Greycoat Row. Lazenger was one of the few men he spoke of with naked deference. She knew the New Britannia Institute was involved in the consultancy payments that constituted the real bulk of their income. And she now knew Russian money had been floating around the organisation. She was starting to get a glimpse of the inner workings. If Lazenger was going to accuse her of trying to access the Bank of Gibraltar account, perhaps she could ask some uncomfortable questions of her own.

Rebecca rang the bell and he unlocked the door from the inside. Something was immediately off. He seemed delighted to see her. Surprised, even.

'Come in, come in. No one else is here yet.'

He ushered her upstairs to his office, past framed photographs of prime ministers. A Union Jack filled one wall of the office, a sofa beneath it. Lazenger sunk down into the sofa and patted the seat beside him. He was clutching his phone.

'Rebecca. I've been so worried about you. I got your message.' An icy dread began to fill her body. She wanted to flee, felt herself paralysed.

'What did you get?' she said. He studied her face, the first uncertainty showing on his own.

'Did you send me this?'

She took the phone from him. An image, cropped from one of the videos: herself, bare breasted, looking down at whatever she was doing with her hands beneath the lower edge of the picture. Touching herself or, more likely, somebody else. The message said: *Call me.*

'I didn't.'

This provoked a flicker of hesitation. A recalibration.

'Oh my dear. But it *is* you.' To her horror, he seemed undeterred. 'Who'd have naughty pictures of you?' he asked, amused. 'You're a dark horse.'

131

'I'm being blackmailed. I'm going to leave now.'

'I don't think that's wise. Given the precarity of your situation.'

'What do you want?' she said.

'What do *you* want, Rebecca? Is it a money issue? Last night, Robert mentioned that someone had been trying to get into one of his accounts. Do you need pocket money? That can be arranged.' He patted the sofa again, and when she didn't sit, he stood up and approached her, inches from her face so she could smell the milky coffee on his breath. 'You know I can help with that.'

'That wasn't me.' Rebecca heard the failure of her lie as she said it, heat rising up her skin.

'I want to help you. You understand that? Whatever your predicament. I can keep it secret. I haven't told anyone.' He met her eyes. Close up, his were surprisingly mild. 'Robert wouldn't mind.'

'Jesus Christ.'

'I know things haven't been easy since the affair.' He touched her hair. 'I don't think you want to be leaving now.'

Was that a threat? Lazenger let his hand fall so that it brushed her breast. Rebecca summoned a grim smile, a reluctant sigh, thinking this air of resignation would be more convincing than sudden enthusiasm. She placed a hand gently on his chest and pushed him back onto the sofa. Then she knelt before him, undid his belt, the clasp of his trousers and tugged them down to his ankles. Lazenger let out a contented purr. She buckled the belt again so that he was incapacitated, and when she was confident he wouldn't be able to walk, got up and left.

'Rebecca,' she heard him call, stumbling to his feet, knocking something over. She moved downstairs fast. Then, as she stepped out onto the cobblestones, 'Rebecca, come back here. We need to talk about this.'

She moved blindly towards Pimlico, feeling sick and terrified.

Had anyone else received supposed propositions from her? The thought turned her stomach. She felt as if she was naked, walking through a bad dream. A young man in a suit and lanyard passed her, his glance lingering over her face, her body. Was she being paranoid? Was she well known enough to attract attention anyway? She was only minutes from the House of Commons; this was dangerous territory.

She tried to call De Souza, but he didn't answer. A message came in as she stared at the phone, from a friend, Alexandra.

I'm here, Alexandra wrote.

Rebecca had forgotten a lunch appointment. She swore. Alexandra was married to an ambitious backbench MP; they met occasionally at fashionable restaurants in Soho or on the South Bank and gossiped. Rebecca called her: 'I'm so sorry, Alex. I've totally ballsed up my day ...'

'What's going on, Rebecca?' Alexandra asked, sounding concerned.

'You've received something?'

'Received something? No. Your voice.'

'Just one of those days.'

'Is it Robert?'

'No. Mostly Iona. She has some kind of fever.'

They agreed to reschedule. Rebecca felt the first real twist of the knife. She had begun making plans for a life that wasn't going to happen. She remembered a line from one of the blackmail investigation websites: *You could lose the trust of friends. They might never look you in the eye again.* What would they see if they did? Your shame? And why is that so hard to look at? Because they are the source of your pain, perhaps. Because it would expose their own fascination. In Rebecca's experience, people flinched from their desires more than their fears. And their own secret desire was to watch you crawl with humiliation, destroyed.

Eclipse finally messaged: *How's your day going?* She felt a hatred rise within her, unlike any she had known before. *This could all go away very easily*, he wrote.

I tried, she messaged back. *You are requiring me to steal money. That is likely to expose me and you will not get anything. You're being stupid.*

Try harder.

The next time she called De Souza, he answered. But he sounded hesitant.

'I've been looking into it. Hang on.' He put her on hold, came back a moment later, said he could share some information, but she needed to come to an office in Hatton Garden. 'I've definitely got a few more questions for you,' he said.

This address was on the corner of Hatton Garden and Charterhouse Street, above a jeweller's. The only sign visible announced The London Gold Centre. Rebecca checked the list of buzzers beside an ornately carved stone doorway. She pressed 'B', as instructed, and was buzzed in, told to come to the first floor. Dingily carpeted stairs led up to an unmarked door with its own video entry system.

De Souza himself opened the door. Beyond him, a man in his sixties with cropped silver hair sat at a bare desk. He was large, straight-backed, in a pale grey suit jacket and open-necked shirt, with a bulky sovereign ring on his right hand. Her first impression was of an undertaker – a discordance of physicality and solemnity. The room had no decorations, just shelves of directories and ring binders. In the corner, a small table supported a kettle and a basket of teabags and single-serve creams.

On second glance, Rebecca read the man as former police or military. She'd seen enough of this type now. Which meant the place was some kind of private investigations company, which explained its caginess.

'This is Andy,' De Souza said. 'We've worked together a lot. He helps me with research. A very well-connected man.'

Andy bowed his head, modestly. Then he smiled at Rebecca. His teeth were very white and straight.

'Thanks for coming in, Rebecca.'

'What have you found?'

'We'll get to that in due course.' He had a copper's steady tone, a faux-reasonableness. 'Talk us through the story again.'

'It's not a story.'

'The events.'

'Let me see what you've got.' Rebecca was still taut from her encounter with Lazenger. She'd had enough of men inviting her to offices just to fuck with her.

'Talk to us first.'

'I came to you. You talk to me.'

Andy and De Souza exchanged glances.

'There's no record of a rape on the police system,' Andy said. This opening felt like a blow, but not a total surprise to Rebecca.

'What about 62 Eaton Square?' she said. 'Did you look into it?'

'Yes.'

'Who owns the house?' Rebecca asked.

'It's been in the Earl of Westmorland's family for some time,' De Souza explained. 'That's not to say they wouldn't have loaned it. The family have extensive military and diplomatic connections.'

'To Opula.'

'Potentially. But we're not seeing evidence of that. Not much evidence of anything that you've described.'

'I checked the police database for any records pertaining to that address,' the private investigator said. 'Nothing came up.' He reached beneath the desk and retrieved a very slim, silver MacBook, like a bladed weapon, which he opened with ungainly fingers. He took some time typing in passwords. Finally he turned it and showed Rebecca a map of Victoria.

'Can you point out where you might have gone?'

'Here.' She traced the route from Eaton Square to the High Street.

'And what do you remember?'

'Very little.'

'Had you been doing drugs?'

'Yes.'

'And your maiden name was Nolan.'

This non sequitur momentarily threw her.

'Yes,' she said.

'There is one thing, Rebecca. But it's caused a puzzle for us.' Again, that side glance at De Souza.

'Go on,' Rebecca said.

'So I looked at the police local system. The local incident system records all daily incidents generated: stray dogs, traffic accidents, you name it, right up to events that police call "occurrences". That means they warrant criminal investigation.'

'And?'

'At approximately 3 a.m. on January 1st 2009, a woman was picked up by an officer in a patrol car at the corner of Buckingham Palace Road and Eccleston Street, a few minutes east of Eaton Square. Her name was Rebecca Nolan.'

'Yes?'

'The attending officer was PC Paul Lockhart.'

'Let me see.'

He angled the screen. She studied the report, grateful that someone, somewhere had taken this seriously. That they had, at least, set it down on record of some sort. She wasn't entirely mad, it had happened.

PC Paul Lockhart. She could see him: the face emerging from the lights and laughter of New Year's morning.

0320 hrs. IC1 female, approx. 20–30 years . . .

Rebecca read on with increasing alarm.

'It says I was detained after acting suspiciously.'

'You were arrested,' Andy said. He peered at Rebecca, as if this should make more sense to her than it did to him. Rebecca's relief evaporated in an instant.

'Why?'

'There's a CAD – a computer-aided despatch number – i.e. an incident number. I managed to access the logs, where any updates are recorded. It seems there was something you told those initial officers that made them concerned enough to arrest you and bring you in for questioning. I can't find any crime report from the front desk. Station office CCTV from that night has gone. The custody sergeant roster is also missing, which means I can't even check to see who was on duty. The log was closed at 11 a.m. on January 1st, following a decision not to charge you. But it's unambiguous: you were the suspect, Rebecca.'

'For what? Suspected of what?'

She heard the jeweller's doorbell downstairs, a cheery greeting as locks were undone.

'You tell us,' Andy said.

'You married Robert a few months after that,' De Souza pointed out, with as much sensitivity as he could muster.

'Yes.'

'Did he know about this?'

'No. About what?'

'I'll be honest,' De Souza said. 'We've never seen anything removed from police records in this way before.'

She read the report again, pressed the two men for more information, but they were waiting for her to reveal something she didn't possess. She was stuck in another nightmare, claustrophobia closing in.

'I need to collect my daughter,' Rebecca said, standing. She looked at De Souza. He appeared at once apologetic and puzzled. The two men were awkward, as if they'd reluctantly fired her from a job; as if she had burst into tears and they needed to draw on compassion that wasn't native to them. But she hadn't burst into tears. And something was coming back to her now under the pressure of rage.

Something to do with Elliot.

Robert had made dinner – his signature carbonara. That took her by surprise, especially as she had half-expected divorce proceedings to be under way. He seemed to genuinely believe the Bank of Gibraltar thing was an attempted hack. He was convivial, which revived Rebecca's gentle, circumspect fondness for him and forced her deeper into the well of her secrecy. No more messages from Eclipse. She couldn't see how she could pay him, and strategy had dissolved to a dull, unrelenting fear. No more messages from Gerald either.

'Heard from Gerald Lazenger today?' she asked, eventually, when they'd eaten and were settled in the living room, Iona with her homework, Robert sifting his red box, Rebecca pretending to flick through a *Sunday Times* supplement.

'No. Why?'

'Just a passing thought. The legal situation.'

'I'm seeing him tomorrow. Something in the papers?'

'Isn't there always?'

Robert looked at her, frowned, then dropped the conversation, returning to the affairs of state. It was always strangely comforting watching him with his box, working through his papers – just the fact that this quaint thing actually existed, and the country was determined by it. The sitting room featured an inglenook fireplace with log burner, which enhanced the cosiness. Doors led out, through a small conservatory, to the patio and afforded a glimpse of tamed garden and wild hills beyond.

Rebecca helped Iona finish an account of life for an

eight-year-old girl in the Iron Age, the back of her mind spinning around words like they were rocks in a stream: *Suspect. Suspicious. Occurrence.* Her memories were a vortex with a gap at the heart of them.

Or was there one face?

Once Iona was asleep, Rebecca returned to the living room and took down *The Mayor of Casterbridge* from the bookshelf, looking for the page she'd been reading when Elliot first spoke to her.

She had noticed him before, of course, and sensed that he played some role in overseeing things. On at least two occasions she had seen him circulating the house, like a head waiter ensuring tables were correctly laid. Quick glances, polite nods at the girls but little interest beyond that. Until he saw her in the garden, on the bench, an hour or so before the party was due to begin, cigarette in one hand, *Mayor of Casterbridge* in the other.

She remembered looking up, catching the flicker of a smile.

'Interesting novel,' he said.

Rebecca waved away a cloud of cigarette smoke, uncertain how deferential she was meant to be. She sensed him appraising her.

'Long,' she said, and instantly felt she'd let herself down, defeated the whole fantasy of who she might be, that the book was meant to prop up. So she added: 'I love how cold it is. Unsentimental.'

'Read any others by him?'

'No, this is the first. I'm studying it.'

'University?'

'A-levels,' she said, and was annoyed by her blush. 'I skipped them the first time around. Bit embarrassing,' she said.

'Why is that embarrassing?' he said with genuine puzzlement. He asked if he could join her on the bench, introduced himself as Elliot. 'Enjoying the studies?'

'Yes.'

'Can't be easy, juggling it all.' By which she suspected he

meant cramming nineteenth-century novels in between jobs as a high-class escort.

'Works quite well,' she said, truthfully.

He nodded. 'I can imagine that.' Never did he betray any sense of surprise or scepticism.

'Then university, perhaps? Reckon you'll take it further?'

'Maybe.' It felt odd admitting this. She hadn't discussed her fantasy of doing a degree with anyone, she who worked among so many secret desires. But he had sensed something: she was looking ahead. They spoke some more and began chatting regularly soon after that, initially before jobs, then they exchanged numbers and began meeting outside of work. Just coffees or lunch. She sensed that he was curious to see if she might be of use to him in some way, but that this was balanced by a genuine interest in helping her. Once, discussing her dreams of a different life, he had joked: 'I wish *I* could get out of my line of business.'

What was that business? How did it connect to the broken shards of memory that occasionally surfaced in dreams, scraping the membrane of her waking life, ones in which Elliot appeared, grim-faced, holding her hands beneath a pair of gold taps, washing blood from them.

Some form of trauma had tried to bury this Elliot, the one who belonged to that fateful New Year's Eve. She wondered if a kind of selective amnesia could work like that. What had she taken that night, to instil an oblivion like a tunnel without lights, out of which, at the farthest end, another man's face appeared, a police officer. One for whom she now had a name.

Paul Lockhart. Belgravia Police Station.

Rebecca eased the patio doors open and stepped out to the garden, away from the windows. A sluggish breeze brought a scent of summer midnight and a vague memory of adolescence, of vodka and other people's mouths and some obscure promise in the nocturnal warmth. She found a number for Belgravia Police Station, hesitated, then called.

'Does a police officer called Paul Lockhart still work there?' Rebecca asked.

'A police officer called Paul Lockhart?' The woman who'd answered the station's phone sounded wearily sarcastic. 'No.'

'He worked there in 2009. I need to speak to him. Do you know where I'd find him?'

Now the woman permitted herself a laugh.

'Is this a wind-up?'

'No. It's quite urgent, actually.'

'I'm sure if you're someone who needs to speak to Paul Lockhart urgently you'll be able to find him, love. Sorry.' They hung up.

What did that mean?

Rebecca searched his name online and saw why the woman had laughed. Paul Lockhart was now Commander Paul Lockhart, Deputy Chief of Counter Terrorism.

According to a brief piece in *The Times* upon his appointment, Lockhart left frontline policing in 2009. That was shortly after his encounter with Rebecca. But whatever that night had involved, it hadn't held him back. His star had shone.

Counter Terrorism Policing were based in an HQ in West London. Rebecca imagined appearing out of the darkness as he had done, reaching out to him. *Acting suspiciously.* Asking exactly what he meant by that. She fantasised taking him by the arm, asking: *what happened that night? Why did you arrest me?* Then she decided that was exactly what she was going to do.

TWELVE

KaneXposed sat there online, waiting for its revelation. According to a site that monitored domain names, it had been set up an hour ago, using a commercial provider. The server was in Iceland, which was less surprising if you knew how resistant the country was when it came to releasing data to international criminal investigations.

The same domain supplier had also been used to set up ElliotShame.com and Elliotkaneserialkiller.is.

No word from MI6. Waiting around wasn't an option. Kane checked the balance of his and Bell's business account again, then called a company called Psionic run by Tim Cunningham, GCHQ's former Director General of Technology.

'Elliot, how's tricks?'

'Not that great, Tim, to be honest. I've got something trouble-some going on and I could really do with you taking a look at it.'

'Want to come in tomorrow?'

'Can you do now?'

Cunningham hesitated. It was last minute, but Cunningham knew that the people who contacted him did it out of urgency. Cyberattacks didn't give you a lead time. He worked for an emergency service, and Kane had been a good client over the years.

'Sure,' Cunningham said. 'You know where our office is. I'm here all afternoon.'

*

Psionic had its main office in EC1, nestled among the financial institutions that turned to it for security. It stood out from them, with a sleek, angular steel cladding that had something to do with energy neutrality but gave it an imposing presence, an impenetrable fortress of cybersecurity beside which the glass of the financial institutions seemed vulnerable.

Walking in, it felt like an art gallery, the illusion only slightly qualified by a set of biometric gates. To one side was a room showcasing digital artworks, then a café that proudly accepted cryptocurrency payments, with a digital currency exchange screen showing real-time crypto rates above the menu of flat whites and protein smoothies.

This was where Cunningham met Kane. He was wiry, boyish, bright-eyed behind frameless glasses. Before his GCHQ directorship, Cunningham had been one of their most senior technicians, part of the secretive team who had inserted backdoors and trapdoors into commercial encryption software, allowing the intelligence services to maintain their edge. They had also developed tools that could get into private messages in most apps and email services. Cunningham left GCHQ in 2018, taking that reputation with him and, rumours suggested, a lot of skeleton keys. These were rumours he was happy to encourage as he set up his own firm, quickly earning millions from banks, blue chips and governments terrified of increasingly professional hackers. Cunningham became known as the person intelligence agencies went to when their own services failed.

'You say you've got a problem,' Cunningham said.

Kane passed his laptop, open on the website KaneXposed.com, with the details of the domain name registration on another tab. Then he talked Cunningham through everything he'd gleaned from his interactions with Eclipse, including details of Eclipse's Whispr and Bitcoin accounts.

'And you want us to shut him down?'

'I need an ID,' Kane said. 'I need to figure out who's doing this.'

Cunningham looked at the website, then the Bitcoin code.

'What's it about?'

'A troublemaker. I don't know what kind, but he needs to be stopped. I think he has access to data stolen from MI6.'

This got Cunningham's interest. It encouraged another few minutes of close analysis.

'Does MI6 know about this?'

'Some of it. Think it's possible?'

'Everything's possible.' Kane could see professional curiosity. 'Russia?' Cunningham said.

'No idea. Doesn't vibe Chinese.'

'They use any email addresses? What's their comms?'

'All via Whispr.'

'Okay. Well, for you, I can take a look. Give me an hour or two. We're just finishing something.'

In the end it was seven hours. Kane had given up on waiting and was contemplating another sleepless night when Cunningham called.

'Got something quite interesting,' Cunningham said. 'You available to pop in?'

It was 9 p.m.

'Yes,' Kane said. 'What have you got?'

'He maintains bad digital hygiene. I don't think it's a state thing, or even a gang. It's an amateur.'

'You reckon?'

'Looks like that to me. Come in now. We need to make some decisions fast.'

Kane drove in. The ground-floor café and art gallery were closed, but Cunningham stood waiting in the gleaming atrium, looking excited.

This time, Kane was led upstairs, past the biometric scanners, to the top floor. This was dominated by the Threat Centre, the heart of the office, a vast, open area surrounded by screens displaying live cyberattack data in real time. Teams of analysts appeared hard at work. Cunningham led Kane past the Threat Centre, across a rooftop courtyard with a vertical garden, a lush oasis with benches and a small fountain, charging stations and solar panels. Cunningham pointed out tomatoes and lettuce amid the greenery, which he said were used in the café downstairs, then the rainwater harvesting system that fed into the office block's toilets.

A door led from the garden into the Cyber Lab, a brighter, barer, calmer space, equipped with the latest hardware, super-computers and virtual simulation environments.

'He's sending people data via Whispr,' Cunningham said. 'That's smart enough. No one's going to get user ID via Whispr. But this website – KaneXposed – you're going to need an email address to verify. So we had a look, and it connects to a Proton Mail address: 3736.protonmail. Obviously, Proton's a pretty robust, encrypted email provider, but we have our ways. So we sneaked a peek into his emails.'

'Really?'

Cunningham led Kane to a man with a ponytail, sitting in front of a double monitor, sipping from a keep cup. He introduced him as Jay. On one of the monitors was a Proton Mail inbox: black menu bar down the left-hand edge, beneath the Proton Mail logo, then the subject lines of the inbox and, in the right half of the screen, the body of the selected email.

'Not too exciting at first. There's not much there, as you can see. This is an account he barely uses. However, there is one thing,' Cunningham said.

Jay clicked to the drafts folder, and clicked an unnamed draft email dated 7 March 2023. It contained a string of twenty capital-ised words: *TIMBER, SWORD, JOY, EAGLE, VIBRANT, RIVER ...*

'A recovery phrase,' Kane said.

'Bingo.' Cunningham smiled. 'Backup password for the Bitcoin wallet.'

Kane felt a rush of hope. This was a breakthrough. Recovery phrases were standard practice for those using cryptocurrency. In case you lost your original password, almost all cyber wallets recommended setting up a backup phrase consisting of a string of words. But unless you had very great faith in your memory, this also needed to be kept written down somewhere: in a safe, in a safety deposit, etched onto fire-resistant materials. Kane could see how the draft folder of an anonymous, encrypted email service would be an ideal place to keep it. Accessible anywhere. Indestructible.

Ideal unless you came up against Psionic.

'It gets better,' Cunningham said. 'Not only is the full wallet ID accessible too, but the money's still in it. Usually you'd expect a professional criminal to take their coins offline, put them into some kind of cold storage to protect any ill-gotten gains from law enforcement. Not this one. Follow me.'

Looking out onto the vertical garden was Cunningham's own office. It contained a digital portrait of his family, who appeared to wave as Kane passed. There was a glass box of insects, finally a floor-to-ceiling view over night-time London. Up on Cunningham's screen was a Bitcoin wallet.

'That's his?' Kane said.

'Right.'

It took Kane's breath. The screen showed the alphanumerical address in the top-left corner, then, in rows below, were all the recent transactions sent and received in the last few days. Eight in total, all incoming, all between ten and thirty grand. Kane saw his own payment, anonymous as the rest. The current balance was 41.33 BTC.

'Three million dollars, by yesterday's exchange rate,' Cunningham said.

The cybersecurity boss wore a look of professional satisfaction. But Kane sensed that this hadn't been a huge challenge for his team. Outside, the City's glass blocks twinkled with other secrets.

'What do I owe you?' Kane said.

Cunningham waved this away. 'If it's a bad person, then I'm glad to have helped. You've got us good contracts in the past, and I'm sure you will in the future. I'd like to take a cut of the coin for a charity we support – the World Land Trust. I propose 10 per cent; only question is what you want us to do with the rest.'

It took Kane a second to realise what was being suggested: that they empty the account. That would be standard, of course, when working with security services or law enforcement, penetrating criminal gangs or terrorists – secret little hits, chipping away at adversaries in a grey legal area.

'Does this tell you anything else? Any identifying details?'

'Sadly not. All it tells us is that he's slapdash.'

'Can you hold off for a couple of days?'

Cunningham shook his head.

'I wouldn't. They could change the password. I'm going to move 10 per cent to our charity account. Where do I transfer the rest?'

It seemed there was no choice in the matter. Kane felt himself lighting a fuse.

'We can see the people who paid in.'

'I can see the wallets that transferred money in, sure. Anonymous, of course.'

'So you could split the money between them, return what they paid.'

'I could. But are you sure? You don't want a cut?'

'I don't want a cut, no. I want Eclipse.'

*

Bell and Mason were sleeping when Kane got back. He sat in the kitchen, watching the darkened garden. At midnight he checked Eclipse's account page on Nemesis. They'd published a new message:

To whoever is fucking with me, you will pay for this. You've got one hour to return the money or tell your government you're sorry, you messed with the wrong person.

Kane checked his Whispr account. Eclipse had sent a direct message to him six minutes ago.

Have you just done something very stupid?

Kane didn't reply. The next message came in as he was staring at the screen.

You've just dug a lot of graves, you dumb motherfucker. Say goodbye to your life and the lives of those you love. I hope you enjoy watching people die.

THIRTEEN

The National Counter Terrorism Policing Operations Centre was housed in the Empress State Building in West Brompton, just north of Fulham, thirty-one floors of soaring 1960s optimism, with a curved façade that made it look like a five-star hotel.

Paul Lockhart was housed inside that. The man who had entered her nightmare and then arrested her. Rebecca sat in her car watching the building. Professional head, she thought, steeling herself. There is no way forward but this – no other way to protect herself and her family but to advance deeper into the horror towards the truth. She approached the entrance, smoothed her hair, straightened her posture, walked in.

She hadn't anticipated such high security. A line of scanners, then electronic barriers, with uniformed guards on both.

'I'm here to speak to Commander Paul Lockhart,' Rebecca said to the woman on the front desk. She felt the security guards watching.

'Do you have an appointment?'

'Yes,' she said, and felt there was some obscure truth in that. The woman studied her screen. 'It may not be down there,' Rebecca said. 'Could you tell him it's Rebecca Nolan? We met fifteen years ago.'

The woman stared at her.

'I can't see an appointment. Can I ask exactly what it's concerning?'

'Something he'll want to speak to me about. I promise.'

After a second's consideration, the receptionist picked up her phone, angling her chair away from Rebecca. She explained that a Rebecca Nolan was here, wanting to speak to Commander Paul Lockhart, no appointment. Waited as this was relayed by her counterpart upstairs, then looked visibly surprised.

'He's coming down,' she said, regarding Rebecca with a new depth of curiosity.

Lockhart appeared a few minutes later. Rebecca recognised him immediately, astonished by this sense of familiarity. Slightly coarse ginger hair, faint freckles – a tall, pleasant-faced man in full uniform, drifting towards her out of the depths of her consciousness, a face from a recurring dream.

The receptionist turned anxiously between them, but Lockhart beamed.

'Rebecca,' he smiled. He shook her hand warmly, and for a second she wondered if he had mistaken her. 'Excellent ... ' His speech trailed off, smile fixed.

'I wanted to have a quick word.'

'Of course. Let's head up.' He tapped impatiently for a visitors' sign-in book. Rebecca signed – she was aware of him reading her name over her shoulder – and was given a lanyard. Now he could lead her into the building, via the bag search, down a long corridor to a lift, quickly. His eyes held a splinter of fear that took her by surprise.

In the lift he studied Rebecca's face openly, reading it like an object.

'Do you know who I am?' she asked.

'Yes.'

'Or who I was.'

He nodded. The lift doors opened directly onto a busy office. Counter Terrorism. Fifty men and women worked intently, glued to screens showing CCTV footage, screens showing social media accounts, speaking on phones or huddled in groups of two or three above paperwork. Lockhart led her rapidly past all this to his corner office, then closed the blinds so they were screened from the rest of his staff.

It was only when he was sat behind his desk that Lockhart regained a certain composure. She saw the layers of his identity: a man with a firm sense of right and wrong, one that had suited him for seniority, a figurehead in a stormy ethical sea. And she saw how seniority had tempered his innate gentleness with impatience and self-regard. He'd been on a journey, and at some point that had involved stepping over her body.

'We met, on New Year's Eve 2008.'

'Yes.'

'You were working at Belgravia Police Station.'

'That's right. I was on patrol. I found you.'

'Found me where?'

'Why now, Rebecca?' He stared at her, moving restlessly on the chair, leaning back then forwards again to clasp his hands, as if searching for the position that would grant him control of the situation.

'Things are happening that connect to that night. I'm being blackmailed. And it relates to where I'd been, what I'd been doing, when you found me. The house I'd been to, maybe to what happened to me there.'

'How does it connect?'

'I don't know, because I don't know what happened.'

'You don't know?'

'I barely have any recollection. I never did,' Rebecca said.

The Commander watched her face again, reading her, trying to decipher her game, like someone sensing themselves the object of a dangerous joke.

'I was coming back from a brawl in a minicab office,' Lockhart began. 'Thought my shift was almost over. You can imagine,

New Year's Eve, not a police constable's favourite night. London was chaos. Then I saw you, on the corner of Buckingham Palace Road. You were ... in a bad way. I could see that at once. Stumbling about. I actually thought you were going to flag me down, but then you saw it was a police car and you backed away. So that got my interest. Something was clearly wrong – you were in a tiny dress and it was freezing. So I stopped and approached you, just thinking perhaps you were drunk, lost your mates, and then I saw the blood on you.'

'Blood.'

'Yes. On your clothes, your arms, your face. It looked like you'd tried to wash at some point but hurriedly. So I didn't know what was going on. I asked if you were hurt, where you were going, where you'd been. I couldn't get anything coherent out of you. You could barely speak, and your phone was dead, so I offered to take you into the station. Do you remember that?'

'I remember a police officer, that's all. Then being in your car.'

'You were resistant at first. Very resistant.'

'So you arrested me.'

'For your own safety. So I could get to the bottom of what was going on. I wasn't leaving you there in the street. It was freezing, for one thing.'

'And what happened at the station?'

'It was like you were having a nightmare and we couldn't wake you up. I've never forgotten the look in your eyes. It was one of the most upsetting things I've seen.'

'Do you think I'd been spiked?'

'That was one assumption.'

'Did you find out what had been done to me?'

'Done to you? Not entirely.' There was something he was holding back.

'And then what?'

'Well, eventually you vanished.'

'What do you mean, vanished?'

Lockhart gazed across his office, at a wall of framed photographs of himself receiving things – handshakes, commendations, an MBE. His body was tense, twisted, as if contorted from within by whatever he couldn't bring himself to say.

'By around 5 a.m., you'd calmed down a bit. We got your phone charged up and managed to ascertain your name and home address, persuaded you to drink some tea and suggested you call a friend. Next thing I knew, you were gone. I was told you'd been de-arrested, no grounds for holding you further. But it was stranger than that. I checked the station's tapes. It looked like you spoke to someone on the phone and they told you to walk out and that was that. Baffled me. Next time I was in, I checked we were pursuing your case, but all the records had been wiped.'

'The CCTV's now gone as well.'

'How do you know?'

'I've been looking into it.'

This made Lockhart very uneasy. 'What do you mean?'

'What do you think happened to the station records?'

'My boss at the time said there'd been a technical issue.'

'A technical issue.'

'Something to do with a coding mistake. Because of the change of year. The system was meant to get rid of old data and it got rid of new data. That was as much as I understood.'

'And who exactly told you that?'

'The Station Inspector. I couldn't see it had affected anything else. And I knew there was something dodgy going on. Leave it, he said. I couldn't understand what he meant. I still had your home address – a flat in Stoke Newington, I think. Is that right?'

'Yes.'

'I did pop round and there were a couple of girls who said they hadn't seen you since the afternoon of December 31st. I tried, Rebecca.'

His desk phone started ringing. He rejected the call. It rang again. He pressed a button that muted it.

'Something's kicking off,' he muttered, eyes flicking to the blinds. She could tell he was keen to move on. 'I also wanted to know what happened,' Lockhart said. 'I have thought about you, considered contacting you. I saw ... I know who you are married to now. So I thought, better not to.'

'Where was I in that time, after I left the police station?'

Lockhart shrugged. 'I had a number for your parents, and I called that and they said they also couldn't find you. You'd gone missing. No one had heard from you since you walked out of the station. Eventually your Mum called me and said you'd turned up, but they had no idea what happened. You wouldn't talk, and I said I wasn't able to enlighten them. I tried to chase it.'

'Did I mention a house on Eaton Square?'

'No, I don't believe so. Not to me.'

'You've had fifteen years to think about this. What do you think happened to me?'

'I've had fifteen years not to think about it.'

'Something was covered up.'

'Yes, that was my reading.'

'Why?'

Lockhart shrugged.

'You never tried to find out?'

'Rebecca, I say this recognising that it sounds callous and complicit: it wasn't my job. Police is a hierarchy. You follow rules. If you don't grasp that, you don't survive.'

'You certainly survived. When did you leave Belgravia?

'There wasn't some kind of agreement, if that's what you mean.' He said it quickly, and she understood, for the first time, why he had agreed to speak to her: not just guilt but fear of potential exposure. How unnerving it must be to construct a career atop a complicity you don't understand.

'But you were promoted soon afterwards.'

'Relatively soon.'

'What did you think about that?'

Lockhart met her stare.

'I wondered who was protecting you.'

'Protecting *me*?'

'You really don't remember,' he said, more to himself. 'The blood, Rebecca. The blood on you . . . ' Then, carefully: 'The whole thing was complicated by what you told me.'

'What did I tell you?'

He sighed and glanced away, as if choosing his words. But there was little choice.

'You said you'd just killed someone.'

FOURTEEN

'Seen this?' Bell rolled over in bed and dropped her phone onto Kane's chest, squinting against the daylight.

She'd paused a video. He pressed play. It showed a fat man lying on a large bed, naked, masturbating. A woman in a black bra knelt on his legs. Something had been stuffed in his mouth. Bell took the phone back and clicked to another video of a man in a hot tub with two topless women, one laughing as she pushed her breasts into his face.

'That's our Chancellor of the Exchequer. The guy with the knickers in his mouth is Admiral Sir Robin Macclesfield, head of the United Kingdom's Armed Forces. There are another twenty videos just been released, all of big names.'

'Released by who?'

'A guy calling himself Eclipse. Heard of him?'

Kane closed his eyes again.

'We've crossed paths.'

'Really? A friend sent me a link to his Gab account.'

Gab.com. Of course. Beacon of free speech, haven of paedophiles and neo-Nazis. It was where you ended up when no other social media platform would have you.

Eclipse had first posted on Gab at 5.45 a.m.: *For decades those in power have hidden behind a veil of secrecy. Recent revelations of corruption have had minimal impact, so let's see how they look naked.*

At 6.30 a.m. he had elaborated: *I have come into possession of highly sensitive photographic and video recordings of 1,098 public figures, taken over four decades: 377 videos; 4,022 photographs. Over the next five days I will release them all.*

The precision was unnerving, and Kane suspected that was the point. Eclipse posted a teaser image: sixty thumbnails with the faces blurred out. He followed this with an initial list of two hundred names, including the Prime Minister, two of his cabinet, five members of the royal family, three members of the House of Lords, several foreign heads of state, religious leaders, media executives, TV presenters.

'Any pick-up from mainstream press?' Kane asked.

'Not yet.'

Kane tried to set up a Gab account, but their servers were overloaded. He got out of bed, splashed his face and made coffee. Then he turned on his laptop and ran a search for Eclipse content across the internet. The first Eclipse accounts had appeared overnight on several social media platforms: EclipseTruth, Eclipse Leaks, Total Eclipse. Kane scrolled through to find those who'd responded to his posts, searching for evidence of a coordinated bot operation by a government or military, but it looked organic.

Next, Kane checked the list of upcoming victims for any agents it might expose or operations it could compromise, but it wasn't that kind of material. Then he searched for himself: KaneXposed, ElliotShame.com, Elliotkaneserialkiller.is. They were all still blank, which was a weak relief.

He'd missed eighteen calls in the last hour, mostly press contacts, some colleagues in rival private intelligence companies, most recently Alistair Godfrey. Kane started with Godfrey.

'Seen it?' Godfrey said.

'I've seen what's on Gab, yes.'

'Eclipse.'

'It's definitely the same person.'

'HQ is locked down. Everyone's been called in. Is this the Research Group material you were talking about?'

'Quite possibly. Has anyone figured out how it might have leaked?'

'No. And there's been no word from any back channels about a state-level operation.'

'Is Broughton putting numbers on this now?'

'I hope so.'

'GCHQ.'

'I'm in contact.'

'Alistair, I visited Tim Cunningham last night. We got into Eclipse's Bitcoin account, emptied it, returned the money to his victims. I think that's what precipitated all this.'

Godfrey was silent for a moment, then exhaled loudly.

'Shit, Elliot.'

'We can get him.'

'I hope so.'

There was another long silence. Kane wondered what Godfrey was thinking. When the MI6 officer spoke again, he said: 'I'm on the list, Elliot. Eclipse's list. My name.'

'I see.'

'Do you know ... Is this ... ' He swallowed.

'It could be your vetting file.'

'Even so ... '

'Let's get him, Alistair. Resources. If I can get his coin you can drill down to an ID. He's an amateur. He's putting himself all over the place.'

Kane called Tim Cunningham at Psionic, but there was no answer. He returned the call of one of the journalists who'd tried to get in touch, Dipa Chand, the *FT*'s Defence and Security Correspondent.

'Elliot,' Chand said. 'I appreciate you getting back to me. There are suggestions that these videos originate with the Secret

Intelligence Service. I wondered if you were able to say anything with regards to that.'

'Who is saying it's from the intelligence service?'

'I can't disclose the source of that suggestion. Would you deny it?'

'I don't know anything about this. But I'd appreciate you sharing what you've heard.'

'I've heard that it's causing serious concern in Vauxhall Cross. Let me put it this way: can you confirm that there *may* have been files on all these named individuals held by the intelligence service?'

'The question is who Eclipse is and why they're doing this.'

'So they're real? The videos?'

'That's not what I said.'

'Would I get knocked back if I wrote it as an intelligence leak?'

It had been a mistake to think his usual press connections might be useful. He wasn't used to being the story.

'Sorry, Dipa, I'm not the person to talk to. I don't work for the intelligence service any more.'

By 9 a.m. there was a lot of speculation online regarding the identity of Eclipse. Guesses included an intelligence official gone rogue, a disenchanted civil servant, a professional hacker, a prankster who got lucky. The mainstream press were tentative. The first few headlines appeared, concerning 'a purported leak', with an emphasis on Gab as disreputable. Kane imagined the decisions being made: national papers had nervous lawyers and close relationships with government. They required multiple sources and fact-checking before running a story. Videos on far-right social media platforms weren't going to leap onto the front page, but it wouldn't be long.

Broughton called, furious.

'Is what I'm hearing right? You visited Psionic last night, stole three million pounds' worth of Bitcoin.'

'I didn't steal it, I returned it.'

'After I told you to keep away from this.'

'I was trying to establish who Eclipse is. Has there been any progress on that?'

'You moved unilaterally when I told you to step away. And you've delivered us a crisis.'

'We've learned something,' Kane said. 'They're not professional. There was carelessness around how they handled the Bitcoin. And this response – it's petulant. They're emotional, immature.'

'You've fucked up, Elliot.'

'I don't see it that way, sir.'

'Don't speak to anyone about this until I call again.'

Bell was in her study, on the phone. Kane heard fragments of conversation: 'I can ask him. We'll see. So far, it seems real. Yes . . . ' He went up to his own office and opened his laptop. A lot of the sites carrying Eclipse material were suddenly disappearing, leaving 404 messages. Kane sensed GCHQ hard at work, maybe government leaning on service providers. But it was whack-a-mole. The same content popped up elsewhere. The leaks were mirrored, available on multiple servers, different domain names, with an official Dark Web version.

Bell walked in, hanging up on her call.

'Eclipse is claiming this is intelligence services footage,' she said. 'Is that right?'

'Probably. Has Eclipse said how they acquired it?'

'No. But apparently they're a victim of MI6. I'm sensing a grudge, or maybe an activist kind of motivation.'

'A victim?'

'I don't know. That's what they've just said.'

Mason came in and stared at Kane's laptop, on which the Chancellor remained, entranced by cleavage. Kane closed it.

'Mason, go and have some breakfast,' Bell said.

'What is it? What's going on?'

'Go downstairs,' Kane said. 'I'll come down in a bit and we can plan what we're doing today, after your session. You want your usual pizza?'

The boy left without replying. Kane imagined similar scenarios playing out across the country.

'Is this connected to what's been going on with you?' Bell asked. 'This is what you've been worried about?'

'It's part of that. There's been a leak of some kind, maybe a cyberattack. It could be a psychological operation, to do with Ukraine.'

'Really?'

'All we know at the moment is that someone or something calling itself Eclipse has accessed files from the MI6 archives. They have a lot. It's not clear who they are, whether it's an individual, what their motivation is.'

'This was all being held by MI6?'

'A lot of it. I don't know about all.'

'What the fuck, Elliot.'

'Every intelligence service collects dirt. You know that. It's standard.'

'There's nothing standard about secretly filming other people having sex. What's the justification?'

'Security. The men in the videos are either people who are a potential security risk or targets we might want to recruit, affiliated with enemy states.'

'And how's the GDPR on that? You archive it indefinitely?'

'Obviously it needs storing. So there's an archive there. That seems to be what's being leaked. I'm not trying to justify it. I'm not interested in that right now.'

'I'm sure. How did it get leaked?'

'I don't know. I'd really like to.'

'Journalists have been approached by Eclipse directly.'

'Saying what?'

Bell brought up an email on her phone. It had been forwarded to her from Alex Colgan-Smith, Investigations Editor at *The Sunday Times*. Sent to him from Eclipse's Proton Mail account.

> All of the material I have been releasing was collected by MI6 against innocent people. This is just the start of what I can reveal about a project grown out of control. There are aspects of MI6 that even the government doesn't know about. I can give you the exclusive story of a lifetime, but I will need financial support.

The message ended with a Whispr number and a Bitcoin address.

'Apparently there's a few of these emails doing the rounds. Think it's him?' she asked.

'Sounds like him: money hungry, manipulative. It ticks the boxes. Eclipse likes being the one who knows the secrets. That's his power. I'm not sure I buy this whistle-blower act.'

'What do you mean?'

'Sounds fake. Like a whistle-blower from a film.'

'But it looks like they might have a point. It's not about tone of voice.'

'Sure. You can be a whistle-blower and a weapon of psychological warfare at the same time. This is not a clear-cut situation. Did Colgan-Smith follow up?'

'He requested more information, then the paper got a call from the Chief of MI6 saying the material was covered by the Official Secrets Act and presents a threat to national security. No one can move on it. The government's come down hard: no media's allowed to report Eclipse because of suspicion that the information is coming from a foreign power trying to undermine UK democracy.'

'I give the tabloids an hour.'

'There's a D-notice.'

Kane shook his head. 'Two hours.' A Defence Advisory Notice was the informal process by which the government told media outlets what was too sensitive to cover. Editors liked to go along with it, stay cosy with government press officers, but the press was a herd and things fell apart. 'You can't D-notice a phenomenon. This is already out there.'

And, as if to prove that they'd moved well beyond anything containable, news sites began changing their front pages:

Biggest release of classified data since Wikileaks.

UK authorities ask: Is No One Safe?

Government and Royal Family in Crisis
Talks over Leaked Videos.

Bell checked her messages and gave a grim laugh.

'Apparently, politicians are being urged not to resign as it would validate the cache.'

'Any more yet?'

'He's giving teasers. Next up is the head of the Metropolitan Police.'

Then someone on Twitter called it 'the shame archive' and within a quarter of an hour that was the title of the *Guardian*'s live feed.

At 11 a.m., with no sign of the situation abating, Kane called Sebastian Rosenquist. Rosenquist was close to both Washington and Beijing, where he did a lot of business. He had his own cyber resources.

'This is an interesting one,' Rosenquist said. 'The markets have started getting jittery. Going to do something?'

'Maybe. But I'd need backing.'

'Elliot, you know I'd always back you. I'm in town right now. Let's talk strategy.'

'Usual place?'

'That's right.'

Rosenquist stayed in a penthouse by Hyde Park when in London. They were both fond of Hyde Park's Italian Gardens, the cool marble and bright fountains. Rosenquist was standing in the café when Kane got there, stirring an espresso. He wore a black polo shirt, Ralph Lauren shades and a New York Yankees cap. His tan had a luxurious depth to it.

'Glad you could meet me,' Kane said.

Rosenquist downed his espresso and they set off around the fountains, a bodyguard at a discreet distance behind them.

'Spoken to the US yet?' Kane asked.

'I just spoke to someone in the Secretary of State's office,' Rosenquist said. 'No one seems to know anything. The Department of Justice is about to issue a subpoena directing social media firms to provide information for accounts associated with Eclipse. They're taking this seriously.'

'It won't help.'

'Something has to. It's having an impact on peace talks. There were two twin-track discussions on ending the Ukraine situation, one brokered by China, one by the UAE. Both have frozen. This is costing. No one's going to negotiate until the situation stabilises and we establish who is behind Eclipse and where it's going. Do you have any idea?'

'It's unclear.'

'Someone who doesn't want peace, is my guess. China would have the capability, but I don't see what they'd stand to gain. That leaves Russian hardliners, people who want the war to continue. Ones with their own hackers.' Rosenquist stopped. He removed his cap and smoothed his hair before replacing it. 'Am I in it? The archive?'

'Not that I'm aware of, Sebastian,' Kane lied. The billionaire nodded, rested his hands on a stone urn and gazed at the fountains.

'It's fucking hot.'

'The situation?'

'The weather. The UK doesn't feel like the UK any more.' He pushed himself away from the stone and they continued walking. 'So what will work? What's the legislation around shutting things down entirely? Would the government go there?'

'Shutting down the internet?' Kane said. 'There's the Civil Contingencies Act. It could be used to order internet service providers to close down operations if it was felt to be a question of national security.'

'But it makes us look like a dictatorship.'

'And it's not going to achieve much. The UK's got thousands of independent service providers, plus a lot of mobile operators and undersea cables. Trying to shut anything down is pointless.'

Rosenquist stopped again, leaned back against the railings.

'So what were these resources you wanted?'

'First of all, speak to Whitehall. You're going to be better received than me at the moment. Tell them to control the narrative, get a psyop going. It's the only front to fight on.

'Speak to your people – here, Washington – and make sure they reframe this as terrorism. People need to be seen manning COBRA. Any whiff of terrorism gives the government a lot of legal powers and it will keep the media and Parliament submissive. Push the line that this endangers intelligence officers and ongoing counter-terrorist operations. That will put a brake on the press for a bit. At the same time, attempt to discredit the whole cache by planting fake material. Suggest Eclipse is a weirdo, that they're out to hurt people. Throw some nasty porn in, scare people away. You want the public unnerved, distrustful, and the press and big tech companies onside.'

'I hear you.'

'But I've got a bigger favour to ask, Sebastian. I'm not bothered about British politicians getting caught with their pants down, but some of the material connects to the recruitment of agents. It can be used to blow them. Once it's known that MI6 has this material, people are going to assume it was used to turn those targeted, even if it wasn't. There's going to be a presumption of guilt. I've got contacts, friends, in Russia, Egypt, Iran, who are going to be seeing these leaks and wondering if their lives are over. I might need to get them out of their respective countries fast.'

'That can be arranged.'

'Private flights and paperwork. You have contacts in those countries. If I need to exfil.'

'Tell me what you need. I'll see what I can do.'

'Thank you.'

They turned back towards Piccadilly. Rosenquist glanced back at his guard then up at the sun.

'What interesting times we live in,' he said.

By the time Kane got home, an Eclipse industry had sprung up.

'We've got our first fan sites,' Bell said. 'Look.'

The Eclipse Files, registered in the Philippines, cataloguing the footage released so far. *Eclipse Tapes* in Russia, which linked to the first YouTube channel collating the various leaks in heavily censored form. Both invited donations to PayPal and Google Wallet. They disappeared half an hour later, only to reappear under slightly different names.

At 1 p.m. Kane received a direct message from Eclipse:

Hey Elliot. I've got a new cache ready: 25 MI6 assets in Moscow, and how they were recruited by the British Secret Intelligence using kompromat. What do you think? How many do you want dead? Get on TV and apologise to me and to the nation for what you've done – for every death you're responsible for.

True to form, Eclipse included specific names: Mariya Shubenkov, Marta Bach, Pavel Kolyada, Mikhail Krotov. Kane knew most of them: Halcyon successes, more familiar by the cryptonyms under which their intelligence product was circulated. He messaged Godfrey: 'Eclipse is directly threatening assets in Moscow. I'm in contact with him. Get me into the war room.'

No answer. At 2 p.m. Eclipse published a video of two male MPs having sex in a Manchester hotel room, and one of a former technical adviser for the International Monetary Fund in a leather body harness. The former Crown Prince of Saudi Arabia was pictured beating one of his wives, and the Iranian deputy foreign minister appeared masturbating at his desk, with a portrait of the Ayatollah behind him.

A lot of the videos contained cross-dressing, with the most impressive being a nuclear scientist from Pakistan who appeared in full evening wear with gloves and pearls. Many showed inappropriate and adulterous drunken advances. Then there were the more niche penchants: one American politician obsessed with masturbating to the image of themselves in the mirror, a Russian dignitary who sought out amputees, two British military officials and a newspaper editor all depicted watching someone else have sex with their wife. Finally, attracting a lot of online attention was a senior civil servant tied to a table, receiving electric shocks from a smartly dressed woman with a cattle prod.

Kane had been aware of many of these people as targets, and knew the rationale behind filming them. Many had compromised themselves with shady deals and inappropriate acquaintances long before they'd been filmed. None of that seemed relevant now. The videos were leverage, never meant to be released publicly, but what kind of excuse was that? He had known, deep down, that every one was an unexploded bomb beneath a life. That was the power. Official secrecy had made them godlike. A god without secrecy was just a very powerful voyeur.

Eclipse knew that. The tone of public response changed again when he threatened to release footage of innocent men and women watching pornography, all supposedly amassed by the Secret Intelligence Service. Alongside this, he claimed to have membership databases of married dating sites and gay hookup apps. He included 500,000 names. Civilians.

Anyone could compile a list of names, Kane reasoned. But it was just about possible he had this: there had been occasions when MI6 used a keyword dragnet. They had the capability to hoover up all visits to certain websites, membership of certain online services, metadata. You'd need additional clearance to then search in all that for a particular person's behaviour. But that didn't mean it wasn't there.

How big could this flood be? That was what people were asking now. This was the question Kane had wondered himself. Unlike most, he had seen the paper archives and navigated the digital ones to some extent. But a digital labyrinth is hard to measure. The paper ones gave some sense of scale; Kane remembered the basement rooms of Vauxhall Cross, soon after they'd moved to the new headquarters, with the boxes and files from the previous MI6 offices on Gower Street stacked up, from a paper world, a cold war, a service making it up as it went along. Down in the bowels of the building, under a feverish, clockless light, the men and women toiling to scan it into a new, digital immortality. The storage rooms adjoined Broughton's psyops department. Kane had to go down there one day, to retrieve a file, and saw a team of Broughton's minions working away, scanners flashing. Kane glimpsed handwriting on the screens and saw it was old love letters. In one side room were black-and-white Edwardian photographs, cine reels, then VHS; technology biting ever deeper into our flesh. All these records had been carried with them from premises to premises. Never exposed to daylight until now.

'We've got our first woman,' Bell said, clicking through to images of Felicity Cribb of the International Atomic Agency, performing oral sex on a man who still wore his white shirt and suit jacket. It was Christian.

Kane tried to call him. Eventually, Christian answered. One of his kids was crying in the background and Amelia was trying to get her husband's attention. He said, 'Give me a second,' and took the phone outside.

'I'm in a few of them,' he said.

'Has Amelia seen?'

'Not yet. Broughton says you're responsible.'

'I'm not the one putting them out there. I would have thought Broughton bore more responsibility. It's his collection.'

'Who the fuck is Eclipse?'

'I don't know, but he connects to Anton Zakharyan's killing. Anton had written the word Eclipse next to a Bitcoin address. I think this Eclipse character was threatening him. I think he released information about Anton to the men who killed him.'

'And what does that imply, exactly?'

'Possibly that we're going to have issues with assets around the globe. I'm trying to do what I can to monitor that situation, get people out if necessary.'

'Did you have any idea there were that many videos?'

'Broughton threw the net wide. We played our part in that.'

'You know the government wants to deflect this shitshow onto us. They're going to nail this as MI6 overreach, launch an enquiry, call us in one by one. Was it all cleared?'

'This is several decades' worth of material from hundreds of different operations. I don't know what exactly was cleared.'

'Someone's going to be the scapegoat.'

Bell knocked on the study door.

'We need to get Mason to his session,' she said. 'Can you still do it? Want me to go?'

'I can do it,' Kane said. Then, to Christian: 'I've got to run. Let's speak again later.'

The therapist's was in a clinic behind the Holloway Road. Kane dropped Mason off and went to his usual café to wait. He checked his phone. The Eclipse story was leading BBC, CNN, Fox, Al Jazeera. The governments of China, Russia and the Gulf States had blocked access to all Eclipse-related sites. Updates appeared stating: *MI6 Deputy General due to speak at a live press conference.*

It was Gillian Rossi. Kane could see why they'd chosen her: she looked human. She stood in front of a Union Jack and the Secret Intelligence Service logo.

'The UK has been hit by an extraordinarily sophisticated cyber-espionage campaign,' she said. 'All evidence points towards a nation state, and, more specifically, to the direct orders of the Kremlin. This is undoubtedly connected to the situation in Ukraine, and to a state that seeks to bully and intimidate those who stand up to it. Make no mistake, the goal is to undermine Britain, to sow chaos. As such, I want to stress that anyone disseminating these images is doing Putin's work for him. Russia uses misinformation as a tool of war, and I implore the public not to take what they see online at face value, and not to share these destructive and abusive images.'

On the ticker at the bottom of the screen, it said: *PM calls defence staff to COBRA Joint Terrorism Analysis Centre.*

Tim Cunningham called as Kane was walking up the stairs to the therapist's office. Kane stopped on the stairwell and answered.

'Is this connected to last night?' Cunningham asked.

'I believe so. What have you heard?'

'It's total pandemonium in the services. Digital 9/11. We're getting asked if we can help in any way.'

'Can you?'

'I can recommend some good divorce lawyers. I don't know what else they expect us to do.'

'You saw everything I had on Eclipse. Are you buying this Russia line?'

'Not 100 per cent. But who's to say? We've been asked to provide a report on Moscow's cyber capabilities in the next two hours. The MOD want addresses.'

'What kind of addresses?'

'Physical addresses: Russia's cyber HQs, target coordinates of related facilities. Elliot, they want to go to war.'

Mason was always subdued after his sessions. Their ritual was Pappagone on Stroud Green Road to debrief over pizza.

'What did you talk about today?' Kane asked.

'Talking.'

'You talked about talking?'

The boy grinned. 'How to do it more.'

'That's an art.'

'What do you mean?'

'I mean, there's talking and then there's just making noise. You know? To talk you've got to have something to say.'

'We talked about you.'

'Really? What about me?'

'How you never get angry.'

Kane laughed. 'I get angry all the time.' As so often, Kane struggled to see himself through the boy's eyes, or even through Bell's eyes. Who was he to them? A stranger who'd appeared one day and enabled a lucrative business idea and then moved the remains of his PhD into a box room. Who had some curious games and anecdotes but never the plenitude of full disclosure.

'You never seem it,' Mason said.

'That's good. Seeming angry isn't very nice. What else do you tell them about me?'

'Nothing.'

'Sure?'

The boy smiled again. Then he stopped. 'Do you think I'm scared?' he asked.

'No. Why?'

'They said I might be scared.'

'I think you're very brave. Doing this, going to these sessions and talking, that's not easy.'

'No.'

'Listen, Mason, want to know a secret?' Kane leaned forward, lowered his voice. 'Everyone's scared.'

The boy studied Kane to see how serious he was being.

'It's true,' Kane said. 'Finish your pizza.'

He resisted the temptation to check his phone while they ate. He needed this time away from the world's meltdown, just enjoying the meal with Mason. Almost like none of it was happening. A war that only existed online, that you could put away in your pocket. For now.

When they got back, Bell was standing in front of the TV, pen and notebook in hand. An MP was saying: 'Britain must retaliate, and not just with sanctions.' Kane knew the politician, previously on MI6's books, now useful inside Parliament.

'How was it, Mason?' Bell said.

'Okay.' Mason kicked off his shoes and went up to his room.

'How was it?' Bell asked Kane, still staring at the screen.

'Good. They're encouraging him to talk more.'

'Not to me, it seems. Government's sounding increasingly certain it's Russia.'

'I saw.'

172

'I'm wondering if Eclipse is even the story here.'

'What do you mean?'

'Whoever's leaking this, they're exposing an extraordinary abuse of surveillance powers.'

'That's true.'

'You agree?'

'Of course.'

Kane checked Russian news for any Eclipse fallout, then word from Iran and China. He couldn't see arrests yet, but he had encrypted emails coming in from friends and contacts in those countries, people asking: *What is this leak? Are we in danger?*

Godfrey confirmed: 'We've lost contact with dozens of Chinese sources. They've all shut down, including WESTWIND, an official high up in the CCP. We're having to cauterise the network.'

Kane compiled a request list for Rosenquist, including private flights out of Moscow, Tehran and Beijing. And he knew it was a gesture, a palliative for his conscience more than anything. When he'd done what he could, Kane went into the garden and tried to steady his mind. He watched planes crossing the sky. Mason came out and stood beside him.

'Hunting?' the boy asked.

'Hiding.'

'From what?'

'I needed some space to think.'

'Want me to go?'

'No, you can stay. Guard the place.'

Mason set about fixing the bivouac. Kane watched him, thinking through the possible upcoming scenarios. Ten years ago, the powers that be wrote up NATO military doctrine for cyberwarfare. Cyberspace was recognised as a war-fighting domain. States had the right to act in self-defence in response to a cyber operation meeting the threshold of an armed attack. All this was very new territory. Kane remembered reading the strategy document when it first circulated and wondering if he was out of touch with reality, or if the concept had evaporated altogether.

Cyber meant fighting invisible enemies on a battlefield without location. The certainty of attribution you needed to start a war wasn't going to come in cyberspace. And if you decided to risk it anyway, what did that involve? People sat in Cheltenham and Corsham and Dorset, the Joint Cyber Units, government's own keyboard warriors, tapping away. NATO Cyber Defence beside Lake Ülemiste in Tallinn, its Cyberspace Operations Centre in Mons, overlooking the scars of World War I trenches, every military exercise now involved them, but for all the war games conducted, full-blown cyberwar was a mystery. Retaliate with your own psyop? Leaking dirt on Kremlin figures? Putin's fifteen-year-old sex slaves? Kane could imagine Broughton trying, but what would that achieve? Which left retaliation through conventional means: a strike against somewhere related to the perpetrators of the cyberattack. Which meant World War III.

Strange pathway to apocalypse. Perfect, maybe. Humanity's blush veiled by a mushroom cloud. The growl of powerful cars stopping outside their home pulled Kane from his thoughts. One car door slammed, then another, then a third. Mason looked towards Kane. Kane nodded. The boy scaled the garden wall to peer over.

'There's two,' he said. 'One Range Rover, one Mercedes S-Class. Six men, I think.'

'The cars are black.'

'Yes.'

Government vehicles. Mason dropped down to the grass. 'Some of the men have gone to the back door.'

'Okay. Good work.'

'Why have they gone to the back as well?'

'To stop me running away.'

'Why would you run away?'

'Exactly. They obviously don't know me.'

Kane was heading inside as Bell entered the garden.

'We've got visitors. They don't look very friendly.'

'I might have to make friends with them anyway.'

'Why you?' Bell said.

'I touched on it. They probably want information.'

'You were involved in collecting this stuff?'

Kane's phone rang as he grabbed his best suit jacket. It was Broughton.

'They're here,' Kane said, answering.

'We need to speak first. I want you to report to VX now.'

'Too late.'

'They are not cleared for information about the Psychological Research Group, and certainly not about Halcyon.'

'I'll be sure to explain that. But I think someone needs to steer them. Do you know what I mean? Before they stumble into all sorts.'

'We don't know that this is all ours.'

'That's your line?'

'Everything with the slightest element of political or legal risk was signed off by the Foreign Secretary.'

Kane knew that was a lie.

'Right.'

'I'm trying to protect you, but I don't know how sustainable that is.'

'Protect me?'

'It's your name on a lot of the paperwork.'

Kane hung up. Broughton messaged as he was putting on his shoes: *F-Sec authorised all Research Group activity. There was no need to clear individual ops. These remain classified.* He attached a link to a lawyer.

FIFTEEN

'I said I killed someone?' Rebecca met the Commander's eyes. She searched for a reflection within them of who she was.

'Yes. You said it multiple times. In fact it was almost all you would say.'

'Did I say who?'

'No.'

'Did you believe me?'

Lockhart considered this.

'I didn't know what to think, in all honesty.'

'Did you investigate at all?'

'I couldn't, as I've explained. You walked out. Next thing I knew it was cleared from the system. I'm sorry I can't help more, Rebecca. I've told you what I know.'

'I don't understand.'

'I never did either.' There was a knock at Lockhart's door. 'This situation you're in now – I'm sorry to hear about it. Obviously, if you think I can help, please let me know. But ... Hang on.' He got up, opened the door and began remonstrating with whoever was on the other side. Rebecca couldn't hear the exact nature of their response, but it silenced him. When Lockhart came back, he looked graver still.

'There's a bit of a crisis,' Lockhart said. 'I have to go. What are you planning to do?' he asked. He looked at her unsentimentally, the Commander's mask back on. He wanted to know what threat he faced.

'I don't know.'

'Will you tell me if you discover anything?' he said. 'I'd like it if this was pursued in a controlled fashion.'

Rebecca descended back down the Empress State Building alone. A controlled fashion, she thought. She was vaguely aware of the receptionist watching her as she crossed the lobby.

You said you killed someone.

'Excuse me,' the receptionist said. Rebecca flinched, as if handcuffs were about to be slipped on.

'Yes?'

'You need to sign out.'

She signed out, marvelling at her two signatures side by side. Less than thirty minutes had passed between them and yet they referred to different people. Outside, the sunshine tickled her skin, as if curious to discover how someone containing nothing but questions could walk.

Why did she say she'd killed someone?

Rebecca didn't know where she was going. There was an area in front of her like a park, a break in the residential buildings. As she got closer she saw it was Brompton Cemetery.

Entering made some kind of sense. It looked big enough to stay in for ever, hidden within the leafy suburbs of the Victorian dead. She went in, through elaborate entrance gates, past colonnades and mausoleums. A city of the dead, from a time when death had been fashionable. Its main avenue converged on the dome of a chapel. She sat halfway along it and felt deep, gnawing envy for those rotting beneath her feet. Life seemed to be a state of horror. The horror of looking into a mirror and not recognising your own face.

Her memories of New Year's Eve were layered.

On the exterior: brightness; arriving at the house, the sense of excitement in the air. The biggest party yet, a pyramid of champagne flutes, a lot of adrenalin. She was wearing a low-cut, high-slit silver cocktail dress, which she had bought the previous week in the Christmas sales, a promise to herself that the end of escort work was not going to be the end of glamour. She had saved up by then. She remembered exactly how much she had in her account – sixty-three thousand pounds – her get-out money. So she, too, was filled with the bonhomie of endings, departures, new things approaching.

Next layer: Russians harassing her. She remembered that. And drinking more heavily than usual, accepting fat lines of cocaine. Usually, it was important to her to keep a straight head. But there was never going to be anything straight about those parties. And coke was everywhere, deep drifts of the stuff, bridging fantasy and reality.

She remembered midnight, balloon pops, a burlesque dancer in a jewelled headdress appearing in a cloud of dry ice, then everyone crowding to the terrace to see fireworks, feeling hands on her, annoyed, needing another bump to get through. The midnight fireworks were the last thing fixed in a timeline; other fragments orbited this moment.

Dancing on a glass surface, high up above people, a table or breakfast bar. One of the Vietnamese sisters, Mai, up there with her, the taste of her mouth, conscious of the eyes on them, the pulsing of the music, the adeptness of their performance. Looking down at her five-inch heels on the glass and thinking she should be scared but knowing she wasn't going to fall.

She didn't remember ever getting down.

At some point her face was forced into a carpet. She was alone in the room with her attacker – this was something she became suddenly conscious of. They were in what the girls called the black room, which was soundproofed. Where, in her memory, was his face? Why could she smell his aftershave, feel his fingers in her hair, but not see him?

She remembered, later, a white-walled room, staring at a fluorescent strip. So she must have been lying on her back. That enhanced the sense that this was somewhere medical. And there were moments when she was in cars, one conspicuously high-end, with leather seats cold against her bare thighs. This car, she had to assume, connected to the last torn patches of memory, ones that began to reattach themselves to her life afterwards. A basement flat somewhere, one that didn't feel properly occupied. A chalky smell of plaster. It was freezing at first, her breath visible. At some point a portable heater was produced. She remembered its glowing bars, which reminded her of her parents' home, and the new smell of burning dust. This place was made more sinister by the various attempts at comfort: tea and biscuits, a bath that she declined. There had been a woman briefly present, attempting some kind of sisterly support, with several sets of new clothes in a Debenhams shopping bag. At some point, Rebecca's own clothes had vanished. When she went to the loo, she saw someone guarding the front door, reading a newspaper.

This was where the man in a charcoal-grey suit and glasses suggested that it was best to forget anything had ever happened. It must have been convincing – she had almost managed.

Could you wipe your own memories? You could certainly pack them away. But out of the black hole of that night, the vortex, arose one certainty: someone had assaulted her. Her body had borne the memory of that long enough.

But it wasn't the only horror that occurred that night.

Two fragments of recollection hung suspended in the darkness, without a bridge between them. There was the voice above her: *Play nice. Don't be stupid.* That was what they were saying. *Or you're going to die. Do you understand?* The hand in her hair, forcing her to nod. Then, like an adjunct dream, the feeling of blood trickling down her arm, and her face in a mirror above a black marble sink, Elliot beside her.

179

It's okay.

Because she'd killed someone?

Sometimes in dreams she saw a man dying. Always the same man, gargling blood on a floor before her, as if her sleeping mind had access to memories she didn't. Did she really remember the sight?

Elliot was definitely involved. This had begun returning to her with greater certainty. The man named Elliot, with the enigmatic smile and inquisitive eyes, who understood her love of literature, washing her hands, his own face streaked with blood.

Somehow, at some point, she was outside again. It was still dark, but the streets were crowded, people having paid their respects to midnight. Their eyes widened, seeing her. *I'm okay,* she was saying. *Thank you.* Walking on. Then the brightness of the police station hurting her eyes.

What had Lockhart said? *I wondered who was protecting you.* Had she killed, and then someone made it all go away? Rebecca pictured an uninvited angel, one that had taken ownership of her soul and now crouched there; a pact she couldn't remember but which placed her life in debt.

She'd missed another message from Eclipse. *First videos up on Pornhub.*

Rebecca watched them, numbly. Two ten-minute clips, with different men but from a similar time period. The Eaton Square era, 2007–8. So she was online now. They each had over twenty views already.

She looked young. That was her first thought. She looked good. But moving from still images to videos was a whole new level of degrading exposure. One thing she had always prided herself on was seeming to authentically respond to punters – physically, volubly. That was what got her the return custom. She knew the men who wanted power over her through pain and those who wanted power through pleasure, and she could deliver the illusion of both. Private performances suddenly visible to the entire world.

A funeral began. Rebecca saw, with a start, the thin procession a few hundred metres away, the coffin slung between pall-bearers, who seemed to be struggling, as if dragging a sack of rubble, a handful of mourners sweating behind them in their unseasonable clothes. She watched, transfixed, glad for some distraction, something indubitable, as the priest said their piece and shovels were distributed. The coffin was lowered into the earth and what she saw disappearing for ever were secrets.

Once the last mourner had departed, Rebecca left the cemetery. She walked through West Brompton into Earls Court, mask on, head down. Eventually she found herself back on familiar territory: Kensington High Street. Which meant she was close to Kensington Central Library.

Kensington had a robust, red-brick central library – muscular and municipal – looking more like a courthouse than a place of learning, but with its own reference room and keen, attentive librarians as old as some of the furniture.

'I'm looking for news from 2008,' Rebecca said.

'Yes?' The librarian was in her sixties, with a slash of magenta lipstick that gave an aggressive glamour to her kindly smile. 'Anything in particular?'

'Particularly the very start of the year – January first or second. London news.'

'What exactly do you want?'

'I want to know if anyone was killed on New Year's Eve.'

This provoked a slight twitch, but the woman's smile didn't fade. 'Interesting.' The librarian led her to a PC. Rebecca had expected a dusty drawer, or even microfiche, but the librarian cheerfully informed her that they subscribed to a digital archive now, and set her up at a computer with access to newspaper articles going back fifty years, local and national, all searchable.

Nothing Rebecca could see in the nationals for the opening days of 2009. She tried the *London Evening Standard*. The headline on 2 January caught her eye:

Body of man 'in his 40s' found in
Thames, near Westminster Pier

Westminster Pier was only a few minutes from Victoria. Rebecca read the whole article.

The Metropolitan Police's Marine Policing Unit were called to Victoria Embankment this afternoon following reports of a body in the water. The remains of a man, believed to be in his 40s, were recovered. Police say the victim remains unidentified, and the death is being treated as suspicious while enquiries continue.

Detective Inspector Steve Markham, of the Homicide and Major Crime Squad, has appealed to members of the public for assistance, releasing pictures of the victim's clothing and possessions in the hope that they jog someone's memory. It is believed that the man may have been a Russian national, and police are appealing directly to any members of that community in London for information.

Rebecca stared at the photo of a blue suit, a label that said Canali Boutique, a Tag Heuer watch. Was he the one? Certainly there had been Russians at the New Year's party – there always were at Eaton Square. And, according to De Souza, they were Opula's main clients. She certainly hadn't thrown anyone in the Thames. But then who had been 'protecting' her? Had they done this?

There was no follow-up story that she could find, not in the *Standard* or any other paper. That in itself seemed odd, as if the corpse had simply sunk back into the water and everyone walked on.

Her phone rang. It was Michael De Souza. She turned it off without answering, suddenly panicked. What story had she led him into? Because there seemed only one revelation of significance now: she was a murderer. And, as such, she was utterly alone. Alone in a blank and icy wilderness, these fragments of memory her sole possession, and they condemned her. She was closing the browser when she noticed a pop-up news alert from the present day – something about leaked sex videos. Her heart gave an anxious punch, but it wasn't about her. Rebecca took a breath, then she saw the full headline:

Eclipse leaks an 'Unprecedented threat' – PM

SIXTEEN

Kane stared out of the window as he was transported through London, at the people glued to their phones, peering into others' hearts, at the world turned inside out. Stared at the military statues casting deep shadow, the blank-faced, bone-white buildings as they entered the government zone. Reporters and protestors had gathered along Whitehall in equal numbers.

He needed leads on Eclipse. He didn't trust anyone else to manage this effectively, not government, not the intelligence service. But he needed some sense of what theories were being pursued behind the scenes. And, as uncomfortable as it was to admit, he wanted to control where they looked.

The armed police on duty admitted their convoy through the black steel gates of Downing Street. They continued past Number 10 to the parking lot beside Horse Guards Road. Kane was led from the car, through the high-security entry system at the Cabinet Office entrance, down to the corridors of panic.

It wasn't COBRA that they headed to but a much smaller conference room, deeper within the shadowy depths of Downing Street, a clandestine chamber with its own security guard and curtains over the windows.

Four people waited for Kane at a mahogany table that almost filled the oval-shaped room: three men, one woman. Kane recognised the Foreign Secretary – tall, slightly manic-eyed – and the smaller, neater figure of Natalie Petherton, the UK's National

Security Adviser. Petherton introduced a silver-haired man in horn-rimmed glasses to her left as Henry Sarratt, the government's chief legal adviser. Finally, there was Sir Roland Mackenzie, former Chief of MI6, now Chairman of the Joint Intelligence Committee, the nexus of MI6 and government. A huge man in a pale suit, pink-faced, he had been Chief for the first ten years of Kane's intelligence career. Kane remembered his welcome talk to the new recruits: the nobility of their mission, its unique personal challenges. Now he studied Kane's face for some omen. Did he remember Kane as a wide-eyed new arrival? Or as one of Broughton's boys? Rumours had always been that Broughton held dirt on Mackenzie, and leveraged it in his jockeying for power.

It occurred to Kane, as he took one of the high-backed leather chairs, that this must be the meeting room for the Joint Intelligence Committee itself. He had thought about this room a lot, while sitting in various less comfortable locations around the globe, imagining his reports being pre-digested for government. No one else from MI6 appeared to be present. They'd got Kane here on his own. They were going to ask him to turn against his superiors.

Petherton handled the preamble, thanking Kane for coming in, asking him to excuse the inevitable haste. The legal adviser, Sarratt, peered at Kane above the rims of his glasses, donnish, judgemental. Kane was asked to clarify the exact dates he worked for the Secret Intelligence Service.

'And for a period, around 2007–2008, you worked in Psychological Operations under John Broughton,' Petherton said, glancing at some papers in front of her.

'That's correct.'

'As much of the leaked material appears to connect to that department, I wondered if you had a sense of how much could be out there?'

'Potentially? Thousands of files. Tens of thousands.'

'I'm told you were one of the first to be aware of this,' Petherton said.

'Yes. You'll have been briefed on the death of a man known as Anthony Zachariah on Sunday night. I believe he was compromised by leaked material. That put me on the trail of Eclipse.'

'And do you have any suggestion as to who Eclipse might be?'

'I don't have an ID. Zachariah was connected with an MI6 operation against the Kremlin,' Kane said. 'Obviously, if Eclipse *is* connected to Russia, they will just say it's criminal gangs independent of the government. From what I've seen today, there's no material recorded after 2020, so they're not in the system now. They've accessed the system previously, downloaded a cache, sat on it.'

This got some interest.

'Any reason they stopped then?' the Foreign Secretary asked.

'I've been told there was a security upgrade to the MI6 system a couple of years ago,' Kane said. 'That's the only reason I can think of. It made it harder.'

'What else have you been able to ascertain?' Petherton asked.

'Eclipse varies their writing styles, but it's a lone individual. I get the feeling they introduce elements to mask their identity: spelling mistakes, sometimes abbreviations, slang from several different countries. Where they use Russian it matches what you'd get out of basic translation software. But they've got an education. The way they've staged this Eclipse phenomenon shows awareness of previous leaks and media coverage. They have familiarity with a wide range of platforms and forums and will have been on at least some of them before under other names, maybe posting on related topics. That's where I'd start looking. They like mischief but, ultimately, I think they want money. We know they're willing to use blackmail to get it, as well as trading state secrets to the highest bidder.'

Petherton was typing this up as he spoke. Sarratt, the legal adviser, slowly uncrossed his legs and leaned across the table towards Kane.

'We're having difficulty establishing the extent of this archive, or how it's organised and indexed. You have authority from me; this meeting is classified as Top Secret. So please share what you know.'

'It's extensive,' Kane said. 'There's material going back to the early twentieth century. I couldn't put a figure on it, but several thousand videos and images were collected each year. Many of those won't ever have been viewed. It's like storing communications data.'

'This is not communications data,' Sarratt said.

'No.'

'Indexed how?' Mackenzie asked.

'As Research Group.'

'What's included?' Petherton asked.

'Video files, photographs, text documents, search histories, bank transactions. Everything, from a target's use of online pornography to visits to prostitutes, infidelities. Anything that made them a security risk.'

'Material on Britain's allies?' the Foreign Secretary asked.

'Yes,' Kane said.

The assembled elite fell silent.

'But what operations are these from?' The Foreign Secretary pressed, after a moment. 'They're not conventionally authorised. I'm told we're finding no paper trail. No one appears to have had oversight. There's no funding sign-off.'

'A lot may have been precautionary. Therefore they wouldn't be linked to a specific operation.'

'We're seeing British politicians caught up in all this,' the Foreign Secretary said. 'That's what I don't understand.'

Kane wondered how much he was going to have to educate

them. Power was dumb, he knew that. It had people know things for it. They weren't here right now.

'An independent judicial body in 2008 established that MPs and other parliamentarians were not necessarily protected,' Kane said.

'There have been operational conventions—' Mackenzie began.

'But not with the force of law.'

'For Christ's sake,' Sarratt muttered. Mackenzie traced a finger across his perspiring brow.

'From my limited understanding, you were one of those involved in acquiring these,' he said.

'I don't have the authority to confirm that.'

'Just to be clear, this is the beginning, not the end, of an attempt to understand what went on here,' Petherton said. 'That process will involve a police investigation. We're here as a line of defence for you.'

They all stared at Kane. But they asked no further questions, so Kane didn't offer further answers.

'Who ran this?' Sarratt said, eventually.

'You don't need me to tell you the chain of command.'

'Under Research Group, you say,' Mackenzie encouraged him. 'PsyOps.'

'Again, details of internal structure and clearance is something you'd have to take up with those currently working for the Secret Intelligence Service.'

'Who chose targets?' Sarratt asked.

'There was ongoing analysis and assessment.'

'And who cleared it?'

'Ultimately, the Foreign Office.'

'You saw that sign-off?'

'It was generally understood.'

More exhalations. Petherton's phone lit up. She showed a

message to the Foreign Secretary and this appeared to signal the end of Kane's questioning.

'We need to brief the PM,' Petherton said, gathering her notes and rising. 'Stay here. You'll be speaking to the police in due course. A dedicated team has been established to look into SIS activity in the relevant period, with a focus on Psychological Research. We're going to need you to list everyone who was targeted. As I'm sure you're aware, in addition to the police's own enquiries, the Investigatory Powers Tribunal gives a right of redress for people who think they've been a victim of unlawful covert investigative techniques. MI6, and any former employees of MI6, are under a duty to provide the Tribunal with all documents and information required. Nothing can be held back for reasons of secrecy or national security.'

'Unless the government says it compromises the functions of the intelligence services,' Kane said.

'We can't cover for you for ever.'

Then they were gone. What documents could the Tribunal demand? The guiding principles of Psychological Research weren't written down, although Kane remembered delivering the lecture to new recruits. *Principle A: everyone has their pressure points; everyone has secrets that their identity is built to hide. Principle B: people transgress by steps, within environments in which new patterns of behaviour are normalised. You see it in war, in business, in every subculture.*

Sex is the tripwire, gateway to the underworld of shame upon which floats the thin crust of daily life.

Dimming the lights. Eaton Square. Their palace on the floodplain of royalty.

One of the Foreign Office's shiny young Special Advisers appeared, chubby, in an expensive suit. He placed a pen on the desk, beside a pad of paper.

'Mr Kane,' he began. 'Right now there's a crisis of governance.'

'I'm sure.'

'It may be better to write who you think *isn't* in the archive.' He wasn't joking. 'We need to know who's safe, who can lead.'

'I'll write whatever you want.'

Kane could hear a TV in the next room: *The urgent questions: how wide was this surveillance programme? Do innocent citizens have anything to fear? How many of us have been filmed and on whose authority?*

The spad said: 'There's going to be a meeting with the Attorney General in the next couple of hours, and we can clear up some of these legal issues once and for all. Hopefully some-one can sort this Eclipse out before then.' And when Kane didn't reply, he added: 'I'm told you're good.'

'Good?'

'You've done ops.'

'Right.'

'Save everyone a lot of trouble if you got the bastard.' The spad smiled and his teeth showed. His eyes, behind the glasses, were bright with madness, or ambition, or both, Kane couldn't tell. The adviser went to watch the TV in the room next door. Kane got up and walked out.

He found stairs, took a wrong turn into a briefing room and backed away, eventually finding a door to Downing Street. It was a lot easier getting out than in. Kane walked purposefully towards Whitehall, buttoning his jacket. Armed police held the gate for him, and in seconds he'd melted into the crowd.

Bell was in the shower when Kane got home. He went to her study. She'd printed out screenshots of a lot of the Eclipse videos, annotated with the target's name and date. Her old reporter's notebook sat beside them.

Get the bastard.

There was only one approach to get Eclipse that he could think of, and it was becoming tantalising.

The shower stopped.

'Elliot?'

'It's me.'

'You're still a free man?'

'So to speak.'

'I'll be out in a second.'

Kane went online. The first disappearances had been reported in Russia. The government official with a fetish for amputees had briefly become an object of public fascination, then disappeared from view, and was now believed to be under house arrest. A former Chief of the General Staff in the Russian military who came up in the Eclipse archive dressed in a wig and miniskirt had been abducted, then found stabbed on the edge of Moscow.

Rosenquist had private security contractors on standby in Iran and Egypt, waiting for Kane to connect them to those in need. Kane had reached out, but it was hard to tell who was in exactly what situation. On Gab, Eclipse was trailing an upcoming release focused on members of the UK judiciary. Kane wondered at what point systems broke down.

He began preparing for the event of a formal arrest warrant being put on him, transferred essential phone numbers to paper, packed a go-bag with several grand in cash, some first aid and a change of clothes. Took a new burner phone from the safe, ensured there was enough in their Channel Islands account for plane tickets and lawyers' fees. He opened a new file on his laptop and typed instructions for Bell regarding emergency communication procedures, then a short message for Mason.

Bell came in, dressing-gowned, drying her hair, and he closed the file.

'Are you okay?'

'For now,' Kane said. She came over and ran a hand through his hair. He tried to smile.

'PM's been leaked,' Bell said. 'Seen it?'

'Not yet.'

'Want to know what he's doing?'

'Fucking someone?'

Her smile faltered. She studied Kane closer. 'What did the government say?' she asked.

'They're scared.' Kane nodded at the notebook. 'Good to see you back.'

'Is it? I can't just watch this happening from afar. I've got people calling me. This is the story I've been waiting for,' Bell said. 'Going to tell me to stop?'

'No. Where's Mason?'

'At his Dad's. Want to tell me how you connect to it all? Before I continue researching?'

'I set some of it up. But with a specific focus on penetrating Russian activity in London. This wasn't arbitrary voyeurism.'

'What's the government saying about Eclipse?'

'No one knows anything. I want to find him.'

'Think you can?'

'I think we can.'

'Oh.'

'The way to trap someone is to offer them what they want,' Kane said.

'What do they want?'

'You.'

'Me?'

'Someone who'll take them seriously.' Bell narrowed her eyes, as if to better see Kane's game. 'As you say, this is what you were waiting for. If there's one journalist who'd be willing to dig into all this, it's you.'

Bell pulled up a chair and sat down.

'If I was working on this, you know the first thing I'd do?' she said.

'What?'

'Find the women involved. The ones used to entrap all these powerful men.'

This took Kane by surprise.

'I'm not sure they'd want that.'

'I don't think you know what they'd want.'

'Maybe. What would you ask them?'

'How they were recruited, if they knew who they were working for, whether there was any safeguarding.'

'They didn't know they were working for MI6,' he said. 'If that's what you mean. What would count as safeguarding? There was no more or less safeguarding than in any sex work.'

'Some of them look very young,' she said, carefully.

'None of them were illegal.'

'And there were drugs.'

'Right.'

'MI6 supply those?'

'Sometimes.'

'Where do intelligence officers get drugs?'

'Where do journalists get drugs?'

'Okay. Did they know what they were getting into?'

'No one ever knows what they're getting into,' Kane said. Bell winced and he felt clumsy. 'There are aspects of it I regret.'

'I'd like their names.'

'Do you think I have them?'

'I think someone does. I think you'd make sure you knew exactly where the women were.'

'You're overestimating us.'

'Well, for a long time it seems I underestimated you.'

Kane got to his feet, then sat down again. The conversation had slipped out of his hands. He could see the multiple stories within the revelations. Part of his job as a field officer, writing reports for HQ, was to choose the story from within a chaos of events. Intelligence work wasn't about information, it was about focus. Bell's work too. He hadn't anticipated this focus.

Bell looked across the images she'd printed. 'A lot of this feels like it's calculated for maximum humiliation,' she said.

'It's not easy to arouse shame these days.'

'Was that your operating principle?'

'It was John Broughton's.'

Bell nodded. Kane was conscious that he had dropped the name into the conversation as a last resort. He was waving Broughton as a lure, a decoy. And it worked.

'This is about him, isn't it,' Bell said. 'John Broughton. He's behind all this surveillance.'

'He was certainly instrumental.'

'Did you work with him?'

'Sometimes.'

'What if a journalist speculated that this archive is John Broughton steadily accumulating power over police and media and politicians – anyone who might ultimately turn against him, who might question some of the things he's done and their legality?'

'Very possible. But right now it's Eclipse who poses the greatest danger. He's the one I care about.'

'I think Eclipse is trying to tell us that something went badly wrong.'

'Eclipse is an attention-seeking sociopath with no concern about endangering innocent people's lives. Last night they were hit by a cyberattack, lost some blackmail money, and suddenly they've reinvented themselves as a martyr. But there are people around the world getting killed because of these leaks. Getting arrested and tortured as we speak.'

'And what do you want me to do?'

'Approach him.'

'Eclipse? Even if I could, he wouldn't trust me.'

'You said he'd emailed Alex Colgan-Smith at *The Sunday Times*. Get Colgan-Smith to reply, to say he wants to run the story but can't: the government's putting pressure on newspapers, his editor's terrified. But he knows one journalist who might be able to help. They're brave and hungry and think this story deserves to get out. He passes on your details. Eclipse comes to you, and you act suspicious at first. You want to do this, you say, but you have to be ultra-careful. Make him prove himself.'

Bell thought this through.

'Let's say it works. What if he gives me something I want to run?'

'Then you're in business.' Bell looked at him hard. 'I'm not expecting to control you,' Kane said.

'What about your people? Do I need to check my brakes?'

'You can't cut brake lines any more, you'd see a warning light as soon as the engine started.'

'I'm serious.'

'The most important thing is finding out who Eclipse is and what their game is. Leave the intelligence services to me.'

'With the greatest of respect, Elliot, I don't think the Secret Intelligence Service is in your control.'

'The more involved we are the more control we have.'

'And the Russia thing? Am I taking on Putin?'

'Eclipse is an individual. Whatever they're connected with, however they got this material, I think Eclipse himself is a wild-card, a loose cannon, one who doesn't know or doesn't care how much damage he inflicts.'

'You admit that this archive should never have existed.'

'Absolutely. But destroying the lives of innocent people is not a justifiable response. That's not how you whistle-blow. Eclipse lost their money and got angry.'

'And if I agree with him anyway?'

'You'll do what you feel is right.'

'I'm not colluding in a cover up.'

'I don't want you to. But at the moment this is a free-for-all. And there are limited options in terms of how we move. We can step away, get shut down or be very clever and proceed in a manner that isn't going to get you arrested. I'm showing you that third option, but I'm not forcing you into it. In some ways I'd much rather you gave up on the whole thing.'

Bell rubbed her wet hair, then folded the towel in her lap and looked at it.

'No other press are going to be able to move on this,' Kane said. 'If Eclipse really has more to share, let him share it with you. We'll take it from there.'

'Public interest would override any legal block from the government.'

'I agree.'

'Stop trying to push my buttons.'

'I've stopped.'

'You're sure your sudden plan isn't MI6 using me?'

'This is my idea. It's nothing to do with MI6.'

'Don't say "trust me", Elliot.'

'I wasn't going to.'

'I'm not doing this for you. I'm not being used. But I will approach him. You will have to step back and see what happens.'

She looked very beautiful then, her wet hair enhancing the brightness of her eyes, eyes for seeking out truth regardless of the consequences, as if truth wasn't a fire.

They drafted an email for Colgan-Smith to send in reply to Eclipse's approach:

> I do believe you have one of the most important stories
> of our time. However, our hands are tied. It's been made
> clear that no one's allowed to pursue your revelations.
> There's intense pressure from government that leaves

me, as an employee of a newspaper, unable to go any
further. If you are still interested in making contact with a
freelance journalist who is willing to investigate this story,
I recommend you contact Juliet Bell.

Bell set up a new Proton Mail account and included the email
address. Finally, Kane typed:

Please do not retain any record of this message.

Colgan-Smith agreed to send it to Eclipse in return for being
kept in the loop. Then all they could do was wait. They had
plenty of catching up on their regular work to do, not least
drafting a report on the implications of the Eclipse leaks for their
clients. At 6 p.m., Bell turned on BBC news. The Prime Minister
stood at a lectern, promising to resign as soon as arrangements
were in place to ensure continuity of governance at this time
of crisis. She checked her phone when the news ended, then
looked at Kane.

'Eclipse has messaged.'

SEVENTEEN

Kensington Central Library had become the setting for a dream, her dream, bizarre as she looked around. Rebecca stood up and circled the room, peering: *Eclipse, Eclipse, Eclipse.* Three of the PCs she could see were on stories about Eclipse. Other visitors were looking at Eclipse postings on their phones. The librarians were watching the checkout desk monitor: ... *we don't know yet the identity of this person, or why they've chosen now to wreak such devastation ...*

Rebecca returned to her computer and brought up the main UK news sites.

UK Rocked by Surveillance Leak

Hunt for 'Eclipse'

COBRA in session

Eclipse's name arose in conjunction with a range of people and their secrets, but not hers. That was disorientating: her own catastrophe had been swallowed by a national one. She remembered Lockhart being called away. *A bit of a crisis.* This must have been it.

The British government seemed to think it was to do with Russia; meanwhile, a lot of the online noise involved criticism of MI6, who appeared to be the source of the material. That gave her pause. She saw Elliot – his ease and charm and enigma – and then heard again Lockhart's account of the erasure of all records. Slowly, something began shifting into place in terms of her understanding of that night.

She clicked through some of the leaked kompromat with a mixture of relief, compulsion and prurience. Once she was sure she wasn't included, Rebecca checked for her husband. Not yet. Indeed, the *Telegraph* had announced that Robert was now 3/1 to be the next Prime Minister.

He had messaged a few minutes ago: *Not sure if you've seen, but it looks like I might be working overtime! Never seen the HoC so crazy.*

On the news, government ministers looked frantic, ashen. Lives were at risk, they stressed. Rebecca needed to tell someone what she knew.

But tell them what?

She looked through the leaked images again. So many came from Eaton Square. And now she had several pieces of that puzzle. Government were hunting Eclipse, but she had been investigating him longer than they had, and had an insight they might lack. Buoyed by this new sensation of power, she typed a message to Eclipse: *Have we met? I think so.* Then she deleted it and tried a bolder approach, seeking to instil some fear in the man who had made her own life so nightmarish: *I know who you really are. And a lot of people are interested, aren't they. They'd be interested in Opula too, in 62 Eaton Square.*

She liked the look of it, sent it, then followed up with another: *I am working with police and press. Now you've gone public I don't care what you do to me any more. You've got a lot more to lose than I do, you prick.*

She didn't get a reply. Not directly, at least. A few minutes later, Robert messaged: *We need to talk. Come home immediately.*

EIGHTEEN

Eclipse's first message to Juliet Bell was concise:

You've got the balls to write this story?

It had come into the email address Bell had passed via Colgan-Smith. Bell showed it to Kane.

'Think it's genuine?'

'Maybe.'

She typed: *If there's been an abuse of state power on the scale you seem to be suggesting then I'd like to report this properly and give you the platform you deserve. I think it is vital that the world is informed, and I would be honoured to help, if you think my journalistic background would lend credibility.* She paused, then Kane took the laptop: *People are saying you're a crank. I don't believe that.* Clicked send.

Let's do this then, Eclipse wrote a few minutes later.

But how do I know who I'm communicating with? Bell typed.

'Ask where he is, roughly,' Kane said. Bell looked sceptical but typed this up. Eclipse wrote back: *You don't need to know any of that. What I need is proof you're Juliet Bell.*

She took a photo of herself, holding one of his messages. Kane checked geolocation was turned off on her phone's camera, and that there was nothing in the image that could tell the recipient anything about her home or its security.

Ok, Eclipse wrote, five minutes after she sent it. *I'm going to get you docs. Hard copies. It pertains to something I believe you will be interested in and will agree is important to get out there. Conditions:*

we do this in a manner of my choosing. And I'm going to need money in order to protect myself and plan for the future – a first instalment of 50k in BTC to show goodwill. As you are aware, by doing this I am placing my life in profound danger.

Of course, Bell wrote. Then Kane took the keyboard: *Can I ask how you acquired this?*

Eclipse replied: *No. I can't go into that.*

Are you, or have you ever been, an employee of a government or intelligence services?

No comment.

It would be very helpful, in terms of bringing this to print, if I knew your nationality.

I am currently a UK citizen, Eclipse wrote. Bell raised an eyebrow. Kane typed: *Can you tell me what inspired you to do this? Why would you take this heroic risk?*

'You sound sarcastic,' Bell said, and deleted 'heroic'. Eclipse's reply arrived a moment later: *Disgust.* Then: *I am not the story. Don't fish for my identity.*

Understood, Kane wrote. *What is it you ultimately want out of this?*

A confession.

'What does that mean?' Kane said.

'Seems fairly obvious what it means,' Bell said.

'Whose?'

'Yours, I guess.'

Kane took the laptop.

I understand your need for anonymity, he wrote, *but at some point I will need to meet you, to verify this.*

Eclipse replied: *You would be the one endangered.*

I can look after myself, Kane typed.

No further reply. Ten minutes passed.

'What's the law on paying him?' Bell asked.

'Right now, it probably counts as funding terrorism,' Kane said. 'Minimum fourteen-year sentence. Let's hold off.'

Still no reply.

'We pushed too hard,' Bell said.

'We would have seemed suspicious otherwise.'

'What now?'

'We protect ourselves from MI6.'

Kane swept the house for listening devices, then ran checks on their phones and computers. They were on dangerous territory communicating with Eclipse behind the backs of officialdom. Eclipse had taken their outreached hand and pulled them over the border of illegality. Bell turned the news on and Kane half-listened:

'In response to claims that MI6 unilaterally assumed the power to authorise surveillance, going far beyond existing legislation, and to demonstrate that its policies satisfy legal safeguards, the intelligence service has been required to disclose internal guidance to staff on the collection of potentially sensitive material.'

The cover of *The Times* had recently been updated to an image of the sun obscured by the silhouette of a male head: WHO IS ECLIPSE? *Daily Mail*: ARE THEY ALL AT IT? *Guardian*: ECLIPSE FILES THROW INTERNATIONAL ELITE INTO CRISIS.

The first wave of resignations broke: the Speaker of the House, the Prime Minister's Chief of Staff. Three executives had stepped down from directorships at banks and technology companies.

Kane received a message from the Metropolitan Police, advising him that a team of detectives from Special Operations 15 had been instructed to investigate historic activity at the Secret Intelligence Service and he was to report to their Central London headquarters to be interviewed by midday tomorrow. He showed the message to Bell.

'Not sure I'd be walking out again.'

'What are you going to do?'

'Go and collect Mason.'

'Are you sure that's safe?'

'I'll take your car.'

Mason's father lived out in Borehamwood, among the tall hedges and electric gates of the mock-Tudor elite. There seemed to be an unspoken agreement whereby he walked Mason to the end of his expensive property while Kane waited on the pavement just beyond. It was like an Iron Curtain checkpoint.

Usually things were civilised. This time the father wore a strange smile, waving his iPhone.

'Your work?'

'See you next week,' Kane said, taking the boy's hand.

'What does Juliet think?' the man said to his back.

'Ask her,' Kane said. Mason climbed into his car. Kane got in and closed the door.

'There's stuff on the news,' the boy said.

'Sure is.'

'My dad says you know about it.'

'Yeah?'

'He says you're not what you seem.'

'Not many people are,' Kane said, and started to drive.

The house was filled with the sounds of protestors when they got in, a crowd turning nasty, chanting.

'We're back,' Kane called. Mason went to the garden. Bell came downstairs, the chanting coming from her phone. 'Any word from him?' Kane asked.

'Not yet. Should we reach out?'

'Let's give it another hour. What have I missed?'

She glanced at her screen, paused the footage.

'Eight members of Sinn Fein just walked out of Stormont. There was an attack on one of them as he tried to get in his car, supposedly because of videos that showed him with young girls. Northern Ireland is currently without a government. The Metropolitan Police Commissioner has stepped down with immediate effect. I can't find the video relating to him. Those are the headline upsets. Oh, and your old boss, Sir Roland Mackenzie, turns out to like sex in toilet cubicles. Thought you might be interested in that one. Wife of the *Times* editor moved out. Someone's killed themselves, blaming Eclipse, and they weren't even leaked yet.'

A lot of the new leaks involved Christabel's, the brothel of choice for MPs and civil servants back in the '90s. One document concerned the former Bank of England Chairman's sexual fantasies relating to gas masks. Several videos just showed men and women masturbating alone in hotel rooms, and at least twenty didn't contain sex acts at all but people crying. Two high-profile businessmen had been revealed as drug addicts. One happily married Labour MP had met forty-three men through apps over a six-month period, and was pictured smoking amphetamines in a sea of toned male bodies.

The police released a blanket statement: where Eclipse material indicated a crime had been committed, they would investigate. A team of officers had been assigned to work through everything released. There were already over two thousand hours of video and more than five hundred photos.

Vigilante groups had sprung up online and manifested physically, gathering in Central London, Parliament Square and at the homes of various members of the establishment to wave placards and shout. On the news you saw protection officers being rushed into place. A leading economist had gone into hiding.

Then came Mackenzie.

'Several videos from the early 2010s have surfaced of Sir Roland Mackenzie, former Chief of MI6, appearing to approach men in public toilets . . . '

There was a surprisingly dignified statement from Mackenzie:

'Carrying these secrets around for so long was infinitely more painful than their revelation.' Then the news cut to footage from outside MI6 HQ, where the intelligence service's LGBTQ group had gathered. Kane had never heard of it before. He turned the volume up.

'As representatives of the LGBTQ community at MI6, we deplore and condemn the intelligence service's historic obsession and exploitation of homosexuality. There is no shame in any sexual orientation, and no place for this kind of activity in a modern intelligence service. We support a full public inquiry.'

Good, Kane thought. But had they not known who they were working for? He switched channels. A burning car lit the screen. 'Sir Stewart Donnington's vehicle collided with the bridge at the Thorpe interchange of the M25. His family believe he feared release of information in the upcoming twenty-four hours ... '

Politics had ground to a halt: debates cancelled, currency falling. Kane turned the TV off, stared at his reflection in the black screen. Alistair Godfrey called.

'Elliot, there's a woman at Vauxhall Cross asking for you. She's causing a scene.'

'Who is it?'

'She's called Amelia, says you saw her a couple of days ago. She thinks you still work here. Can you speak to her? Ask her to leave?'

'Christian Rivera's wife?'

'Maybe.'

'What is she saying?'

'She's just asking for you. She's pretty distraught.'

Kane felt a new depth of dismay. Amelia came on the line.

'Do you know about this?' she asked.

'About what?'

'The video I got sent, of Chris with another man?'

'It's from a long time ago, Amelia. Where did you get it?'

'The kids saw, Elliot. The kids, for God's sake.'

'I'm sorry.'

'Did you know he was gay?'

'I don't think he's gay.'

'They said they're going to send it to my parents. They want money.'

'Who?'

'It came to my Facebook. I don't know who.'

So Eclipse was still hustling; in the midst of his firestorm, blackmail remained a source of profit. He needed money. Now more than ever, maybe. Amelia began crying again. Kane listened to her and he was transported back to Cambridge, circa 1999. She'd just had an argument with Christian about the way he treated her. Kane told her to leave him and she replied: *And then who am I?* He thought of that every time he wondered the same question, heard her clarity of insight that had seemed, briefly, the revelation of a different person.

'Where's Christian now?' he asked.

'With some fucking reputation manager. I don't even know what that means. Who's doing this to me?'

'Is the reputation manager called Lucy Piper?'

'Yes. Piper and Chatsworth or Chatsby or something.'

Kane closed his eyes wearily. Of course, he thought. Piper and Chatsby, masters of the dark arts. Trust Christian to take that route.

'About these videos?'

'About MI6. Says he's going to go public before the police arrest him. He's got some stupid plan. He's been trying to get hold of you. What exactly does he want to go public about?'

Piper and Chatsby. Kane drove towards their Chancery Lane office, cursing Christian. Kane had always admired him for his performances – of masculinity, of competence and gregariousness – and had based much of his adult identity on that façade, but Christian wasn't in control. That was the difference between them. His charm floated on petulance and, occasionally, unbridled rage. Kane had first seen this just before finals when Christian attempted to steal money from a social club, then, upon being discovered, had trashed the college bar. He was sent down before he could take his exams, exposing, once and for all, his lack of intellectual distinction. Everything Kane would subsequently learn about Christian was there: rage as a vehicle for escape, destruction as a pretext for reinvention, a slipping away from judgement. But it made him a man eternally on the run. Kane had only encouraged that.

He could imagine Christian trying to go public and making a bad situation a lot worse. And he had no expectation that Christian would try to protect those he was close to. Christian was a con game, and like every good con, the trick was to make you think you were on the inside, you could see how it worked and weren't going to get played. Kane's fondness for Christian had always been nihilistic. He was there for the spectacle, and it was only as such that he had avoided harm so far.

The reputation managers' office hadn't changed since the days it catered to the newly arrived oligarchs Kane was so interested in. That was how it had first crossed their radar. Kane climbed the narrow stairs to the etched glass door, past photographs of other success stories: dictators, oil companies, bad pharma. So this was the company he now found himself in.

The office was airy and modern. A smiley young receptionist said they were in a meeting.

'Me too,' Kane said, and walked in. The meeting room featured a glass conference table surrounded by white chairs. The walls were covered with abstract art. Chatsby and Piper sat beside each other, Christian pacing at the front of the room as if rehearsing a role. He turned when Kane entered, bright-eyed, one of those men who thrive disconcertingly on crisis. Lucy Piper was in her usual authoritative splendour of blow-dried hair and red lipstick, Chatsby hunched beside her, hair slicked straight back from his brow, eyes haunted, as if his intricate legal talent was a form of illness.

'Elliot,' Piper said.

'You heard?' Christian said.

'Yes.'

'Are you in?'

'Do I have a choice?'

Everyone laughed at this as if it was funny.

'Have a seat,' Chatsby said. 'This is going to be as pertinent to you as to anyone.'

Kane sat down. Christian had pulled out the dream team. Chatsby handled the legal side of reputation management: law as a pillow over the face of truth. Piper was a former journalist and government press officer – she handled PR via her network of media contacts and more shadowy internet manipulators.

'Big point,' Christian said, taking a seat at the head of the table. 'Trying to retrieve evidence of how it went down? Witnesses? It's not going to happen. Trying to prosecute the intelligence service, it's like shooting into water. We're not there.'

'I wasn't quite so forthright,' Chatsby said.

'Okay. Correct me if I'm wrong,' Christian said. 'But the central question is how we perceived the framework in which we were operating; what the government had agreed to. We can't just say they told us to do it.'

'It seems clear to me,' Chatsby said, 'that whatever process happens now, in the wake of Eclipse, it's going to be first and foremost at the level of the institution. And all the secrecy will be a great help. No prosecutor will be able to access adequate documents to build a case against an individual employee.'

Piper chipped in, with an eye on Kane: 'Problem is this isn't going to be fought in the courts.'

'We need to take control of the narrative,' Christian said. 'Frame it.'

'Get on the front foot,' Kane said, to spare him the effort of any more clichés.

'TV interviews.' Christian's eyes lit up. When they were recruiting him into Halcyon, Broughton said that sometimes in espionage you look for whoever is the centre of attention; they are the ones people are blinded by. People were blinded by Christian. He blinded himself.

'There's a piece being written as we speak,' Christian continued. 'A journalist asking around about the good old days, using our names. *Our* names, Elliot. I don't want them being the ones who put me into the public domain. I want to control how that happens.'

Kane wondered about the identity of this purported journalist. Wondered if it was someone very close to him, and whether Juliet Bell would really be using his name.

'Okay. Maybe we can talk in private, Christian.'

'I think that's a good idea,' Piper said. 'Let's reconvene a bit later. Obviously, we don't have much time to waste. But you want us to take this further, is that right?'

This question, it seemed, was the pretext for asking Christian to sign a contract, which he did standing, bent over the table, without reading it very closely.

'We'll get you in to do some test recordings later,' Piper said. 'If there are interviews, I want them to be our interviews.'

'Yes.'

'And Elliot, you should think seriously about how you'll fit into all this. You're a crucial part of the story.'

Everyone shook hands, then Kane and Christian hit the stairs.

'You've heard from the police?' Christian said.

'Yes.'

'Did you know, to be counted as a sex trafficker, you don't even have to force someone to come over?' Christian said. 'It's enough if you've exploited their vulnerabilities. If you've used your charm.'

'I can believe that.'

'I mean, there's a lot of sex traffickers out there. You know what I mean?'

'I've just been with Amelia. She's upset about some videos she's seen.'

'I know. She's leaving me.'

'I don't think she's leaving you, Christian.'

'Eclipse is setting the agenda. This is how we fight back. You get that?'

'Maybe.'

They left the building, into the bustle of Chancery Lane. It was sweltering.

'Is she really bad?' Christian said. 'Amelia?'

'A little shocked. She went to VX to find me.'

'Oh, Christ.'

'I think she'll pull through.'

'Not this time. Breakfast, she opens her phone, looks at Facebook, and there I am having my cock sucked by some Saudi prince. Let's get a drink.'

They strode through Holborn to the Princess Louise, a palace of Victorian shadows with stained-glass windows, gilded wall mirrors and an island bar the size of a boat. An oasis of seclusion, neglected by those in the sun outside.

Christian ordered two large gin and tonics, and they took a table at the back.

'I think I may be able to bring Eclipse out into the open,' Kane said.

'And what are you going to do then?'

'Stop him.'

'Heroic, if it works. But you can get Eclipse and we're still fucked. Do you see that?'

'I have my priorities.'

'Chatsby thinks I should pre-emptively sue.'

'Sue who?'

'MI6.'

'Sue the Intelligence Service?'

'For what they did to my life. I'm in a mental health crisis. I have been since I got involved.'

'Okay. That's going to be messy.'

'You don't think Broughton's going to go messy? Hang us out to dry to save his neck?'

'I'm not sure even John would do that.'

'Over three hundred people have come forward with complaints regarding their inclusion in MI6 databases. They've got the big human rights lawyers on board talking class action, gross violation of the public's right to privacy. If it goes to a tribunal we're fucked. If it becomes a criminal matter we're really fucked. I need you onside, Elliot. Come in on it. Penitence, cooperation, amnesty. That's the plan. The law will do us a deal.'

'You don't know that.'

Christian sighed and gazed out across the permanent dusk of the pub.

'What were we doing back then? Whose demons were we chasing? You have to see there are two opposing forces here. The Service is going to throw us to the wolves. We've got to be clever. Chatsby's exploring legal immunity in return for full disclosure.'

'There is a limit to what will be forgiven.'

'I don't care about forgiveness. I want a deal. I don't want to go to prison. The government follows the public, the press. We have to risk putting ourselves out there or we're just sitting around asking to be fucked. What hand are we playing, Elliot? That's

211

the question.' He shook his head. 'You're not a gambler,' he said, finally. 'This is how you win.'

'Maybe.'

Christian looked around the room, then back at Kane. 'It's not just about surveillance, Elliot. We killed people.'

Kane was suddenly very conscious of the dusty silence that surrounded them. Those fantasies of reunion with his old colleague – that was the bit they didn't say. Now Kane understood why. It wasn't because of modesty. Christian watched his face. Eventually he continued.

'People are saying there was an inquiry before and John got it closed down. Buried.'

'I've heard things along those lines.'

'There are senior police and members of the Crown Prosecution Service under Broughton's thumb. You know who we filmed, you know what they were doing.' Christian sipped his G&T and considered his reflection in the mirrored wall. Again, Kane thought of Christian being sent down from Cambridge and the extent to which this had been a calculated performance. A man, cornered, who burns his own house down, grinning, clutching the box of matches. My house, my fire. The man who shoots his family, then himself. Kane remembered why he had cut ties with Christian on their last job together, in Russia itself. The final disagreement was superficially about Christian driving around unnecessarily, sightseeing, high on the situation, which meant they ran low on petrol, which meant having to either steal a new car or risk the cameras of a petrol station. You don't draw attention to yourself when on a mission. But something else would have served as pretext for parting ways if it hadn't been that. They had come to the end of a friendship which had always been more an exploration. Kane had tried every way of enjoying Christian Rivera, of discovering a core that might redeem the artifices. There was no core.

Kane remembered waking one night to see Christian sitting at the end of his bed, light on his collarbone, shadows between his muscles, studying him. *You're lucky*, Christian had said, then smiled and walked away. Kane never asked him what he meant, but he had an idea. He initially thought of Christian as lucky – good looks did that – but Christian was dependent on luck, which was different. The gambling to which he was addicted wasn't an attempt to escape his situation but an affirmation of it, a trust game with the universe: catch me; prove your love for me. Back in university days he'd lose hundreds in bad deals and ill-advised punts in the town centre, and the wealthier students would pool resources to rescue him. Women especially bailed him out with a persistence that led Kane to believe there was some masochistic enjoyment to be had in it. That was ruthless, not lucky.

'Are you sure you want your face out there?' Kane said.

'We don't have a choice. You know what Lucy said? It's very easy to scapegoat someone without a face. I like that. I believe it's true.'

'There's a limit to what anyone's going to write off.'

Christian appeared to ponder this, turning his glass on the table and wiping a bead of condensation.

'Is your hesitation something to do with that night?' he asked.

'Which night?'

'New Year's Eve.'

New Year's Eve. The end of so many things. A night that Kane did not dwell on too often.

'New Year's Eve,' Kane said, 'was part of a bigger project which, I think we can say now, sprawled beyond our control. None of it involves stuff we can just televise our way out of. These are complicated things.'

'Like I say, people are on the scent. Fleet Street's remained pliable, but there's a reporter over here who's got backing from

213

pro bono lawyers – Spotlight on Corruption lawyers. They've won big cases against the government before, and the attitude is: let the people decide. They'll find a newspaper willing to take the leap eventually. Publish and be damned. Except we're the ones damned.'

'Got a name for this reporter?'

'Juliet Bell, the one who was sniffing around back in the day. The one who did the Saudi torture story. She doesn't give a fuck. And she's got a point this time.'

'Yes.'

'So you hear what I'm saying: we're on TV soon, whether we like it or not.'

Bell was on a call out in the garden when Kane got back. He searched for signs of contact with lawyers or charities – recent emails, phone calls, notes. Nothing that he could see, which didn't necessarily mean she was hiding it from him, but she hadn't mentioned it either. He felt the ice on which they stood begin to crack. But then this was what he'd suggested she do: chase the story.

He went to check on Mason. His bedroom door was jammed shut. Kane forced it open and the boy jumped. He was looking at Eclipse leaks on his PC.

'No!' he said. 'Why did you come in?'

'I wanted to check you were okay.'

He stormed past Kane, into the bathroom.

'I'm not angry,' Kane said. Then Bell appeared.

'Oh shit. What's he been looking at?'

She tried the bathroom door. 'Don't lock it, Mason.'

A second later they heard his body slump to the ground. Kane managed to get the bathroom door open, and cushioned the floor around Mason's head with towels as the boy fitted. Don't restrain him, Bell had said. Just let it burn itself out. Urine spread across the tiles and Bell moved a towel to stop it. Her phone pinged as it was all going on, but it was another twenty minutes before she could check it, once the boy had come back to consciousness and they'd got him washed and changed. Finally, Bell picked up the message. She stared at her phone screen then at Kane.

'What is it?'

She showed Kane the message. It was from Eclipse. *Due to considerable time pressure, I have decided to agree. I will meet you. Go to the phone box on the corner of Archway Road and Southwood Lane, near Highgate Station. Midnight tonight. Be alone. I have something you'll be very interested in. I will know if you are not alone and I will call it off. You'll receive further instructions when you are there.*

'This is crazy,' Kane said.

'This is what you asked for.'

'You're going to go?'

'Of course.'

'Not in the middle of the night. It's power games. He knows exactly what he's doing. It's a wind-up.'

'Only one way to find out. He has no reason to cause me harm.'

'You're putting a lot of faith in his powers of reason.'

'Maybe. But this is what he's offering. I can't throw away this chance. Trust works both ways.'

'We need backup,' Kane said.

'We don't have time. And I don't want him arrested or shot or whatever.'

'There's no way I'm letting you go there on your own.'

'You don't control me.'

'I'm coming with.'

Kane called Tactical, the private security company, to see if they could provide any kind of discreet protection, while Bell called around babysitters. She had better luck. There was no way Tactical could pull together a team in time. To properly observe and tail someone without being detected yourself you needed at least fifteen people across multiple forms of transport. Team members would need to be briefed and kitted out with hidden communications equipment. That would take at least twenty-four hours to set up. Kane and Bell had fifty minutes. They were on their own.

The babysitter arrived at 9 p.m.

'This is a late one,' she said, dropping her coat and bag on the sofa. 'Off somewhere nice?'

'Work-related,' Bell said. 'Hence the last-minute panic. We appreciate it.' Mason came downstairs, looked at Kane, dressed all in dark clothing, and his mother in a hi-vis jacket.

'I need to go do something, baby. I'm on a story.' Bell went to kiss him and then held him very tightly.

'Mum?'

'I love you,' she said. 'I'll be back soon.'

NINETEEN

Back into the Chilterns, eye on her phone, the lights of London behind her. Into the darkness and quiet of the countryside, which used to feel such a refuge. In the glare of her headlights, the signs to villages seemed like frantic warnings she was ignoring one by one.

Robert needed to talk to her. That was all his message had said, and it made her very nervous. She was nervous at having confronted Eclipse, and already wondering if that had been a big mistake. What did Robert want? But he was right, she needed to talk to him, tell him everything. It was a time of revelation, after all. Honesty was strength.

As she pulled into her drive, Rebecca saw the cars parked up: three of them, gleaming beneath her home's security lights. She let herself into the house quietly, glimpsed a huddle in the kitchen, all staring at a mobile phone. A cabal, in silence. Then the silence was broken by the sound of her own carnal moans. They came from the phone speaker. Unmistakeable.

Robert's new private secretary broke away to take a call. Marcus Bothwick, head of comms at Conservative Party HQ, didn't raise his eyes from the screen. Holding the phone was Gerald Lazenger, of course. Then there was Robert, the only one sitting down.

'No, it's worse than that,' the private secretary said into her phone. 'Tell me the headlines.'

'Excuse me,' Rebecca said. 'What the hell are you all doing?'

They turned to her. Someone had the decency to pause the video. The aide hung up. Robert looked gaunt. She could smell the whisky on him.

'Where's Iona?' Rebecca said.

'I sent her to my parents,' Robert said.

'Without telling me?'

She felt a new rage starting to build. These were not the people she wanted huddled in her kitchen watching her fake orgasms. Bothwick stared at her, dull-eyed, looking like someone past midnight given an impossible task.

'Rebecca, we've got a somewhat pressing situation,' he said. 'We're going to need to move quickly, and we're going to need some ... insight from you, with regards to how we play this.'

'There are aspects of your past you haven't been entirely open about,' Lazenger said.

'I'll speak to my husband first,' Rebecca told them.

'We'll give you ten minutes.'

'You'll get out of my fucking house is what you'll do,' she snapped, closing with a smile. This got a reaction from the team: surprise, new caution. Behind it all, the fear of loose cannons. They hadn't seen her like this before. Nor had Robert. She hadn't been like this for quite some time. 'I'll call the police.'

'That's not going to do anything,' Lazenger said.

'If I say you assaulted me this morning, Gerald? How would the press react? Know which journalists I'm in touch with?'

He eyed her warily. 'Tell us, Rebecca, exactly which journalists are you in touch with?'

'Where did you get that video?' Rebecca said.

'Robert's being blackmailed,' Lazenger said. 'It was sent to his constituency email. Want to shed some light on its origins?'

'I used to fuck people for money. I think that's fairly obvious.

It was the happiest time of my life. Marcus, do you want to tell the press or shall I?'

Bothwick paled. The private secretary had frozen, phone in hand.

'What do you mean Gerald assaulted you?' Robert said, catching up. Lazenger laughed.

'She came to me, Robert, asking for financial assistance. So I'm wondering what exactly this blackmail is about and who's behind it.'

'Why would I ask you for financial assistance?' Rebecca said.

'Why would you try to steal money from Robert's Bank of Gibraltar account?' he said. 'That's the question. You came to me, trying to seduce me into helping.'

Beneath the nonsense of his accusations, Rebecca could sense a deeper strategy forming. It would be useful to make the story about her; deflect from Robert – from 3/1-next-PM Robert Sinclair. She wasn't letting that happen so easily.

'What if I told you that the video you're watching connects to a company called Opula?'

This divided the room. Robert and Gerald grew very still. Marcus and the private secretary turned to them, puzzled and ignorant. Rebecca took advantage of the stunned silence of both sides.

'Russians. Let's talk about them – Robert, Opula, Russians, Eaton Square . . . '

'Enough,' Robert barked.

'Get a grip, Rebecca,' Lazenger said.

'What is this?' Bothwick asked.

Lazenger said, quietly: 'Get her phone.'

Rebecca took a step back. 'You just try.'

'What's Opula?' the private secretary asked.

'Get out of my home,' Rebecca said. 'Or I'll call the police and then Michael De Souza.'

Gerald laughed. Robert looked at him, then laughed.

'Robert,' she said. 'We need to talk.'

'Yes indeed.' He wiped his bloodshot eyes as if the mirth was overwhelming. 'I can deal with this,' he said to his team. 'Please. Leave it to me.'

The cabal of four spent several more moments in hushed confabulation, then they left. Rebecca heard the cars drive off. Robert stood at the kitchen window, watching them go. She realised she was scared of being alone with him.

'I'm going to get Iona,' she said.

'Are you on something?' he said, looking at her reflection in the glass.

'On something? No.'

'You're acting very fucking strange. Can you talk to me?'

'You don't send my daughter away without telling me.'

He turned. 'We're going to start on things we haven't told each other about?'

'The party where we met. Opula.'

'Yes.'

'Who are they?'

'A networking thing. Oligarchs, hangers-on. Why? What's this got to do with anything?'

It seemed clear to her that Robert really didn't know much more. Not for the first time, she was granted a sense of his ignorance, and an understanding that he would never achieve true wickedness because he lacked depth.

She tried to call Robert's parents, to speak to Iona. Her mother-in-law said: 'What's this I've heard about a video?'

'Let me speak to my daughter.'

Robert grabbed the phone off her.

'Don't worry,' he began. He turned away from Rebecca and when she tried to grab the phone he elbowed her in the face.

The movement was lazy. So she was surprised to find herself

on the ground, temporarily blinded. When she opened her eyes, Robert was staring down at her.

'Shit,' he muttered, then, into the phone: 'Mum, I've got to go.' He hung up. 'That was an accident,' he said. He tried to help her up and she shrugged him off. Rebecca went upstairs and locked the door of the bathroom, right eye throbbing. She inspected herself in the mirror. Never had anyone hit her.

She sat on the edge of the bath, contemplating her next move. Robert knocked at the door, called her name, then descended to the living room again when she told him to go away. Rebecca closed her eyes and began to cry, and only opened them when she heard a door banging downstairs. Was Robert going out? Then, before the thought was complete, she heard a curtailed cry and the sound of something heavy hitting the floor.

TWENTY

They agreed that Bell would take her Mitsubishi Outlander, Kane would follow in the Audi but stay out of sight when she went to meet Eclipse.

Kane persuaded her to wear a hidden mic, camera and a miniature GPS tracker, size of a key fob, in both coat and bag. The mic and camera were to record Eclipse. The trackers were in case she was abducted. Both mic and camera were barely visible, the size of SIM cards: wireless, with three to four hours' battery. Kane could monitor from his phone. He might just see Eclipse's face.

Kane brought binoculars and an expandable steel baton, just in case. They parked away from the phone box, out of sight, in the Tube station car park. The night had an unwelcoming, metallic darkness, its sickly half-moon dimmed by clouds. Bell went ahead, Kane stayed fifty metres behind. As he approached the main road, Kane could see why Eclipse had chosen the spot: he could position himself almost anywhere and watch to see if Bell was alone. The phone box to which he'd directed her was exposed, beside an open traffic junction, hushed by the seventy-acre expanse of Highgate Woods adjacent to it. Kane called Bell and suggested pulling out.

'Not now,' Bell said. 'Not when we're this close.'

Kane checked the mic, the tracker, ran through emergency procedures. If comms went down for more than two minutes he was intervening.

'Stay there,' she said. 'Don't blow this. Stay back.'

Kane checked the High Street, saw scaffolding in front of a charity shop and scrambled up – less than thirty seconds from the box but concealed. He was seventy or eighty seconds' sprint away from her. He wanted to maintain that proximity. The streets were quiet but not deserted. Kane put a headphone in to hear her.

Bell's mobile rang on the dot of twelve. She answered immediately.

'This was your idea,' a man said. 'Sure you're alone?' It sounded like he was speaking through a voice changer app – robotic, distorted.

'Yes.'

'You trust me?'

'I don't know you. I'm here to find out.'

'I need you to trust me. I'm going to ask you to head into Highgate Woods.'

Kane got to his feet. Fuck that, he thought. Highgate Woods was dense, unlit, deserted at night. He went down to the pavement.

'I'm not comfortable with going into the woods,' Bell said. 'You need to trust me too.'

'If you want what I have, then you need to do as I say. Go down the hill to the first entrance. Follow the left-hand path into the woods. Follow it straight for five minutes in the direction of the playing fields. If I think you are alone, you'll get the next instruction. No light, no torches.'

She hesitated, then said: 'Okay.' Eclipse hung up. Kane tried Bell's mobile as he moved towards her, but she didn't answer. By the time he got to the junction she was walking towards the woods. When he got to the entrance to the woods, Bell was disappearing into the trees.

He followed.

The ground was a carpet of dead sticks, crackling beneath his feet. Every step seemed deafening. Kane moved slowly, holding back. Then he saw Bell had stopped too. She was at a crossroads where two paths met. There was a bin, a bench, a signpost. No trace of anyone else that he could see.

Her phone lit up, the screen's glow appearing and disappearing. Whatever the new message said, she moved behind the bench. No, Kane thought, not into the trees. But Bell crouched and began clawing at the ground. After another moment he saw her retrieve something from among the leaves and soil. It was a large plastic bag. She peered inside, looked around.

He stepped forward. No sign of Eclipse. Bell raised a hand. They waited another minute, frozen, like trespassers caught in a searchlight, then she walked back towards Kane.

She carried an unmarked black carrier bag stuffed with papers. It had been in the ground for some time by the looks of it. Which suggested, whatever game Eclipse was playing, he wasn't currently present after all. Bell removed a sheet. She clicked her torch. Kane recognised the format immediately: an MI6 internal report. The cover sheet announced Above Top Secret classification.

Subject: *Rebecca Nolan: concerns and request for heightened surveillance following events of New Year's Eve.* Dated 1 Jan 2009. Marked: *Halcyon Eyes Only.*

Compiled by *E. Kane (PRG 23678).*

Bell glanced at him then back at the name. Kane walked up to the bench, the shallow excavation from which the file had been plucked, then shone his torch into the surrounding trees and bushes.

He continued past the crossroads, straining his ears. There was no sound; no one he could see. The paths here took you to at least seven potential exit points from the woods. And he had no idea when the file had been left or from which direction Eclipse came or went.

'Let's go,' Bell said.

TWENTY-ONE

Rebecca froze. It had been the sound of a body hitting the floor; some primal instinct told her that was what she'd heard.

She slowly unlocked the bathroom. Silence downstairs. She walked to her bedroom and found the hunting knife. Only then did she call out: 'Robert?'

No reply. Had he fallen? She climbed slowly down the stairs. Halfway down, she felt a breeze. The living room drapes were moving. The doors to the patio had been opened.

Another two steps and she saw her husband.

He lay on his back on the floor, one arm up around his head as if waving. A small pool of dark blood had begun to form beneath his head. It looked like something had smashed into his right temple. She stood over his body, then a hand touched her arm.

'Rebecca.'

She spun around. The man was dressed head to toe in black, a balaclava obscuring his face. His eyes were blue and beady, and in her peripheral vision she was aware of rope looped onto his belt, white shoe coverings on his feet.

She slashed with the knife. There hadn't been time to calculate what exactly to do with it, and her broad swipe gave him a split second to move back, out of the way. But it had indicated that she meant business, and the knife remained firm in her grasp. Next time: straight into his stomach. He was aware of her determination. The eyes in the balaclava had become bright.

'Don't be stupid,' the man said.

He stood between her and the front door. But she could feel the breeze from the garden at her back.

Rebecca ran for it. Her mind raced through eventualities. There was a gate out of the garden, but it would take two or three seconds to unbolt it and he would be on top of her by then. The knife required too much positioning. She grabbed a can of wasp spray from the shelf beside the conservatory door.

Surprise him, she thought.

Halfway across the lawn, Rebecca turned and sprayed. It was a perfect shot. He was a foot away, and the pesticide blasted directly into the gap where his anxious eyes peered out. The man swore, then lashed out, bundling into her, knocking her to the grass. She dropped the knife, but was already staggering back to her feet while he was still spluttering. It gave her a second to move past him, back into the house to the front door and out to the road.

Rebecca was sure he was behind her. She ran, barefoot. The road itself was bright and straight and bare, so she tumbled into the trees at the side, roots snagging her, trying to grab her ankles and break them. Into the putrefying mulch of dead bluebells, rising between her toes.

In the darkness she heard that voice. *Don't be stupid*. And she knew, with a knowledge in her bones, her gut, it was the voice she'd heard fifteen years ago, saying the same words. *Don't be stupid. Play nice. Say thank you.* The voice of the man pressing her down into the carpet. Was that possible? Was she going mad?

Rebecca heard a car drive away from her home, fast. But it was only after another five minutes that she let herself stop and look back. The darkness throbbed in time with her heartbeat.

No one.

Cautiously, she made her way back to the road. Headlights blinded her as they came around the bend. She jumped back, terrified, then recognised the Volvo of a couple who ran the post office in Watlington. It swerved to a sudden stop.

'Rebecca?'

She blurted out something about an attack, asked them to call the police. She could see the glow of her upstairs windows through the trees. The woman got through to an emergency services operator.

'Is he breathing?' she asked Rebecca.

'I don't know,' she said, and this ignorance seemed horrendous. 'I don't know. I need to find out.'

'Wait,' the woman said, but Rebecca was running back now. The front door of her home was open. No movement inside that she could see. She stepped in, saw far more blood than had been there before.

Smeared down the hallway, expanding in a bright lake around Robert. He lay in the same place as the last time she'd seen him, but the head wound was now insignificant alongside a dozen or so stab wounds from head to toe. He had been knifed in the cheek and neck and stomach and groin. His eyes were open, lifeless, as if tired of all he'd been subjected to.

Rebecca knelt and cradled him. Then she saw her knife on the rug a few feet away. Slowly, she released the corpse to the floor. Rebecca got to her feet, sticky with blood. A moth with pink and brown markings entered from the garden, and circled the living room light.

She was standing there, watching it, when the first police arrived.

TWENTY-TWO

Bell kept hold of the file as they left the woods. Kane couldn't see anyone watching or waiting. They sat in her car for a moment and she looked at the papers again, at Kane's name.

'Should I not read this?'

'You can read it, but we should get out of here,' Kane said.

'What is this, Elliot? Who is Rebecca Nolan?'

'She's someone who was involved in something. She became Rebecca Sinclair, Robert Sinclair's wife.'

'The Conservative politician? Why are you recommending surveillance on an MP's wife, fifteen years ago?'

'Because of what we'd done. Let's talk at home.'

Mason was awake but exhausted when they got back. The babysitter looked relieved to get out of there. Kane put Mason to bed and the boy was asleep as soon as he lay down. When Kane returned to the living room, Bell had the pages spread across the table.

Rebecca Nolan: concerns and request for heightened surveillance. Halcyon Eyes Only.

The file contained a brief statement of Kane's concerns about the whereabouts of Rebecca on New Year's morning, followed by a psychological assessment of her, conducted by MI6's in-house psychiatrist. It described her mental instability, erratic behaviour, recreational use of narcotics. This was followed by Kane's recommendation to place her under surveillance in case of any further issues, including the monitoring of phone calls. Finally, he had requested research into her movements and contacts over the course of 1 January 2009.

But there was something not quite right about it all – more pages than he remembered inputting – and he searched through for additional material.

'Is it authentic?' Bell asked.

'Yes.'

'Want to tell me what happened?'

'I'd like to tell you everything. It's probably about time. Can it go without saying that this is incredibly sensitive, that very few people even within the Secret Intelligence Service know about this, and that some of those who do will go to significant lengths to stop it coming out?'

'I just risked my life, and this is what I got given. I don't need to be warned off now. I need to know why I have it.'

'I'm not warning you off, I'm just warning you. But I feel sure now – this is what Eclipse connects to somehow. He's playing some kind of game. This is too much for coincidence.'

'Please talk,' Bell said. 'Because I've got a feeling that what you don't tell me, Eclipse will.'

Kane suspected that was right. He just wondered where to start.

He moved their phones upstairs, put on some music, allowed himself a moment to gather his memories. Rebecca Nolan. New Year's Eve. The end of it all. He could tell her that. The question, as ever, was where to begin. But, of course, the answer was with Anton Zakharyan himself, and the success of Opula.

For eighteen months Anton Zakharyan had given them gold: not just on the political powers controlling Unit 22195 but the killers' techniques, training, financing, even the addresses and phone numbers of men involved. Meanwhile, Unit 22195 kept getting more brazen, intoxicated, it seemed, by their own impunity. The founder of a website called Russian Democracy, who had been researching Putin's overseas killings, vanished along with his wife and three-year-old son; two healthy Russian men in their forties, both journalists, collapsed with heart attacks a few weeks after speaking to British officials; a scientist appeared to stab herself after an intelligence-gathering mission to Moscow. And then there were the falls from balconies, roof terraces, fourth-floor windows; an epidemic of defenestration, whose cause seemed to involve exposure to the circles around Putin. The Russian assassins, it was becoming clear, were adept at disguising murder as suicides. Sometimes they went a step better and used drugs and psychological tactics to drive targets into genuinely taking their own lives. But their very success gave them visibility. And MI6 had a man on the inside now.

How do you stop someone behaving with impunity? You punish them, Broughton said.

What they needed to do was on the far edge of the law. But law was made of language, and it was with words that you could pick its lock. Kane's report to the Joint Intelligence Committee was crafted for maximum impact: men and women in Britain's capital were being assassinated by state-sponsored killers. He requested paramilitary support for a deterrence operation, arguing that they had a right to protect innocent citizens.

The MOD remained nervous, but they knew the political circumstances had changed, and withdrew objections during the planning stages. The Defence Minister ordered the military to assist MI6 in any way it required. Kane was given eight men from E Squadron – a composite of the Special Reconnaissance Regiment and 22 SAS Counter-Terrorist Team. His team were classed as an independent asset reporting directly to MI6, authorised to use lethal force if necessary while occupying a space between recognised protocols. Upon joining Halcyon, men were formally detached from their parent unit, seconded away from the armed services so nothing technically counted as British military action. The government, as tradition had it, neither conceived of nor approved covert action.

Broughton impressed upon the team his philosophy of mirroring: you needed an army to defeat an army but a gang to defeat a gang – small, informal, operating by its own rules. It gave Kane a glimpse of Broughton as he must have been in Belfast, the man he knew from anecdotes. From the first day, Broughton insisted on there being no differentiation between the Special Forces and the Secret Intelligence Service officers. No ranks were used, all pitched ideas. When Kane first met the soldiers it took him a moment to realise who they were. One was suited, one bearded in jeans and trainers. None looked like military, which was the point, of course. It was only as he got to know them that the men's distinctive nature became apparent: quiet and self-assured, companionable, with a sense of readiness. Kane realised what else distinguished them from other military: no one ever spoke about past jobs. They adapted easily to Halcyon's operating procedures: no phone calls or messages on any system, just those meetings away from HQ as they trained for action and waited for their opportunity.

On Boxing Day 2008 it came. Kane met with Zakharyan at Ashness Bridge, where they had the views of Derwentwater to themselves. A white collar of ice pinched the remaining darkness at the centre of the lake. Frost coated the grass and bracken, and their breath steamed.

MI6 had helped the Russian set up a second home in the Lake District, well away from prying eyes, and Zakharyan's regular weekend visits provided good opportunities to make contact. Loweswater, Loughrigg Fell – it was amid those stark, soaring landscapes that he had given Kane an organisational diagram of Unit 22195, complete with a list of non-declared officers in Russia's UK embassy and eleven agents under deep cover among the émigré community, on hand to assist in various ways. Zakharyan also spoke to Kane at length about Russia's retained stocks of chemical weapons and nuclear poisons.

Thanks to Zakharyan they knew the enemy inside out, every detail of their MO: how they paid for flights and accommodation using debit cards issued by a Russian company called Payoneer, whose CEO was a military veteran, how they used mobile phones routed via a number in Austria that served as a switchboard of sorts. Kane established a number of passports used by Unit operatives: Georgian, Ukrainian, Moldovan. With phones, passports and bank accounts Kane's team could start mapping the movements of Unit members within Russia and internationally; the techniques of killing, travel routes, documentation, counter-surveillance.

That Boxing Day, beside the frozen lake, he told Kane they were coming over.

The Unit's target was a prominent businessman from Odesa, Maxim Repilov, who lived in Hampstead and had been trying to set up a Russian-language satellite channel critical of the Kremlin.

'They're coming over and they're going to kill him.'

The target, Repilov, was well known to Kane. Indeed, he was one of the Opula party crew, a sex-addicted bon viveur like so many of those risking their lives in the name of democracy. Zakharyan said a team of three men would arrive in London on 30 December; that they planned to kill the businessman in the first week of January. Zakharyan had been asked to play his usual role providing cover, introducing the killers as sympathetic dissidents looking to invest in Repilov's media empire.

On 27 December, three members of the Unit reserved flights to London, arriving on 29 December, two men flying via Istanbul, one from Malta.

This time they weren't going to get away with it.

The Halcyon team was well prepared. They'd acquired non-military weapons, including imitations of those known to be used by the Russian mafia in London. They had vehicles with false plates. It was agreed that if it came to physical intervention, all recording equipment would be switched off.

Kane remembered waiting in their London operating base – one of MI6's satellite offices, behind Charing Cross – radio updates coming in from the watchers at Heathrow, waiting for the planes to touch down, butterflies in his stomach. Every member of the Russian unit was tailed from the moment they arrived in the UK. They were in his sight, the cold-blooded psychopaths who had left such misery in their wake. And he was in a position to stop them once and for all.

Late on 29 December, Zakharyan sent an urgent message: *They want invites for the Opula New Year's Eve party.*

Of course they did.

It was the peak of Opula's notoriety, and every filthy millionaire in London wanted an invite to the New Year's party. That included Repilov himself. Which gave Kane and his team a jolt of anxiety.

Were they intending to poison him at the party? Zakharyan didn't believe so, but his knowledge of the exact assassination plan only went so far. He believed they would keep the target under surveillance on New Year's Eve and kill him the following day at his home.

If the Russian plan was to stick to their target, the UK plan was to stick to the Russians, even as they submerged themselves in depravity.

Opula. Their baby, the jewel in the crown of Operation Halcyon. The ultimate honeytrap. Kane, alongside Broughton and Christian himself, had created an oligarch magnet. They were almost too good, victims of their own success. Within a couple of months of Christian launching this elite concierge service for London's high net worth individuals, Russians were walking into his office on the Strand with half a million in cash in Harrods bags. Opula was where they bought London itself. The idea of a concierge was perfect, Kane thought; from the Latin *conservus*, fellow slave. Kane pictured London as a deferential creep turning a blind eye to his new master's vices. The city's age suggested sophistication, but the elderly could also be jaded, dependent on others, worn into cynicism. The façade of tradition was an indicator of harmless senescence; someone too far gone to judge you, limping around their own antiques. Russians wanted to meet the establishment and the establishment fell to its knees.

The parties were simply the truth of the matter laid bare, a ritual of shared amorality. We're all on the inside, they said, in the candlelight. And, of course, it supplied MI6 with kompromat by the bucketload.

Late 2008 was the peak of Christian Rivera's notoriety. He was the face of Opula, and people had started becoming members just to meet him, to get invites, introductions. Christian had planned the New Year's party of a lifetime: burlesque performers, a trapeze in the double-height entrance hall, fire-eaters, live music. The guest list was insane: politicians, diplomats, minor royalty, some musicians and actors. Kane remembered decorating the place with gold, with circus equipment, five grand's worth of caviar, fifty of alcohol.

By then he had spent three years watching the excess, on the sidelines of an orgy. Nights at Chinawhite, Russians topping up Chateau Petrus with Diet Coke, smoking Cohiba cigars; dinners at Sketch, lap dancing, men blowing twenty grand in a night. A bonfire of offerings to dubious gods. The Russians were terrified, he came to understand. The elaborate legal and financial structures they built were their mausoleums. Every night was their last. So they partied hard. Stringfellows, Sotheby's, grouse shooting, then a jet to the Maldives. In his memories of those years, Kane was travelling at a hundred miles per hour, through excess the likes of which he would never see again, towards one night: New Year's Eve.

The girls were ready. They knew it was going to be big.

Rebecca Nolan was ready.

Rebecca.

He had shut her away in the less accessible vaults of his memory, as we do with someone who threatens us by lingering. In the knowledge that they will not fade, and so a door must be involved. There is forgetting and there is locking a door.

They had met up on the afternoon before the party. This was one detail he had disregarded in the aftermath of what subsequently occurred. Rebecca had asked to meet Kane somewhere 'away from Eaton Square'. This itself seemed startling now; he had forgotten their closeness. In the whirlwind of Halcyon, he had neglected a genuine friendship forming. But he had liked her. She was watchful, clearly intelligent. A lot of the international guests were attracted to her because, he discerned, she represented some ideal of English femininity, but also because she had poise, and there was something unobtainable in her bearing. Kane knew she wanted more from life, and wanted to help her. She was studying. That meant she was discontented, with an eye on bigger things.

It had been snowing when they met. A thin, hard snow lay across Green Park. Wrapped up, without make-up, Rebecca looked very young. Kane had to rendezvous with Christian in ten minutes to drive to a final briefing. He remembered being impatient, and conscious of this, of how emotionally cold he must seem. Slow down, he thought, you can't afford to alienate people in this game. *Manage her*: that was the duty he felt. He was surprised when Rebecca took his arm.

I think I've come to the end of this. New Year's resolutions. I wanted to tell you personally.

Of course, you leave when you want.

Want to come with? She smiled, joking but not joking. That also surprised him. He wondered if she was high, and disliked himself for the thought process. *You once said you'd like to show me Italy.*

Did I say that?

You don't remember.

His thoughts were on the trained Russian killers already in London. He didn't have time for this. Everything is coming to an end, he wanted to say. Don't worry. And, out of guilt, out of impatience to get back to the op, he wrote his name and mobile number on a piece of card.

This is my personal phone number, in case you need it. Don't use the other one.

Okay.

One more party. Then, if you'd like, I can put you in touch with a couple of my old tutors. I'd be happy to make an introduction ...

They got to Green Park Station. Christian pulled up in an Aston Martin, threw the door open. When he saw Rebecca, he raised an eyebrow – a gesture which seemed more dismissive than it had any right to be. Christian had always had doubts about Rebecca, who he believed wasn't as 'professional' as the other girls, though he never elaborated on this word. He knew she was clever and ambitious, Kane suspected. Cleverer than Christian.

'Not protocol,' he muttered, when Kane was in, and their car was leaving and Rebecca was somewhere behind them in the disorientated snow.

The three Russian killers travelled from their hotels at 8 p.m. sharp on 31 December, met at the bar of the Savoy, went on to the party at 9.30.

One member of the team stayed outside, waiting in a hired BMW. The senior officer, Grigoriy Nechaev, went in, accompanied by his second-in-command: a six-foot-five-inch thug they'd codenamed PARTISAN. Nechaev himself was shorter, with the physique of a soldier who'd got out of shape: pot-bellied, with a heavy brow and receding black hair. Kane recognised him from a catalogue of atrocities; he was the man laughing on airport CCTV hours after breaking the legs of Kane's source with a sledgehammer.

From that moment, Kane's memories were bright fragments. A band at the start of the night, a lot of champagne being consumed, three of his own team disguised as catering staff, two as guests, one monitoring communication signals from a van parked around the corner. Kane remembered Christian steering the debauchery along, encouraging everyone to play.

Then the Geiger clicked.

Kane's team picked up the first traces of radiation around quarter to midnight. One area in the lounge, where Nechaev had been sitting, gave an alpha-radiation reading of more than 30,000 counts a second. The Halcyon team ran scans on the vehicles used by the Russian unit and picked up further evidence of nuclear materials.

'They've got something with them.'

Nothing had suggested another nuclear poisoning.

A rapid debate over the radios followed. Get all guests out? Get the Russians out? Kane couldn't risk blowing the whole operation; he couldn't risk the death by nuclear poison of several hundred elite guests either.

'Who's carrying it?' Kane asked.

'Strongest readings around Nechaev,' the lead Special Forces officer confirmed. 'He's got an object in the right pocket of his jacket, hip-flask size. He's reached in there several times.'

Kane had seen the studies from military toxicologists in the wake of Litvinenko: one gram of polonium-210 could be enough to kill fifty million people. It did so through provoking what they called cell suicide, spreading through the body, destroying your very DNA.

237

Isolate him, Kane thought.

He had replayed the following moments again and again over the years, without ever determining how exactly things must have unfolded. The house was chaos to operate in: dark, loud, filled with bodies.

'I managed to steer Nechaev briefly away from people,' Kane told Bell. 'I said one of his friends was in trouble and needed to speak to him. I had a knife with me. There were double doors that led from the main party room to a hallway and I got him through those and closed the doors. One of my team, a Special Forces officer, was waiting. He got Nechaev's arms and we dragged him into a room at the side, one of the bedrooms. Then I saw Rebecca.'

It was loud throughout the house, music and voices. Kane remembered assessing the volume as they forced Nechaev into the room: *loud enough. The black room's soundproofed.* The Special Forces officer was armed, but Kane wanted to avoid discharging weapons, even ones fitted with silencers. He had no idea how many of these calculations were woven into memory retrospectively, embroidering what had been sheer panic and instinct. When he later sat down and tried to establish a timeline, he estimated that the whole thing must have taken less than two minutes.

'This is what I think happened. Rebecca was in there already. She was sitting at a dressing table. I think she'd been crying, her make-up was streaked. But we didn't see her until we were inside with Nechaev. The room was kept low-lit, black sheets, black furniture. By the time we saw Rebecca it was too late. We had Nechaev on the ground. But this is the bit that I've never understood. She came over. She didn't even seem fazed. I told her to stay away, but she tried to grab the knife and do it herself, to kill him. It was crazy. Then I thought I saw Nechaev going for the polonium and we finished the job. And then it was a question of what to do with Rebecca.'

'Hang on. You "finished the job". What does that mean?'

'We killed him. I cut his throat.'

He said the words while trying not to dwell on them. He didn't want to think about that moment. Kane remembered his relief at getting Nechaev into the bedroom, away from the other guests, and then seeing that it was already occupied. Momentary relief again when he recognised Rebecca – at least it was someone he could control. Except he couldn't. At some point she must have bitten the Russian's hand. He'd seen the teeth marks sunk deep into the man's skin.

Bell had stopped writing.

'You murdered him.'

'If you want to put it that way.'

'What happened then?'

'We cleaned ourselves up. I arranged to move the body. I told Rebecca to wait, but she didn't. At some point she slipped off. Hence the report. I don't know where she went.'

'The party continued.'

'Everything had to continue.'

Kane saw Rebecca's hands in his own. He remembered being grateful that the room was en suite, with a tasteless black marble sink and gold taps. He had to hold her hands under the taps as she began to shake. *Nothing's going to happen to you.* Telling her to fix her make-up, searching for the polonium and finding nothing. Starting to realise what was later confirmed: minute traces had triggered a false alarm. But his immediate concern was how they could transport Nechaev's body to the caterer's van that the Special Forces had equipped for this eventuality.

'What about the other Russians?' Bell said.

'We faked an arrest on the guard outside, the one waiting in the BMW. The man who had accompanied Nechaev into the house was bundled into one of our vehicles. They were both taken away.'

'And killed.'

'Yes.'

Kane got up, momentarily exhausted, poured himself a whisky to wake up, and then one for Bell. He stayed by the bottles for a moment, remembering. London that night had never looked so vivid, glistening like entrails. Rain had polished the streets to a reflective shine, and all the neon shimmered in the ground. Men and women launched themselves into the world, holding one another, falling into 2009.

Kane remembered driving with Staff Sergeant Terry Ashman in their caterer's-van-turned-hearse, trying to avoid police. At that moment, London felt more alien than Grozny or Aleppo. In foreign cities you knew you were going to leave; they gave you cover, nothing was quite real anyway. But not London. It felt like killing someone in your own home. Seeing the Christmas lights reminded him of visiting Oxford Street as a child, seeing the crowds and wondering if he would ever look as purposeful. And here he was, transporting a still-warm corpse through the revelry.

Where had Rebecca gone? That was the question that grew in significance as a new day dawned. Rebecca, who had just become the closest of acquaintances, who had shared the intimacy of murder. Her phone was off. At around 5 a.m. Kane drove past her home, but she wasn't in.

He returned to Eaton Square around six. They'd managed to wind the party down, empty the house. The fantasy had turned putrid: wine spilled, drugs on the floor, broken glass in the jacuzzi. Someone's Versace jacket had been used to wipe up lubricant. And that smell: the lingering cigarette smoke and sulphurous firework gunpowder; the perfumes of the women and the briny hum of the Beluga caviar.

Kane arranged the MI6 cleaners. There were those who attended to the physical clean – their anti-forensics team – who told him there was a limit to what they could achieve now blood had been spilled. Blood could never be 100 per cent erased. And then those who scrubbed the other traces: parking records, CCTV, mobile phone data. A remarkable job, with one loose end.

He had visions of Rebecca running around London, sequinned, bloodied. Christian had gone on to a New Year's Day breakfast at a private club in Soho. Kane found him on the rooftop with two models in evening dress. Gas flames flickered in pyramid-shaped heaters. Everyone was giddy with exclusivity. But when Kane summoned him away from the crowd, Christian looked drawn.

'Are they dead?' he asked.

'Yes.'

'All of them?'

'Yes.'

'Congratulations.' And then, seeing Kane's face: 'It's a war, Elliot. The world's a better place now.'

'Any idea where Rebecca went?'

'No. I thought I saw her leave the house around two, or two thirty. Why?'

'Was she alone?'

'Yes, I think so. But I wasn't sure if she was just getting some air or something. She didn't have a coat. That's why I noticed her. Why?'

'She was there when we killed Nechaev.'

'Seriously?' Christian groaned. 'How did that happen?'

'I don't know.'

'How did she react?'

'She was shocked, of course. But she was already drugged to the eyeballs. We need to find her before she talks to someone.'

'You think she'd do that?'

'I don't know. I would, if I was her.'

They agreed to stay in touch. Meanwhile, Broughton invited

Kane to the Foreign Office Building on King Charles Street, to toast their success. Kane stepped down Whitehall at 10 a.m. on 1 January, through the river of bottles and cans that flowed from Trafalgar Square. He was met by a security guard at the side entrance and led inside, through the stale Victorian grandeur to the Locarno Suite.

The room was vast, with a barrel-vaulted ceiling and marble fireplaces. Named for the Treaty of Locarno, Kane assumed, the one that was meant to bring peace to Europe after World War I. Was that why the room felt sad? A suite for a failure? Broughton arrived carrying champagne and two glasses. It was the only time Kane saw him smile. The champagne tasted bitter.

'One of the girls is AWOL,' Kane said. 'Rebecca Nolan. She was with me when it happened. I think she's in a bad way.'

'I heard. I've not had any suggestion that she's caused us problems yet. We'll find her, don't worry. How do *you* feel?' he asked Kane. It seemed an odd question from Broughton, and Kane struggled to answer honestly.

'I feel like I want to finish the job,' Kane said. He remembered hearing his own voice, its willed determination, its suppression of anxiety. 'There are other key members of the Unit still out there, internationally. We said we'd damage them so they couldn't operate again.' He wanted an end to it all – that's what he was feeling and this seemed to be the way to reach it: more bloodshed.

'There is time,' Broughton said. 'They're in our sights. They're not getting away.'

'There won't be much time now.'

'We'll move fast.'

The disinformation op over the next few days was Broughton's finest hour. Two of the Russians were found naked together in a hotel room, another floating in the Thames. Broughton flooded intelligence channels with rumours that the men had been planning to defect, that they had information they wanted to exchange in return for UK citizenship. It looked like a series of Russian-on-Russian hits. He initiated a hunt for the mole who must have exposed them, accused the Kremlin of killing their own citizens where they had sought refuge. Obviously, the Kremlin couldn't disclose the true mission of the three victims. Checkmate.

Kane remembered the buzz in the office the following Monday. People shook his hand. The fightback had started. Those hostile to Broughton's methods stayed quiet, uninvited to the celebration, but they had to acknowledge the mission's audacity. Kane reminded himself of the lives saved: not just those who would have died at the hands of Unit 22195 but the bigger context, the doctrine of casual assassinations that they had surely stopped in its tracks. He had placed a spanner in the works of a killing machine. That was what he believed at the time.

On 3 January, Kane got confirmation from the surveillance team that Rebecca was alive and well. She'd been staying with her family, they said, but had shown no desire to speak about what happened. She still didn't answer Kane's calls, and maybe that was for the best, he thought. Opening the newspaper a year later and seeing her marriage to Robert Sinclair it felt strangely as if he had been right when he suspected suicide. She had ended her life and begun a new one. And there was a strange satisfaction to be had in the fact of having indirectly introduced her to the MP; that his creation of Opula meant their paths had crossed. Three funerals and a wedding. It wasn't everyday he proved a successful matchmaker.

A week after the killings, the bodies of the three Russian men were flown on a charter flight to Moscow. MI6 watched carefully for a response; security was heightened on all active officers and agents. But nothing happened. The perfect crime is one no one wants to talk about.

But Kane talked about it now. He led Bell through the rationale behind Halcyon, the legal clearance. He told her about Rebecca Nolan. When he'd finished, she took a long time thinking through it all. He could see her deciding what to say.

'It is extra-judicial killing,' she said, 'however you frame it. I'm trying to see this dispassionately.'

'Loosely speaking.'

Bell turned to her laptop and began googling. Eventually she clicked through to a Russian news website. It showed headshots of the three men they'd killed, taken from family photographs, looking a lot younger than they'd been when they died: Stanislav Vitsenko, Fyodor Taktorov, Grigoriy Nechaev.

'Is this them?'

'Yes.'

'What does it say?' she asked. 'You read Russian.'

'It says they were buried with military honours. There was a medal ceremony. Russia's launched a murder inquiry but is complaining that British authorities are refusing to pass on crucial evidence. Families of the dead men have been paid some money by the Russian government. One of their mothers thinks it's insufficient.'

Kane looked across the faces of the men, then those of their grieving families at the ceremony. He heard Christian's voice: *It's a war, Elliot.*

'What happened to this concierge front?' Bella asked. 'Opula? The one that initiated the party?'

'It was eventually moved out of our hands. Sold. I think it survived under new management until the recent sanctions.'

'But a lot of the material being released now connects.'

'Yes.'

'You're very exposed here,' Bell said. 'Like, prison exposed.'

'Possibly, possibly not. The Intelligence Services Act allows MI6 to engage in various tasks on top of spying. It protects

244

officers from prosecution, so long as what they were doing was authorised. And can you imagine the government putting SAS soldiers on trial for protecting the UK?'

'I missed the declaration of war.'

'There was a judicial finding of state-sponsored terrorism on behalf of Russia. Behind closed doors, obviously. But that gave us some legal room to manoeuvre.'

'The government signed off a kill list?'

'An operation.'

'But you had named targets.'

'Not formally.'

'Did anyone have qualms about all this?'

'It wasn't a widespread discussion. I don't remember all the details,' he lied.

'Elliot, the details determine whether you're facing a murder charge.' Bell looked away and he saw that she was holding back tears.

'You've got backing to write an article? Lawyers?'

'How do you know?' she asked.

'I hear things. Be careful, but keep going, that's what I wanted to say. I need you to. Ask me questions.'

Bell cleared her throat.

'When did you last speak to Rebecca Sinclair?'

'That night. I've thought about her over the years, considered getting in touch. To apologise.'

'For what?'

'Putting her in a situation that wasn't a nice one and shouldn't have arisen. I'm glad she got away, established a new life for herself. That's what I always thought.'

Kane turned back to the papers that had been left in the woods. 'You can see why I think Eclipse is revenge of some kind. In terms of me, of us, this memo is one of the most destructive, sensitive things he could show you. It implicates me directly.

It's personal. Eclipse has targeted too many people involved in Halcyon for it to be coincidence.'

'Yes, I can see that.'

'But they're showing us something more.'

'What do you mean?'

Kane lifted the final page of the report.

'According to this, Rebecca went to the police. I've never heard anything about that. No one ever told me there was any contact between Rebecca and the police in the aftermath of what happened. And it says her family were looking for her. I didn't know that either. I was told the opposite: that she had been with them following the killing, when I thought she was missing.'

Kane read the written account again.

'There's a request here to the police, regarding the destruction of any records pertaining to Eaton Square. It's got my signature, but I've never seen that request before.'

Bell came over and read it beside him.

'Think it's genuine?'

'Yes. Eclipse knows something I don't. Contact him again, thank him for this. Say you want to know more about what happened that night.'

Bell typed: *Thank you for the information. I now realise the full significance of what you have to reveal, and the precautions I will need to take. Let me know if you are still willing to work together.*

Kane added: *I am going to ensure you are amply compensated for the inconvenience this courageous action will bring you. It is clear you have a story of international and historical importance.*

He opened his laptop, went into the Coinbase cryptocurrency exchange and bought fifty grand's worth of Bitcoin using the funds in their Atlantic Bank account. Then he sent them to Eclipse.

And that was that. They were in his hands. *I know more about your life than you know yourself.* He was right. Kane saw Rebecca's eyes in the black room, glimmering; several Rebeccas, broken into individual selves around the mirrored walls. Why was she crying? There was no shortage of explanations, and so he had never sought one.

Kane checked news updates on Eclipse. No progress as far as he could see. Bell began typing. Over her shoulder, he read an email to a *Guardian* journalist, Michael De Souza:

Mike, it's been too long, and now we're in the midst of a porn apocalypse. I've been chasing things and wanted to pick your brains. You once asked me if I'd come across Opula …

Kane stood behind her, but he felt Bell's breath on his own neck, coming at him from his past. And his instinct was to let her research, to excavate the truth, scoop it all out, as if this would supply the honesty he was yet to provide himself.

He went out to the garden and called Christian. His former colleague answered amid laughter.

'Can you speak?' Kane asked.

'I can speak. I may slur.'

'Eclipse knows something about that New Year's Eve.'

'What do you mean?'

'He's supplied us with MI6 documents about Rebecca Sinclair that don't tally with what I know of events.'

'Really?' The laughter faded as Christian moved somewhere quieter. He sounded more sober too.

'Broughton ever talk to you about it?' Kane asked.

'About what?'

'Rebecca, the forty-eight hours after the party, what happened to her.'

'Yes, but I thought you were the one overseeing it all.'

'Overseeing what?'

'What happened to Rebecca.'

'What do you mean?'

A door opened somewhere near Christian. Laughter blew out like a gust of wind.

247

'I can't hear you very well, Elliot. And my phone's dying. I promise you, if you don't know about this, I won't.'

'It sounds like you know something.'

'Well, that would be a first.'

'Overseeing what?'

'The cool-down, or whatever you call it.'

'Christian, where are you? I need to speak to you.'

'Well, come and speak to me, Elliot. Buy me a drink while you're at it. You won't believe where I am, and it hasn't changed a bit.'

TWENTY-THREE

Two uniformed officers walked into Rebecca's home, a man and a woman, nervous, radioing for police and ambulance support as soon as they saw the body.

'What happened? Who did this?'

'I don't know. Someone broke into the house.'

'Do you know where they are now?'

Rebecca shook her head. She saw the dance of their gazes around the room: the curtains, the whisky bottle, the knife on the ground. She felt the first knot of anguish and dispossession spreading across her chest.

'Are you injured?'

'No.'

'Can you step towards us, away from the body?' The male officer had severe acne, which made him seem more adolescent than he was. His female partner was shorter but more robust, her stare intense. Rebecca became aware of sirens in every direction, beyond Christmas Common and north of Watlington, growing louder. She realised she had to say something else, and whatever she said would determine much of what happened next.

'Eclipse,' she said.

'Eclipse?'

'The man on the news – he's been blackmailing me. I'm sure it was him. He was wearing a balaclava. He was in the house. I sprayed him with wasp spray and ran.'

The explanation didn't sound as helpful or sane as she'd hoped.

'How long ago was this?' the man asked.

'Maybe half an hour. I'm not sure.'

'Any idea which way he went?'

Rebecca shook her head. 'I left him here. I ran, then stopped a car – Neil and Patty from the post office. They were the ones who called you. He was gone when I got back.'

'Know if the attacker had a car?'

'Maybe. I didn't see it, though.'

'Can you describe him in any more detail?'

'About your height.'

'Black? White?'

'White.'

The woman began to radio through these details. A police car pulled up outside and all the windows flashed blue.

'My daughter—' Rebecca began. This got a look of alarm from the officers.

'Is she here?'

'She's with Robert's parents.'

'Okay.'

'I need to get to her.'

'Yes.'

They led her out of the home entirely. Two more police cars and an ambulance had arrived. Ahead, up the darkened road, she could see someone beginning to tie police tape to a fence.

Rebecca was handed over to the paramedics, a pair of efficient-looking men who encouraged her to sit inside their ambulance.

'I haven't been hurt.'

'Just precautionary, check you over.'

'I need my phone.'

'Where is it?'

'In the house.'

'It will be part of the crime scene now. Is there someone in particular you'd like to contact?'

'My daughter.'

'We'll make sure that happens.'

They left the ambulance doors open. She could see more and more people sweeping in: specialist homicide teams and forensic officers. There was a strange beauty to it, like a well-functioning machine, everyone knowing their role.

And what was her role?

She was conscious of shock beginning to encase her. Don't let it close in yet, she thought. She needed to remain in some form of control. She wasn't safe.

The Borough Commander appeared, marching from his car, pulling on his cap.

'Rebecca, what happened?' Behind him, Firearms and Territorial Support Group vans screeched to a halt and armed officers climbed out. Meanwhile, the forensics investigators were pulling on protective suits, creating a team of white among the black combat uniforms.

Rebecca got out of the ambulance, to reclaim some stature, but her legs were weak.

'A man,' Rebecca said. 'He got into the house ... '

An officer with an assault rifle approach out of the darkness. He was striking: over six foot three, with silver stubble against brown skin, eyes alert, enhanced by conspicuously long eyelashes. He stared at Rebecca, and remained fixated on her as he spoke to the Commander. The question, it seemed, was whether this was to be classed as an act of terrorism. The classification determined who was in charge, and Rebecca sensed that she herself was a significant factor in making that decision.

The counter-terrorism officer angled his gun away.

'Did you see anything to suggest the suspect's still inside?'

'No.'

'Any kind of device?'

'No.'

'Bag with them?'

She shook her head. Evidently he had no time for the rigmarole of sympathy. She appreciated that. He was all mission.

'You said something about Eclipse, to the first attenders.'

'He was blackmailing me. I think this is him. I threatened to expose him. He knew where I lived.'

The man nodded, but the expression in his eyes didn't change, as if he was computing a million possibilities and this barely grazed them. She was released back to the paramedics. They asked about her vision, any dizziness, felt tenderly along the bones of her face. She remembered the blow from Robert's elbow. A strange souvenir to leave her, the wrong memory, confusing the sense of loss that had begun to bite, the idealisation of grief, the incomprehensible reality of his not existing any more.

'Is he dead?' Rebecca asked. It was bizarre hearing herself, in the voice she used for dealing with unhelpful customer service advisers. *Excuse me, could someone please tell me if my husband has been stabbed to death?*

'Yes,' they said.

And all their voices and lights in her garden. Someone had got the security gates open. Her home was rinsed in waves of flashing blue. Only it wasn't her home any more, it had been requisitioned by homicide.

Target is around six foot tall, dark clothing ...

House is clear.

My last message to Eclipse, Rebecca thought, the mention of Opula, Eaton Square – it had spooked him. She connected him to those parties and he hit back. Again, she heard that voice: *Don't be stupid.*

She was the one he had wanted dead.

A helicopter hovered in the night air. She craned her neck to see it, its searchlight combing the woods as if what happened connected to some evil that had its home among the trees. People were watching her, Rebecca knew, but when she met their eyes they looked away.

Eventually they put her in the back of an unmarked Škoda. In the front, dutifully buckling up, was the Commander and a woman with jet black hair who introduced herself as Detective Inspector Kelly Anderson, from the Major Crime Unit. They said they were going to Aylesbury Police Station.

It was a half-hour drive east, along the edge of the Chiltern Hills, which had gathered under the cover of paying their respects to steal a last glimpse of her. Down narrow, unlit country roads for the most part, where the silenced blue lights made the whole world seem mute, every sullen field and overhanging tree caught up in the crisis.

Radios cracked endlessly, announcing nothing: *Watlington checked, Benson and Stadhampton clear; blocks set up on the M40. No indication from the helicopter's thermal camera. Traffic camera footage collected; dashcam checked.*

No sightings, no witnesses.

Rebecca understood that with every negative report her significance in the back seat grew; the world of possibilities was being whittled down. Twice, DI Anderson lowered the volume of her radio set as if it was giving the game away.

Most of the local police stations had been closed in the last few years. The political drama of these closures had forced itself into her domestic life. Aylesbury had been earmarked for the same fate, and it was Robert himself who had achieved a quiet stay of execution. 'Cost me brownie points with the Home Office,' he had grumbled. And here it was, three storeys of ugly brown bricks, looking like sheltered council accommodation, saved to serve as Major Incident Control Room for his murder. Rebecca got the feeling that it didn't see many homicides.

A small crowd had already gathered outside, people chatting amiably to the uniformed officers on the front steps. It was only as they drove past and Rebecca saw a camera flash that she realised who they were.

She was strangely calm. Calm enough to make a mental note not to seem too calm. As they passed a mirror on the wall of reception, she caught a glimpse of herself and was shocked by her black eye, which was surfacing like a false confession, gaining a silky, luxurious sheen.

A whole other team had begun assembling here at base camp. Several officers offered condolences as she was led into a side room with comfy chairs and a box of tissues. Who would she like to phone, someone asked. Her parents? She could imagine their response, the news of Robert's murder awful but also part of the strange fate that had been laid upon them the day she was chosen. 'No,' she said. Robert's parents, of course, were on the road, heading this way; on the road to incomprehension and heartbreak. And where was Iona? Not contactable right now.

'Iona's fine, and we understand it's your priority seeing her. Leave that to us.'

But who would break the news to her? She was fatherless. Half-orphaned. Rebecca was all she had now. Who would try to explain, and what would the girl understand by it? By murder? These were not questions due to be answered at this moment in time, it seemed.

Anderson and the Commander disappeared and Rebecca was briefly alone, then Anderson reappeared. With her, to Rebecca's surprise, was the tall counter-terrorism officer with the eyelashes. He had removed his bulletproof outer layers and was unarmed, as if she had met him first in a dream and here

254

was the reality out of which she had concocted such a ridiculous vision.

They pulled up chairs across from her. Anderson, Rebecca saw now, was her own age, in a navy trouser suit she recognised as Jigsaw. The black hair was surely dyed. She had pretty green eyes, which didn't detract from an air of tough competence. She asked if Rebecca had been offered water, tea, adequate medical attention, all the time studying her face as you might watch a window to see the weather changing.

'I'm going to be one of the lead investigators on your husband's murder,' she said, once assured of Rebecca's comfort.

'My name's Mohammed Nasser, from Counter Terrorism,' the man said. Both had notes of some kind, and Rebecca felt bare without any. 'Can we call you Rebecca?'

'Yes.'

'Rebecca, I wanted to say how sorry I am about your loss,' Anderson said. 'I know how hard this must be.' The DI stared at her, unblinking. 'I know words won't be adequate for what you're going through right now, but all I can do is promise that we're putting everything into finding the person who did this.'

Rebecca admired the act: those who deal with extremes of experience and learn their humanity like a script.

'Thank you,' Rebecca said.

It was explained to her that they'd established a command chain. Due to Robert's importance, and the extensive public and political interest in the case, it was to be led by Chief Superintendent Roger Ledbury, the overall head of Major Investigations, but the nitty-gritty would fall to DI Kelly Anderson and her team. Ledbury would manage the politicians; Anderson would oversee the investigation on the ground. Rebecca was reassured that hundreds of officers were crawling around the Chilterns, that the PM was due to be briefed any minute now. The police force's Intelligence Unit was keeping an eye on terrorist channels. No footage or claims had surfaced online yet, not by Islamists, not by right-wing extremists. Rebecca idly imagined the excitement in Westminster. Everyone would want in on this: Number 10, Home Office, Police Commissioner. It was a big opportunity.

Then Anderson produced a tape recorder and Rebecca realised they were to get down to business.

'It would be very helpful if I could ask you a few questions now, to clarify what you saw.'

'I understand.'

'Do you mind if I record this? So we don't miss anything?' Anderson placed her dictaphone beside the tissues.

'I don't mind.'

Anderson pressed record.

'This is Detective Inspector Kelly Anderson, interviewing Rebecca Sinclair, pertaining to the murder of Robert Sinclair. We're at Aylesbury Police Station. It's 2.20 a.m. on Monday 18 July. With me is Sergeant Mohammed Nasser. To confirm, Mrs Sinclair: you're not under arrest, you're free to leave at any time, and you don't need to make a statement now if you're not ready, but you understand the consequences of making a false statement. You're fully entitled to have a lawyer present. Do you have any questions?'

'No.'

'Can you confirm you're happy to proceed without legal representation? And that you've given us permission to ask you some questions and to record this interview?'

Rebecca nodded.

'Are you able to consent out loud?'

'Yes, I consent.'

'Rebecca, it would be very helpful if you could describe in as much detail as possible what happened. I realise this is upsetting, but there might be something that helps us catch this person, so take your time.'

She described the sequence of events as precisely as possible, from hearing the sound of a body falling to the arrival of police, initially keeping it simple. The hard facts. That was what they liked, she knew.

'I had a knife,' she said at the appropriate moment. She said it quickly, clearly. 'That was the knife on the floor when the police arrived. I brought it downstairs with me but dropped it in the garden.'

'Right,' Anderson said. 'Where do you usually keep this knife?'

'It was in my handbag. I bought it to protect myself, when I first thought I might meet Eclipse.'

She told them about Eclipse, the blackmail. 'But you won't find trace on my phone. The messages disappear.'

And suddenly it became very clear what he'd done. The trap clicked shut.

'When did you buy this knife?'

'Recently.'

'How recently?'

'The day before yesterday. At a camping shop in Central London.'

'Do you think Robert had already been stabbed when you first encountered the attacker?'

'No.'

'But he was on the floor.'

'Yes.'

'Did you notice any blood on the attacker?'

'No.'

Nasser sat back, puzzled. Then he leaned forward again.

'You reported concerns about someone who might have been watching the house a few nights ago,' he said. His eyes, she had noticed, held a glint of mischief that he tried to tame into seriousness. She imagined the camaraderie of Counter Terrorism: men and guns; a thirst for action, for the clear-cut. 'Did Robert's security guards find anything?'

'No.'

'Had Robert mentioned any threats?'

'No, not to me.'

Nasser nodded.

'Let's go back to a bit earlier in the evening,' Anderson suggested. 'I know several people were at your home before this all happened.'

Rebecca talked them through that, brutally honest: arriving home, seeing them, hearing the video.

'And then there was a call.' Anderson checked her notes. 'At around midnight, from Robert to his parents.'

The investigation had moved fast, Rebecca realised. She wondered if it was possible to move faster than the truth.

'Yes. That was after they'd gone.'

'Robert's mother heard something, something that made Robert end the call abruptly.'

'He caught my eye with his elbow.'

'I see.'

'It was an accident.'

'But you must have been upset about it.'

'I was generally upset. It was, as you can imagine, quite an upsetting evening.'

Anderson nodded and became silent again. Rebecca imagined her realising, long ago, this was her weapon. An interview is erosion. Truth was what you were left with when everything else crumbled away. Friends and family will have told her she was too quiet for the police, but it was silence people hanged themselves with.

'What happened after you'd run?' the detective asked, eventually.

'I went into the woods at first, then back to the road and raised the alarm. Then I went back into the house.'

'Why go back in?'

'To save Robert.'

'Weren't you scared?'

'I don't know. All I know is that I had to see Robert. I had to go back.'

'And what did you find?'

'Him. What you saw.'

'I know this is difficult. Can you describe it as clearly as possible?'

'Robert had been stabbed. He was on the floor. He'd been stabbed a lot.' Rebecca was very conscious of her steady voice and dry eyes.

'With your knife,' Anderson said.

'That was my assumption.'

'Has he ever hit you before?'

'No.'

'Did you drink last night?'

'No.'

'Was Robert drunk?'

'Yes.'

She tried to tell them about Opula, and Eclipse, and how they might connect. But she didn't know, and her teeth had begun chattering. She was shivering now, struggling to get the words out. Anderson regarded this with an almost-sympathetic expression. She leaned forward until she was in touching distance.

'Rebecca, I can understand you're going through a lot right now – more than anyone should have to deal with. No one is expected to go through this alone. Can I be honest?'

Rebecca nodded.

'I see everyone gathered around you, your marriage, the spotlight you live under. Your husband was an important, public figure, and all that must make it incredibly difficult for you to talk about what you've been put through. But people would understand. I'm a homicide detective; one thing I've learned is that people need to speak to someone. Look at me, Rebecca. A lot of what happens from this point on will depend on how honest you are with us. I want to help you *whatever* happened last night. But I need you to help me. Do you understand? Because there's no way you can keep it all inside.'

Was this it? The exquisite double injustice of losing a loved one and then being cast as their killer. The thought was exhausting. And Eclipse still out there.

'I've told you.'

The police officers nodded and relaxed their posture, as if some conclusion had been reached. Rebecca felt as if she'd failed a test. Nasser remained bright-eyed, amused, watching her face as if a sniper's bead was dancing across it. Anderson gathered her papers and straightened them.

'Okay. Thanks, Rebecca. I'm sure we'll have more to talk about soon, but right now we're going to take some samples from you, before you shower or anything. We'll need your clothes as well, but we'll make sure you have replacements. Does that sound all right?'

'Of course,' she said.

The first daylight was knocking on the station's dirty windows when they led her out, along a short corridor to a brighter room where a female forensics officer greeted Rebecca, snapping on gloves.

A sense of déjà vu became more pronounced with every step.

'We're going to take a few bits and pieces from you,' she said, 'Mostly to assist in the process of elimination.' She went on to explain that, by this, she meant eliminating Rebecca from any other results they retrieved, but the word caught in Rebecca's agitated mind. Eliminate entirely? Was innocence elimination, and only guilt that made us present? She lay down. The light hurt her eyes.

Her déjà vu came to a point.

Perhaps because she was about to be eliminated they took mementoes. From under her fingernails, her hair, her skin. The blood on her skin was removed so carefully it might have been gold. The technician worked with the patience of someone restoring frescoes. And Rebecca was transported back to the white room of her post-traumatic flashbacks: New Year's morning, the fluorescent light above her. It wasn't an operation, she thought now, not a hospital at all. It was in the police station. They weren't doctors, they were forensics officers like this one.

Samples were taken.

When it was all done, Nasser and Anderson appeared, politely deferential again, as if any accusations of being a murderer remained in the small room with the tissues.

'We'll need you back in a bit to chat some more. Where would you like to go in the meantime? We can suggest a hotel nearby. Now we've got the samples you can shower, freshen up. Your parents are already there.'

'My parents?'

'And I know Robert's people are very concerned and want to offer their full support. They'll want to check in on you.'

Dumbly, and because for the moment she couldn't think what other courses of action were open to her, Rebecca went along with this. A hotel, a recommendation, yes. Once she'd acquiesced, the officers reverted to business mode.

'There's quite a crowd outside now. Let's leave via the back. We've got an unmarked van we can use. Blacked-out windows.'

The blacked-out windows seemed a good idea. Still, as the van left the station, Rebecca heard cameras click, saw flashes flash.

Her parents. That was bizarre. When she entered the Premier Inn, they were the only people present: her father rooting around a coffee machine in the darkened restaurant, her mother stiffly, fretfully, in an armchair at the side of reception. The hotel was joyless, indestructible, hermetically sealed. And temporarily unstaffed, it seemed. Her police chaperone went to try and rustle up a receptionist.

Rebecca knew there would not be condolences as such from her mother or father, not for the loss of a son-in-law who had never seemed entirely real to them. She hadn't been entirely braced for their hostility, though.

'Becky,' her mother said. 'Oh my God.'

'Mother.'

'What on earth is going on, sweetheart?'

'Robert was stabbed.'

'What happened?' her father asked, marching out of the restaurant's shadows with an empty coffee cup.

What happened, she thought. Where to start?

'Do you remember me coming home after New Year's 2009? I'd been missing for some time.'

Her father's face scrunched into a frown.

'What?'

'We got sent some troubling things yesterday, Becky,' her mother said. 'Your father wondered if it's connected.'

'And now we've had police asking us about them, about you,' he said. 'About Robert.'

'You've spoken to the police?'

'What on earth were those videos?'

'You were sent videos?'

'Are they real?' her mother said. 'You wouldn't do that.'

'What would you say if they *were* real?' she asked, cold curiosity slicing through the dismay.

'Oh, Becky,' her father sighed. 'What have you done now, you silly girl?'

A receptionist was unearthed and bestowed upon them a grey plastic key card. They went up to their room. Rebecca looked around the cigarette-burned carpet, the view through shatterproof glass over the hotel car park to Aylesbury train station. She couldn't be here, not with her parents; it was like she'd been buried alive and they were in the coffin with her. And Robert's people on their way. She couldn't bear to think what that would involve.

Her mother lay down on the bed. Her father tossed his jacket beside her. Rebecca watched him enter the small bathroom and regard himself in the mirror, alert to signs of his ever-deeper humiliation. He saw her watching and closed the door.

'Is there a kettle?' her mother asked.

Rebecca took her father's car keys and phone from his jacket.

'I'll be back in a second,' she said.

A heatwave sun had mounted the sky above Aylesbury. The circus was in town. Four broadcasting vans sat beside the green, blocking the village centre, along with half a dozen satellite trucks and a row of people carriers with open-sided canopies crammed with sound equipment, TV monitors and lights.

A queue had formed outside the one café – The Railway Tea Shop – which had opened early, men and women with phones glued to their ears. Rebecca drove past them fast, in her father's Peugeot, heading to the M40, the chemicals from the forensic swabs still tingling on her skin.

Samples.

If she was right – if Eclipse was the man who had attacked her fifteen years ago – then the fact she'd received forensic attention after the event gained a whole new level of significance. She had already caught him once, perhaps, within the very ridges of her body. *Samples were taken.* What happened to those?

TWENTY-FOUR

Three a.m. at the Clermont Club, Berkeley Square. If Mayfair had a grey, clogged heart, this was it: a private gambling club in a Grade I listed mansion including restaurants, a dance floor, a theatrical staircase and Grand Saloon. Former members ranged from Lord Lucan to Lucian Freud, and the atmosphere fell somewhere between the two. You could toss away your family's fortune on baccarat or blackjack, punto banco or roulette, and do so in the historic Club Room or Pavilion Rooms or on the smoking terrace itself. The bored, the spoiled, the desperate; chandeliers and thick carpets. Christian was right, it hadn't changed, with all the ambience of an out-of-season hotel, its season being the 1960s. Yet it was soothing. Nothing real could happen here, and even bankruptcy was painless as a dream.

Christian stood at one of the raised tables, clutching a champagne flute. He was in a group of six men, all expensively dressed. Christian rattled casino chips in one hand while someone told an anecdote. There was a cigar in his top pocket. When Kane got there, Christian introduced him as 'my brother', to more laughter. He was coked up. Everyone was drunk.

'Shall we go smoke that cigar?' Kane said.

They wandered off to the terrace.

'Remember this place?' Christian said.

'Hard to forget.'

'When were we last here, do you reckon?' he said.

'August 2008.'

'I only stopped for a shower. Lucy Piper says we should do the interview tomorrow morning, before anyone can turn us into pariahs. I spoke to Broughton. This Juliet Bell situation isn't going away. And half of those videos out there are from Opula parties, no injunction will hold. Have you seen the *Mail*? Notorious party mansion, that's what they're calling it, 62 Eaton Square. They're going to dig until they get to more than they expected.'

Through the windows, a screen on news: *military on high alert. Five thousand officers hunt Eclipse.*

'What a mess,' Christian said. He clicked a lighter and held the flame to the end of the cigar until it glowed.

'It's New Year's Eve I need to talk to you about.'

'So you said.'

'Someone I know got shown classified MI6 documents that talk about Rebecca Sinclair going to the police. I never knew anything about that. What's this cooling down you mentioned? What do you know?'

'I know someone raped her.'

It hit Kane from the side, slamming in out of the blue, out of his blind spot.

'Really?'

'You told me she'd gone AWOL. I didn't trust her. I went to Broughton, said what the fuck is going on. He told me it was under control.'

'He said someone had raped her?'

'Not in so many words. She'd gone to the police about some harassment, something like that. Someone had got heavy-handed. It was clear what he was talking about. Which meant obviously we had a problem – you can imagine, the police start pulling on a thread ... ' Christian puffed on the cigar, exhaled a thick cloud of smoke.

'Tell me exactly what Broughton said.'

'She had had contact with the police. Broughton managed to persuade her to leave the police station. Obviously, there'd just been the situation with you and her and Nechaev . . . '

'Did you ever get any sense of who attacked her?'

'No.'

'Any guesses?'

'There were more than a hundred people at that party. If they were well-behaved, pleasant people they wouldn't have been there.'

'Who did you see her with?'

'Everyone. You know how it went. Around 1 a.m. she was with two guys; I think one was a military chief, one was the Home Secretary's adviser.'

'So what did Broughton do?'

'Looked after her,' he said. 'She was held somewhere.'

'Held?'

'I don't know.'

'Held where?'

'A safe house. One of the coolers.'

The thought made Kane's stomach turn. MI6 maintained premises for activity they needed to keep out of HQ: interrogations, sensitive debriefs. Room 40, they called it. There were a handful of Room 40s across London.

'You never mentioned this to me?'

'Elliot, I was told it was on your instruction. I was the one who shouldn't have known about it. Broughton only told me because I was making my own threats of walking, turning my back on the whole thing.'

'Broughton was nowhere near Eaton Square that night,' Kane said.

'No. But he must have come in when he heard Rebecca was freaking out.'

'What were they doing to her in these facilities?'

'Keeping her quiet, I assumed.'

'A pay-off?'

'Pay-off, or just made aware of the extent to which she was implicated in a killing, that she could go to the police but it would mean spending the next decade behind bars. She was an accomplice. If she went to anyone, spoke about anything, there was nothing we could do to protect her from prosecution. That kind of thing. Bullshit, of course. But, as far as I'm aware, it worked.'

'I didn't know about any of this.'

'That wasn't the impression I was given.'

Kane thought of his meeting with Broughton in the Locarno Suite. No later than 10 a.m., which meant he must have come straight from wherever Rebecca was being held.

'Why do you think Broughton never told me?'

'Because you have a moral compass. Broughton never trusted you. He loved you, because he knew, if you believed in the cause, you'd do things other officers wouldn't. But he didn't trust you. And he knew you liked Rebecca. Did you ever fuck her?'

Kane stared through the windows at the gaming tables, head spinning. Christian laid a hand on his shoulder, offered the cigar.

'This TV interview,' he said.

'I'm not doing an interview.'

'I really wish you'd consider it. It's your story to tell. What am I in all this? Someone following you around, doing what they're told. It's the same feeling I've had since uni. I'm in your wake. You're doing what you want, and I get capsized.'

'Go home, Christian. Speak to your wife.'

'Say what?'

'Maybe sorry. Explain some things.'

'Do you think there's an explanation for everything? You think everything can be put into words? Whatever I need to say to Amelia can't be put into words.' Christian laid the cigar in an ashtray and stared into the blue smoke, then turned to Kane, clammy, red-eyed. He ran the nail of his thumb down the stubble of Kane's cheek, halfway between a caress and an incision.

'Elliott . . .'

'Sort yourself out, Christian.'

Kane was outside, crossing Berkeley Square, when his phone buzzed. It was Bell. The message said: *Seen news re Rebecca Sinclair?!*

TWENTY-FIVE

Her father's car was a creaky old Peugeot 307. Rebecca's recent life didn't involve cars like this. It took some getting used to, but sheer desperation to put distance between herself and Aylesbury kept the vehicle moving. When she felt she'd got far away enough she found the number for Anti Terrorism HQ and persuaded the switchboard to put her through to Lockhart. It went to his voice mail.

'It's Rebecca,' she said. 'I'm on my father's phone. Eclipse connects to that New Year's Eve and what happened to me then. I think there were forensic samples taken from me. Do you have any idea where they went?' She gave her new number. The message she chose not to include explicitly: *You let him go.*

Lockhart called her back within seconds.

'What happened?'

'It was him. Eclipse killed Robert. And I think he was the one who assaulted me on New Year's Eve.'

'Where are you?'

'On the M40.'

'Your car?'

'My father's.'

She heard an exhalation. 'Where are you planning to go?'

'To you.'

'Go to Marylebone. Park near the station. Find Boston Place,

269

on the east side of the railway station, where there are bike racks. I'll be there in half an hour.'

Boston Place was a small alleyway. The area around the station was busy by the time she got there, but no one in the alleyway itself. She found the bike racks. No sign of Lockhart. Her father's phone rang.

'You're at Marylebone?' Lockhart said.

'Yes.'

'Keep going, down the alleyway to the High Street at the far end. See Gino's Coffee Bar?'

'Yes.'

'Cross the road towards it.'

He was waiting away from people and cameras, shades on. When Rebecca got to him, Lockhart said, 'Follow me,' and led her fast down another side road to where his own car was waiting.

'Get in.'

She jumped in. He began to drive.

'What are the police saying?' he asked.

'They think I did it.'

'And you're sure you didn't?' She stared at him. 'I have to ask. You wouldn't believe what I'm hearing from my people on the scene. They're not sure Counter Terrorism need to be there at all.'

'It was Eclipse.'

'Okay, so you're claiming. But how on earth does what happened on New Year's Eve connect? Why was it covered up? I'm struggling here.'

Rebecca outlined her speculations since their last meeting: the fact that the Eclipse leaks connected to MI6. That, she said, was why everything on New Year's Eve was covered up. It had something to do with the intelligence services.

'Did you take forensic samples from me? On New Year's?'

'Yes. We had a specialist suite in the station by then.'

'Do you know what exactly was done?'

'The standard, I think. Initial swabs: clothes, mouth, genitals. I didn't conduct it, of course.'

'But I was a suspect.'

'We wanted to ascertain what on earth was going on.'

'Do you know if those samples were ever processed?'

'I've no idea. Obviously, within a few hours, nothing had ever happened, according to the police system. So I don't know where the samples would have gone.'

'You don't know if they went to the lab?'

'No.'

'But it's possible they did?'

'Anything's possible.'

Lockhart's radio crackled with updates. The terrorism threat level had been raised to severe. His phone bleeped endlessly with messages coming in.

'When will they notice you're gone?' the Commander asked.

'My parents may already have told them.'

Lockhart drove into a council estate and parked in a sheltered corner. He scrolled through messages, then called someone, asked them to direct queries to his deputy. He told them he was pursuing a lead. Then he started ringing around labs asking after samples from 2009.

'Yes, this relates to the Eclipse investigation. It's urgent.'

As the calls mounted up, it became clear that the forensic samples taken from Rebecca in the early hours of 1 January 2009 could have been in a number of places. Lockhart walked her through the likelihoods, managing expectations. It was possible they'd remained at Belgravia Police Station, never sent for analysis – every station with a CID unit had a property store with freezers, and these were frequently cluttered with old samples. They could have been destroyed, of course. Alternatively they could have been submitted to a laboratory, in which case there was a bigger chance they'd been retained, but they would need to establish which lab was used.

Belgravia Police Station drew a blank – they couldn't find any record of the incident, of course, and there was no separate record of samples, but they reminded Lockhart that their contract for forensic testing then, as now, was with a company called Eurofins Forensic Service, who had laboratories in Teddington.

Lockhart typed the address into his satnav. It was forty-five minutes' drive away. A new all-units alert went out over the radio as he stared at the map: *Rebecca Sinclair. Missing from Aylesbury, believed to be driving a grey Peugeot 307.*

Lockhart clicked his radio.

'Received. Any indications where she got to?'

'None.'

'Okay. Any leads on the murder of her husband?'

'No.'

'Can you keep me in the loop?'

'Yes, sir.'

He clicked the radio off, checked his watch.

'Where did you park your father's car?'

'Marylebone station car park.'

'I'm meant to be speaking to government about the terrorism threat level in half an hour.' He closed his eyes, his nostrils flared. Finally, he opened his eyes again.

'Do you have another police interview scheduled?' Lockhart asked.

'Not yet.'

'Who is your lawyer?'

'I don't have one.'

'Seriously?' Lockhart checked the satnav. She saw the strain: a man walking out of his life, a good police officer, willing to run into burning buildings; brave, decisive.

He made a final call and delayed the briefing, then they hit the road again.

The labs sat between Richmond Park and the Thames, a faceless slab among the genteel homes, with four storeys of mirrored windows stretching over a square kilometre. Its unattractiveness was mostly hidden behind trees and shrubbery.

When they'd parked, Lockhart explained the odds again. Even if this fortress of forensics contained the samples from that night, they may never have been processed. There was a good chance they'd been filed away without examination, usually because of a lack of funding. Science was expensive. Sexual assaults generated endless exhibits. Even in homicide investigations you couldn't process everything.

'Stay in the car,' he said.

'No.' Rebecca said. She accompanied him in. The laboratory's reception area was small, with a single, swipe-operated door leading out of it into the premises beyond. It was manned by a security guard. Police weren't meant to just turn up here. But Lockhart carried seniority and crisis with him. He explained they were there to check the stores, that he'd sent an email, that it pertained to a live investigation. The guard looked at Rebecca.

'She's with me,' Lockhart said.

Had they seen the news? Could she carry off the role of a detective? The guard made a call and a few minutes later a young woman in a lab coat arrived. She introduced herself as Faith Amusan, head technician. She said she'd just seen the email from Counter Terrorism. Lockhart said that was right, that he couldn't say any more at this moment in time, as she'd understand. The woman asked them to wait. After ten minutes, she came back holding a piece of paper and two sets of white coats and face masks.

'Sir, the samples are here,' she said. She hesitated. 'This is terrorism related?'

'Yes.'

She gave them the protective clothing. 'Please, put these on and come through.'

She led them down white corridors, past rooms signed Evidence Examination, Digital Forensics, Audio and Video Analysis, down a flight of stairs to a door marked Biological Evidence Storage. Key card access. Amusan opened it and the temperature dropped as they walked into a vast storage area with rows of stainless-steel freezer units. The technician marched between them, slowing as she reached the right numbers. Then she opened one.

And there it was: a small box with the contents written on: *1/1/2009. R. Nolan. Bayswater.* An urn of her ashes.

Amusan removed the lid. Rape kit; individual bagged pubic hairs, nail clippings, samples of bodily fluids, a full set of swabs. Belgravia had done a thorough job. It looked like it could have been done yesterday: a horror frozen in time.

'Was it processed?' Rebecca asked. Amusan checked the attached paperwork.

'It's ticked as processed.'

Lockhart turned to her.

'Any positive results?'

'Let's see.'

This discovery afforded them access to a new realm of the laboratory kingdom. They returned the box to its storage, left the refrigerated area and went up to the third floor, to an office with windows along the side and several high-powered computers. Amusan logged into one, spent several moments navigating records, then turned to Lockhart.

'We isolated several distinct DNA profiles.'

'Any have a name attached?'

'Possibly. Not on here.'

'Who did the results go to?'

'No one. Not according to this. I don't understand that, to be honest.' The technician seemed concerned, as if this might have been a mistake at their end.

'I believe the investigation was terminated prematurely,' Lockhart said. Amusan glanced at him. She read something odd going on.

'That would match what I'm seeing.'

'Send the DNA results through to Counter Terrorism. We'll run them for an ID.'

Neither Rebecca nor Lockhart spoke as they returned to the police officer's car. Lockhart called through instructions to his team regarding the incoming DNA results, then started the engine.

'Let's get the bastard,' he said.

TWENTY-SIX

Kane stared at the photo of Rebecca Sinclair that led most news: Rebecca being whisked away from Aylesbury Police Station in an unmarked car 'following questioning about the murder of her husband last night'.

It was the only thing that could have placed a dent in the Eclipse coverage:

CONSERVATIVE MP ROBERT SINCLAIR
DIES AFTER ATTACK AT HOME

Kane read the initial reports, trying to discern what on earth was going on.

> Police confirmed that no arrests have been made and a crime scene remains in place at the address. They have warned the public to be alert, while assuring local residents that over a hundred officers are patrolling the area.
> Counter Terrorism are assisting Thames Valley Police, who have emphasised that they are keeping an open mind as to motives. Anyone with information should contact the anonymous helpline.

The Prime Minister led politicians in offering sincere condolences. Robert Sinclair's family described themselves as being in profound shock. Friends described Sinclair as an 'incredibly intelligent, joyful, loving person'.

Kane remembered Robert Sinclair as a useful idiot, valuable for establishing Opula as a gateway to Britain's political class. So enamoured of Opula and the billionaires it introduced him to that he agreed to hire the Churchill Room at the House of Commons for an Opula welcome event for new members. Kane remembered meeting Christian's eye as Robert Sinclair gave a speech among the busts of Churchill, knowing that they were thinking the same thing: it didn't get better than this. Opula had been perfected. Looking around the room at fifty or sixty of the most venal men in the world, wormed into the cradle of democracy, gleeful at getting into the House of Commons as if it constituted a refuge from corruption. None of whom realised the extent to which MI6 was burrowing into them.

Opula paid Robert Sinclair 400k over three years and it had been some of the best money the intelligence service ever spent; Sinclair, embodying the British establishment as pliable, needy, servile. The MP had no idea what they were really up to, of course. His murder made no sense in that respect.

The news showed footage of Rebecca among police, looking dazed; Rebecca *who miraculously escaped the attack and managed to flee the property before raising the alarm* . . .

'What the hell is this about?' Bell asked, when he called her.

'I don't know.'

'A bit too much for coincidence.'

'Yes. Have you been able to ascertain anything beyond what's being reported?'

She told him what she'd gleaned from her own contacts: no traces of a third party had been found; there were several witnesses to an argument between Rebecca Sinclair and her husband in the hours before his death, possibly involving leaked footage of Rebecca, part of the Eclipse files. This wouldn't be the first domestic incident Eclipse had detonated.

'I need to speak to her,' Kane said.

'Elliot, the police are also asking after you. They visited. They say you're not answering their calls.'

'Did they say which of my crimes they wanted to speak to me about?'

'No.'

'Do you think any of your people could establish a way for me to contact Rebecca? Where is she now?'

'I don't know, but I can't see how you'd get through to her. I can ask around.'

Christian was in a taxi heading back to Barnes when he picked up Kane's call.

'Rebecca,' Christian said.

'Yeah.'

'Did you know about this?'

'No, I've just heard.'

'Why Robert Sinclair? Was it her? You think she did it?'

'I don't think so.'

'From what I can tell, it's not a wildly different attack from the one on Anton Zakharyan and his wife.'

'That's what I was thinking.'

'But what does that mean? Are we still talking about a hit team? Or something to do with Eclipse? And why Rebecca?'

'It connects to Eclipse. I think he kills when things go wrong, when something threatens him.'

'Have you spoken to Alistair Godfrey recently?'

'Why?'

'I got a strange call from him. He was asking about you, and that journalist I was talking about, Juliet Bell. Is that the person who got shown the classified MI6 report about New Year's Eve?'

'Yes.'

'Alistair says you're in a relationship with her. He's kidding, right?'

'No.'

'For Christ's sake, Elliot. You're being played.'

'What else does Alistair say?'

'That Bell's in trouble. She's not going to be working on this for very long the way things are going. She will end up dragging you down.'

'What kind of trouble?'

'I don't know. Those were his words.'

Godfrey answered on the first ring.

'Elliot, just the man.'

'Let's meet,' Kane said.

'Yes,' he said. 'There's something I need to tell you about.'

TWENTY-SEVEN

They were on the A4, heading back into Central London, when Lockhart received a call that made him pull over and get out of the car. Rebecca watched him speaking, turning, buffeted by the passing traffic. She watched his expression darken.

'What is it?' she said, when he got back in. Lockhart sat silently for a moment, staring through the windscreen, then he turned the car around.

'We need to go somewhere.'

'Why? What was the call about?'

'A result of sorts.'

The 'somewhere' they needed to go was a brutalist grey block above a bookmaker's in Paddington. A discreet sign announced this as an outpost of the National Crime Agency. They were met at reception by a petite, serious-looking woman who introduced herself as Detective Inspector Lindsey Derringer, and stared at Rebecca with a mixture of fear and wonder.

'Show us what you have,' Lockhart said.

Derringer led them upstairs to an empty, open plan office, then into a smaller room at the side, windowless and bare and hot. They took seats at a desk with a file in the centre. Derringer looked intently at Rebecca again, as if she was a rare creature, long sought, with a value of which Rebecca herself remained unaware.

'The sample results,' Lockhart said.

'Take a look.'

To Rebecca's frustration, this invitation was directed at Lockhart. Lockhart opened the file and began to read. It felt like having junior doctors visit her bed in hospital, whispering about her.

'Who raped me?' she said.

'Rebecca, before we get to that, could you talk us through what you remember?' Derringer said. 'A New Year's Eve party. Is that right?'

So they were going the long way around. Still, it was a relief to start here, in 2008, to have this recognised as the origin of everything. Rebecca told them what she could about that incident, which wasn't much. Derringer, with Lockhart's gentle accompaniment, pressed for any possible physical description of the attacker and, when Rebecca didn't have any, his possible nationality, his accent, then questions about the international nature of the party. She could answer the last, but the rest was still inaccessible to her. They were particularly interested in her loss of memory, and Derringer even tried to get Rebecca to specify the nature of her amnesia.

'Can I ask,' Derringer said, tentatively, 'why nothing appears to have proceeded in terms of an investigation?' This was to Lockhart more than to Rebecca.

'For now, that's a separate issue,' Lockhart said, 'which I'll be pursuing with the relevant parties.'

'I've told you what I remember,' Rebecca said. 'Can you tell me why we're here?'

'She has a right to know,' Lockhart said.

Derringer studied Rebecca's face once more as if assessing her resilience, then stood up.

'I'll show you,' she said, and led them back through the open space, past rows of desks to the far corner, where she unlocked a glass door in a glass wall obscured by slat blinds. Derringer turned the lights on inside and Rebecca saw why they kept this room screened from the rest of the office. Flashing into life was a strange museum, walls papered with photographs and diagrams. The photographs showed four women. Each had her own map. Each map was overlaid with concentric circles, creating a radiating heart. Beneath the maps was a different realm of photography; bruised flesh against leaves, mud, grass; images which Rebecca saw and chose not to look at again.

'We don't have a name,' Derringer said. 'But the DNA profile of the man who attacked you connects to several incidents over the last fifteen years. They all involve sexual assault, with three of the victims murdered and one missing, presumed dead.'

Rebecca felt her breath go. She wanted to look at the faces on the wall but couldn't move. She felt them watching her. From a side cabinet, Derringer produced four heavy box files and lay them on the table.

Top sheet of the first file: a picture of a smiling young woman, dark hair cut in a straight fringe.

'November 11th last year, the body of a woman was found on Wandsworth Common. She was identified as a twenty-year-old student, Evie Inglewood. The pathologist determined death by asphyxiation, specifically compression to the neck. She'd been raped. Her clothes were found in a pond nearby. Inglewood had been walking home from a friend's party at around 1 a.m. when she disappeared. One of the search team found a surgical glove in a skip nearby. Several hairs were recovered from inside it, one of which had a root with tissue attached, which made it possible to obtain a DNA profile. That profile is a 99 per cent match with the semen swab taken from yourself in January 2009.'

Rebecca stared at the woman's face. In the hush of this beige-furnished memorial chapel, a new alternative reality emerged, alongside the ones where New Year's Eve hadn't happened at all: one where it was the last thing that ever happened to her.

Derringer continued: 'The Wandsworth Common attacker has been linked to several similar crimes over the last fourteen years: Victoria Lewis in 2010, Irena Podolski in 2011, Rosa Martinez, 2015. All involved use of a ligature, at least two of them involved the placing of the victim's clothes in nearby water and a rudimentary attempt to clean their body after death. Victoria Lewis, a business consultant aged thirty-three, was reported missing from Blackheath, south-east London, in September 2010. Her body was discovered three days later on a building site near the Millennium Dome. The body of Irena Podolski, thirty-four years old, was found in woodland outside Guildford in March 2011. Rosa Martinez was twenty-nine, a nurse at West Middlesex University Hospital. She went missing on 20 April 2015, after a birthday party in Hounslow. No body has ever been found, but there are still connections we can make to the other cases: sightings of a dark, high-end vehicle and a well-dressed white man.'

Ghost sisters. Some of their names had a vague familiarity, floating out of Rebecca's peripheral consciousness, news stories skipped over as too painful and too common to read closely. Derringer turned to an even bulkier file marked 'Profiling' and explained that her own team at the NCA was called in when the Senior Investigating Officer in the Rosa Martinez case established that it was part of what police called a linked series crime, and the public called serial killing. The National Crime Agency put their specialist teams to work: geographical profilers, behavioural analysts, the entomologists and soil experts. But none of this had produced the breakthrough they needed. The most valuable lead, instead, had come in September last year, when one woman appeared to have got away.

On 3 September, Casey Kehler, a twenty-two-year-old student at the Royal College of Art, had been found at three in the morning, walking along the side of a road outside Waltham Forest, very confused. It was later established that she'd been abducted, and was on the verge of being assaulted when something disturbed her assailant and he fled.

Kehler possessed little recollection of what happened. She had a vague memory of talking to a man about travels. At some point she was in a vehicle. She wasn't sure why she got in or where she thought she was going. The man was in his late thirties or early forties, she believed; white, clean-shaven. He spoke quietly, and she thought he might have been putting on an accent. That was all she recalled.

'Her memories were gone,' Rebecca said.

'Yes.'

'Why?'

'It's a good question.'

Police had torn their hair out trying to fathom the apparent compliance of some of the victims. In the case of Irena Podolski, a witness saw the victim speaking to a man in Guildford town centre, close to the Friary shopping mall, before accompanying him away. In the hours before the disappearance of Rosa Martinez, a dashcam caught two figures on a residential road in Hounslow. Derringer retrieved the image from the file. All you could see clearly was that Martinez was unrestrained, walking beside him, hands in her pockets. The NCA's behavioural analysis team devoted hours and a lot of ink to speculation about how the killer might have inspired trust. No conclusion was ever reached.

Then Kehler was able to give her hazy account and the focus shifted.

'Have you heard of scopolamine?' Derringer asked Rebecca.

'No.'

'Scopolamine comes from the seeds of a South American plant. It's used medicinally for treating motion sickness, but with powerful side effects. They include memory loss and an ability to act, but without resistance to suggestion. We've seen very few criminal cases involving it in the UK. It's difficult to get but not impossible. It's one theory.'

'Do people hallucinate on scopolamine?' Rebecca asked.

'I'm not sure. I've not come across that.'

'Could you remember things that never happened? Confess to something you hadn't done?'

Lockhart sensed what Rebecca was chasing and sat forward, watching Derringer as if the detective's response could be crucial for both of them.

'Possibly. Again, that's not something I've ever heard about.'

'Have people been persuaded to kill while on scopolamine?'

Derringer met Rebecca's stare. She appeared unwilling to answer until she knew where this was leading. Then her phone rang. She answered, frowned. 'Okay, hang on.' Derringer turned to Lockhart and Rebecca. 'Apparently, there are some people downstairs looking for you.'

'No one knows we're here,' Lockhart said. 'Is it police?'

'I don't think so.'

The Commander got to his feet. He turned to Rebecca. 'Stay in this room. Let us deal with this. You're not going anywhere right now. Not until we've decided on a course of action.'

The two officers went to speak to whoever was downstairs. Rebecca remained in the room of horror, looking at the walls, the space where her face could have been. She read the notes on the table:

Linked Series. Operation Michaelmas. AC156

The suspect is on the border of organised and
disorganised personality types. Their attacks are
impulsive but professional, showing no loss of control,
and performed to create the minimum noise or
mess possible. But there is a consistent element of

opportunism: time of day varies, as does geographical
location. These are indicators of high confidence.
The cleaning of bodies, disposal of clothes and use
of protective equipment all spell advanced forensic
awareness ...

Voices returned to the main office. Rebecca moved the blinds
to peer through. Lockhart and Derringer were accompanied
by a smartly suited man, authoritative, bespectacled. Derringer
led him into the windowless room on the far side of the open-
plan office.

But not before Rebecca had seen him.

She recognised him, although it took a second to process. Then
she was transported back to the unheated basement flat of New
Year's morning. The man who told her to forget everything that
had happened. Here he was.

A sense of dread returned. She got to her feet. Instinct said
flee. She opened the door, then turned back and grabbed the
report on scopolamine. If anything belonged to her, it was
this. Walking through the office, she heard raised voices in the
side room.

'I would need to receive orders from within the police,'
Lockhart said.

And the voice of their visitor: 'This is a long way beyond the
remit of police.'

Then she was in the corridor, heading for the lift. At the ground
floor, the doors opened and she glimpsed an awkward stand-off
between the building's in-house security and four thuggish men
who must have belonged to the visitor. She recoiled, pressing
herself to the side of the lift, punched the button for the lower
basement level, emerging eventually in an underground car
park. Rebecca ran through the strip-lit gloom, found the ramp to
street level and ducked under the barrier, still clutching the file.

TWENTY-EIGHT

Alexandra Palace. Kane was there first this time, staring out over the burning city. Godfrey drove in a moment later, fast, parked askew and threw his passenger door open. Kane climbed in.

'People are saying you have an ID for Eclipse,' Godfrey said.

'No.'

'But you're in direct contact. Or, at least, Juliet Bell is.'

'Yes.'

'You never told me you were in a relationship with her.'

'It's not a secret.'

'The boy I saw in your car . . . '

'He's called Mason. He's her son. I know you spoke to Christian. Why's Juliet Bell in trouble?'

Godfrey sighed. 'I think you've been deeply naïve.'

'Well, it makes a refreshing change.'

'It's not funny, Elliot. We've got a matter of hours. Tell me what you know.'

'Why hours?'

'Eclipse is in contact with Russian intelligence. He approached Iran and China too, but the Russians bit first. The deal is he brings his files and they get him set up a long way from the UK. He says he can bring a terabyte of data in return for protection and five million dollars.'

'How would he get there?'

'Flight from the UK to a third country, accompanied by

Russian security from there. Given that currently no one has any idea who he is, that's not going to be much of a problem. But something's made Eclipse think his time is almost up. He says he's got twenty-four hours to get out of the UK.'

'Because he killed Robert Sinclair.'

'Maybe. Why would he do that?'

'My suspicion is that it was Rebecca he was after, for the same reason as he killed Anton Zakharyan: they were onto him. Is this Russian plan from a solid source?'

'Solid as we've got.' That meant someone in or very close to the Kremlin. Kane thought: this is what Eclipse's whole whistle-blowing act was about – marketing themselves, positioning for an escape.

'Who's he speaking to in Russia?'

'The head of Russia's Main Intelligence Directorate, Igor Kostyukov.'

'Think Moscow will play it straight?'

'Fuck no. But they'll string him along. They want the data, they could do without the person. He claims to have over ten thousand MI6 files on an external hard drive, all unreleased yet. Given what we've seen so far, there's no reason not to believe that.'

'Any progress on figuring out exactly *how* he has all this?'

'Not that I'm aware of. If you told me what you know it might be a help.'

'At the centre of Eclipse's obsessions is Operation Halcyon. I don't know how much you know about Halcyon.'

'A lot more than I did a few days ago, when I started looking into you and Anton Zakharyan. Although I can't say the records you've left behind are very informative. I know it involved the killing of three Russian operatives in London. A New Year's Eve party.'

'That's right. I think Rebecca was raped at that party. It got

288

covered up along with everything else. Broughton's work. I was never told – not until Eclipse told me. So that's what I've got. It means Broughton is a potential problem.'

'Why?'

'Because this is now a very real, personal threat to him. This would be the beginning of his undoing. And without the protection of his role, he's facing criminal charges.'

'How do you know Broughton had any knowledge of this?'

'Christian told me.'

Godfrey shook his head wearily. 'You know about his TV plans?'

'Yes. Going to try and stop him?'

'We're a lot more worried about Juliet Bell.'

'I trust her.'

'To do what?'

'The right thing.'

'I'm sure. What I'm wondering is if she trusts you.'

'What's that meant to mean?'

'We're monitoring her. We know her speculations. Have you told her the real reason you crossed paths in the first place?'

'Is this a threat?'

Godfrey paused. Kane began to subtly scan the other vehicles in the car park, in case his former colleague had brought backup.

'She's in touch with Michael De Souza. They're doing something on Opula for the *Guardian*.'

'Well, maybe it's about time.'

'She has an agenda.'

'What's her agenda?'

'It's the agenda of whoever – or whatever – is steering her.'

'Right. You're not good at this, Alistair. I'm going to go now.'

'I'm trying to help you, to protect you from Broughton.'

'No, you're trying to protect Broughton from me.'

Godfrey shook his head again, firmer this time.

'In the next few hours, Juliet Bell will be arrested for assisting a foreign intelligence service. I'm telling you as a friend.'

'What foreign intelligence service? That will blow up in your face.'

'Broughton has a file ready.'

'What's in this file?'

'Question marks over time she spent in Russia in the late '90s, for one thing.'

'She was reporting the war in Chechnya, for fuck's sake.'

'Is there any reason Juliet Bell would have access to an offshore account? The Atlantic Bank in Belize?'

Kane suddenly saw where this was going.

'I set it up. It connects to our private intelligence work.'

'To your knowledge, has it been used to transfer any money to Eclipse?'

A hot rage flushed through Kane's body.

'You know why Broughton's doing this. She's onto something that will bring him down.'

'Be that as it may, the point is Bell's up to something beyond what you know about. And it places her at risk. Her, you and Mason.'

Kane gripped the handle of the car door, on the point of leaving. His arm tensed.

'Tell whoever's feeding you this: fuck with them and I will talk. I will blow the whole thing.'

'That's not your choice to make.'

'Try me.'

Kane drove back home, stopping when he saw the police cars outside their house. It was being raided.

Six police vehicles on the road, his front door open, men coming and going, carrying paperwork and computers in transparent evidence bags.

So it had started. Had Godfrey's invitation to meet been a ploy to allow for that? Kane reversed away fast. He tried Bell but she wasn't answering his calls. There was a whole range of potential disinformation and mindfucks that could lie behind that, or it could be nothing. The last message he'd received from her, two hours ago, was an odd one now he looked at it more closely: *Mason's with his dad. I've got to pop out for a second.*

That was uncharacteristically vague.

Kane parked behind a pub on Highbury Corner and managed to get through to Mason's father. He confirmed that Mason was with him and agreed to put the boy on the line: 'I'm sure he's got plenty to say to you.'

Mason came on a few seconds later.

'Elliot?'

'Yeah. You're okay?'

'Yeah.'

'Know where your mum is?'

'She said she was going to work. A meeting.'

'A meeting with who?'

'I don't know. The people you work with.'

'Clients?'

'I don't know.' The boy sounded upset. 'Why is this the last time I can speak to you?'

'Who says that? It's not true. And it's not for someone to tell you who you can speak to.'

'Dad says you were lying to us. Me and Mum.'

'Well, that's not true either.'

'He's going to tell Mum you lied to her. He's been told stuff. About how you met. Says she won't be happy with you.'

'That's a shame, but it's not the end of things. Trust me. Just try to relax, Mason. Don't listen to what people say. Everything's going to be all right.'

'I don't care if you lied,' the boy said. Kane heard his father laugh.

'Hang up now, Mason,' he said.

'I'll see you soon,' Kane said. 'I promise.'

He called their clients.

'Is Juliet there?'

'No, haven't heard from her for a while. She was meant to get back to me, in fact. Is the report ready?'

'I think so. Did you have a meeting lined up?'

'No. Why? What's going on?'

Kane tried Bell again. This time he left a voice message: 'Our home's being raided. You're being framed as some kind of Russian asset. I also believe people are trying to divide us, spreading false information. This is what they do, Juliet, please understand that. Call me, and don't believe anything you hear in the meantime.'

He checked the go-bag in the boot of his car: passport, twenty grand in cash. Options, perhaps. But none of that was what he wanted to take with him.

Still no reply from Bell. A final thought occurred to Kane. He opened the tracking app on his phone and checked the trackers Bell had put in her coat and bag when they went to Highgate Woods. The one in her coat wasn't broadcasting. The one in her bag remained on. It was currently in South Tottenham.

What was in South Tottenham?

Kane stared at the flashing dot on the map. It was static, among what looked like a lot of warehouses, a derelict industrial zone. He waited for it to move but it stayed there, like a beacon, calling for help, so he went to his car and began to drive.

TWENTY-NINE

Rebecca clutched the file as she marched through Paddington. She didn't dare turn until deep in the crowds around the train station.

No one was following her that she could see.

An aggressive heat had settled, liquid against the skin. Rebecca fanned herself with the file. She was as bare of possessions as she'd been in Aylesbury Police Station. But she had her wallet. She withdrew five hundred pounds, bought a pay-as-you-go phone, some water, some more disguise – cap, T-shirt. She dumped her father's phone in a bin outside McDonald's.

Paddington. It had been a while. Rebecca knew the area. She kept going, away from the shops and cafés into the shabby side streets. Walk on the seedy side and you discover Paddington. It always felt like a border town to her, shitty, transient, centred on the railway station with its express Heathrow connection, so part of the sprawling estuary of air travel too.

She knew places you could lie low in Paddington.

The Suffolk Plaza Hotel remained where it always had been, on a rundown crescent in permanent shadow from the monstrous plane trees in the neglected park opposite. She'd sometimes suggested the place to men in town who didn't want to use their own hotels. You could pay by the hour, cash, no documents required. Perfectly cooperative with police but never very helpfully so.

They'd redone the gilt of the signage since her last visit, and put a sticker advertising free Wi-Fi in the front window. There'd been some new paint but not enough. The young man on the front desk wasn't anyone she recognised, but then they wouldn't have remembered her anyway; part of the etiquette was not looking at your face. Right now they were transfixed by the news on the small TV next to their computer monitor. Rebecca glimpsed Aylesbury Police Station behind the reporter.

She gave them a fake name, said she just needed a couple of hours, paid cash, got a key.

Up to the second floor. She even remembered the room. It had a view to the street at the front. She opened the window to ensure she could hear any cars pulling up downstairs, then closed the curtains. The room had crap air con, for which the standing fan unplugged in the centre of the floor seemed to be some kind of apology. Rebecca checked the end of the corridor, the fire escape. The door said it was alarmed. It appeared to be unlocked, ready for a quick getaway.

This is a long way beyond the remit of any police. That man, the basement with bars on the windows, the portable heater and the guard by the door reading a newspaper. It flooded back to her again: the food that came in, the bath she never took, and the warnings that had implanted themselves in her unconscious: forget this happened.

As if she could remember it anyway.

Scopolamine.

She pulled up the room's sole chair to what passed for a desk: a narrow piece of wood supporting a plastic kettle and a dog-eared brochure for local tourist attractions. Rebecca spread the notes from the file, then turned on her new phone and searched 'scopolamine'.

Devil's Breath.

According to a medical website, scopolamine, or Devil's

Breath, was part of the deadly nightshade family. The drug was known to produce pliability, used to subdue and manipulate people. The borrachero tree from which it derived was disarmingly beautiful, with white and yellow orchid-like flowers.

A handful of cases had been reported in Europe, involving robbery and rape. In Colombia, where it originated, there were hundreds a year. People were giving up their kidneys, handing over babies. Rebecca detected an element of exoticised panic, with stories of South American tribes administering the drug to the wives of dead chiefs so they could be buried alive with their husbands, accounts of criminals blowing the drug into the faces of victims, leaving them physically functioning but mentally unable to resist orders.

One detail in particular made the drug distinct: scopolamine blocked the brain's acetylcholine receptors, which meant it stopped memories from forming. Victims had no recollection of what happened to them, and couldn't identify their attackers. Which was frustrating for law enforcement, because the longer it took to report the crime, the less likely it was that the drug itself would be detected. Scopolamine showed up in bodily fluids for only a few days.

Rebecca's hypothesis: whatever happened on New Year's Eve 2008, it gave her attacker a taste. He was at that party, he assaulted Rebecca, he was some kind of VIP. And he got away with it. And, after that, there seemed no reason why he would not get away with anything. A gate had been opened that would not close. The world was his oyster. Life and death were in his power. She remembered Derringer's questions about the international nature of the party, her attacker's accent. An appendix to the file discussed possible international leads, other scopolamine-connected cases sourced via Interpol. One came from Israeli police. On 29 January 2009, a twenty-nine-year-old woman was murdered in a coastal neighbourhood north of Tel

Aviv. Dana Lahav was a waitress at a beachside café, found stran-
gled behind some rocks on the beach. Forensic analysis detected
traces of scopolamine in her blood. That was just three weeks
after Rebecca's own assault.

The next intriguing parallel came from St Petersburg. It concerned Carolina Byshkina, a twenty-five-year-old woman found
partially undressed and disorientated in Rzhevskij Forest Park
on the morning of 2 July 2009. A sample of the victim's blood
had been processed at St Petersburg's Department of Forensic
Medicine and came back positive for traces of scopolamine.

The appendix included police contacts listed at the respective
international liaison offices in Israel and Russia. Could you still
call Russia? Rebecca wondered. Were we at war with them? She
tried. In the end, both phones rang unanswered, so all she could
do was read through the reports again. They seemed so partial
and deficient. Rebecca searched for something to grab onto, a
way forward, then one detail caught her eye. Dana Lahav had
been missing for over a day when her body was discovered, and it
was only discovered then because of another police investigation
nearby. She was found by sniffer dogs involved in the investigation of 'a car bombing at the Sea View Apartments complex'.

Rebecca opened up Google, typed 'car bomb Tel Aviv
2009' and got the *Jerusalem Post*, an English-language paper.
Underneath the photograph of a vehicle's blackened shell, tipped
on its side, was a short account:

A car bomb exploded shortly before 16:00 outside a
residential block in Netanya, killing two men and leaving
two critically wounded. The individuals were all of
Russian origin. No groups have claimed responsibility.
    54-year-old Mikhail Panzhinskiy, a biochemist who has
been resident at the luxury Sea View complex for only
a few weeks, was approaching the parked SUV when a

bomb planted in a spare tyre on the back of the vehicle
exploded. He was killed instantly. His companion, Daniil
Gusev, died several hours later at Ichilov Hospital. Police
believe the device was triggered remotely.

The story didn't get much coverage that she could find. By
early February it had vanished from the news. It looked odd to
her – not terrorism but a targeted killing of Russians.

A strange thought began to form. She checked another story
that had faded from public sight, the *Evening Standard* report
from the day after her own assault: *Body of man 'in his 40s' found
in Thames, near Westminster Pier.* Another Russian. Rebecca had
been assaulted the same night as a Russian was killed in London,
and here was a similar pattern in Israel.

Next, Rebecca looked for events in St Petersburg around the
time of Carolina Byshkina's rape. The result gave her a chill.
It felt like seeing a pathway open up, along which no one had
walked before.

At half past midnight on 2 July 2009, a few hours before
Carolina Byshkina was found wandering disorientated in
Rzhevskij Forest Park, a senior Russian official had been shot
dead on Nevsky Prospekt, a few kilometres away. This one made
international news. Headline in the *Telegraph*:

Top Russian Official Victim of Shooting

A leading political ally of President Putin, Major General
Oleg Gorevoy, believed to have been responsible for the
president's overseas covert operations unit, has been
shot dead in St Petersburg, Russian officials say.

An unidentified attacker in a car shot Mr Gorevoy
four times in the back as he returned home to his luxury
apartment building on Nevsky Prospekt.

Russian President, Vladimir Putin, has condemned
the murder. According to a Kremlin spokesman, Putin is
assuming 'personal control' of the investigation into the killing.

This killing managed to stay in the news. Coverage continued for several weeks.

On 1 August, Russian authorities released a possible image of the attacker. The driver of a vehicle seen near the location where Gorevoy was shot had been caught on petrol station CCTV earlier that evening. He wore a white baseball cap, bomber-style jacket, FC Zenit St Petersburg T-shirt. The image was blurry, but Rebecca recognised him at once.

Elliot.

Surely not, she thought. But he was unmistakeable.

Rebecca called Lockhart but there was no answer. She messaged De Souza via his Twitter account with her new number, praying he saw it: *I need to speak to you, urgently.*

He called a moment later, sounding cautious, blunt.

'Did you kill your husband, Rebecca?'

'No.'

'Police are looking for you. This call could be considered aiding and abetting murder.'

'I know who Eclipse is.'

De Souza paused. 'No,' he said, finally, 'I can't do it,' and hung up.

She felt a wave of despair. Her last roll of the dice gone. Then her phone rang – a mobile number she didn't recognise. When she answered, it was De Souza.

'I think my phone's been tapped,' he said. 'Don't use that number again. Let's meet.'

'Yes.'

'How are you travelling?'

'I can get a taxi. I'm masked up. I've got shades, cash.'

He gave her an address in South Tottenham and said he'd be there within an hour.

She caught a black cab from the rank by the station. The taxi driver was the indifferent type, Bluetooth earpiece in, conducting a conversation in Arabic. London unspooled beyond the windows, but all she could see was Elliot. Rebecca recalled all their conversations and tried to imagine them as a veil for evil. She didn't know what to believe. She thought of the mild-mannered professors and writers and even priests who had used her when she was for sale. After a few months working for Platinum she began to think she could tell which men used prostitutes just by looking at them. After another few months she gave up. It could be anyone and everyone. The world was unveiled in all its depravity. She had been braced for the burden of her own secrecy and ended up overwhelmed by the amount of other double lives that underpinned the world. Every man lived a lie. And therefore any of them could be a rapist? Was that a syllogism she was prepared to defend?

The driver uttered his first words to Rebecca as they arrived at the address she'd given him, when he said: 'Are you sure?'

They'd stopped in the midst of a former industrial site behind Seven Sisters Road. Windowless buildings looked down on them from all directions, peering over razor wire and rusting steel gates.

'I hope so,' Rebecca said as she handed over her cash and got out. The car departed slowly, as if guilty at abandoning her. Then she was alone.

'Rebecca.' A woman stepped out of the shadows across the road and approached her. She was tall, middle-aged, with dark hair tied back.

'Yes,' Rebecca said.

'My name's Juliet Bell. Michael's waiting for you. Follow me.' She led her through the rusting gates into the warehouse complex itself. OMEGA WORKS. Faded signs for an old piano factory. The place sprawled, a maze of brown brick semi-derelict structures, perilous fire escapes, graffiti. As they continued, Rebecca saw it wasn't all abandoned. Some thin attempts at homeliness appeared: painted picnic tables, plants in an oil drum. Some ground floor windows showed offices and studios. A young man stood smoking in the shade of a wall. Bell opened a metal door into one of the central depots. They took bare concrete steps up to a dingy, third-floor corridor. From the signs beside heavy iron doors, it seemed various companies and organisations sheltered here as if it was a post-apocalyptic refuge. The woman turned and smiled reassuringly at Rebecca as they continued beside cracked windows to a door with more locks than some of the others and a smaller sign: SPOTLIGHT ON CORRUPTION.

Bell knocked, stood in front of the spyhole, and the door opened. De Souza ushered them in, closed the door and locked it.

The office was cluttered and cramped with mismatched furniture, boxes and papers everywhere – on a stained carpet, a coffee table, a sagging sofa. No other staff present. The place stank of cold filter coffee. On the wall, several dense, webbed diagrams showed interlocking names of banks, law firms and politicians. At the back was a small editing suite, with a poster tacked to the wall above it: NO DEMOCRACY WITHOUT TRANSPARENCY.

'Rebecca,' De Souza began. 'I don't know what to say.'

'Say you believe me.'

'Yes, and so does Juliet. This is Juliet Bell. She's also a journalist. She's been working on Opula, on what we believe are MI6 connections to Eaton Square. I thought you should meet. We're going to be trying to get this story out together. We have legal backing and the approval of my editors. So, don't fear. We can do this.'

Now that they were inside, Bell looked graver, more focused.

They offered Rebecca a seat, then asked what was going on. Rebecca showed them the NCA file, the scopolamine links, then the Interpol appendix on similar incidents in Israel and Russia. She asked to use one of the office's PCs and brought up those news stories on the killings that accompanied them. Finally, she showed them the blurry petrol station shot.

That was when she felt Bell tense.

'I think he works for MI6,' Rebecca said.

Bell continued to stare. Rebecca saw her scan the date, the news story. De Souza also sensed tension.

'Know him, Juliet?' he said.

'Yes, I know him.'

'How?'

'He lives with me.'

An awkward silence filled the small office.

'He lives with you?'

'What else do you know?' Bell asked, staring straight at Rebecca.

'He's called Elliot,' Rebecca said. 'He was around Eaton Square, back in 2008.'

'Elliot Kane,' Bell said. 'He's former MI6. He's not a serial killer.' Rebecca wondered at her certainty. What other explanations were there? De Souza turned to Bell.

'When did you meet him?' he asked.

'Elliot? Why?'

'Roughly when?'

'A couple of years ago.'

'Around the time you first started researching John Broughton, working on MI6.'

'He was *helping* with that,' she said, but her voice trailed off. Finally she straightened herself. 'Where did you get this?' Bell asked, gesturing at the police file. Rebecca told them about the NCA, her visit to the Teddington forensic labs and then DI

Lindsey Derringer in Paddington, how they were interrupted by the appearance of the very man who had warned her into silence fifteen years ago.

'He was there that night. He must work for MI6 and it's MI6 who have swept everything under the carpet. He told Lockhart to stop investigating this.'

'He's there now, at the NCA office?'

'He was when I left.'

'I'm going to make some calls,' De Souza said. He went to check on the institutional war going on. Bell continued to probe about New Year's Eve and its aftermath. Rebecca described the flat she was taken to, the fragments of conversation she remembered. Bell pressed for information on who exactly might have been present.

'Elliot said he didn't know about it: the missing hours, after you left the party. Did you see him at the flat?'

'No.'

'You're sure? This is important for me, personally.'

'I'm sure.'

De Souza hung up and turned to them: 'Lockhart's raising an army. He's put the case in for Rebecca's innocence with regards to last night, and vowed to take on any obstructive sections of MI6 in his pursuit of Eclipse, who is now being classed as a serial killer. There's ambiguity over the current status of the Special Forces travelling with John Broughton. That ambiguity leaves us vulnerable, because it seems we're on their list of people to be stopped. But Lockhart has control of two regional counter-terrorism units, including firearms officers and search teams. They are liaising directly with him. He just needs to know who Eclipse is.'

'Not Elliot Kane,' Bell said.

'Maybe not,' De Souza said. 'But he'd know. He needs to explain this picture. He was clearly in St Petersburg at the time.'

Bell lifted her phone. 'He's calling now.'

'Put it on speaker,' De Souza said. Bell answered.

'Elliot. I'm with Rebecca Sinclair and Michael De Souza. You're on speaker.'

'I'm outside,' Kane said. 'They've got you trapped.'

THIRTY

When he got to the warehouses it was already too late.

Kane recognised the threat of the vehicles at once: two tank-like Land Rover Defenders and a bulletproof Jaguar XJ Sentinel rolling up Vale Road towards the former hives of industry with a malicious gleam.

It told him one thing: they didn't already have her. Bell was hiding, not held. For now.

Kane parked his own car right across the main entrance. That was one route blocked. He ran into the complex, trying to gauge the layout, the potential exits and where she might be. Finally, Bell answered her mobile and he broke the news.

'There are at least three vehicles. The men are probably armed. You need to get out of here. The Vale Road exit is blocked.'

'Elliot, there are some serious accusations against you.'

'Okay, let's go through those when we can. Right now they're going to try to arrest you as a Russian asset and I don't want that happening before you've got your story into the public domain.' He kept moving, deeper into the decay, looking for safe routes out. 'Where exactly are you?'

'The offices of Spotlight on Corruption.'

'What floor is it on?'

'Third floor.'

'Do you have a view outside?'

'Hang on.'

Kane brought up a map on his phone. The warehouse district had at least six exits. Bell came back on the line.

'It looks like there's someone pulling up at the back,' she said. 'A big fuck-off Land Rover.'

'That will be them. Where's your car? Is it inside the warehouse complex?'

'No, it's on Hermitage Road.'

'To the west.'

'Yes, just a minute outside.'

'I think you can get to it if you move fast. There's no one there. Go. There will be more on their way.'

But as he got closer to the side gates he saw one of the Land Rovers approaching from the right. Kane moved to the side, into a loading bay filled with huge metal waste containers. He saw Bell and De Souza appear from the warehouse building with Rebecca following a second behind them. They saw the Land Rover, turned towards the gates and ran.

The car picked up speed, heading straight for them. Kane kicked a steel bin into its path.

It swerved, slamming into the bin. The bin slammed back into Kane.

He lifted an arm in self-protection and felt his wrist smash as the force of the metal sent him tumbling to the ground. His head smacked something as he fell. The container was on his legs. He managed to push it off and crawl out. His right leg was a mess of torn fabric and blood. But it was his left arm that splintered with pain. He knew, with sickening immediacy, that bone had broken, but pushed the thought to the back of his mind as he clambered to his feet. Could he move? Yes. He used the shock and adrenalin to stumble away, deeper into the recess, in case anyone was coming for him. No one came. After a moment, Kane pulled his phone out. It had survived. It rang.

'Are you okay?' Bell asked, breathless, terrified.

'Yeah. Go, drive. I'll get out.'

'We lost Rebecca,' she said.

THIRTY-ONE

Rebecca had followed the journalists as they ran down the stone stairwell, trying to escape the warehouse. She stumbled at the bottom. That second's difference meant Bell and De Souza were ahead as the Land Rover tore in.

She saw it smash into a toppled waste container, which gave her a second to sprint across the courtyard into the shelter of a doorway.

But it meant she was stuck.

Bell and De Souza made it out of the complex. The vehicle followed them, delayed only slightly by its collision, but maybe enough for them to reach Bell's car. It was followed a few seconds later by a second Land Rover and a Jaguar. Then Rebecca saw Kane.

He stood on the other side of courtyard, watching her. His forehead was bleeding. He lifted a hand, checked the space between them. When he was sure there were no men or vehicles, Kane limped across. He winced as he walked, and when he reached her she saw the beads of sweat and his ripped clothes.

Still, she took a garden fork from one of the plant pots near her. Just in case.

'Rebecca.'

'Elliot.'

He glanced at the fork in her hand. 'We need to get out of here,' he said. He had a map up on his phone. Then the screen lit with Bell's name. He hit answer.

'I'm with Rebecca,' he said. 'She's here. She's with me.' Kane peered across to the gate. 'Get word out. That's the most valuable thing you can do right now.'

Rebecca heard Bell say: 'I'm not leaving you there. We're coming back.'

'You won't make it. Keep going. We'll figure something.' He hung up.

'Will we?' Rebecca said.

'Maybe. If we're quick.'

They found a doorway into the building behind them, followed a corridor past studios and emerged again. There was a side exit from the complex here, directly into a residential road. One direction was blocked by a Thames Water treatment plant. The other direction led them past a Carpet Warehouse and around the back of Sainsbury's and Argos.

She saw Kane searching for a hiding place. His speed was slowing. Eventually he sat down with his back against the brick wall of a car park.

'You go,' he said to Rebecca. 'Get somewhere safe. Reconnect with Juliet and Michael.'

'No.'

'We're too exposed here.'

'Let's see if we can get a bit further. There may be somewhere on the High Street.' She helped him up. Kane groaned with pain, then looked around.

'The Kurdish centre,' he said.

'What?'

'There's a Kurdish community centre near here. It may be open. Keep going, past the car park.'

So they hobbled, her arm around him, to a small, stand-alone building signed KURDISH ASSEMBLY. Kane tried the door and it opened. Inside, the lights were off but chairs had been laid out in the main hall. The red, white and green Kurdish flag dominated the back wall, alongside banners and posters: WOMEN RISE UP FOR AFRIN; THE MARTYRS ARE IMMORTAL. Beneath them, forty or fifty photographs of people's faces, most of them in combat fatigues.

Rebecca put Kane in a plastic chair and rifled the cupboards of the centre's kitchen until she found a green first aid box. She patched up his forehead first, so the blood didn't get into his eyes, then put his arm in a sling, bandaged his leg. Kane flexed it.

'I don't think the leg's broken.' He felt up his right arm with his left hand. 'The arm's got multiple fractures. Did we leave a blood trail?'

She glanced through the front window. No blood was visible. A helicopter prowled the blue sky.

'No,' she said. 'I can't see a trail.' Rebecca sat down opposite him. For a moment they just looked at each other. She wondered how long they had left, and knew he was thinking the same thing. Finally, she said: 'Are you Eclipse?'

'No,' Kane said. Then: 'Did you really think I could be?'

'I didn't know what to think. I still don't.'

Kane also heard the helicopter now. He sighed. And she understood that they were trapped, this was it.

'I didn't know what happened to you that night,' Kane said. 'That you'd been attacked.'

'Did I kill someone?'

'No, I killed someone. I think that was shortly after the assault on you. You were present, that was all.'

'What about the others?'

'What others?'

'In Tel Aviv, St Petersburg.'

Kane stared at her.

'What do you know about Tel Aviv and St Petersburg?'

'You were there in 2009.'

'Yes.'

'Wherever you go, Russians die and women get attacked.'

'Tel Aviv and St Petersburg?' he said, quietly, staring at the paper tablecloth. And suddenly Kane's face contorted with a look of realisation, as if he'd been physically hit again. Just then, the centre's lights flickered on. Kane turned. There were voices in the hallway: men's voices.

Kane looked like he was thinking fast. He got up, walked over to the wall of martyrs and glanced across the faces, then looked back at Rebecca.

'Do you drive?' he said.

'Yes.'

Kane reached into his pocket and found an envelope. Inside, she saw a wad of cash, several thousand pounds.

'Give me a minute.'

Kane stumbled out of the hall, into the arriving crowd. For a second there was a startled hush, then she could hear Kane talking, though not in a language she recognised. After another few moments, the men began responding audibly with cries of what might have been anger or sympathy.

Eventually, Kane was carried back to her between two tough-looking young men. They were followed by a small, elderly man with a grey moustache, holding Kane's envelope of cash and a set of car keys. He gave the keys to Rebecca.

'Please, go speedily.'

'Apparently there's a back door,' Kane said.

At the back was a white van. The crowd watched them get in. They called out: cries, exclamations.

'Always liked the Kurds,' Kane said.

'What on earth did you tell them?' Rebecca asked, putting the key in the ignition.

'I told them we had something very important to do.'

THIRTY-TWO

Waves of pain crashed through Kane's body as they began to drive. He watched Rebecca getting used to the van's set-up, wrestling the gear stick, picking up speed. Kane directed her onto Green Lanes; told her they were going to head west towards Barnes.

He sat with the pain and the patter of memories, beating, flashing: everything he should have seen. Netanya, with the Mediterranean glaring like fire, the steep cliffs above the sand, and their target, Mikhail Panzhinskiy, Unit 22195's nuclear and biochemical weapons specialist, emerging from the sea. Christian passing the binoculars. Halcyon had become a well-honed killing machine by then, and more than one other person worked with Kane as part of those international teams, but it was only one face he saw.

He saw the wall of Anton Zakharyan's living room, blood-daubed. Anton had Christian's details. They were taken when he was killed because he was on Christian's trail. There was no Russian hit team, the graffiti was just misdirection. *He thinks he's smart enough to get away with it. And that he deserves to.*

But another memory intruded, more terrifying for being early and innocuous enough to lie at the root of all subsequent horror. Kane was walking Amelia home through the beauty of Cambridge on a spring night. She was drunk, tearful, trying to tell him something. 'He's not as nice as you think.' That was all she managed to say. He had registered the understatement, something unspoken behind the words, but not their import. The message had seemed so obvious as to be entirely forgettable and now seemed the only message in Kane's life that he had needed to hear.

He saw St Petersburg, stranded in its undarkening night, Christian's strange behaviour, and their parting ways, Kane knowing he would never see fault in himself. Never, couldn't, acknowledge the harm he did to others, holed up in his cave of narcissism.

Christian's Porsche Cayenne was missing. The front door of his house stood open. Kane and Rebecca followed the sound of cartoons to a play den where the kids were on beanbags with a lot of sweet wrappers across the floor.

'Is your dad about?' Kane asked. They shook their heads and turned back to the screen. 'Amelia?' Kane called.

'Someone's upstairs,' Rebecca said.

They climbed the stairs to the top of the house where Amelia stood in a loft-conversion study, searching through a pile of papers on a roll-top desk.

'Where is he?' Kane said.

Amelia was very pale. She stared at Rebecca, then at Kane's bandaged arm, but not as if these apparitions were the first horrors of the day. Kane looked around the mess. In the centre of the floor was a fifty-round pistol ammo box.

'He has a gun?' Kane said. Amelia continued sifting the papers.

'So it seems. And his passport. Some of my jewellery is missing.' Her voice was flat. Kane checked the paperwork she was holding: *Notice of Default under standard security. It is important that you read this letter. Your home may be at risk of repossession.*

There were more letters across the desk: a two-hundred-grand loan from a company called Horizon, several credit cards, court letters. There were car payments, mortgage payments, loan companies.

Rebecca picked up a family photograph and studied Christian. Then she gestured at a letter on the desk. It was from Eclipse Debt Solutions Ltd. Amelia began to wail, then she stopped, wiped her mouth with the back of her hand.

'This is you,' she said, turning to Elliot.

'Yeah?'

'He worshipped you.'

'Amelia, you once said Christian wasn't as nice as I thought. Do you remember that? Walking back after the May Ball.' She stared at him. 'What did you mean? Was it something specific he had done?'

'You know what I meant. Everyone knew.'

The kids called her from downstairs. 'Mummy?'

'What do I say to them? What do I do, Elliot?' She wandered out, clutching the door frame as if she might fall, then straightened and made it to the stairs. Rebecca showed Kane a sheet of paper from the pile, a P45 from Vaultec, dated six months ago. *Termination of Employment.*

'He'd lost his job,' she said.

Kane called downstairs: 'Had Christian been fired recently?'

'I don't know,' Amelia said. 'I don't know anything.'

Kane dialled the phone number on the Vaultec paperwork.

'My name's Elliot Kane. I work for the Foreign Office. I'm calling about a former employee of yours, Christian Rivera.'

'Yes? What exactly can I help you with?' The receptionist sounded cheery, and impenetrable as rock.

'Was he ever involved in any way with contract work for the Secret Intelligence Service?' Kane asked.

There was a pause.

'We wouldn't be able to discuss details like that. Who did you say this was?'

'I've told you. I work for the government. Could you put me through to someone with the necessary clearance to speak to me?'

'I'm sorry I can't help.'

'Okay. Could you inform whoever's in charge that armed police will be attending your Kingston offices in the next hour or so and it's vital that staff cooperate. I repeat that these officers will be authorised to use armed force if necessary.'

'Hang on, sir.'

Kane was put through.

'This is Pete Kruger,' a man said.

'My name's Elliot Kane. I'm involved in the hunt for Eclipse. MI6 had an IT security system upgrade some time around 2020. A significant amount of data was taken around that time. Could you confirm if Vaultec had that contract?'

A few seconds' stunned silence as this was digested, followed by Kruger clearing his throat.

'Any work for the government is obviously classified,' he said.

'So were the files you let leak.'

'Can you give me some details?' The CEO sounded increasingly nervous.

'Why was Christian Rivera fired a few months ago?'

'Christian? Well ...' He weighed up the sensitivity. 'There were several issues of improper behaviour, retention of data. And we had some money go missing.'

'And you were involved with the Secret Intelligence Service upgrade.'

'We have done work for all areas of government. I would need to go through formal confirmation of your identity before I—'

Kane hung up. 'Let's go,' he said. They went back downstairs. Amelia was in the kitchen, buttering bread, eyes glazed.

'What's going on?' she asked.

'When did you last see Christian?'

'A few hours ago.'

'Where might he have gone?'

'I've no idea.'

There is one certainty in your mind: you will get away with it until the end. Because you deserve to.

'Paul Lockhart,' Rebecca said, when they were back in the car. 'We need to speak to him.'

'Who is he?'

'Deputy Chief of Counter Terrorism. He's been helping me. He knows Eclipse connects to what happened at Eaton Square. He's prepared to take on MI6. We need to contact him.'

'Got a number?'

'I can try.'

While she called Lockhart, Kane got through to Alistair Godfrey. Godfrey began to speak before Kane had a chance.

'Elliot, you need to turn yourself in. The police are after you. Were you at an incident in South Tottenham?'

'Yes. Do you know if Juliet Bell and Michael De Souza are still free?'

'I believe so. For now. But they won't last long. They're being tracked. Broughton is personally onto them.'

'We need to be quick, then. The MI6 computer systems were upgraded a couple of years ago,' Kane said. 'Broughton told me. Was it external contractors? Vaultec?'

Godfrey paused. Then he said: 'Why?'

'It was Vaultec.'

'I believe so.'

'Were they security-cleared for access to the MI6 servers?'

'Yes.'

'What level?'

'Top level, I imagine. System administrator privileges.'

'So a Vaultec employee with adequate clearance could check MI6 files, unaudited.'

'As far as I'm aware.'

315

'And move them, if necessary.'

'They *were* moving files. That was the job: updating the system, correcting corrupted user profiles. Is this to do with Eclipse?'

'It's Christian Rivera. He was on Operation Halcyon, he worked at Vaultec. He's Eclipse.'

The penny dropped. Hard.

'Christian—' Godfrey began.

'He got away with an awful lot of horrendous things because Broughton covered up a crime against Rebecca Sinclair fifteen years ago.' In the silence that followed, Kane sensed an ethical compass turning. A professional one, too.

'Oh my God,' Godfrey said, eventually.

'Broughton's closing down the people set to reveal this. You need to stop him.'

'I'm not in a position to do that.'

'You can connect with Paul Lockhart, the Deputy Chief of Counter Terrorism. He knows the score. He's got authorisation to move on this.'

'Where is Christian now?'

'I'm going to find out and get him. I'm the only one who can.'

'How?'

'I've got an idea. But if I catch Christian, I need Lockhart and his team to be the ones who get to us first. I don't trust Broughton and his militia not to do something stupid – to me, Juliet, all of us. This is the end of his reign. You need to decide who you're siding with. Tell Lockhart that MI6 is split and you're in charge. Tell him to be ready for more information soon.'

'I don't know to what extent I can personally slam the brakes on John Broughton. He's still Chief of MI6. He went to the Director of Special Forces and has been granted his own team.'

'Yeah, I met his team. Can you slow them down in any way? Divert them?'

'I can get in contact with Lockhart. That's all I can do. But how do we stop Christian? He'll release the files and flee. We know Russia is ready.'

'I'm going to try something.'

Kane hung up and checked the sky. Burning blue, not a cloud. Flying weather. When he was sure there was no one behind them he told Rebecca to follow signs for the M25. Then he called Jim Irving, a pilot with his own airfield on the border of Kent.

'Jimmy, it's Elliot.'

'Elliot, how the devil are you?' Irving was an aviator, former military, one of those eccentric, semi-retired thrill seekers beloved by the intelligence service. His private airfield occupied a few acres of scrubby grassland in Kent.

'Busy. Got an urgent.'

'How urgent?'

'Now urgent. Can you fly?'

'I'm around. Could be a nice afternoon for it.' Kane felt the old reassurance at Irving's phlegmatic style. He knew that for an international flight Irving would need to submit the flight plan an hour in advance. But that rarely delayed things.

'Where are you going?' the pilot asked.

'Across the Channel. On to the continent. Anywhere, really.'

'One of those.'

'Exactly.'

'How many passengers?'

'Two.'

'The Skyhawk's got full tanks. I'll file for a flight to Le Touquet. When can I expect you?'

'Anytime. Won't be long.'

Kane tried Christian's mobile again. When he couldn't get through, he messaged:

Things have heated up. Do not try to use an airport – I've just been tipped that they have us on a no-fly list, they will arrest us at the gates. I can get us out of the UK. Call me.

Christian called from an unrecognised mobile number in less than a minute.

'Elliot?'

'Where are you, Christian?'

'Tell me what's going on.'

'An all-ports border block, both our passports. We're in trouble.'

'Who's with you?'

'No one. I'm as isolated as you are.'

Behind Christian, Kane heard piped music, voices, lift doors pinging.

'I just heard your name on the news,' Christian said. 'They're looking for you, Elliot. You and Juliet Bell.'

'Right. Pretty soon they're going to be looking for you too.'

'What do you mean "get us out of the UK"?'

'I took the liberty of making us some arrangements,' Kane said.

'Like what?'

'Jimmy's at Red House Farm.'

'Jim Irving?'

'He's got a Skyhawk ready.'

'You're kidding.' Christian was breathing hard. He was on the move again.

'I owe you this,' Kane said. 'I'm sorry I dragged you in.'

'You fucked my life.'

'I know.'

'Where will we go?'

'Monaco. Catch our breath, get our story out there. Then it will be up to us. But we've got to be quick, Christian. This is our only shot.'

'You're coming with?'

'Going to have to.'

'Like old times,' Christian said.

'Like old times. That's the idea.'

THIRTY-THREE

Rebecca kept her eye on the mirrors as she accelerated. She turned the radio on – *unprecedented manhunt under way* – wound the window down to listen for sirens.

Kane was on the phone to Bell: '... Red House Farm. It's an airfield in Kent, about a mile west of Sevenoaks.' Then he stopped, turned to Rebecca. 'My phone's died. Juliet's still with Michael De Souza and they've managed to reach Paul Lockhart. Can you get in touch?'

Rebecca called De Souza's new number, put it on speaker.

'Rebecca,' De Souza said. 'Are you okay?'

'Just about.'

'Can you put the Commander on?' Kane asked. Lockhart came on the line a few seconds later.

'Elliot Kane?'

'Speaking.'

'You have an ID for Eclipse?'

'It's a former MI6 officer called Christian Rivera. Have you spoken to Alistair Godfrey?' Kane asked.

'Yes. We are trying to contact John Broughton. He's not responding.'

'I need legal guarantees: Rebecca, Juliet Bell.'

'I will do everything in my power to protect them. I can't make promises about you. You have been very involved with John Broughton, from what I understand.'

'That's fine. Come and get me then. But let us stop Eclipse first. I need you there before Broughton.'

'Where?'

Kane gave coordinates for Red House Farm and rung off. Rebecca took the van to 110 miles per hour. She could see blood seeping through Kane's bandages.

'Are you okay?' she asked.

'Lightheaded. Thirsty. Got any water?'

She checked the van's glove compartment. 'No. Want me to stop?'

'We don't have time.'

Kane directed her from the A2 onto smaller roads. The land either side of them grew flat, marshy, blurring towards the sea into a haze of non-existence. A mile later, just after Edenbridge, he told her to slow. Still no one behind them. A pub stood at a small junction beside a red phone box and crumbling drystone walls.

'See the track about five metres to the right of the pub?'

'Yes.'

'That's where we want to go. But stop for one second.'

Rebecca stopped at the junction. Kane got out, went around to the back of the pub and came back with a rock the size of a fist, which he secreted in his sling.

'He's got a gun, Elliot. What are you going to do with a rock?'

'Go.'

Rebecca turned sharply down a dirt track with an old sign for Red House Farm. The bouncing of the car on the rough ground made Kane wince. After another few minutes she saw the airfield behind chain link and barbed wire: a windsock, an old hangar of arched corrugated steel. She could see the yellow-brown grass of the landing strip runway, the four-seater Cessna Skyhawk waiting.

A minute later they arrived at the gate. Christian's SUV was half obscured among the trees.

THIRTY-FOUR

Kane told Rebecca to hang back, out of sight.

'I'm meant to just wait?'

'Give me a moment.'

He went through the gate, past a rusted RAF rescue helicopter. Jim Irving strode over with a twinkle in his eyes that became a look of concern when he saw Kane's injuries.

'You all right, my friend?'

'Skiing accident.' Kane winked. 'Thanks for working with the late notice, Jim.'

'The way of these things, in my experience. Sure you're in a fit state?'

'Hope so.'

'Travelling light, I see. That's how I like it. Don't want to have to charge you for excess baggage.' He grinned. 'Christian's here. We're good to go.'

Christian was beside the Cessna, staring at Kane. He had a carry-on suitcase at his feet. No sign of the gun.

'Give us one second,' Kane said. 'Stay here by the gate.'

Irving frowned. 'Need some time?'

'Just a minute.'

'If you say so, boss.'

Kane walked over to Christian. Christian looked at Kane's injuries.

'What happened to you?'

'They already tried to arrest me. I'll tell you about it on the plane. Go, quick. Get in.' But something had unnerved Christian.

'If this is some kind of fucking ploy ...' Kane watched for where his hands tensed.

'Christian, I'm not inclined to stick around a moment longer than I have to.'

'What's Jim doing?'

'He's getting his headset. He said to get in. Let's do this.'

Still no sign of Lockhart. Noticing Kane glance back, Christian also turned. He took a final look at the UK, then began to step into the plane.

Kane took the rock and slammed it into his skull.

He aimed for the temple. The idea was to connect sweetly, slam the brain against the skull's lining causing blackout. It almost worked.

Christian toppled. Kane moved aside as he fell from the steps to the grass. The gun spilled from his jacket, a black Tokarev pistol. Kane kicked it away and was turning back when a boot to his right knee collapsed him. A second kick connected with his broken arm.

Christian had clambered to his feet. He drove a fist into the side of Kane's head. Kane struggled to stand and failed. Through the ringing in his ear, he heard Rebecca say, 'Stop.'

Both men turned. Rebecca stood a few meters away, silhouetted against the low sun, pointing the Tokarev at Christian.

'Rebecca,' Christian said in disbelief. He looked at Kane as if Kane might be equally shocked by this apparition. 'Rebecca,' Christian said again, 'put that down.'

She eased the safety off, held the pistol steady. 'I will shoot. And you know why.'

'Don't be stupid.'

'You think it would be stupid?'

She fired. A puff of dirt rose up from the ground a foot away from Christian. The shot echoed across the flat field.

'Stupid like that?' Rebecca said. She took a step closer and fired again, just to the side of him, so that Christian flinched. 'Getting stupider?' Christian raised his hands. Kane got to his feet.

'Lie face down, Christian,' he said. 'Hands behind you.'

'Elliot—' he began, then saw Kane's expression and did as instructed. Kane removed his sling and used it to bind Christian's hands behind his back. Only then did he allow himself to breathe. But Rebecca stepped closer, gun still cocked.

'You don't need to kill him, Rebecca,' Kane said. 'He doesn't deserve to die.'

'No?'

'It's not worth the trouble it will bring us. We've got him. Paul Lockhart will be here any second.'

As if in answer, there was the sound of vehicles arriving. But it was the wrong ones.

THIRTY-FIVE

They swept across the thin grass, right up to the runway: two Land Rovers and the Jaguar. Rebecca watched them screech to a stop. The doors flew open and out poured five men, three with pistols, two carrying assault rifles, all with body armour over their T-shirts.

John Broughton emerged last.

'Throw the gun away,' Kane said. 'Now. Put your hands up.' Kane raised his own hands as the men drew closer. 'Put the gun down,' he said again. But Rebecca didn't want to. Firing it had felt good. She thought she could keep going. How many bullets did it hold? 'They will shoot you in about three seconds' time,' Kane said.

Rebecca tossed the pistol aside. Then, before she knew what was going on, someone kicked her legs out from under her, smashing her face into the dry ground. A knee dug into the small of her back. A minute later she was hauled to her feet again and instructed to kneel with her hands behind her head, facing away from the plane. Kane was forced down beside her in the same position.

A shot rang out behind them. Crisp, definitive. Rebecca flinched. Kane sighed. Another two shots followed, more muffled. When she glanced at Kane, he'd closed his eyes.

He was lifted up, one man either side of him.

'She's done nothing wrong,' Kane said. 'There's no need to hurt her.'

Rebecca twisted round to see Christian, dead on his back. The sling that bound his wrists had gone. He had been shot twice in the chest and once in the face.

Kane was also looking at this, the men either side of him awaiting some instruction from Broughton. Then the first police cars appeared.

First one car, lights flashing, then another two, then there were six and more sirens could be heard turning off the main road. Rebecca saw Broughton's men fastening holsters and tilting rifles down as they watched the squad cars spread themselves across the airfield: ten, then fifteen and still coming. Broughton was also staring intently at these new arrivals. He lifted a hand, level with his waist, as if to say 'let's see'.

Paul Lockhart was the first out, appraising the scene, a crowd of men and women climbing out of their vehicles behind him, armed counter-terrorism officers. Then, from among the black vests and caps, Juliet Bell and Michael De Souza appeared. Bell tried to run towards Kane but was held back.

Lockhart walked over to Christian's corpse, glanced across it, then looked at Broughton. Rebecca wondered if Kane would say or do something but he was staring out, past the plane, at the trees up on the hillside, watching a pair of buzzards circling above the woods.

Lockhart approached Broughton accompanied by two police officers, and there was some intense but quiet discussion at the end of which Broughton was permitted to make a phone call. When the call was over he was led to a police vehicle and climbed in. This was watched closely by his team. There was an immediate change of energy.

The police turned to Kane. He was searched and handcuffed. Lockhart spoke to him and Kane nodded, said something back, and Lockhart led him over to Rebecca.

'You're all right?' Kane said.

'Yes.'

'You saved the day. I owe you my life. It was good to see you again.'

'What will happen to you?' she asked.

'I'm going to have to answer some questions,' Kane said. 'Tell Juliet I'll be in touch.'

'I will.'

'Tell her I'll see her in Tuscany.'

And then he was steered away. Officers led him to a van. He folded himself in, stiffly. Lockhart told Rebecca to wait.

'We'll get you cleaned up in a minute. You'll be home before too long,' he said, and she felt a desperate laughter rising within her. No credible image of home came to mind. And in that absence, a strange sense of freedom began to blossom, replacing the laughter; connected, somehow, to the long horizon and the buzzards wheeling. She could go, she and Iona. Anywhere. Their old lives had burned away, but they themselves remained, unhindered. There was an empty future to be filled.

The body on the floor stared at the sky. Its blood had already been swallowed by the parched ground, leaving a dark shadow. The earth must have thought it was rain, she thought. It must have gulped it down and been left maddened. Christian Rivera's belongings were in better shape, arranged neatly alongside the runway: clothes and chargers and paperwork. Rebecca had been vaguely aware of police searching the grass, entering the plane, emptying the suitcase. Now one of the officers straightened.

'Sir,' he called out. He held a small, black portable hard drive. At once, the entire scene, the hundred officers, the dry, sprawling landscape, all rearranged itself around those few centimetres of black plastic. Over the next five minutes, Rebecca watched it inspected, photographed, bagged and boxed, then escorted towards the police vehicles. It got an armed guard of its own. The five officers walked carefully, in procession, as if to drop it would be to spill the secrets it contained. The sun was at the treetops now, and their shadows were distended. They walked as if they knew they were going to have to carry this load for a long time, and were still uncertain whether to bury it as deeply as possible or place it somewhere high, out of reach, to be worshipped.

In the end, they laid it gently in the back of a police car. It was another minute before the armoured car began to cross the grass towards the gate, with a vehicle in front and a vehicle behind and a helicopter tracking it from above. All moved slowly, magisterial, shimmering in the heat, stately with fear.

ACKNOWLEDGEMENTS

Many thanks to Sarah Butler, David Hutchinson, James Ellson, Nick Quantrill, Veronique Baxter, Clare Smith and, especially, Jihyon Kim.

ACKNOWLEDGEMENTS